A Million
Dollars
An Ounce

by M. John Lubetkin

Printed by CreateSpace, An Amazon.com Company

Book design and cover art by Katie Goldberg

Other books by M. John Lubetkin:

Road to War: The 1871 Yellowstone Surveys.
Custer's Gold (fiction)
Before Custer: Surveying the Yellowstone, 1872.
Custer and the 1873 Yellowstone Survey: A Documentary History.
Jay Cooke's Gamble: The Northern Pacific Railroad, the Sioux, and the Panic of 1873.
Union College's Class of 1868: The Unique Experiences of some "Average" Americans.

To my father, Jacques Lubetkin, and my cousin,
William H. Green, who got me interested in stamps.

Prologue: March 29, 1945.

The *SS Gruppenführer* is not looking forward to the day's executions. These people, some of whom he had known for almost three years, are mostly decent Dutch and German, all with the bad luck of having insufficient Aryan blood.

It is shortly before 10 AM. The Gruppenführer, a one-star general, sits in the back of a black touring Mercedes as it leads two army trucks past a Y-shaped, ten foot high barbed wire fence and into a small compound in Berlin's northeast suburbs. Inside is a two-story suburban home and adjacent carriage house, as well as almost two-dozen Jews transferred from concentration camps. The prisoners are guarded by a dozen elderly conscripts, a small staff, and four German shepherds. Locked inside one room are some ten million dollars' worth of priceless stolen postage stamps, looted over the past five years from Nazi-occupied European countries.

Inside, the prisoners individually identify, sort, visually and chemically test, and value each postage stamp; then record their findings in duplicate. With the price of gold at thirty-five dollars an ounce, each stamp that is selected for keeping is worth at least four ounces ($140) of gold. Almost half the stamps are valued at more than a pound of gold, and some are valued at over a hundred pounds ($56,000).

The workers' day has been routine until the General, a man of average height, soft chin, and wearing a black leather greatcoat enters the building. "Out, out with you all!" he orders, as he enters, slapping his riding crop on the back of chairs as he walks into the large workroom. "Everyone, stop what you are doing! Slowly place everything at your work stations and stand at attention! Good. Now get out! Get out this second!"

Twenty-three prisoners, wearing only thin, cotton black-and-white striped pajama-like clothing line up in front of a small covered truck. An icy Baltic breeze seems to increase in intensity as each prisoner's name is called off and checked. Then all are squeezed into a space that normally holds eight.

"Where will they take us?" they whisper to each other, alarmed. But no one knows.

"Guards," the SS General orders, "Bring your rifles and knapsacks, hurry!"

This contingent of guards is made up of shopkeepers and pensioners, men who haven't cleaned or shot rifles since the Kaiser's days. The second truck will take them to the forward lines. All are fated to disappear when the Russians unleash their final offensive in April.

"Schmidt. Where is Schmidt?" the general asks, looking around for one of his two assistants. Ulrich Schmidt is a muscular short man who lost an eye outside Sevastopol in '42. Even by Nazi standards, he is overbearing and conceited, but he knows his stamps well and handles Jews firmly. Finally, he comes bounding out the door, a tight smile on his face, trying to avoid the general's exasperated look.

As the guard dogs howl, the staff and SS pile into two cars, in front and following the prisoner's truck. Sitting in the first car, the general gives directions to his assistant, *Hauptmann* Rudolph Spangler. All are armed with Schmeisser submachine guns. The weather is sufficiently overcast to prevent Russian fighters flying, for the little caravan is otherwise an ideal target. Cautiously, it follows an eastern zigzag route through pine barrens for forty-five minutes. Then, with the Red Army only ten miles away, the general has the driver pull over.

Here, where ancient glaciers once scoured the ground, the soil is sandy. A short trench has been dug, piled-up dirt creating a low mound. Immediately east is a forest of evergreens, and, in the distance, all can see occasional flashes of light followed by the dull thuds of artillery.

"Five at a time, women first," The general orders. Then he takes out two packs of Camels, taken from an American supply truck during their Ardennes Offensive (the Battle of the Bulge). "Schmidt, give them each a cigarette," he says. The prisoners scream, beg and cry, but the general is as nonchalant as if waiting for a trolley. While the drivers and guards stand by, Schmidt leads the first five to the pit's side. The general and SS men unholster their pistols and take their stances.

The general stands behind a tiny woman, the wife of a Berlin stamp dealer who is mumbling in Yiddish. As she kneels he gently strokes her hair with his left hand while whispering softly into her ear. Then, he pulls up his Walther, places it a fraction of an inch from her head, squeezes the trigger, and shakes his head. Perhaps, if she had not known so much, her execution would not have been necessary this late in the war.

Seeing the woman's head explode, one of the SS—an otherwise brutish looking man—vomits and is unable to shoot the woman kneeling at his feet. The general walks up to him, takes his pistol, slaps him in the face, then uses the man's pistol to shoot the trembling woman.

"If you don't shoot, you will be the next one who kneels. Do you understand?" he asks. Between gasps, the man nods and the general returns his pistol.

It takes less than ten minutes. After the first twenty are shot, the final three male prisoners are given shovels and told to cover the bodies. When this is done, they too are shot. The general turns around, picks up a shovel and hands it to Schmidt. Schmidt is about to protest when the general reaches into his back pocket and removes a flask of Schnapps.

"Have some while I hold your coat and jacket," he says pleasantly.

After Schmidt has been shoveling five minutes, the general laughs, "Stop digging, my friend. You've been throwing dirt on the bodies too quickly and you're sweating like a lunatic. There's no point in getting sick this late in the war, is there?" he says.

Everyone laughs.

"Here, have another drink," he says solicitously. But when Schmidt takes another swallow, the general refuses to take the flask back. "Keep it and have another. Is it good? I hope so, Schmidt because it will be your last. Ja?"

Everyone does a double-take. *Schmidt's last drink?* "Yes," continues the General, as if reading their minds. "Schmidt has been stealing stamps from us. Before our SS friends arrived—now pay careful attention, Schmidt—on my orders, they searched your apartment. Do you know what they found and what I just discovered in the pockets of your jacket? *Our* stamps, Schmidt; mine and those of my brother and our associates. No, my friend; you've been far too greedy, I'm afraid," he says, shaking his head in mock sadness.

Schmidt's face is white. He has just started to beg when the General shoots him below the navel. The bullet's momentum catapults Schmidt on top of the murdered Jews. There he moans and thrashes wildly, between screams imploring the general not to shoot again.

"For God's sake, control yourself," the general says, laughing at Schmidt's contortions. "Neither my brother or I appreciate your stealing what belongs to us. Do you wish a final shot, brother?" the general asks, handing the Walther to his brother, a lower ranking SS officer with a limp. Schmidt continues screaming until a second shot rings out.

The general looks around and nods with satisfaction. His morning's work is completed. "Please collect the shovels, but don't bother to cover Schmidt," he says to the lowest ranking SS man. "However, I'd suggest that you go through his pants pockets. Then we'll return. The wind is picking up and I need something warm to eat."

After lunch at the compound and removing the stamps there is a final clean-up and building inspection. SS General Franz Alfred Seis, who supervised the murder of fifteen thousand Jews in Smolensk, personally shoots the dogs and then sets fire to both buildings.

Now, however, with most witnesses dead or about to die on the Eastern Front, he still faces the biggest question of all: how does he safely get his stamps out of Berlin and through American and British lines?

Part I: May 2, 1945.

.

Chapter 1: Dawn, Ludwigslust, Germany.

There is that mystical moment in the early morning when twinkling starlight gives way to the dawn's first pale light. Mist rises from the cold dew as Captain Harry Strong, a captain in the Eighty-Second Airborne Division, rolls over, trying to get a few more minutes of sleep. He is just to the east of the idyllic, agricultural community of Ludwigslust. Here are cobblestone streets, immaculate houses white-washed or painted in light yellows, and flowering red, pink, and white geraniums nestled in window sills and from hanging baskets.

That morning, yards from the convergence of roads from Berlin and northern Germany, Harry commands five jeeps, a lieutenant, three sergeants, fifteen enlisted men and a stray collie named Hans that has somehow adopted them. Harry's lightly armed force carries standard weapons; two .30 caliber machine guns, bazookas (useless against heavy German tanks), Tommy guns, and carbines. These few are the spear tip of the 82nd Airborne Division's 504th Parachute Regiment's 3rd Battalion.

Harry's jeep includes Corporal Ernie Manfredi, his driver; a wiry, worldly high school drop-out who is second-generation Italian-American from the "Dago Hill" neighborhood of St. Louis. In the back is Russ Tonstad, a private first-class, blue-eyed and blonde, whose parents own a dairy farm near Perham, Minnesota. Harry's third man is Pete Zilina, also a PFC-1, from the mining town of Donora, PA. Pete went through grade school with baseball star Stan Musial. Between them sits Hans, who constantly sniffs the air but seems to bark only when it's safe.

The previous day, without sleep, the fast-moving forward elements of the Eighty-Second cross the Elbe River and advance thirty miles across post-card-perfect countryside. Blossoms are fully out on magnolia trees and small, neat orchards contain blooming apple, apricot, cherry, peach, and pear trees. Riding into the town's tiny center that afternoon, Harry is astonished to see freshly painted "Kilroy Was Here" cartoons: a large head and huge eyes just above a horizontal line with Kilroy's large phallic nose dangling over it. First seen in Sicily, no matter how fast a town is liberated, Kilroy always welcomes fellow GI's; the "artists" taking incredible risks to paint this icon across Europe.

To Harry, Ludwigslust's most distinguishing feature is its medieval insignia showing a grinning dead bull with a crown on its head, its large, bright red tongue hanging out. The bull traces back to some long-forgotten pre-Christian ritual. Three miles north is the Grand Duke of Mecklenberg's palace, untouched by war. Trudging west are tens of thousands of women, children and elderly men, pulling handcarts or carrying valises and blankets. They wear their warmest and best clothing, all motivated to cross the Elbe, the demarcation line between Western and Soviet control, before the river's east bank falls to the Russians.

To Harry's surprise, their arrival is greeted with sighs of relief and smiles. The reason, he discovers, are the throngs of begging, terrified refugees who carry tales of Russian barbarism. Then he learns that the last of Himmler's SS have disappeared only an hour earlier. Their final gifts to Ludwigslust are the bodies of a half-dozen Wehrmacht deserters swinging from town square telephone poles.

Harry's small unit cautiously moves east of the town and eats cold rations—food offered by residents is rejected based on false rumors of poisoning. Only then is Hans fed and petted; he'll be the one on guard-duty. Harry's last thought, before his eyes close late that Tuesday is the fervent hope that tomorrow, May 2nd, will be a quiet day: a shave, perhaps a bath later, something fresh to eat and, with the war almost over, staying alive.

▲

Awakened from a deep sleep by noises he can't quite identify, Harry throws off his blanket, scrambles to the top of his jeep for a better view, and pulls out his "liberated" Zeiss precision binoculars. Seeing movement eastward, he now recognizes the noise of diesel engines cranking up. How deeply was he sleeping? Could the Eighty-Second's light armor have passed him? And why, his still-sleepy brain asks, are the engines so loud?

Rising from the fields on either side of the tree-lined road, the quickly lifting mist making them look ghost-like, are hundreds, then thousands of German soldiers. Scanning from north to south Harry spots Tigers, Panthers, Mark IVs, and ferocious looking *Jagdenpanzer 38* tank destroyers. While they are all on tank carriers, they can be unloaded in under a minute. There are also scores of "88" artillery that can shoot down a bomber or blow a hole in a Sherman tank. Beside them are innumerable trucks and horse drawn wagons, undoubtedly carrying German wounded. The procession fills the tree-lined road, spilling over for fifty yards on either side. Meanwhile, infantrymen carry *Panzerfausts*, rifles, light machine guns, and blanket rolls. Collectively, they walk head down, the marching songs of their glory years forgotten. Most baffling to Harry are two regiments of Hungarian cavalry, Hussars dressed as if on 19th century dress parade.

"What do we do, Cap?" asks Manfredi, as the gap between the paratroopers and the Germans narrows.

"Tell the boys to stand down. No funny stuff. We can't run and we can't hide. Let's—"

A *Kübelwagen*, the German equivalent of a jeep, speeds forward, horn honking as it zig-zags along the road, coming to a stop fifty feet in front of them. Two officers, a brigadier general and a major, step out and walk over to Harry, saluting.

Thank God, Harry thinks, if a general is saluting me he won't have us shot.

"You are General Gavin's paratroopers, yes?" the general says in excellent English. He has shaved that morning and his field-gray uniform is pressed, immaculate down to his polished boots. In contrast, the major has clearly slept in his leather coat. Harry knows that the general is fully aware that American paratroopers tuck their pants into their boots in a unique, baggy fashion; his question has been rhetorical.

"I'm one of General Gavin's paratroopers and I speak German," Harry answers in German.

"And with a Swabian accent, too," the general smiles as the major registers disgust.

"I'm from Stuttgart," Harry says, ignoring the major who is turning red with anger.

"And the Nazis drove your parents out, yes?" the general asks.

Without warning Hans begins to bark. Only now does Harry realize that Hans has been quiet up to that moment and muses if Hans has switched sides again. After looking at Hans for a second and shaking his head in mock disgust.

"Our guard dog," Harry explains as the general smiles.

"In Stuttgart," Harry continues, "*Oberbürgermeister* (Lord Mayor) Strölin personally 'suggested' to my father that he might want to leave Germany."

"The mayor himself? I know of him. A dedicated party member with Hitler in '23."

"And my father's first cousin, sir." The word "sir" can't hurt when you're outnumbered a hundred to one Harry thinks.

"Might I inquire why you left?"

"The Strölin family is descended from generals and Lutheran ministers. My father and the mayor strongly disagreed about the treatment of Jews."

"So stupid. So very, very stupid," the General mutters. "We needed soldiers like you."

Harry smiles, thinking it better not to mention that he's half-Jewish.

"Nevertheless, you're a traitor," hisses the major, unable to contain his rage. Putting his hand on his holster he advances towards Harry.

"*I* am the traitor?" Harry answers, snarling in return as he clenches his fists. "Do you—"

"Major!" commands the general, stepping between the two. "We are here to save our comrades." He is barely controlling his own anger at the humiliation of having to surrender. "You will do nothing except follow my orders. After we've completed the formalities of surrendering, I will explain to you why the captain and so many other Germans like him left the Third Reich. We have *lost* the war, in large part because of the stupidity of our late Führer and his sycophants. For the next few hours, before we enter captivity, you will devote yourself exclusively to rescuing some of Germany's remaining men. If you feel this is impossible you will immediately surrender your pistol to me and face a field court martial."

The major bows his head. A field court martial means immediate execution.

He takes a step back, places his hands behind him in an "at ease" stance and says nothing.

"Thank you," the general continues. "Captain, let me apologize for the major's temper. Perhaps your lieutenant and the major will drive to the end of our column in one of your jeeps with a large American flag? With luck, we won't be bombed and it will facilitate our men's morale. I need not say how distraught they are after five years of fighting and now, quite candidly, they are frightened by the thought of Russian captivity. What do you Americans call it, a 'one-way trip' to Siberia?"

Harry, red-faced and still angry, nods to the general. Thank God, somebody is calm and has his priorities straight, he thinks.

"Will you be the officer at the surrender?" Harry asks, attempting to be courteous.

"My commander, *General der Infantrie* (Lieutenant General) von Tippelskirsh is willing to surrender his 21st Army Group, but only to an officer of appropriate rank. Not a captain certainly, yes?"

"Not me, no," Harry smiles again, otherwise keeping a poker face. Army Groups are huge. "If I might ask, how many men do you have and where are the Russians?"

"General von Tippelskirsh commands 160,000 men, although, as you can understand, we have not had time for roll call this morning."

That's fifteen times larger than our Eighty-Second, Harry thinks.

"With Hitler dead," the general continues, "our desertions would be enormous were it not for the Russians. At best, they're thirty-six hours behind us, and this flat land offers little in the way of defense. The canals are not deep and mostly flow east to west anyway—"

Harry puts up his hand. "Sir, I will take you to General Gavin. I'll also radio back to headquarters and let them know what's happening. We'll do our best to make sure that there's no accidental bombing. After your men arrive here, have them stack rifles and remove the firing pins—just so there's no confusion. However, in case the Russians get too close, send some of your 88's and heavy weapons to the rear."

"And General Gavin? He is near here, yes?"

Harry nods; out of the corner of his eye he has just seen a half dozen mud splattered jeeps advancing from the west.

"Very near here, sir—"

Harry stops as the column of jeeps pulls up alongside them. A slim, youthful looking officer all but springs from the lead jeep's passenger seat, mud-coated and bleary-eyed, and walks up to Harry. Although carrying his trademark M-1 rifle and not a carbine, he is indistinguishable from any other paratrooper.

"What's going on here, Strong?" asks General James M. Gavin.

"General von Tippelskirsh wishes to surrender his Army Group, sir."

Baby-faced Jim Gavin, just over six feet tall and thirty-eight, is already a legend. Despite his illegitimate birth, lying about his age to enlist in the Army, and not having a day of high school, almost miraculously he is admitted to West Point at eighteen where he impresses all. Gavin is among the first Americans to see the potential of parachute and glider attacks, which leads to his role in organizing and training the first American airborne division—the Eighty-Second. "Jumping Jim" believes in leading from the front, which translates that officers like Harry are the first to parachute from each plane and the last to eat in chow lines. The result is exceptionally high morale.

"On behalf of Lieutenant General Kurt von Tippelskirsh I wish to speak to General Gavin," the German general says.

"And you are?" Gavin asked.

"*Generalleutnant* (major general) Graf von Shilling."

Gavin takes off his helmet, his thick hair making him look even younger, spits on its mud-covered front and wipes his helmet with his sleeve. Only then do his two-major general stars appear. Both Germans instantly salute, clicking their heels.

The conversation takes minutes. *Pro forma* surrender negotiations are to begin that afternoon at Wobelein Palace, von Shilling to inform von Tippelskirsh of the details.

Chapter 2: Wobelein, Germany, May 2, 1945.

"Strong," Gavin asks Harry after the officers leave and, his face slowly changing from a smile to a quizzical look, "Does anything smell funny to you?"

"No, I think they're sincere. They're scared—"

"Not *that* kind of smell," Gavin smiles. "Your nose, your olfactory senses."

A light breeze is beginning to blow from the north. Harry sucks in a huge breath through his nose. "Oh shit," he mutters.

"Take some half-tracks, mount a platoon in trucks, include some engineers and a communications team," Gavin orders. There is no need to say more. The breeze carries the odor of dead flesh. Beginning in April, the Allies have discovered one concentration camp after another; Hitler's crumbling Germany no longer able to hide its mass atrocities.

Most of the time, the men in Harry's jeep grumble when he is given a forward assignment. "Hey, why such a shit job, Cap?" they ask. Harry invariably answers, "Because you guys are so fucken ugly the general doesn't want to look at you again, why do you think?" Today, however, as the stench increases, there are no jokes.

▲

As a combat officer, Harry has drawn outstanding reviews. Some lieutenants have slightly more stamina, are braver, or are academically brighter but, Gavin realized, none combine these traits and better understand Germans and their language. When it comes to front-line prisoner interrogation, Harry is peerless. No one is more adept at playing "good cop;" offering cigarettes, sympathizing, and speaking German to usually frightened prisoners. Also, the fact of the matter is that many prisoners are ardent Nazis. With so few Americans speaking unaccented German, prisoner interrogation is often handled by German born refugees who look Jewish (because they are) and who take a visceral dislike, and vice versa, to those they are questioning. Harry *looks* Nordic and, almost invariably, can quickly—a figurative and literal lifetime for front line troops—have hostages turn over critical front-line intelligence.

But join Gavin's staff? When asked, Harry demurs. For post-war promotion, it would've been a strike against him, but Gavin understands Harry's wartime attitude and admires him for it.

▲

The original purpose of the hamlet of Wobelein, three miles north of Ludwigslust, was to house many of those working for the Grand Duke of Mecklenberg. As Harry's column drives past empty fields, neat looking homes appear deserted and, except for the distressed sounds of unmilked cows, silence surrounds them. Harry, in the lead jeep, stays under ten miles an hour. Sitting over his jeep's front wheels are two engineers looking for mines. With the war winding down, nobody wants to be the last to die or to have his legs blown off.

Without warning, the unit rounds a wood-lined section of road and, less than a mile away, Harry sees guard towers.

"Spread out" he shouts, "we've been spotted." As the GIs leap from their vehicles, Harry pulls up his binoculars and slowly pans the landscape. But, because of other buildings and a low hill, what the towers are guarding can't be seen. Strangely, Harry sees no movement in them.

"Hey, Zilina," he calls, beckoning for Pete Zilina to come over, "you've got better eyesight than I do. Do you see anything?"

Zilina looks carefully, then shakes his head. "Nobody's in them, Cap." To sighs of relief, Harry's men re-form and move forward again, but even slower than before. Are they being set up for an ambush?

Any question as to what they'll find ends as the odor of bodies and excrement grows. Harry hopes that they'll find dead animals but his instinct says that the chances of that are between slim and none. On the north side of Wobelein are shiny railroad tracks, an indication of frequent use. Blocking their view west is an empty freight train. An old engine, judging by its nineteenth century smokestack, sits in front, wisps of steam indicating it had been fired up earlier that morning, then abandoned.

Once past the locomotive a high barbed-wire topped fence faces them. Approaching the gate they see hundreds if not thousands of bodies. Usually, the Nazis stack up bodies like cut wood, but at Wobelein it appears that they fled even before even this began.

Approaching on foot, Harry's men tie handkerchiefs or scarves around their noses. Only then do they see that some bodies seem to wiggle, more and more of whom try to stand. The living corpses are Jews, Gypsies, Hungarians, French, and anti-Nazi Germans who shakily arise as, holding onto the fence, they watch Harry's column approach in eerie silence.

As Harry reaches the gate, the prisoners, far too weak to climb over the barbed wire, begin to hideously laugh, cry, or try to clap. To a man, their skin is stretched tightly over skulls, usually yellow-greenish from jaundice and scurvy. Some can only sit, plaintively holding out their hands. Few have shoes and many are naked. Two nearby tarpaper shacks swarm with flies. Harry knows no one in them is living. There is no water or sanitation. When did the guards lock the gates and flee, he wonders?

Harry, sickened, has the communications team reach Gavin. He tells the General what they've found and reports that there are no mines. Getting his small group to pool its rations and candy bars, he sends others searching for water while he cautiously drives around the camp, only to find another nasty surprise. In the camp's northwest corner, hidden from the main road, is a small quarry. Bodies—at least a thousand, Harry thinks—have been stacked and pushed into place by a bulldozer. Staring into the open eyes of one corpse, Harry vomits. As he soon learns, the Nazi's planned to let the prisoners starve to death, then burn the bodies.

On entering through the main gate, Manfredi and Zilna next to him, a living skeleton staggers forward, saying something that Harry can't make out.

"He's speaking Polish," Zilina says. "He wants to thank you."

"Tell him we'll get him food soon," Harry says, speaking slowly and smiling at the man.

Zilina repeats in Polish what Harry has said, and a broad smile crosses the man's face. Then his body, almost in slow motion, sags to the ground.

"Jesus Christ, Cap, I think he's dead," Zilina says, crossing himself.

As Harry stands, hands on hips shaking his head, another officer, Jim Megellas, joins him. "You know," he says half to Harry, half to himself, "until I saw this I don't think I ever fully understood what we were fighting for. Those bastards..."

▲

Gavin reaches Wobelein ten minutes later. Trailing him are jeeps full of food that Ludwigslust's Nazi mayor had hidden in case of a later food shortage. Feeding the camp's inmates was never considered. However, once more of the Eighty-Second reaches Ludwigslust, "scavengers" quickly find black bread, canned hams, cheeses, and so forth—which begins arriving minutes after Gavin.

To Harry's horror, the sight of food proves too much for the skeletal prisoners and a riot ensues. Some are crushed to death or die expending their last bit of energy running for the food. Worse, the solids prove a horrifying killer for those who gulp down too much, too quickly. Finally, medics arrive and a field hospital is quickly assembled.

▲

(The next day, with the question of what to do with the bodies, Gavin forces Ludwigslust's remaining adult male and female population to march to Wobelein, listen to a sermon, then walk through the camp. After that, Ludwigslust's remaining men will bury the corpses just inside the gates of Mecklenberg Palace's carefully manicured grounds.)

▲

Gavin has been at the prison camp for perhaps an hour when a call arrives from an officer in Ludwigslust: a man, believed to be a high-ranking Nazi, has been captured but nobody can identify him. With surrender negotiations soon to begin, Gavin sends Harry back to Ludwigslust to interview the man.

"And get some sleep afterwards, you look terrible," Gavin says, patting Harry on the shoulder. "How much sleep have you had recently?"

"Maybe nine hours," Harry grins, "in the last four days."

"Then it becomes an order. See who this person is, then hide somewhere—but let me know where just in case."

Back in Ludwigslust, MPs have established a reasonably smooth traffic flow. The German army stretches east as far as the eye can see, but there are also American ambulances, first aid stations, and gasoline tankers placed at strategic locations along the road. Overhead the air buzzes with one-engine Piper "Grasshoppers" flying in and out of a makeshift airstrip, many carrying wounded German soldiers to Army hospitals west of the Elbe. Hope the bastards are grateful, Harry thinks.

Walking over to a knot of MPs, Harry is directed to where three men are being guarded. Next to them is another captain, Phil Belfield, who Harry knows slightly. Harry has his jeep crew find some chow, then turns to Belfield.

"What's up?" Harry asks, gratefully accepting donuts and a cup of decent coffee.

"Well, it hasn't been very quiet since you left. We just learned that Ludwigslust's mayor just killed himself, his wife, and their teenage daughter. Turns out he knew all about the camp and purposely withheld food. Nice guy, wasn't he?"

Both shake their heads as Belfield continues. "The civilian," Belfield points, "walked up to the two German officers and they suddenly saluted, which I thought odd. When I asked, they both denied saluting, then said they'd mistaken him for someone else. My German is piss poor so I had all three arrested and called for help. You're the help Harry, sorry about that."

"No problem," Harry says, thinking about getting some sleep. "Here's what we'll do. Get me three MPs and have each Jerry"—as a German himself Harry has learned to say *Jerry*, but never the insult *Kraut*—"separated, and guarded. Then bring me the civilian first."

To Harry's surprise, he can't get to first base. The man claims he's Helmut Nortlander and is a mid-level official in the Food & Agriculture Ministry. Nortlander claims to be fluent in six languages, is a trained agronomist, and managed F&A's translation department. Yet the man looks familiar to Harry, someone dating back to his Stuttgart youth.

"Do you know who you remind me of?" Harry suddenly asks. "Surely you must've known Reich Minister Walther Darré. He was already famous when I left Germany."

"Of course. He was the Reich Minister for Food & Agriculture when I joined it in 1935."

"He was responsible for *all* agricultural production and food distribution. Not just in Germany, but during the war from Norway to Crete. Unfortunately, Herr Nortlander, any association with Darré will not go well for you."

Harry sees Nortlander involuntarily stiffen, his last energy draining. A week earlier, he says to Harry, his eyes telling the truth, he'd fled Berlin with his long-time mistress, his wife sent west weeks earlier. The two walked west, pushing a baby carriage with clothes, blankets, and food, indistinguishable from thousands of others. Out of nowhere came a swarm of B-25 two-engine bombers, attempting to destroy a bridge a hundred yards in front of them. Amidst the explosions something hit the woman. As best he can, Nortlander squeezed her into the carriage, then walked miles until reaching a makeshift first aid station. A doctor performing triage took one look and shook his head, but Nortlander stayed with her until the end. Telling the story, he does his best not to cry. Harry listens, unmoved. "Darré hated Jews, Catholics, Slavs, and almost everyone else. He was the one who first advocated and then taught Hitler about Rasse und Raum (Race and Space), the cornerstone of their Lebensraum (expansion) policies. Didn't he say something like what the Nazis really had in mind was a modern form of medieval European slavery?"

"He often spoke in haste and excess, Captain. Jewish newspapermen were only too happy to repeat his ramblings. In my relations with him, Nazi or not, he was a good man to work for; always polite and restrained. He led by example, not by kicking and cursing those under him. If you find him he'll certainly vouch for me."

"Regardless, I'm afraid that we'll have to detain you, at least until your personal documents can be fully verified. However, you'll be pleased to know that your interrogation will be west of the Elbe. Rest assured, you won't have the Russians to worry about."

As Harry finishes, Nortlander lets out a sigh of relief.

"OK, Phil," Harry calls, "bring out the two officers." Then he whispers that he wants Nortlander cuffed. "He *is* somebody high up and I think I know who. He seems to be nice enough in person, but, if I'm right, he murdered five million people. Be careful, we don't want him killing himself."

Harry has a third chair brought up as well as donuts, coffee, and two packs of Camels. He also gets two pencils and paper. The three sit like old friends, Harry letting them enjoy the food and cigarettes. "However," he says, "this man calling himself Nortlander will be sent to Allied Headquarters where, sooner or later, we'll identify him. If you two continue protecting him, Harry explains, you'll be taken east by jeep until... Do they understand?" They do for, without exception, nothing is more frightening than Russian captivity. When Harry asks each to write down "Nortlander's" actual name, Walther Darré's emerges twice.

Chapter 3: Ludwigslust, 3:30 PM.

Leaving the two German officers to rejoin their army, Harry turns to go and then all but runs into Ludwigslust's newly minted mayor. Standing in the town square, wringing his hands, and bowing unctuously to every American, the middle-aged, clearly frightened man asks in a falsetto voice and broken English if he can be of assistance. Harry sees no point mentioning Wobelein or Darré. Besides, he's under orders from General Gavin to take the afternoon off.

Which doesn't mean he must do nothing. Harry has always collected stamps and this is the opportunity to acquire more. He can't remember his age when he first noticed his maternal grandfather placing little pieces of colored paper in an album.

"What are they?" the little boy had asked.

"They are stamps. And stamps tell you stories."

"They do?" Harry said, excited for he took his grandfather's comments literally. Standing on his tip toes he had put his head on the stamp album, hoping to hear a story.

"No," his grandfather had laughed. "They only tell you stories when you're old enough to read and write."

"But I know this is a blue choo-choo train."

"But it is not any choo-choo. Do you know what else? It is an American train. And look at the chimney."

"It's silly looking," said Harry, giggling.

"That's because it's old-fashioned. This stamp's even older than I am, it was printed in 1869, almost seventy years ago. That cone shape is what a smoke stack looked like long ago."

From then on, whenever Harry visited his grandfather, he would look at the stamps and pick one he liked, often from far away countries. And the stamps did tell stories; about animals, people, geography, and historic events. The stamps whetted the little boy's interest and, as he grew older, he found himself wanting to own stamps himself.

▲

Harry has collected stamps from other liberated countries and was now determined to find more stamps before the latest jolt of coffee wore off. Thus, he politely asks the mayor where he can "buy" stamps and is directed to a nearby butcher shop.

The location didn't surprise Harry, although it would most Americans. In Nazi Germany, the location for stamp *sales*, versus the distribution of mail, varied and often wound up at a political favorite's store. Ludwigslust's butcher shop is owned by a dedicated Nazi who, likely having little legal meat left to sell, had been rewarded with the local stamp sales monopoly.

Harry and his three men park their jeep at the store's entrance. They cautiously enter the empty building looking for booby traps or for signs of death—suicides being commonplace among Nazis. Upstairs they find three immaculate bedrooms. The first floor's combination butcher shop and stamp sales office are equally clean; an empty meat counter with old-fashioned scales on one side. On the other a twelve-foot long, three-foot high display case. Behind it are two chairs and a square card table. Peering down from whitewashed walls is the large, obligatory Hitler poster. In this rendering, the Führer is on horseback in silver armor, a look of determination as he faces the future, all the while holding a large Nazi banner. Nazi calendars also hang in sight, but, although it's May 2, April is still displayed.

A hallway leads to a 12' by 18' meat locker with enameled walls and floor, a water hose on one side. On the other side lies a family kitchen, dining room, and bathroom. There is no running water, gas, or electricity. In the back yard, two new wood fences run twenty-five yards, ending at the Rögnitz Canal. Harry suspects that with meat in short supply, the butcher built them to protect against thieves. Reaching the canal's edge, Harry is surprised to see that the water, which had been placid, now has a weak current indicating a break somewhere west.

Harry sends Manfredi and Tonstad upstairs to bring down mattresses, pillows, and blankets and collect the butcher's knives while he examines the postal counter. One after another, he opens the drawers, each containing scores of

Nazi stamp sheets. Many of these, he knows from his stamp collecting days, represent the highest quality engravings. To his surprise, a large pile of stamps portraying Adolph haven't been sold. He wonders if the Germans been voting with their feet. Nevertheless, he is pleased with the variety of stamps he'll add to his collection. Someday, these and stamps he acquired in Nazi-occupied countries might be valuable. Soon, his standard officer's briefcase is bulging. To him, this is merely souvenir hunting, no different than acquiring a Nazi flag, helmet, bayonet, or medal. Nobody has been hurt and these are the spoils of war.

"Hey fellas!" Manfredi yells, charging in from the back yard. "Guess what Hans found? Four fuckin' cases of buried Lowenbrau! And the bottles are cool!" Manfredi and Tonstad drag the beer inside as Pete pulls open one drawer after another until finding a bottle opener.

God damn, if this doesn't taste great, Harry thinks as they happily race to see who can finish their bottle first. "Give some to Hans, Cap," Zilina happily yells, then drains his bottle without stopping.

To hoots and hollers, Harry is the slowest, also spilling some of it on his shirt. Knowing that they'll be in Ludwigslust for only a night, Harry has Tonstad and Manfredi look for boxes to fit into their jeep and hide as many bottles as possible. As for Zilina, the quartet's junior, Harry sends him, sans Lowenbrau, outside to discourage any unexpected arrivals.

As the Lowenbrau cools him off and the cumulative effect of a pack of cigarettes works through his system, Harry sits against a wall and lets the tension slowly drain. He looks around, smiles with gratitude for being unwounded yet another day, and begins another bottle.

Harry is one of the boys yet not one of the boys. In the field, there's no saluting like the Germans officers had done with Darré. Being saluted in a liberated town is guaranteed to draw a sniper's attention. And, after days on the move, limited sleep, and with all his men equally filthy, there's no need to acknowledge rank. While it's one thing to have a spontaneous drink with his men like this, Harry would never consider going out drinking with them and thus cross a subtle demarcation line.

▲

"Cap, we have a customer," Zilina shouts ten minutes later as he opens the door from outside. Harry glances at his wristwatch, noticing it is almost 4 p.m.

Like so many other refugees, a well-dressed but haggard and unshaven man of about fifty, limps in holding an attaché case. His shoes are dirty, a ludicrous pair of driving goggles hang at his neck, and an unbuttoned expensive wool overcoat reaches well past his knees. Underneath is a tweed suit, sweater-vest and loose tie. Bicycle clips around his ankles indicate his mode of transportation.

"May I enter with my bike?" he asks in poor but understandable English. "No matter how careful your men are; bicycles are very—"

"Zilina," Harry shouts, "bring in his bike before somebody swipes it." He then explains to the cyclist that he speaks German. The man, breathing rapidly, is ill at ease, trying to adjust to the calm of the butcher shop versus the madhouse outside of a 160,000-man German Army Group and its equipment squeezing through Ludwigslust's bottleneck.

"Water? A cigarette?" Harry asks in German, wanting to put him at ease. He asked to see us, Harry thinks. But what Harry immediately notices is that behind the man's eyes, despite his fatigue and embarrassment, is barely controlled anger. Maybe he's going to cause trouble, Harry thinks, catching Manfredi's eye.

"Real American cigarettes?" the man answers. "Thank you, it's been weeks now."

Weeks? This guy must be high up, Harry thinks. For the average Jerry, it's been years. Harry picks up a chair, carries it over, and pulls out a pack of Camels. The man, hands trembling slightly, pulls out an obviously expensive stainless-steel lighter embossed with a blood-red oak wreath encircling a black swastika. God, Harry thinks, this guy isn't very subtle, is he?

"What can we do for you Herr—" Harry pauses.

"Doctor; Doctor Hermann Seis, I am an agronomist—"

The second agronomist this afternoon. Something's fishy, Harry thinks.

"And please take the pistol out of your pocket," Harry says, "it makes us nervous."

Standing twenty feet away, Manfredi holds Harry's Tommy gun, which is aimed at Seis's chest. On the other side of the room Tonstad stands with his carbine, also pointed at Seis, eyes following the doctor's every move.

"Of course, gentlemen, of course. I forgot, pardon me" Seis says, nodding, then smiling at all three. "I am your prisoner. But until now I needed something to protect myself, *Ja*?" Seis carefully removes the weapon, barrel in his hand, which trembles as he turns to Harry.

"Cap, is that a real Luger?" Tonstad asks. "Can I have it as a souvenir?"

"No," Harry laughs, "it just looks like a Luger. It's a long-barreled Walther P-38. You'll just have to keep hunting."

With the German disarmed, Hans begins barking and cautiously approaches Seis. The German smiles at the dog, whispers something, and lets his hand be smelled by Hans, who stands still and shivers in pleasure when Seis gently massages his neck.

"Dogs and children are war's most innocent victims," Seis says, looking at Harry.

This bastard's attempting to look as virtuous as possible, Harry thinks. He sure as hell wants something from us.

Chapter 4: Berlin, April 20, 1945.

Twelve days earlier it is April 20, Hitler's fifty-sixth and last birthday. Hermann Seis is in Berlin, a city sliding into terror and chaos with the unleashing of the last Russian offensive. As fires burn uncontrollably, Russian artillery shells plunge indiscriminately into neighborhoods. Essential services—water, phone, the courts, fire, police, transportation, communications, and entertainment—began to twinkle out. Theaters give final shows, the Berlin Orchestra performs Wagner's *Twilight of the Gods*, radio broadcasts became sporadic, and newspapers (other than a Propaganda Ministry's two-page sheet) cease publication. As streets fill with rubble, trolleys stop in mid-run, ransacked cars and trucks sit immobile, and bodies lie everywhere. Grocery, clothing, hardware, and liquor stores are ransacked. Next to food, the most precious items are shovels; banks, shopkeepers, and citizens begin burying valuables; jewelry, gold, silver, coins, cash and family heirlooms. Priests and nuns look to hide crucifixes, vestments, relics, and paintings. It is unnecessary to say that the Russians will take it anything of value.

The SS and municipal police, often drunk, indiscriminately shoot looters, hang army deserters from lamp posts, and open the jails—freeing some while executing others. The last of Berlin's military units are augmented by tens of thousands of hardline Nazi volunteer soldiers from other European countries. These fascists are without a homeland and under no illusions regarding capture. They drink, loot, then dig defensive positions hoping to kill one more Russian before they too will be overrun and, if lucky, die quickly.

On Sunday, April 22, Seis bicycles to Falkensee, a dozen miles west of central Berlin. There he meets with his brother, SS General Franz Seis, and their accomplices. The group has made its escape plans, but impatiently awaits Martin Bormann's representative. As the day passes, the Russian attack grinds forward while massive columns of T-34 tanks race westward in gigantic arcs, overcoming increasingly feeble German defenses defending the city.

The next day, Nauen, twelve miles northwest of Falkensee, falls, and with it the Nazis' last international radio transmission facility. It is time to leave, the conspirators agree, with or without Bormann's man. Better to explain later why they left, although, in fact, the man has died in Berlin. It is agreed that Hermann Seis has the best chance, so he is given the stamps which weigh less than two pounds. Hermann and his brother Franz immediately split up. Walther Darré (soon to be captured by Harry Strong) meets his mistress. Herbert Backe, the Reich's Food & Agriculture minister, heads north to the Baltic. The fifth person is Rudy Spangler, the Seis brothers' stamp expert. Because he knows so much about stamps, and with Franz Seis always suspicious, he isn't allowed to carry them. Everyone agrees to meet in one year at noon, April 23, 1946 at the southeast corner of Munich's historic *Hofgarten*.

Yet, even now, escape is possible. Russian infantry, on foot and subject to simplistic delaying actions, are days behind their tank columns. The tanks' first priority, however, is to break up remaining armored forces and strong points, then seizing and holding critical river crossings, roads, and railroad sites. While a dozen T-34 tanks defensively parked at a crossroad can stop all vehicle traffic, they do nothing to prevent refugees cautiously but openly circling past them. Nevertheless, as every German knows, soon enough Russian security police vehicles will screech to a halt and establish checkpoints to catch Hitler's flotsam and jetsam.

Hermann Seis, the man now carrying the stamps, is overjoyed finding himself alone. Now he plans nothing less than to double-cross everyone. Hermann is confident that his, and other Nazi doctors' wartime "medical" research, is invaluable and will give him a persuasive bargaining chip with Allied physicians. After crossing the Elbe, his plan is to hide the stamps and then surrender to the Americans.

Chapter 5: Ludwigslust, May 2, 4:00 PM.

Harry Strong moves the small table behind the postal counter to the center of the room where he motions Seis to sit. He wonders who Hermann Seis really is, for the name means nothing.

"So, how can I help you?" Harry says, pulling up the second chair and straddling it backwards. Cigarettes or not, this is not a chat among friends but, Harry wants Seis to understand, an interrogation.

"I need to cross the Elbe before the Russians arrive," Seis begins.

"You and a half-million others. But you're doing fine. Even in this mess, you should reach Bleckede Bridge before nightfall. And how did you get past the SS? They've been hanging men your age right and left."

"Oh, they stopped me too, but I have no right foot," he says, pulling up one trouser to reveal a wooden prosthesis. Harry also notices a slight lisp to his speech. "But perhaps I haven't been clear. Let me start over. I'm an employee of the German government, now administered by *Staatsoberhaupt* Admiral Karl Dönitz. I work for the *Reichminister* of Food & Agriculture, Herbert Backe, and have orders to report to Flensburg, that's just south of Denmark."

"I know where Flensburg is," Harry says curtly. Something about the man's attitude grates him, although he cannot explain why. "However, before we go any further would you please *very slowly* open your attaché case and put all its contents on the table?"

Seis is about to protest, but looks around and sees Manfredi and Tonstad, both grim-faced and carefully watching, their guns are pointed at him. Without options, he removes a dozen reports. The top paper, Harry sees, concerns growing potatoes three times a year in varied climates.

"So Backe needs these papers in Flensburg? About *potatoes* while your Third Reich is collapsing?" Harry says, grinning. "And I read German too, you know. Hell, I *am* German," he laughs along with Manfredi and Tonstad who, while not knowing German, think Hermann Seis's astonished look is hysterically funny.

"Well, actually this report doesn't make much difference, does it?" Harry continues. "Guess who I was speaking with just hours ago, Herr Seis? None other than Backe's predecessor, Walther Darré himself. He's a nice gentleman but a terrible liar. In fact, I had the distinct pleasure of interviewing him, confirming his identity, and arresting him."

Seis is shaken, his shoulders involuntarily slumping.

"Had you arrived an hour ago, you could have seen your former boss, perhaps even ridden with him. He's heavily guarded and on an express jeep west. However, he was captured because he was looking... For you? Were you delayed?"

"I had no idea Darré was here," Seis replies, so dispiritedly that Harry believes him. "I'm not here to meet anyone. I would've been here a week ago, but I fell and badly twisted my only ankle. Do you know how difficult it is to bicycle with only one foot, and one that is injured?"

"I'm sure you're telling the truth about your ankle, but why shouldn't I arrest you now? Something funny is going on. You and Darré being only hours apart doesn't add up."

"Please, I have money to give you and your men. I am so close and so tired and you are so poorly paid. I am forty-eight. My foot... you have no idea. I need help and you're interested in stamps. You're a stamp collector, *Ja*? I heard you ask the mayor, which is why I'm here now. I can offer you valuable stamps and your men money. Please understand, I'm just carrying out orders as best I can. You cannot begin to comprehend the responsibility—"

Responsibility, now that's an interesting word, Harry thinks. Responsible for what?

"You Americans control Bleckede. From there it is only fifteen kilometers west to Geesthacht. I'm to meet friends there tonight. They have a car and gas, and we'll drive to Flensburg, *Ja*?" his attempt to smile fails as his lisp becoming more noticeable.

"If I took you across it would cost you a lot of money. Why can't you go yourself?"

"You people have lists," Seis says as his voice rises, "and my brother's name is on them. People might think that I'm him, an *SS Gruppenführer*."

It is all Harry can do not to laugh. Wow, these jerks are terrible liars. They're so used to taking things, he thinks. "Dr. Seis, or whatever your real name is—"

"It *is* Seis—"

"Well, we Americans we don't get paid very well. Everybody's going home soon. The army will say thank you and give us some cheap medals. Nothing else. So, let's get to the point: How much would you pay us to take you through with your 'research' papers? You know, that we'd be in deep shit if we got caught so we'd expect more than a few dollars from you."

Harry catches Manfredi's eye and winks.

"Can we reach a bargain, captain? Leave my research papers with me but take my American money. That would be fair, *Ja*? And for you; earlier I put together a small package of valuable American stamps in the event I met a fellow stamp collector."

"Herr Seis, let's put the stamps aside for a minute. I've already suspected that you have American dollars. However, I want to know a little bit more about your research; potato studies don't strike me as being worth very much, nor would they be useful in Flensburg."

As Harry continues, he takes the pile of papers, moves them to his side of the table, and opens the second report.

"Wait," says Seis, his voice breaking. "Before you jump to any conclusions; when the war began, the *Wehrmacht* needed to know physiological reactions to starvation and wounds, men with and without drinking water; all of this in different climates. What was the minimum caloric intake needed for men in various survival modes? The difference, say, of men who were besieged versus men for whom long marches were required. Alternatively, after falling into a coma, when did death become irreversible? Field hospitals and combat medical teams making triage decisions cannot hesitate. These were *scientific* tests with results that will be of high interest to your army's physicians."

"And you used Jews, of course."

"Jews? *Jews?* No, not ever!" He is already angry and now, too tired to care, loses his self-control. "Even Jews like you captain. You see, I can tell this from your cranium's shape because I'm also a certified phrenologist. No, not Jews, rather Dutch and Norwegian prisoners. After all, these men are Nordic, and, like our young men, admirable physical specimens."

Harry senses that Seis is about to explode and makes eye contact with Manfredi and Tonstad, who nod back.

"The average *Jew*," Seis continues, spitting the word out, "was useless; what could be learned from a race of cowards and slum dwellers? Jews die quickly, whereas young men of Nordic blood might survive for additional day. I told Himmler to his face that our studies would be skewed by using Jews or Poles for testing. He immediately understood."

"And you personally conducted this research?"

"I personally *led* the research; I had fourteen assistants."

Seis stops abruptly. Reaching inside his jacket he fumbles for something, then remembers the guns pointed at him. "Of course, gentlemen, of course," moving his hand slowly and emerging with American stamps in a 2½" by 4¼" glassine envelope.

Harry quickly studies them. There are a dozen classics, all pristine, never mailed or even mounted in albums. Pre-Civil War issues include two green and one black Washington, reddish-brown and redbrick Jeffersons, and reddish-brown Franklins. Harry spots Lincoln blacks, Franklin oranges, a complete set of 1893 Columbus commemoratives. Harry's memory of values isn't that good, but he estimates the stamps' worth at more than $5,000. As he examines them, doing his best to look impassive, Seis carefully removes eight $500 bills, the stern visage of President William McKinley looking Harry in the eye.

"I was a bank teller," says Manfredi. As Harry nods Manfredi takes a flashlight, holds it behind each $500 bill, sniffs them on both sides, pours some precious Lowenbrau on them and lets the beer fizzle. Then he gently pulls each bill at both ends. Removing his wallet, Manfredi takes out a crisp American ten, puts it on the table with the $500 bills and shuffles them. Then he crumples each bill next to his ear, listening for any difference in sound. Next, he shuts his eyes, takes each one in his hand, separately throws them into the air and listens as they drop on the table. Finally, he runs the fingertips of his right hand over each bill.

"This is how we spotted forgeries," Manfredi continues, speaking rapidly in English so Seis will have trouble following. "I don't have a magnifying glass, but so far I can't find anything wrong. If they're counterfeits, then they're damn good ones. Also, do you know what I'm thinking? It's this: if our so-called 'scientist' friend is already flashing this much cash and those stamps, he must have more on him. I say we strip him and go through his clothing."

Harry, despite a splitting headache, has been thinking the same thing. What they haven't realized is that Seis understands English quite well. As Harry and Manfredi talk, distracted by the money, Seis slowly reaches into his jacket sleeve. Perhaps it is a sixth sense, but Harry springs forward, knocking Seis out of his chair with a crunching tackle and grabs him in a stranglehold. A tiny two-shot Derringer falls from Seis's coat sleeve. Like a cowboy with a rodeo-like rollover maneuver on a calf, Harry throws Seis on his back while Manfredi falls knees-first on Seis's chest, knocking the air out of him.

"We're hog-tying the bastard," Harry says, pinning Seis down, then gagging him with his own scarf.

"Drag him into the meat locker and we'll strip him there," Harry orders.

Seis bucks and kicks, but is no match for Harry, Tonstad, and Manfredi. The three larger paratroopers drag his squirming body into the meat locker, leaving the door open for light. As Seis's jacket is yanked off, a second Derringer falls out.

"This guy's a fuckin' one-man arsenal," Tonstad says, then notices a bulge under Seis's vest. Tearing off the vest, then ripping open the shirt, they see a homemade brassiere-like money-belt. There are two wide compartments, each filled with packages of stamps. In Seis's pockets are more large denomination American dollars, British pounds, and worthless Nazi marks.

My God, Harry thinks, forgetting about the cash, what are these stamps worth?

As the three begin sorting through the piles of money and stamps, Seis's gag works free.

"We should have killed more of you Jews!" he screams.

Harry feels his face turning hot, then Wobelein's sights come into focus again followed, to his amazement, by their smells. For a second he feels dizzy. Closing his eyes, he sees sparklers hissing and burning. Opening his eyes, he takes Seis's Walther, flicks off the gun's safety, and with a straight-arm movement smashes the barrel deep into Seis's mouth. Just as suddenly he yanks the Walther out, bringing with it a gush of blood and parts of broken teeth. Seis chokes for a few seconds, then throws up.

A few seconds after Seis's last heave, he looks at Harry, hatred glowing in his eyes.

Harry feels himself slumping from exhaustion. Seemingly out of nowhere, comes the memory of being with his mother as her lungs filling with fluid. He recalls the sounds of her extended death rattle, like a motorboat propeller churning in thick, muddy water. His anger mounts again, bought on by the arrogance and hatred of this Nazi "scientist."

How many deaths has this man overseen? Harry wonders.

Hans, knowing something is wrong, begins to bark.

"You Jews deserved to die," Seis says as he gasps for breath and spits out more blood. "Because of you we've lost two wars and I lost my foot. You are still the scum of the earth—"

Harry pushes the Walther back into Seis's mouth. From somewhere very, very far away he hears Tonstad and Manfredi shouting at him, but Harry is focused on Seis's eyes. He has never seen so much hatred, or pupils so enlarged.

Teeth barred, Harry hisses at Seis. "*Du Affe!*" he says, and pulls the trigger.

Later, Harry will remember Seis's head thrown back against the wall, the man's eyes still focused on him. Then, as Seis's head involuntarily turns, Harry notices a huge hole, blood pumping out for another few seconds until Seis slides over on his side.

What have I done? Harry thinks, disoriented. For seconds, he isn't sure if it is *he* who has somehow been shot and the rest is a surrealistic dream. Is he the dead man?

"What did you say to him, Cap? What did you say?" the astonished Manfredi asks.

Harry, still in a daze, hears himself saying, "There's nothing similar in German meaning to 'fuck you!' Our greatest insult is to call a man an ape. That's what I called him, an ape."

Harry reverses the Walther and, holding the warm barrel, gives it, handle first, to Manfredi who stands mouth open. Tonstad is also speechless and Hans has stopped barking. Then Harry tries to recall the shot's noise that so reverberated off the meat locker's tiled walls, but he is unable to do so. The only sound he hears comes from the retreating German Army as it rumbles over the cobblestones.

Harry Strong has no possible way to know it, but he has just taken possession of the most valuable collection of stamps stolen by the Nazis during World War II.

Part II: Heinrich Strölin.

Chapter 6: Harry Strong.

Heinrich Strölin's early childhood is the happy-go-lucky Stuttgart, Germany equivalent of a Tom Sawyer or Huck Finn. Blond, rambunctious, mildly rebellious, he is quick to learn and fast to laugh. When soccer teams are selected, he's chosen first and usually made captain. Harry's first to be called on in class, and always the proud protector of his two-year younger sister who has their mother Anna's jet black hair.

Children pay little attention to politics and Heinrich is no exception. He knows that on his father's side the Strölins were Lutheran bishops and Prussian generals, but his Jewish mother's side receives scant attention. Heinrich is only ten in 1930 when, the Depression rampant in Europe, the Nazis became Germany's second largest party after receiving two-and-a-half percent of the vote two years earlier. But neither his father, Rolf, nor his maternal grandfather, who owns a company manufacturing industrial inks, can hide their concern. Street fighting and anti-Semitic acts increase well beyond often-indifferent police control. Changes are equally apparent over the next three years. Heinrich's circle of friends shrinks, then vanishes. Even playing soccer, he becomes aware that he is the object of dangerous hits that should draw a referee's yellow flag, but do not.

In January 1933, Adolph Hitler becomes Chancellor and Hermann Göring the nation's top policeman. Soon books are burnt, attacks on Jews multiply with Jewish businesses picketed by Hitler's bullyboy Brownshirts. Somehow, Heinrich learns self-control. He throws up when neighborhood toughs pin him down and pour Listerine down his throat, and, yes, he winces when a burning cigarette is pushed into his arm. Nevertheless, his tormentors can take no other satisfaction; he says nothing, and refuses to cry or beg them to stop.

During the winter of 1933-34 Harry's mother, increasingly depressed by events, falls ill and, bedridden, contracts pneumonia. When Rolf Strölin arrives at Stuttgart's main hospital—which had dismissed all Jewish doctors earlier—he is told that there are no unoccupied beds. By prohibiting hospital treatment and the newly available, German-discovered antibiotic sulpha drugs, Anna Strölin is left to die at home, her horrified, weeping family at her bedside. Before she lapses into a coma, she is unable to talk, her eyes fearful as she pleadingly looks around for help. It is an image that Heinrich will not, nor does not want to forget. As far as he is concerned, the Nazis have murdered his mother.

Heinrich's father, Rolf, is a World War I combat officer whose short-cropped hair is still thick. He proudly wears his Iron Cross and leads his company at regimental reunions. Rolf does not hesitate to approach the Lord Mayor of Stuttgart, his first cousin, Karl Strölin, about his children. In January 1933, with Hitler's support, Karl marched into city hall with a cadre of SS, arresting the man who defeated him by 100,000 votes the previous year. Then, like Napoleon who placed his emperor's crown on his own head, he installed himself as mayor.

The mayor listens to his cousin, then shakes his head when Rolf asks that his children be protected. "While your daughter remains in your house," he replies, "she will be safe. But there is nothing that I can do for Heinrich, much as I love him."

"Nothing?"

"How many times did your family tell you not to marry a Jewess? She is dead now and I am sorry for you, but your two children are half-Jewish. My best advice is to leave Germany. Rest assured, cousin, each day will be worse for them than the one before. Soon Heinrich won't be permitted to attend school. Or hold a job. Leave now, before I am powerless to help. You served your country well, but Jewish children are not wanted in the Third Reich. Nor by the Mayor of Stuttgart."

That May, Heinrich, his sister, and father leave Germany and, after a circuitous route, arrive in the U.S. They have little cash, but Harry's Jewish grandfather's stamp collection proves easy to hide and remains valuable, even in Depression America.

▲

Ten years later, Hienrich Strölin has become Harry Strong. He is a 6' feet 2", 215-pound captain in the Eighty-Second Airborne. Had Germany not declared war on America days after Pearl Harbor, Harry would've been *cum laude* at Amherst. One of his advisers, Professor Ellicott Staples, a Harvard graduated Spanish-American war veteran, is a bow-tie, three-piece wearing, old boy network member who tries to recruit Harry for American intelligence.

Harry demurs. He feels he is meant for the battlefield, not hunched over some desk analyzing data. Staples makes some calls, later admitting that he himself hadn't received his father's blessing when he joined the Rough Riders. With a provisional Amherst degree, Harry is soon in Officer Candidate School. From there, it is onto the newly formed Eighty-Second Airborne—Staples having called in many chits to get Harry this sought after posting.

▲

March 30, 1943. Harry jumps first from the third plane in front of not only the Army's top brass but also a score of British onlookers including Winston Churchill. Floating down, Harry can see the reviewing stand. But had *he* actually seen Churchill so he can tell his grandchildren? He still hasn't made up his mind when, one hundred days later, he is in combat, thoroughly scared, puking on the plane's floor and hands shaking uncontrollably.

But Harry is an officer and it quickly shows. He does not just lead his men, but has an instinctive feel for combat. He is cautious yet aggressive, never demanding the impossible, and always taking care of his wounded. Additionally, he is a good listener who respects his men, and they don't mind coming to him with problems or battle concerns. Above all, Harry is lucky; very lucky. Fighting means that half the paratroopers' second lieutenants never became first lieutenants due to death, wounds, capture, accidents, or incompetence. For similar reasons, most first lieutenants never become captains.

Twenty months later, Harry has survived a concussion, a broken arm, frostbite, innumerable cuts and gashes, broken noses (one nose, three breaks), and two hand-to-hand encounters. Harry wins one and is saved the second time when the German on top of him is bayoneted. In Sicily, Italy, Normandy, Holland, the "Bulge," and now Germany, Harry sees screaming men plummet past him when their parachutes fail to open, bodies blown to bits, men squashed by tanks, and untreatable gut wounds. One man, shot through the head, continues to be lucid for fifteen seconds. "Holy shit, I think I've been killed," he says, clearly puzzled. And, of course, he sees dead civilians by the hundreds.

As for German prisoners, all black-shirted *Waffen SS* are killed on sight—and vice-versa. In one case, at considerable risk, Harry and others pull six *Waffen SS* from a burning half-track (wheels for steering in front, tank-like tracks in the rear) and give them water and cigarettes before shooting them. Harry's attitude towards the *Wehrmacht*, the German regular army, varies by mood, whether the captives are German, and if a prisoner's eyes have a "killer look." The latter are always executed. However, teenage and older Germans—members of the *Volkssturm*—or impressed Russian, Romanian, French, Italian, and Slovak troops are sent to the rear. Killing these poor bastards is more than Harry can stomach.

Chapter 7: The Seis Brothers.

Hermann Seis's stamps, now in Harry Strong's possession, have resulted from years of careful planning, good luck, extortion, and outright theft. He, and his more celebrated younger brother, Franz, had begun thinking about acquiring stamps even as the last Polish radio station was playing *Mazurek Dąbrowskiego* ("Poland Is Not Yet Lost") in 1939.

As Franz and Hermann Seis watched Poland's thirty-day conquest, they became fascinated by the booty taken from banks, museums, churches, synagogues, and Jewish and gentile homes alike. To them, the most surprising aspect was the interest in stamps. Although Hitler and Dr. Goebbels considered stamps useful propaganda tools, they never comprehended the monetary value of rare stamps. It was only after walking through an intact Warsaw mansion that the Seis brothers, avid philatelists, realized that Polish stamp collections were theirs for the taking. Which, to the extent possible, they quietly did.

After Poland, the brothers, with no objection from Franz's mentor, SS *Obergruppenfüher* Reinhard Heydrich, developed a philatelic strategy for western Europe, quickly implemented after France's fall. The countries of Belgium, Holland, Luxembourg, Norway, and Great Britain's Channel Islands included some 225,000 Jews. France itself contained some 150,000 identified Jews, half of whom were German, Austrian, Polish and Czechoslovakian refugees.

The brothers knew that, for Jews who had suffered persecution for centuries, the beauty of stamps was that it was much easier to flee if your wealth weighed only ounces. Thus, as stamp interest grew in the late 1800s, Jewish collecting was disproportionally high. In Nazi conquered nations, Jewish philatelists numbered in the tens of thousands, while Jewish dealers represented the majority of each country's stamp merchants.

For a substantial percent of the Seis brothers' "take," Food & Agriculture Ministers, first Walter Darré (until mid-'42) and then Herbert Backe, gave them their full support. Aided by stamp magazine subscription lists and club memberships, the two began requisitioning collections from large cities. In lightly bombed Amsterdam, for example, within days of the Dutch surrender, the brothers procured an *Opel Blitz*, a light, 75 horsepower one-ton truck. The brothers were so busy that they ultimately made numerous trips. Each load was filled with unopened albums, or boxes into which stamp dealers' inventories had been unceremoniously dumped before being sent to a storage site in Berlin.

If the Seis brothers never doubted their Führer, they did ask themselves: can his luck continue? On December 11, 1941 Franz Seis lay in a Berlin hospital. He had lost two toes from frostbite on the eastern front, and now, he heard, heart sinking, Hitler's unnecessary declaration of war on the United States. To Franz, as he cautiously discussed with Hermann, this meant only one thing: barring a miracle, eventually the war will be lost.

Franz regarded Hermann, twelve years older, with equal parts admiration and sadness.

He had idolized Hermann, who had been hit in the mouth in 1915 by a ricocheting bullet that tore out two teeth and a small chunk of his tongue. Despite speaking with a slight lisp, Hermann voluntarily returned to his regiment, only to have a foot blown off at Verdun. Hermann received his doctorate in agronomy after the war and, with his father in 1922, proudly joined the Nazi party. With his limp and lisp, Hermann gave the impression of being "slow." After Hitler's takeover, he joined the Food & Agriculture Ministry. While his superiors thought his work excellent, advancement was slow despite his being an SS member. (If outsiders were baffled by the Nazi overlapping organizational structure, most upper level F&A officials, like Hermann, Darré, and Backe were also in the SS.)

Unlike Hermann, and until the Russian disaster, Franz Seis had been a rising SS star, and his mentor, Heydrich, was a brilliant, amoral figure. In 1940, as planning for Great Britain's invasion, Operation Sea Lion, developed, Franz was chosen to lead all six *Einsatzgruppen* (death squads) that would follow behind the Wehrmacht as it advanced across the country. His role, as head of Britain's *Gestapo*, was to immediately capture or summarily execute 2,400 of Britain's key government, business, clergy and educational figures,

Communists and, of course, leading Jews.

After Sea Lion's postponement, with so much of Russia to conquer in 1941, Franz found himself leading *Einsatzgruppen, Vorkommando Moscow.* If the panzers captured Moscow, his future was assured. That summer and early fall proved heady days for the Third Reich. Despite heavy fighting and occasional delays, the Wehrmacht had advanced hundreds of miles into Russia. Better yet for Seis, he thought, was Stalin's refusal to evacuate the Red government from Moscow. At night, Seis saw himself as *the* person capturing hundreds of Red officials. For the rest of his life he would day-dream about the lost opportunities; if only...

Until the gates of Moscow were reached and winter enveloped the *Wehrmacht*, Seis's leadership was a textbook elimination of Jews, Russians, Party members, and Gypsies. In one operation alone, outside of Smolensk, he played a key role in killing over 15,000. Seis was so "effective" that he was singled out by Himmler in a fall, 1941 letter of promotion. However, for philatelists, Russia proved useless; Stalin's purges had decimated the upper middle class and the cities Seis entered were too destroyed to offer anything meaningful.

▲

For the Seis brothers, stamp acquisitions became dependent on support from Food & Agriculture Reich Ministers Walther Darré and his successor, Herbert Backe. With Himmler's approval, concentration camp records were scoured for Jewish stamp dealers. On average, they oversaw between fifteen and twenty of these former concentration camp prisoners, with a slow turnover due to disease, breakdowns, and incompetency. The operation also utilized eight to ten Jewish women as record keepers and cooks, frequent replacement caused by pregnancies, madness, and suicide. The prisoners were managed by two disabled combat veterans, both philatelists: Ulrich Schmidt (no left eye) and Gottfried Kessler (three fingers of his left hand lost), as well as several older male guards.

The site, formerly a Jewish-owned home, sat on two acres of lightly wooded ground in the northeast Berlin suburbs. Two stories tall, it contained an un-finished basement, 40' by 50,' an equal sized first floor, and a smaller second floor with four bedrooms. Worker-prisoners were locked in the basement at night, while guards not on duty slept or lounged on the second floor. Sexually accommodating females received extra food.

Most important of all was stamp protection. A concrete reinforced corner room was built and two large safes requisitioned. As dampness is stamps' greatest threat, air conditioners were installed, a 65° temperature maintained. The prisoners' work sorted, selected, then gave each stamp a preliminary value. Stamps worth less than $140 (American) were set aside and later sold in Switzerland and Sweden, the cash used for bribes and the Seis brother's secret accounts. Assisted by a large library of rare, looted books of stamp minutia, the grading of each stamp was by microscopic examination, then followed by examining paper quality, color density, previous usage, and overall condition. Afterward, each stamp was filed and cross-classified by nation, date of issue, and value. Trusting no one, the Seis brothers had the prisoners work in groups, unknowingly double-checking each other.

▲

After America entered the war, French resistance and British raids in occupied France increased. Hitler become livid when a March 28 commando raid at Saint-Nazaire destroyed the Nazi's largest Atlantic Ocean dry-dock, effectively prohibiting repairs on battleships and heavy cruisers. Hitler felt he'd been too gentle with the French and determined to move forward with an iron hand. The SS, he decided, would prove better policemen that the Wehrmacht. And who is more effective than Seis's mentor, Reinhard Heydrich? After all, hasn't Heydrich so subdued the Czechs that he rides through Prague in an open car without bodyguards? First, though, Franz Seis is sent to Paris to administratively prepare the way for Heydrich's transfer.

Late afternoon May 27. Seis is sipping coffee outdoors near the Paris SS headquarters at the Hotel Residence Foch. His new position will entail coordinating SS intelligence, counter espionage, and police for the *zone occupée* (occupied France). On one hand, Seis is looking forward to a meaningful assignment; on the other, he realizes his stamp collecting days are over. Then comes news that Heydrich has been seriously wounded by an assassin. Heydrich lingers a week, then mysteriously expires after Himmler's personal physicians arrive.

Caught in Paris, Seis is not recalled to Berlin until weeks after Heydrich's death, thus being absent during a period of vicious SS political infighting. Ultimately, he is shouldered aside by his former assistant Adolph Eichmann and sent to the Nazi equivalent of Siberia: performing desk work as a war rages on. However, this ill wind blows Franz Seis much good. Vichy France had been off limits for the Seis brothers' stamp operations. Cooling his heels in Paris, Franz Seis uses his time to research the French stamp market and discovers that a huge amount of trading continues. Better yet, new philatelic journals are being published in Vichy France (*Bulletin Philatélique Mensuel*) while the decades old *L'Echo de la Timbrologie* resumes. With these resources, Seis begins to pinpoint future stamp acquisitions. Following Hitler's occupation of Vichy France in November, immediately behind the troops are the Seis brothers. By year's end, the brothers have acquired another huge haul.

Chapter 8: Martin Bormann.

If the number of people involved in the Seis brothers' operations is small, no such work goes undetected—the Nazi hierarchy can sniff out money-making prospects. Thus, it comes as no surprise to Seis when he is told that Martin Bormann, Hitler's personal secretary, gate keeper, and *Parteikanzlei* (Nazi Party leader) wishes to visit the stamp compound.

When the short, double-chinned Bormann arrives in his armor-plated, six-seat Mercedes Benz 540K, Franz Seis is fully prepared. Wishing to make the best impression possible, Seis has fed the workers well for days and distributed fresh prison uniforms. The facility is so spotless that even the German Shepherds have been cleaned. Bormann, shrewd but no philatelist, slowly goes from room to room. He has no idea what he is inspecting, but grunts approvingly when he realizes that it will be another source of money for himself and the Führer.

Following his tour, Bormann and Franz Seis sit in a small room drinking Columbian Coffee and eating French pastries with heavy cream and real chocolate. Then Bormann begins the civilized but one-sided negotiations.

"Your workers certainly look content," Bormann remarks. "All Jews?"

Seis nods and Bormann continues. "Being here is like visiting a hospital; clean uniforms, the smell of detergents, and real oatmeal for the prisoners if I'm not mistaken."

Seis' smile answers the question. "We have civilian neighbors on all sides; unlike the concentration camps we try and set a reasonable standard."

"But those bathrooms for prisoners? Even where they sleep. Isn't that over-doing it?"

"Just like women perfume love letters, stamps acquire odors. How could we sell a stamp for $5,000 if, say, when a buyer closely examines it with his magnifying glass, the stamp literally smells like shit?"

Bormann slaps his knee with pleasure, becoming red in the face when he cannot stop laughing, then continues, "But if I arrive next week, will the conditions still be the same?"

"If you come back unannounced next week they will be wearing the same uniforms, and they will be day-dreaming of the food they received before your visit."

After this hearty laugh, Seis continues that they are being fed horsemeat, days-old sweetbreads—nothing wasted in wartime Germany—and leftovers including fat drippings from the Food and Agriculture mess hall. Overall, Seis explains, they receive two, perhaps three, times the calories of concentration camp inmates.

"But won't all those fat drippings kill them some day?" Bormann asks, a marvelously funny joke that Seis repeats for months. "And what about the Jewesses? Are they separated from the males?"

"We see no reason to separate them. It would only cost money to build partitions and they would find a way to rut anyway. They're surprisingly good at that, you know," Seis replies as Bormann laughs so hard that tears fill his eyes.

"And are they good looking? Many are I understand?"

"Yes. Most are young, comely, and *exceptionally* grateful to receive extra rations."

"Ah yes, so now we are back to them getting fat, aren't we?" Bormann jovially says.

As Seis smiles, Bormann snaps his fingers without warning. "Oh, amidst our pleasurable discussion I almost forgot the purpose of my visit. My sources indicate that your stamps might be worth over ten million American dollars —"

"Far closer to five. And there have been considerable out of pocket costs."

"We can compromise on a nine-million-dollar estimate. And, unless I am mistaken, your 'out of pocket' costs have been met by the Food & Agriculture Ministry, is that not so? All properly accounted for, I assume?" Bormann asks with a wicked smile.

Seis says nothing. Both know that every penny from Food & Agriculture has been taken illegally.

"You know," Bormann continues, looking Seis in the eye, "when we win the war, and with Britain and America brought to their knees, there will likely be very few people left with which to buy stamps. Some people might even believe your efforts are a sign of defeatism."

Seis is stunned, have all his calculations been for nothing. Might he be shot?

"However," Bormann says smiling, "under the circumstances, let me suggest that my share should be twenty percent."

Franz Seis nods and smiles. The twenty percent is not negotiable even if Bormann never tells the Führer. But behind his smile, Seis groans. He is already paying off Himmler through Walther Darré and Herbert Backe. When the stamps are finally sold, each penny will be meticulously recorded by accountants on Himmler's staff. And will someone else, perhaps Goering, shake them down next?

▲

Prior to Bormann's visit and before all of France was occupied, Franz Seis added a third man to his staff, another injured veteran, stamp expert, and Nazi party member, Rudy Spangler. The angular, homely Spangler, with a bulging Adam's apple and big ears, was thirty and worked for years in his father's stamp and coin store in Munich. Spangler was an elite *Fallschirmjäger* (paratrooper). A lieutenant in 1940, he was one of eighty-seven men who landed *on top* of Belgian's Fort Eban Emael and, blocking their air vents, captured twenty times as many defenders. With this came an Iron Cross with Oak Leaves. In May 1941, he jumped into Crete with the First Assault Regiment, the same unit as legendary boxer Max Schmeling. Here Spangler badly broke his hip and thigh and Schmeling was shot in the knee, the injuries leaving both unfit for further duty.

Across occupied western Europe, Seis, in his black SS uniform, and Spangler with a cane and in his Luftwaffe blue-gray jacket and gray pants make an effective pair. Spangler, multi-lingual, open faced, and with a pleasant smile, begins all conversations in a sympathetic, low key manner but with ample technical questions so that the stamp collector or business owner knows he isn't talking to an amateur. After ample coaxing, if there is still not satisfactory cooperation, Spangler sadly shakes his head and nods to Seis.

Seis's approach is to ask personal questions about the man's family, then state his goal: to examine the man's stamps. If cooperation isn't forthcoming, Seis sighs, shrugs his shoulders, and removes a ball-peen hammer and a square, bloodstained small wooden platter from a large black doctor's bag. Spangler takes the platter, places it on a table, shaking his head before placing the man's right hand on the platter. Seis solicitously asks which finger he would like to have smashed first, then carefully takes aims. In fact, the dried blood is from a chicken and, perhaps disappointingly for Seis, no philatelist ever calls his bluff or complains to the police.

At times, Seis and Spangler are far too late. When it comes to the truly wealthy such as French baron Alphonse James de Rothschild, that family's legendary collection had arrived in New York even before Paris fell.

In late 1944, months following the D-Day landings and with the war clearly lost, the question facing the Seis brothers becomes how to retain their most valuable stamps. Ideally, they would be placed in Swiss banks, but since the Gestapo are, if anything, more vigilant at the border, that option isn't available.

Franz Seis's only choice is to wait until almost the end, then have trusted associates carry the most valuable stamps west *through* Allied lines. He needs two men who are likely not on Allied "wanted" lists, can mix with civilians and safely pass through SS check points. Equally paramount: they can't know too much about stamps and be tempted to keep on running.

One of the two men that Seis selects is Bormann's representative who, Franz Seis will learn years later, was killed in Berlin. The second is his brother Hermann whose injuries, Franz hopes, will protect him. While Spangler isn't allowed to carry stamps, his role on April 23 is to certify the stamps for the others: even as this late date Franz Seis makes sure that lower grade stamps haven't substituted. While the Seis brothers discuss killing Spangler—after all, he knows too much—his expertise and proven discretion will be needed after the war.

Franz Seis is fully aware that it will be one thing to evade the Russians, and another to safely cross the Elbe. Like salmon, smaller Nazi fish have begun leaping one hurdle after another, helped along their way by anti-Semitic European and Vatican sympathizers. Yet the higher the official, the greater the likelihood of capture. For years, most were treated like mad sultans—whatever street skills they'd possessed now eroded by desk jobs and fine food.

On April 23, the five shake hands and go their separate ways. In ten days, Darré will be captured and Hermann Seis killed. Rudy Spangler, not on anyone's wanted lists, safely reaches his parent's Munich home. Herbert Backe is taken prisoner in late May while Franz Seis, wanted by the Allies, evades capture.

Chapter 9: Germany, Late Spring—Early Summer, 1945.

An hour after Hermann Seis's May 2 death, his identification and research papers are burnt. Harry and Manfredi jump on his corpse, forcing out any remaining air. Hans stops barking and happily licks blood and brains off the tile floor. With the canal now fast flowing because of a break before the Elbe, Seis's unclothed body is heaved into the canal followed by his clothing and shoes. Next, Seis's bicycle is placed outside and disappears in minutes. The meat locker is cleaned, Lowenbrau the only available disinfectant. U. S. dollars and British pounds are divided 30-30-30 for Manfredi, Tonstad and Zilina, the final ten for Harry. He also keeps the stamps and, rationalizing his actions, tells himself that the other three would never be able to get their minds around the concept that the stamps could be worth tens of thousands of dollars. In fact, not until months later does Harry realize how woefully he underestimated their value.

▲

As summer begins, Harry's most important tasks are fielding a good company baseball team and forgetting about losing his temper and murdering Seis. He realizes that he isn't a good player, nor does he have managerial instincts, but he is a damned good *watcher*.

Doing nothing for long periods, sitting under a tree in his brown under-shirt, sipping a coke and listening to birds chatter, Harry thinks, perfectly tests his leadership abilities. Daily shaving is another treat. Then, one July morning, after word comes that the Eighty-Second is being transferred to Berlin, he examines himself closely in the mirror. For a split second, he realizes he has the same look in his eyes that Spencer Tracy, playing Dr. Jekyll, had as he scrutinized himself for traces of Mr. Hyde.

Harry starts to laugh, "Well, I'm not *that* crazy, am I? I'll be OK. Hell, I *am* OK." Which might or might not be true.

▲

To every paratroopers' dismay, instead of the Eighty-Second going home, Eisenhower selects it for Berlin occupation duty. That summer, the city holds over two-million Berliners and another million refugees from eastern Germany, Poland and the Baltic countries. Additionally, there are tens of thousands of stranded Jews, Gypsies, French, Hungarians, Czechoslovakians, Ukrainians, Russians, and Germans released from Nazi concentration and forced labor camps.

The first day that Harry goes on patrol in his jeep, the decimated city seems like a silent movie produced in sepia tones, the scurrying population wearing the clothes they slept in, the stench of over 3,000 unburied dead hanging over subways, bomb shelters, and piles of rubble. Along the main boulevards and streets, long lines of *Trümmerfrauen* (rubble women) pass buckets by hand down a line, gradually clearing streets while building mountains of waste for American bulldozers and dump trucks to remove.

Harry is more than aware that, during the previous three months of Russian occupation, the Soviet Army has become a gigantic, million-man raping machine. Seemingly every healthy woman between fifteen and fifty has been raped, often gang-raped, and usually for days on end. Some one hundred and twenty-five thousand women, a fraction of those raped, need emergency hospital care. Fighting off an attacker or screaming for help results in beatings and often death. Paradoxically, Russians like heavier women who are often the wives and daughters of well-fed Nazi officials. In all, at least 20,000 women are murdered or commit suicide, there are tens of thousands of hospital abortions, all of which is followed by a huge spike in live births and abandoned babies in early '46. No one is spared. When the wives and daughters of German Communists who'd lived in Russia since Hitler's ascendency finally return to Berlin, they too are indiscriminately raped.

Within days of the Eighty-Second's arrival comes the first U.S.–Russian showdown. It is common for Russians to rob and even kill for wristwatches— their spoils of choice. A point of pride for Soviet soldiers is to wear as many wristwatches on each arm as possible.

One evening, Harry and Manfredi, who is now his driver with Tonstad and

Zilina reassigned, are accosted by a very drunk Red soldier. The man's soft cap is on sideways, he holds a submachine gun in his right hand and cradles a bottle in his left. Stepping in front of their slow-moving jeep, he waves his left hand for them to stop and get out of their jeep.

"Watches ... watches," he mumbles in English, pointing to his right wrist on which he wears a trio of them. Harry gets out and walks to within arm's length of the wobbling soldier.

"*Ya ploha gavaru pa Ruski,* (My Russian is bad)," says Harry, as slowly as possible. Then carefully pulls up his jacket sleeve to show his standard army-issue Bulova wristwatch.

"*Da! Da!*" the Russian grins, forgetting about Manfredi, as he leans forward to examine Harry's watch. It is the last thing he does before the butt of Manfredi's .45 pistol smashes into his head. The two drag the unconscious soldier to a pile of rubble, remove the ammunition drum of his sub-machine gun, but leave the liquor bottle. Harry has no interest in what will happen next. At night, feral German Shepherds roam the street and murderous gangs operate with impunity. Indeed, a few fanatical Nazis, calling themselves *Werewolves*, still harass the Soviets, one night freeing 500 Germans from a Russian holding pen slated for Siberia.

Days later, another drunken Red soldier attempts to rob a paratrooper's watch and is shot dead. This singular lesson, despite vehement Soviet protests, is not repeated. The paratroopers' verbal orders are to take no risks: when in doubt, shoot. Soon Berlin's turmoil subsides as the paratroopers' presence, cigarettes and Hershey bars—to say nothing of America's dropping two A-bombs—more than trumps Russian fear.

Harry's occupation role is to act as one of General Gavin's informal sets of eyes and ears. He and three other 82nd captains are billeted in the untouched two-story home of a respected widow whose husband died in a bombing and whose three sons are buried in Russia. The widow takes an imaginary poodle for long walks, putters around the house, and sleeps in the servants' quarters. Manfredi proves his uncanny ability to procure anything, including an elderly cook and a comely fifteen-year-old housekeeper. Both are only too happy to work in exchange for safe sleeping quarters, food, cigarettes, and a few American dollars each week.

As for the stamps, Harry can only leave them in his room. Theft in homes billeting U.S. officers are rare, so he simply gets four manila envelopes and tapes them to the bottom bureau drawer. Harry knows that this is an unsophisticated hiding place, but he can't think of anything better and certainly doesn't want to ask anyone—Manfredi included—for help. As for a thief wishing to enter the room, which cannot be locked, he leaves Hans. His superior bark is the best deterrent Harry can think of.

Chapter 10: Berlin, August 21.

It is 9 AM when Harry has Manfredi slow down and stop as they come to a line of Berliners queued up at a Red Cross distribution kiosk of freshly baked bread. At least two GIs are scheduled to be stationed at sites where food is doled out, but Harry sees no one. Harry telephones for GIs to be sent over, then he and Manfredi park their jeep fifty yards away, sitting in the cool morning shadows of a bombed-out church and watch.

Everything seems orderly for fifteen minutes until a man, not noticing the jeep, ambles up to the line's front, waits until a thin, teenage boy receives his allotment, then violently knocks the boy down and takes his bread. Flashing a large knife, he dares anyone in line to interfere. Satisfied, he saunters off in the direction he has come, a smirk on his face.

"Get the bastard," Harry orders Manfredi, who needs little encouragement. There is a loud squeal of tires, the man pivots, but in seconds the jeep is blocking his way, Harry's carbine pointed at the man's stomach.

"Please, I have a wife and children..." he says, pleading in broken English. Then his voice trails off as Harry cuts in and begins speaking in German.

"Drop the knife and give my friend the bread," Harry says. Looking at Manfredi, he smiles and then asks in English, "Do you see an eagle up there?" It is an old trick.

Manfredi nods, takes the bread, picks up the knife and shouts, "Look at that!" pointing towards the empty sky. His actions, the English words meaning nothing, nevertheless instantly draw the attention of everyone in the bread line, the Red Cross workers, and even the thief.

As they all look for something, Harry rams the carbine's butt into the thief's stomach. When the man doubles over, Harry gives an uppercut to the jaw with the rifle. Harry is about to smash him a third time when he stops in mid-motion; he is afraid that a third blow might hospitalize him. Smiling, Harry thinks of the old army line: no thanks, too much paperwork. Instead, he pushes the man to the ground.

"This didn't happen," Harry whispers. "Do you understand me?" The man, sitting on the pavement, his hands on his bleeding jaw, nods. Only then do the Berliners standing in line realize what has occurred and applaud Harry's actions.

"Make sure this prick is gone, pronto," Harry tells Manfredi. Harry takes the bread and walks back to where the boy is sitting on the ground, head in his hands, cap half off, apparently in a daze. Except, as Harry realizes when he squats to ask the boy if he is OK, he is looking into the magnetic blue eyes of a young woman.

▲

The girl wears frayed socks and sneakers, American dungarees, a rope belt, the standard white blouse of female Nazi employees, and needs a bath. Her thick black hair, at first hidden under a Greek Fisherman's cap, is filled with grease and dirt. As Harry learns in bits and pieces, like a half-million other Berlin women, she has slept in the safety—from rape, not bombs—of air raid shelters. Around her neck is a small plastic purse containing aspirin, toothpowder and Vaseline which Berlin women learn to apply in the few seconds prior to being raped. She also has safety pins which have replaced needles and thread to hold things together. Since May, she has lived on raw potatoes, soup, and bread given to rubble women and bartered her body for boiled meat.

Somehow, Harry has chanced upon a combination of a twentieth century Charles Dickens' street urchin and a young woman needing a protector. Needing *him*. A moment later, when she jumps to her feet and smiles, Harry knows he has been hit by lightning.

"You're coming with me," he says, his German perfect, his voice unsteady. She will later tell him how relieved she was to see no lust in his eyes.

"You're German," she answers surprised.

"Of course, I'm German. I just happen to be an American." He says, but blushes when he realizes how nonsensical and flummoxed he sounds. "Do you have anything else with you?"

When she shakes her head, he motions for her to sit in the back of the open-air jeep.

She says nothing, simply following Harry back to his jeep and then to Frau Zollinger's house. Barely seventeen years old, for three months she has been raped, bartered, and beaten, suffering a broken nose and, what to Harry sounds like a concussion. She has lost so much weight that even the Russians have lost interest in her. She has learned when and when not to defend herself. On one occasion, she tells Harry later, she scared off two teenage boys with an animal snarl. Like 75,000 other Berlin women, she'd walked into the American sector the day the Eighty-Second arrived.

The jeep's open top makes conversation impossible as they drive back to the Zollinger house. "By the way, my name is, or at least it was Heinrich Strölin," he says as the jeep pulls to a stop. "I'm from Stuttgart. It's Harry Strong now, but everybody calls me 'Cap.' That's because of my rank," he says awkwardly, holding out his hand.

"And mine is Ilse Wallbillig," she says, hesitantly returning his handshake.

Once inside, Hannah, the cook, says nothing—although her look of disgust makes it clear that she disapproves. Harry doesn't care; he quietly orders her to prepare soup and soft food for Ilse.

▲

In the confusion endemic in the American occupation, there is a constant tug-of-war for supplies. Predictably, most company-sized military units have at least one man who drives pencil-checking, clipboard carrying, supply personnel bat-shit. Manfredi is such a "can do," thoroughly larcenous man whose shrewdness and personality derive maximum pleasure not just cutting through red tape, but taking the tape home as a souvenir.

After Ilse sits down in the kitchen, Harry gives Manfredi a list of items she needs, few of which are to be found in the Eighty-Second's PX. Manfredi knows that he is expected to *liberate* or otherwise acquire the articles via black market bartering. Harry doesn't have to remind Manfredi that, if Manfredi had found similar items for his fifteen-year-old housecleaning mistress now living in the Zollinger house, he can surely do as well for Ilse.

By evening, courtesy of Manfredi, Harry's room has increased by one army cot (with mattress, pillows, sheets and blankets), a full complement of women's toiletries and towels, and German civilian and military clothing without insignias (wearing American army clothing is strictly forbidden for civilians)—shoes are still on order through the black market. Of his own volition, Manfredi has also acquired a lime-green Hamilton Beach milkshake mixer and a six-month supply of malt ("Cap, she's way too thin," he whispered to Harry), pajamas, and a bathrobe. Days later, when it is discovered that Ilse used to play in a Königsburg Orchestra, a violin appears.

Chapter 11: Harry Strong.

Despite his self-possessed demeanor, Harry Strong did not understand women. He had grown up without daily mentors or confidantes; his mother had died before his teenage years, his sister was younger, and his father was always away. At the Mount Hermon boarding school in north-central Massachusetts, as Harry was about to begin his maturation, he possibly knew even less about the birds and bees than any of his fellow freshmen. Wide-eyed, he and a half-dozen dorm mates had painstakingly scrutinized a deck of playing cards with pictures of sad-eyed nudes in provocative poses. The rest of their knowledge was based on rumors and tidbits gleaned from upperclassmen's "advice" and sexual bragging which were, of course, mostly lies by those equally unknowledgeable.

Like all teenage boys, pimples emerged, Harry became gawky, hormones began raging uncontrollably, his voice changed, shaving (finally!) began, and girls slowly fell into place. As a freshman, Harry had to be dragged onto a dance floor by girls his own age who had zero interest in him but needed a partner. Then, late in his sophomore year, square dancing gave way to shy hand-holding when the music stopped, and hand-holding gave way to furtive kissing. By Harry's senior year there were fleeting minutes of intense petting while standing in the shadows of campus buildings. Promptly at 10 PM, busses separated the sexes, whisking them to their respective campuses five miles and the Connecticut River apart. Then, miracle of miracles, while at his roommate's house over Christmas his senior year, the boy's attractive sister, a junior home from Vassar, sneaked into the family guest room one night and then returned every night for a week.

At first, Harry's language skills had left him fearful of ever getting into a college. During Harry's first two years his grades were mostly "credits" for taking the courses, his English too poor for formal marking. Then, almost suddenly, his brain made the critical transition from translating everything he heard from English to German and back again, to understanding and responding to what he was hearing the first time he heard it.

At Amherst, he found himself gravitating to older girls. At first, he had little control over the affairs, never realizing that a three year older co-ed might be using him for sex just as much as he used her. Gradually, he became the equally experienced partner, but there was something in him that he always held back. Most of his girlfriends sensed it but didn't care, but, if they brought it up, the relationship soon fizzled. Harry could drink, dance, sing (when drinking), and laugh, but nevertheless there remained an undefined emptiness that made him think of Hamlet's melancholia, the Shakespeare play he most identified with.

Over the 1940 Christmas holiday, Harry met and fell in love with a Radcliffe junior, Stephanie Chatsworth Pringle whose mother looked more British than Queen Victoria. In fact, she was British; the daughter of a financially strained family who married the grandson of a railroad baron. For eighteen months, the two were inseparable and then, after a soccer game in which he scored the Lord Jeff's winning goal, Harry asked her to marry him. But, Stephanie enquired, even if America doesn't go to war, what do you want to do? You're majoring in history. That means teaching or the State Department. I love you and enjoy proving it, but the fact of the matter is that I also like living in Greenwich, Connecticut, and that my parents have money and keep horses. While I think Robert Donat is pretty damned cute; no, I'm not interested in a Mr. Chips. What would I become: a dried up old woman counting pennies, eating corned beef and cabbage, and having a squeaky old husband at some god-forsaken boys preparatory school? Thanks, but no thanks.

To Harry, Stephanie's attitude had not just been a shock, *hurt,* and hurt badly. He'd been rejected and felt humiliated because he didn't financially measure up. Nor, he realized, was it likely he would he ever be able to do so. While he could bed society's upper crust, there were expectations that he could never meet. Harry didn't want to admit it, but, six weeks after Stephanie's rejection, he almost welcomed America's entry into the war.

▲

During the war, most of Harry's sexual experiences in the States, Great Britain, and France were in brothels. Germany was different. Once the Eighty-Second entered the Third Reich, its paratroopers began to routinely rape German women; even nuns on one grim occasion that Harry knew about. To Harry, the moral lines had become blurry. On occasion, he stopped paratroopers from raping screaming, crying girls who looked like they were thirteen or fourteen. However, like most officers, he usually turned a blind eye to what his men were doing. "Tone things down," he'd say which, he very well knew, wasn't the same as "No."

And, truth be known, twice after the fighting in the Bulge ended, the emotionally spent Harry selected an attractive *fraulein* for himself. The reaction on each occasion, as he had correctly hoped, was one of passive acceptance versus active resistance. In both cases he left money and cigarettes, his way of clearing his wartime conscience. Had his advances been actively rejected, he knew he wouldn't have continued. Some men can rape a woman, but in the back of his mind, he is certain that he cannot.

▲

Outside Cologne, in March, as his company beds down in a small suburban village, Harry notices a classically stunning, mid-twenties, long-haired woman, Maria, who is standing in her doorway. Instinct taking over, he makes a bee-line for her, figuratively brushing aside two otherwise aggressive sergeants jockeying for her attention. After briefly talking with her and discovering that she is a childless widow, Harry taking her by the wrist and walks her into her own house. Once inside he is struck by the perpendicular outline of now-empty spaces on the walls of the hallway and living room. Pictures of the Führer, he wonders?

In the woman's bedroom is a photograph of a young girl with long blond pigtails, curtseying and handing a bouquet of flowers to Hitler.

"Is that you?" he asks as Maria proudly nods.

"You won't hurt me, will you?" she asks. But it is a rhetorical question; her eyes bright with expectation, not fearful.

"There's no way," Harry says, letting her hand go and noticing the beginning of a sly smile on her face. Maria pulls the shades down and, standing near the window, not accidentally lets Harry watch her magnificent silhouette as she slowly undresses. The fact is that both have been instantly drawn to the other. In bed, Harry's slow foreplay quickly rockets them to mutual passion. Harry is as aroused as he hasn't been since he proposed to Stephanie Pringle; Maria is the woman that he's genuinely wanted for years.

Sitting on the bed together, it takes all his will power to put on a Trojan. Amused, Maria watches until he finishes. As they embrace, she tells Harry that it will be her first sex since her husband left for Stalingrad.

▲

"You're marvelous," she whispers in Harry's ear after they both climax. It is as if they've been lovers for months.

"What are you thinking about?" she asks. Harry is lying on his back, thoroughly contented.

"I want to see more of you. Right now, I'm going over in my mind ways to keep my company here as long as possible," he says, affectionately kissing her ears and nose.

"Will you come back afterwards?"

"Wild horses couldn't keep me away," Harry says, his voice serious as he lights another cigarette for her.

"I'd like that," she whispers back. After they finish their cigarettes they kiss again. Harry wants to hug her but Maria playfully pushes him away, laughs, and crawls between his legs.

Only then, as her mouth encircles him, does she realize that Harry's been circumcised.

"Does this mean you're Jewish?" Maria asks in a high-pitched, panicked voice, the word *Jewish* voiced with disgust. Almost gagging, she jerks her head back up and looks at Harry, her anger obvious despite the darkness.

"Yes," Harry answers. He is half-amused, but one hundred percent furious at the Master Race in general and Maria in particular. "It means that you can tell your grandchildren you were fucked by a Jew and absolutely loved it."

Maria's answers by scratching Harry's face, slapping him, and then begin screeching obscenities. Harry explodes and slaps her back. He pushes her on her back, forcefully spreads her legs, then shoves himself between her sticky thighs. Once inside Maria, he hopes that each angry thrust will hurt. However, biology being what it is, his second ejaculation takes far longer. When he's done, she sobs she might be pregnant with a Jewish child. Harry's cold answer is he'll be back in nine months to see for sure.

The incident is beyond Harry's wildest comprehension. Hurriedly he leaves the house, finding himself thoroughly depressed. Has Hitler destroyed us both, he wonders? Why did she have to say what she did and why wasn't I any better? I could have fallen in love with her. Harry stops, thinking about returning to Maria's house to somehow make amends, then decides he doesn't know what to say. Perhaps by morning some idea will come to him. He can't just walk away from a woman like that, can he? Head down, he walks to where his troops are quartered and goes into a fitful sleep, only too happy not to remember his unpleasant dreams.

The next morning Maria, one eye swollen and purple, is found hanging in her family's carriage house. She has committed suicide. It is Harry's job to certify her death. To his horror, as he watches Maria's body being cut down, he finds himself thinking of how much he liked her. As disturbing, the men he is closest to know that he was with her the previous night. They avoid him for days, neither looking him in the eye or speaking to him unless spoken to.

At Amherst, Harry had prided himself on being attuned to the women he dated, especially understanding when "no" meant "no," and more happily, when it meant "yes." Yet, somewhere along the line, has he lost touch with reality? These actions are something he doesn't understand and can't explain.

Chapter 12: A "Holy Joe," Late March 1945.

Maria's unnecessary death all but overwhelms Harry's will to live. He knows that suicidal feelings are common for those in combat, and over the next few days he is tempted to put his .45 in his mouth. In desperation—after all, he doesn't really want to die—he seeks out a regimental chaplain—that this "Holy Joe" was Catholic made no difference to either.

"Welcome to my parish," the priest says, ducking into a dirty, frayed canvas pyramid tent that has two-fold-up chairs, a standard chaplain's foot locker, and a rolled up sleeping bag on top of a poncho. Harry pours out the story as best he can (toning down the sex, of course) as the priest listens sympathetically, nodding and grunting occasionally.

"So, tell me about yourself. When you were little, what did you want to be?" Harry realizes that this seemingly innocuous question isn't chosen at random for, most likely, the priest wants to put Harry as ease and draw him out. Which it does.

"I wanted to be an American cowboy, like Tom Mix," Harry laughs. "Strange as it might seem, father, when I got older my goal was the ministry or teaching. For a while, I was interested in Union Theological Seminary in New York. There were numerous German refugee theologians on the faculty. Nothing against Catholicism, of course, but it's a lower-key church, what I think is more of-this-earth Christianity. I'm comfortable with it. Someone once said, 'The place where men meet to seek the highest is holy ground.' That's how I feel. It isn't the vestments or what you say that counts in God's eyes, but the humbleness and thought behind your actions. One meaningful Hail Mary is better than a hundred by rote."

"Ah yes," the priest smiles. "The parable of the Pharisee and the Publican, Luke 18:9. We all ask ourselves the same question. But you also said that 'for a while' you were interested in Union Theological. What changed your mind?"

"The Nazis. They made it easy for me, didn't they? It never crossed my mind not to fight. To me, it was the only thing that made sense."

"You mentioned earlier that you felt they killed your mother. What about revenge?"

"In the abstract, yes, but not anymore. I don't have the make-up to fly a B-17 and drop bombs killing people who-knows-where. With some people it's the Marines, God bless 'em, but with me it's the paratroopers and taking advantage of how well I know German. I've got no scruples when things get tight and I sure as hell won't apologize for my anger—"

Harry stops as the priest smiles and pushes his hands down, all but saying "calm down."

"Do you know how many times I've seen dead paratroopers that were captured and tortured before being shot?" Harry continues. "They kill us in cold blood and we... But it's that German girl that killed herself after I—"

"Do you get this angry all the time? I mean with women after fighting's over?"

"No, father. Never. What set me off was how much she hated Jews. Nothing like this ever happened. I've been forceful—"

"Forceful? As in slapped or punched? Ones that you beat up, perhaps?"

"No. Forceful, as in taking by the elbow. I'm scared of myself these days. That's why I'm here."

"I'm going to switch subjects, captain. Do you sleep well?"

"As long as there's nothing 'incoming.'" Both men laugh as they imagine themselves huddled in a foxhole during an artillery bombardment.

"Constant nightmares?"

"Some, but certainly not constant."

"How guilty do you feel about all this?"

"I was born and spent half my life in Germany. I don't know what would happen to me if I killed someone I knew years ago, but getting rid of these Nazis comes first."

"Take my word for it," the priest said smiling, "Sigmund Freud would throw you out of his office for wasting his time. I'm going to send you over to the medics and they'll give you some pills so you can sleep better."

"That'll be more than enough, padre." The guy is nice enough, Harry thinks, there's no point saying that the pills will be just extra-strength aspirin.

"One other thing, captain. Do you have a pet?"

"A dog we call Hans, he acquired us last week."

"Keep him. Make him yours, that's an order. And we have an officers' showers over there," the priest said, pointing and smiling. "Then grab some chow and get back to work."

Harry realizes that this Holy Joe senses that he's still capable of leading GIs in combat and that he's being sent off with a bottle of aspirin and a pat on the back. Oddly, in the back of his mind, he remembers the child's song, "Skip to my Lou." So, I'll just take a shower and skip back to work, he thinks. Hopefully, he won't crack up again. But, as Harry well knows, the fact of the matter is that there just aren't enough experienced officers available for the front. Getting combat vets back to the front lines is the Army's and the priest's absolute priority.

As Harry heads to the shower stall he notices the priest opening his tent flap and looking around. "Who's next?" he hears the priest call.

Chapter 13: Berlin, Late Summer – Fall, 1945.

Returning to his room that August 21st night with Ilse, Harry cannot help but think of Stephanie Pringle and Maria, whose last name he never knew. Too often, circumstances have either been beyond his control or he's made a terrible error, he thinks.

Harry feels Ilse cautiously watching him, apparently waiting for the signal to join him in his bed. Instead, he points to the cot Manfredi requisitioned. Hans trots to the middle of the room between the two, walks in a tight circle three or four times, then plops himself down.

"That bed's yours. Hans will guard us both."

"The bed is mine?"

"Yes, to sleep in," he smiles at his own bad joke. "In America, we say *snooze*." He puts his hands together as if praying and then places his cheek on them. Then he pretends to snore loudly, stopping a few seconds later when Ilse begins smiling, then giggles like a child.

The first smile, Harry thinks, wondering how long it's been for her.

Ilse cautiously sits on the cot, pats it in the middle and then one corner, examining the bed like it was a large St. Bernard she's meeting for the first time.

Harry realizes that she's doing her best not to show emotion.

"I haven't slept in a bed since last year," she blurts out, but has barely finished the sentence when an almost visible cloud crosses her eyes.

Harry winces as the mood he's tried to establish instantly evaporates. He doesn't want to know what Ilse's remembering; was it being raped, watching her family slaughtered, or both?

Their third night together, realizing that she wouldn't be thrown out for not having sex, Ilse begins asking innocuous questions. When Harry answers, he makes it a point to ask her something similar, purposely not going too far. Let her lead, he thinks. This is working too well to screw it up.

Week by week the relationship grows as Ilse begins gaining weight and confidence. One afternoon, out of the blue, she tells Harry she knows some English; she wants to learn the language better and know more about America. The two go to the Army's Post Exchange (PX) in Berlin, the system than in its fiftieth year of operation. Here they look over a thin collection of books, both deciding they want nothing about the modern world. Ilse insists on *Gone with the Wind* which she's heard so much about. For her, Harry chooses more than a dozen *Classic Comics,* picking stories by Dickens, Baker, Twain, Cooper and other British and American writers.

Understandably, Ilse remains petrified of going out alone. Finally, half as a game and half to get her out, Manfredi suggests having her sit in the back of the jeep and pretend to act as Harry's translator. Harry's memory still burns from his murder of Hermann Seis, Maria's rape, and Wobelein's concentration camp; he is only happy to play the role of counselor and psychologist. Or, Harry wonders, is it the other way around?

▲

Late one night, a month after Ilse's arrival, Harry lies in bed, an unlit cigarette dangling from his mouth. He wants—hell, he needs a smoke, but is afraid that the noise of thumbing his cheap Zippo lighter will wake her. Sleeping on her narrow cot, six feet away, Ilse lies on her side, almost invisible in the dark, her breathing regular and deep, her head on a pillow, her right hand tucked under her head, and her legs drawn up in a fetal position.

I need her more than she can ever know, Harry thinks. Every night, in the last minutes before sleep, Harry's mind is like a rider on a too-fast carousel, his thoughts jumping from one unexpected idea to the next. Like all GIs, he worries about returning to the real world. Is he sane? How will he feel without a .45? If provoked, can he control himself? He is fully aware that by being bigger, faster, and knowing so many ways to kill, he is a dangerous person.

Will the tension ever be completely gone, he wonders?

"Are you alright, Harry?" Ilse whispers. "I heard you mumbling something, were you sleeping? Why don't we share a cigarette?" She is now twenty-five pounds heavier, none of it fat. The week before, he raced her to the PX when her first menstruation in months began, and, the other day, he had, for the first time, noticed a confidence in her eyes.

Harry starts to get up.

"No. You sit down. I can sit on your bed, it's wider than mine."

Harry's bed is closer to the window and despite the dark he easily makes out her silhouette; long dark hair that has been cleaned but not cut, the brown, baggy, large-size army undershirt she wears over the panties Manfredi procured. For whatever reason, she refuses to wear American pajamas.

Hans wakes up and growls ever so slightly as Ilse tiptoes around him.

Harry, lying on his side, gives her a cigarette and then lights them both. For a few seconds, they inhale deeply. Harry blows out a smoke ring, something Ilse has never mastered and which always makes her smile.

"You talk in your sleep often. Do you know that?"

Harry mumbles in the affirmative.

"You're still afraid, aren't you? Didn't you expect to live?" she asks.

"No, not ever. I didn't care, or I didn't think I'd care what would happen."

"But you saved me. Doesn't that help?"

"And killed others," sitting up and shaking his head.

"Will you tell me?"

"No."

"But you didn't save me to have sex, did you?"

"No, not at all. It was something else. I can't describe it, but I'd do it again and again."

"Good," Ilse says, taking Harry's hand and putting it under her T-shirt where he finds himself cupping her warm breast and swollen nipple. Then she pulls off her T-shirt.

"You will kiss me first, won't you? Isn't that how it's done?»

Harry is as nervous as if it were for the first time. For Ilse, romantically, it is.

▲

The next morning Harry feels as if a slow-moving fever has finally dissipated. He instinctively knows that, by helping Ilse, he has benefited equally.

At times Harry shows her some of the stamps he has acquired, but he never discusses their value, as he points out faces, events, and landscapes. In fact, the stamps prove an easy way to teach Ilse English. One evening he even brings out the famed American 1918 upside-down (inverted) Blue Jenny airplane stamp as Ilse laughs at how silly it looks.

Other than the evenings when he is duty commander, the two attend the wide variety of available entertainment. For the GIs, there are Hollywood movies and USO entertainers, although the two prefer the frequent Berlin Philharmonic concerts. The world-famed orchestra is still in business having survived both the war and the accidental shooting to death of its conductor by an American soldier.

At night, they wedge a chair in front of the door, place Harry's larger mattresses on the floor, and make love. When Ilse suggests something different one evening, Harry is slightly taken aback by her boldness, but she simply giggles, "Last week I asked Manfredi to get me some books, but only if he wouldn't tell you. He found *How to Attain and Practice the Ideal Sex Life.* The author was a Dutch doctor who's been dead for thirty years, but it turns out that human anatomy hasn't changed that much since he died, has it?"

"No, it hasn't," says Harry, gasping for breath after one chapter of the deceased doctor's suggestions are completed.

Chapter 14: Leaving Berlin.

Then comes the inevitable day of reckoning. Harry receives orders to report to General Gavin. "Pronto," the messenger says, without explanation. Has someone found about my stamps, Harry wonders?

"Strong," the general said in his office after minimal pleasantries, "you are aware, aren't you, of General Eisenhower's orders concerning no fraternization with German women?"

"Yes sir," said Harry, trying not to breathe a sigh of relief when Gavin says 'fraternizing.' Now, Harry's thoughts concentrate on the posters and notices he has seen or personally distributed. Of course, the fraternization policy says nothing about Gavin's well-known affair with Marlena Dietrich, or, for that matter, Martha Gellhorn, Hemingway's third wife. What was it Metternich had said? "Power is an aphrodisiac."

Inside Harry, a rebellious little voice squeaks, I dare you: go ahead and tell him Dietrich is a German. Harry stands still and says nothing.

"And do you want to guess what I have at HQ in abundance?" Gavin asks.

"Busybodies, sir?"

"Precisely. One of whom graduated from West Point a few months ago and missed all the fun we had in the Ardennes."

"Yes, sir."

"So, you know what I told him?"

"No sir, I don't."

"I said that since you were born here, in Germany, it stood to reason that this is the country where many of your friends and relatives were still living. That is correct, isn't it?"

"Yes, sir."

"I also said that Ike's orders related to contact between German women and American men. However, I neglected to tell him that the concept of fraternization doesn't apply, for example, when a four-star American general and his pretty British female jeep driver see each other after their car is parked, does it?"

Harry smiles; Ike's affair with Kay Summersby is one of the war's worst kept secrets.

"Sir, if I might personally ask, have you met her?"

"I have and she's a knockout. Nevertheless, to continue with *your* problem. I also told that same busybody that, some weeks ago, you told me about your cousin from— "

"Königsberg, sir."

"Precisely. You see, I thought that if two English-speaking people aren't considered to be fraternizing, the same theory should apply to two German speaking persons who are distant cousins. Correct?"

"Absolutely, sir," Harry nods, privately applauding Gavin's preposterous logic.

"I think that you also told me that she was homeless and had had a rough go of it from the Russians. You remember that conversation, don't you?" Since Gavin's statement safely covered ninety-nine percent of Berlin's women Harry sees no reason to correct him, although he has no memory of a previous conversation with Gavin concerning German women in general or Ilse in particular.

"Yes sir, of course."

"Well, that's it then, Strong," Gavin smiles. "Oh, and off the record. Your personal life is none of my business, but when we head home—and that'll be in December—she can't sail with us on the same ship, even if you two are married by then. You have told her, haven't you?"

"Yes, sir. And she'll be staying in Germany, sir. I'm— "

"The less I know the better," Gavin says with relief. "And by the way, Strong, you've done a helluva good job. I appreciate it." Later, Harry will learn that after he left, Gavin jotted down two words on a note pad, "Promote Strong."

"You know, Strong," Gavin continues, "other than our Ruskie friends, it seems that most of my problems these days come from our idiotic fraternization policy; it drives me crazy at times. Every week I'm ordering condoms by the caseload, but half the men don't want to use them and the other half don't know how. If I were a really mean son-of-a-bitch, I'd transfer you so you could sit behind a desk and answer 'Congressionals.'"

"Congressionals?" Harry asks, seeing no need to mention to Gavin that cases of condoms are in a footlocker under his bed, a key commodity in Manfredi's bartering operations.

"A *Congressional* is usually a condolence letter or when a dick-head private falls in love with the first real blonde he ever screwed. Then he writes his mother saying he's in love and getting married. After that the perturbed mother writes her Congressman to have him *order* me to do *something*. Naturally the Congressman's letter reaches me twenty-four hours after the girl discovers she's pregnant."

Harry smiles, thinking of a boy in his company from Kansas.

"I have to answer," Gavin continues. "So, somebody, in my case a busybody '45 West Point grad, writes for my signature a letter to the mother with the good news, copying the Congressman, of course, that she's got a lovely daughter-in-law and 'congratulations!' on your forthcoming grandchild. Now, get the hell out of here before you get yourself in trouble."

Harry is about to go out the door when he hears Gavin's voice and turns around.

"By the way Strong, is she worth it?"

"A real knockout, sir."

▲

Short-lived affairs are always poignant and Harry and Ilse know that, sometime soon, he will return to America. Neither is sure if they love the other or if their relationship is just the passion of frightened, lonely people. It is said, Harry knows, that a quarter of all paratroopers think about sex every ten seconds; the rest more frequently. Harry, not twenty-five, is in the majority. That they need each other is beyond question. In November, Harry does not propose as much as discusses the subject of marriage. Yet, in the back of his mind he wants more time. What he cannot say is that, like so many men, his old-fashioned side remains bothered by her rapes—something that Ilse is just now beginning to talk about. Another part of Harry worries that he has become a war-created Frankenstein—or has it been there all along?

If he can never atone for what he has done, the incomplete thought in his mind is that he will teach his children what is *good*. From his Judeo-Christian upbringing, Mount Hermon's four services a week and Amherst's equally painful chapel program, he knows right from wrong. Their children, he is sure, can make up for his failures.

But when Harry mentions children, which he thought he had done in the abstract, Ilse bursts into tears. It is the first time he has seen her cry. "I'm too young to have babies. You know I'm only seventeen. I never had what you Americans call a 'boyfriend.' I knew boys liked me, but they all went into the Wehrmacht. Only one ever kissed me just before he left, but then his letters stopped..."

"I want to go to the United States with you. But how will *we* survive? How many times have you said how little you understand America? I've lost my home, my family, and my bearings. And you want me to also have the responsibility of babies?"

▲

What Ilse cannot get herself to say is that, like so many German women, she loves the idea of marrying an American. Her concept is of a huge, powerful nation, an almost endless land of milk and honey with perpetual sunshine and happiness, and—best of all—safely beyond the reach of the Russians. And she loves Harry for restoring her faith in herself. To her, their nightly sex becomes an affirmation of her attractiveness, a daily boost to her ego and the joy at being alive as she enthusiastically matches kiss with kiss and thrust with thrust.

The Harry she knows is filled with doubt and self-anger. And despite his best intentions, can he be a good father? Moreover, she is certain that, with the war over, each will grow in different, unforeseen directions. They are, she has become increasingly sure, two ships that, if not passing in the night, will have docked in the same port for only a few days before sailing in different directions.

"Harry," she tells him, eyes still wet, "I am still German while you're a soul at sea. You have become too American to be a German, and I'm certain that some American woman who loves you will say that you're too German to be an American."

Harry nods knowing that this is sadly true.

▲

Helped by Gavin's staff, Harry, now a major, procures translation work for Ilse at Army headquarters in Munich, the largest German city under U.S. control. Working there means regular food, safe living quarters, and good monthly pay. For Ilse, it's a better arrangement than most Germans can hope for in 1945 and it will also give Hans a nice new home.

In Berlin, Harry worries about being caught with the stamps, only to learn that U.S. Customs will be non-existent. The Army prints a double column, multi-paged list of prohibited items, focused on preventing accidental explosions coming from, say, long-handled German grenades or shootings from loaded weapons. Once the word gets out that officers' wooden footlockers will not be inspected, they become filled with Third Reich "souvenirs."

On their last night together, the two quietly pack Ilse's suitcase and Harry's standard wooden footlocker. Neither speak. Minutes drag. Other than parachuting, Harry has never felt as tense, his mouth dry, and stomach knotted. After four months, each of Ilse's few items hold memories and she begins silently crying. Harry swallows hard, fighting every instinct not to cry himself. This is love, he now understands, but he is too afraid of the future to tell her.

Part III: New York, West Germany, 1946 – 1947.

Chapter 15: New York, Saturday, January 12, 1946.

Coming home on the *Queen Mary*, the majestic ocean liner camouflaged and refurbished to carry the entire Eighty-Second Division, Harry's thoughts of Ilse are replaced by his desire to get home and begin his new life.

Normally Harry hates marching, especially with the temperature dropping, wearing the short jacket Eisenhower popularized for late spring and summer use. But, today, bands are playing as the Eighty-Second begins the country's formal victory parade. Together for the last time, as fighter planes and C-47's with gliders fly overhead, 13,000 paratroopers are accompanied by Sherman tanks, 155mm self-propelled howitzers, and other armored equipment. The parade begins at Washington Square and marches four miles up Fifth Avenue, past more than two million New Yorkers and the reviewing stand at the Metropolitan Museum of Art, as Harry proudly leads his company.

This is an easy way to catch pneumonia, Harry thinks as the wind seemingly picks up every mile they march, but the paratroopers experienced far worse a year earlier in the Ardennes. Confidently, they march and sing sanitized versions of favorite marching songs. To gales of laughter, someone occasionally shouts a "clover!" or "Schlitz!"—the lead word in an off-color song ("Roll me over, Yankee soldier" and "Knew a girl with two big tits; one gave milk, the other gave Schlitz"). Nevertheless, with hundreds of thousands of children watching, the songs actually vocalized are all circumspect.

And then, almost suddenly, it is all over. It is a moment that every victorious combat soldier dreads: the poignant separating and saying goodbye for the last time. There are final handshakes, hugs, strained laughter, lip-biting, and some tears as three years of training and fighting abruptly ends on Fifth Avenue and 86th Street.

▲

Back in his father's single bedroom apartment just west of Broadway on 112th Street, Harry is very, very alone, his sister in Michigan and his father in New Mexico. A quiet apartment and a short note from his father taped to an empty refrigerator is his welcome home. Harry's few possessions and clothing hang in the hall closet with two of five bureau drawers emptied for his use. On the bureau is a blurred photograph of his mother, whom he now can barely remember.

For the first time in Harry's American life there is no school or college, no summer job, and no Eighty-Second. He knows in thirty days (as mandated by the Army) he must shed his uniform and become another civilian among New York's 7⅔ million residents. With his father in Los Alamos on a classified government project, the apartment is more claustrophobic than inviting, the stairwells ominously dark, and Broadway's noises disconcerting. Sleep is equally difficult, not that he has nightmares but rather, for the first time, he'll have to wake himself up. Alone, he feels like an orphan, the memory of Ilse increasingly illusive.

Monday morning, in uniform, he wanders over to the nearby Columbia University campus and graduate school of business. Here, he double checks to make sure his acceptance and the paperwork he received in Berlin is in order and is told that there will be a special two-day orientation beginning Thursday, February 7, with classes to begin the following Monday. "Welcome home, Major," the registrar says.

Late that afternoon Harry walks six miles down Broadway until he absently realizes he is at 14th and Irving Place, across the street from Lüchow's, New York's best-known German restaurant. Is he here by accident? Half in a daydream—he still daydreams in German—he orders *sauerbraten, kartoffelkoesse,* and *rotkohl*—pot roast, potato dumplings, and red cabbage—surprising the waiter that a man in a paratrooper's uniform knows German. Harry finishes his first draft beer when the abstract thoughts that had been bothering him finally coalesce.

Come to terms with what happened, he tells himself. Remember what Manfredi said about Seis: that his death was a form of suicide. Why had he taken so long to reach Ludwigslust and why did he stop when he could've easily reached the Elbe? And why had he so antagonized Harry? And Maria. She didn't need to wind up with a purple eye hanging in that garage, did she?

Explaining to her quietly that your mother was Jewish wouldn't have hurt, would it? Yes, you're fully to blame for your quick temper, but hadn't she been yet another casualty of the Führer's madness? Had curtsying to Hitler as young girl doomed her? Did it destroy her brain just as thoroughly as if she'd been infected with syphilis?

Harry smiles sardonically to himself remembering the old line, "intensive thought leads to extensive confusion." Boy that's for damn sure, he tells himself. Then, like a boxer shaking off a punch, he shakes his head and signals for the waiter for another draft. Think about your stamps, he tells himself, they're real. Maybe there's some way you can make amends with them.

▲

The shoeshine parlor managed by Izzy Cohen consists of a dozen raised seats just inside Grand Central Station's main, upper level waiting room. Year-round, five days a week, "Izzy" and the Negroes working for him begin each day's drudgery when the first commuter trains arrive. Not until fourteen hours later will their labor end. Nevertheless, whatever the time, Izzy also sells "numbers," acting as the bank. Each "book" holds 999 numbers, a winning ticket based on the last three digits of the San Francisco Stock & Bond Exchange's daily sales volume, the exchange selected because it doesn't close until 7 PM.

Across New York, numbers books are split up, for no one person can sell 999 in a day, but Izzy and his shoeshine boys daily sell between two and three. Izzy also books college and professional sports events around the country, although horse and trotter racing is prohibited by the mob.

Emptying into Grand Central multiple levels each day are 500 railroad trains and twelve subway trains per *minute*. Izzy owes his strategic location not just to paying rent, but also to his kickbacks to Grand Central's operations manager, the police, and, of course, to the mob. Late morning and early afternoon, when traffic is slowest, a mob member occupies the last booth to discourage even the stupidest robber. Three times a day, a uniformed policeman and mob member escorts Izzy or his son to the Bowery Savings Bank building, just across 42nd Street. There Izzy deposits his cash-filled carpetbag. Afterward, it is not unusual for the mobster and policeman to have a cup of free coffee—cops never pay—at the adjacent Automat; after all, many of them grew up together on the Lower East Side or in Brooklyn.

As for the frail, humble-looking Izzy, born in Odessa sixty years earlier, he is the youngest of ten. Given the increased frequency of pogroms, he and three brothers were sent to an uncle in Brooklyn. Gradually, Izzy gains a reputation for honesty and being a wizard with numbers, basic mob requirements for running such an operation. Izzy, an encyclopedia of the city's underworld, never forgets a name and is friendly with everyone, from immigrants to WASP commuters. Moreover, he is careful not to make waves; like his shoeshine boys, he has learned his place in the world and is outwardly satisfied.

Growing up, Harry's father had always stressed that shined shoes made a good impression. Faithfully, Harry stopped at Izzy's establishment every time he went to or came from Mount Hermon and Amherst or before meeting a date under the clock at the Biltmore Hotel. Today, Tuesday, January 15, in uniform, his starched pants tucked into his boots paratrooper style, he proudly walks up to Izzy's. Izzy, already on his second pack of cigarettes at 10:30 AM, happily shakes Harry's hand. Many of his employees, remembering Harry, smile from ear-to-ear.

"You're in the number one booth with Earl," Izzy says. "Welcome home. We've been thinking about you for years. When the 82nd marched up Fifth Avenue Saturday, we were hoping you'd be with 'em. And you look great, no problems for you I hope."

"A few, but that's what are doctors for, right?" Harry says. Answering questions and enjoying the adulation, he lets it all wash over him. When the shine is finished, he gives Earl fifty cents, refusing to let the bent old man brush away his tip.

Then he turns to Izzy, whispering that he needs a favor. After a short walk to the Grand Central Station Oyster Bar & Restaurant, both order creamy New England-style chowder. Harry, who hasn't had Bluepoint oysters in years, orders a dozen first, quickly polishes them off, and then downs a second dozen.

"Izzy," Harry begins, "in Germany I got hold of something that I shouldn't have—"

"Off a dead German, I hope," Izzy says facetiously.

"Yes," Harry smiles as Izzy stiffens. This is for real and it makes Izzy nervous. "The man was a high-level Nazi. I have no idea who or what he really was, but what he had was valuable. Far more valuable than—"

"I don't want to know about it."

"Nor would I think of telling you. However, I need to know who I could work with in selling this something. There's no reason for you to be involved any further."

Izzy slowly exhales. Other than giving a name, he will have no obligations or any knowledge of what the "it" is. However, a frown suddenly crosses his face.

"Does it have to do with the Russians?" he asks. The NKVD has long arms and it is common knowledge that they are active in New York.

"No," Harry says as he sees Izzy fully relax. "It has to do with something that the Nazis stole from Jews. It—" he stops for Izzy is smiling.

"So, you stole from the Nazis something that they took from Jews. Good for you. I like that, Harry. My entire family in Odessa is gone; murdered by those bastards."

Harry nods as Izzy continues. "When you were in Germany, did you find out if any of your mother's family survived?"

"From what little I could find out, and I was in Stuttgart in November; not one of them. I went to the neighborhood where we'd lived and no one—or so they said—remembered my family. I even visited Freddie Porsche in jail in Nuremberg. He couldn't have been friendlier; told me how much I looked like Dad, asked after his health, and what he was doing. Dad helped him design the Volkswagen, you know. However, when I brought up my mother's family he shook his head, 'Don't ask; the few Jews that Hitler didn't kill are broken people today.' "

"But now you have something of theirs, good," Izzy says. "Here's what you must do. Every so often, a man will drop by and ask me where he can find an honest card game. If they look like they have money I say that there *are* honest games, but the people in them are professionals playing for high stakes. For a new person, a "good faith" entrance fee requires $500. If they're still interested

I ask for a business card and say I'll make a call, but that I can guarantee nothing."

"Next, I call my friend, Meyer Lansky. If he's in town I tell him. Then, and only if he's interested, he'll drop by to get his shoes shined and talk. The important thing for you to understand is that Meyer knows people with money—big money. And he works well with the Italians. He and Lucky Luciano grew up a block apart: would you believe it? The Italians trust Meyer because he combines a very good mind with common sense, and he doesn't get involved in their shootings. His family came from Lithuania and he told me that his family is gone too. He's always hated the Nazis and could see what was coming."

Izzy pauses, slowly going over in his mind what more to tell Harry. "But you must remember this: Meyer doesn't need money. He's the type of person who likes to do interesting things to keep his mind busy. And don't try to haggle with him; if you tell him you've never done this type of thing before he'll be fair with you."

"Anything else?"

"For God's sake never lie. He'll have lots of questions. Don't be evasive or too quick with your answers. Straight answers; no curves and no sarcasm. Whatever you have, he won't need it. You have to make him *want* to help you."

"Will you make a call for me then?"

"There's no need to. He has lunch every day at Dinty Moore's restaurant, 216 West 46th. Go over there today, as you're dressed, but don't get there until 2 PM. He always eats late. And don't take any shit from anybody. A lot of stars eat there and Dinty's people can stick their noses in the air. Insist on speaking to Jim Moore, that's Dinty's real name. Say that Izzy sent you and it's important. Oh, and one other thing, uniform or not, do *not* make any fast moves with your hands; most of those hanging around Lansky have bodyguards."

Chapter 16: Dinty Moore's Restaurant, January 15, 2 PM.

With nothing to do for three and half hours, Harry wanders over to Fifth Ave, gets on the second level (enclosed in winter) of a double-decker bus, and rides north to Fort Tryon Park and *Spuyten Duyvil* ("Spit on the Devil"), where the Hudson and East Rivers meet. In uniform, as he looks around, he feels somewhat strange acting like a tourist, even though he has taken this bus route a dozen times over the years. Everywhere, the streets are jammed with pedestrians, but with gas rationing still in effect there is a dearth of cars and a lack of exhaust fumes. A cool breeze moves in from the ocean, giving the January air an unusual sparkle. All but alone, Harry stretches out on the front two seats, taking in the sights and smells of Manhattan and feeling himself unwind.

Dinty Moore's is one of the city's "in" restaurants. Damon Runyon, the legendary writer, chronicler of Prohibition New York, and creator of such characters as Nathan Detroit, Goodtime Charley and Harry the Horse holds court daily as literary and sports writers, gossip columnists, Broadway personalities, ball players, and boxers drop by to say hello. Later in 1946, after Runyon dies of cancer, Dinty will rearrange the dining room tables so that Runyon's view can never be duplicated.

At 2:05 PM, Harry walks past the potted shrubbery and white exterior, finishes his Camel, braces himself, and walks in. A uniformed doorman opens the door smiling—everybody smiles at his officer's uniform and major's bars, he thinks—then he sees Dinty Moore's famous long bar, polished mahogany with its brass footrest. An overweight, stocky greeter in an expensive, double-breasted striped suit with a rumbling voice wheezes up, shakes hands, and promises to take Harry's message to Dinty.

"There'll be a few minutes wait, but go up to the bar, Major," he says. Then he looks carefully at Harry's medals and Airborne patch. "And tell Sam, he's the bartender, that Frank said—that's me—that drinks are on the house."

Standing at the bar, sipping Jack Daniels, Harry finds himself worrying.

How can a man so high up in mob business possibly be interested in stamps? Did he make a mistake asking Izzy? Harry begins wishing that Hermann Seis had kept on bicycling that afternoon.

And then comes the tap on his shoulder. It is too late for regrets.

Nevertheless, "Dinty" Moore proves friendly. Portly but borderline obese, he still has black hair parted in the middle and wears a bow tie. He quickly walks Harry to the back of the restaurant where he knocks loudly on a door. "I'll be damned, it's his own place and he has to knock," Harry thinks. Then he follows Dinty into the cigar-smoke filled room.

"Excuse me, Meyer—" Dinty says looking at Lansky. Almost instantly Dinty is cut off by the Hollywood handsome man sitting next to Lansky, wearing a checkered sports jacket.

"I know you from somewhere," the man says, staring at Harry, "where did we meet?"

"And I remember you too," Harry replies, nodding and equally astonished. "Yes, we've met somewhere, but—"

"It's Benjamin Siegel, Major."

Over the years, Harry became used to unexpected turns, but it takes all his self-control not to register surprise that the man he is talking to is America's best-looking mobster, the notorious steely-eyed killer, "Bugsy" Siegel.

Chapter 17: Yorkville, 1938.

Looking at Siegel, Harry instantly recalls Saturday, October 29, 1938 when he was a freshman at Amherst College. When classes ended at noon, he hitched the eight-mile ride to Northampton and taken the New York train. One of the few sections of the city that he knew was Yorkville, where he, his father, and sister occasionally went for authentic German food. The neighborhood includes Irish (Jimmy Cagney's birthplace), Hungarians, Czechs, and Slovaks. Along and adjacent to 86th Street, Germans and Austrians predominate, the street filled with the sights and smells of restaurants, delicatessens, grocery stores and small shops.

Hitler's rise to power in early 1933 sent shock waves through Yorkville. A pro-Nazi "Bund" was formed, its members anti-Semitic, isolationist, violent, and slavish followers of the Nazi line, complete with German manufactured Brownshirt uniforms. More rallies in Yorkville's streets and restaurants were held, brute force the usual method of silencing hecklers, police needed to keep peace. Then, in early '38, two anti-Nazi American Legion war veterans, from the famed 69th "Irish" Regiment, were viciously assaulted. New York's Irish-dominated police were enraged, their anger intensifying when the Brownshirts beat a lone priest senseless. That fall, the Bund, feeding on the oats from Hitler's Munich Peace Treaty, scheduled and publicized a march along 86th Street for Sunday, October 30, "German American Day."

It is October 30, 1938, and one of those planning to attend the march is Harry, a still-thin 195 pounds. For him, the Sunday morning walk from his father's Morningside Heights apartment is swift. Reaching Park Avenue at 86th, he chooses to walk on the street's south side to keep the sun behind him. Here he finds himself open-mouthed. Three blocks east are scores of Americans in *Stormabteilung* brown uniforms, brandishing swastika flags as well as the stars and stripes as a band practices the *Horst Wessel* song, the Nazi Party's anthem.

Harry closes his eyes. Too often, as a little boy in Stuttgart, he saw Brownshirts beating up political opponents and Jews, breaking windows, stealing; always contemptuous of the police. Now, only a few years later, the Brownshirts have again become real. Harry is at their parade for one reason and one reason only: to bash some fucking heads together; to give those bastards a taste of their own medicine. How he'll do it, he doesn't know.

Harry is fifty yards east of the Second Avenue when he notices a short, well-dressed man fifteen yards away. Expensive clothes are easy to spot in the Depression and this man wears a double-breasted camel's hair overcoat, a black-banded pearl grey hat, silk shirt, bright tie, and polished black wing-tip shoes. At first, other than his clothing, he doesn't look distinguished; a soft jaw, indiscernible cheekbones, and overall features that are more rubbery than firm. Harry would have guessed him to be a waiter at a second-tier restaurant, or an accountant. Yet the man's brown eyes are remarkable; dominated by intelligence—piercing, constantly darting, slightly laughing, and fully commanding as they take everything in.

On the man's left side stands a taller, square-jawed man with an athlete's carriage and no hat, which showcases his thick hair. He is wearing a bright sport coat and slacks, and unconsciously pounds his fist into his hand. To the short man's right stands a red-faced, ski-nosed uniformed police captain, fifty and thick around the waist, nodding "yes" as the little man, pointing and animatedly talking with his hands, making "suggestions" to him.

Harry watches as men line up next to the captain, nodding as the captain introduces them, then accepting the twenty dollar bill the short man hands each. Only after seeing Billy clubs and handcuffs in their back pockets does Harry realize that they are off-duty police, being paid half a week's salary for *something*. Then the captain steps away, purposely turning his back as a large heavyset man comes up. He also quickly bows his head, but the procedure is similar; a brief introduction then cash being passed.

The little man turns suddenly, catching Harry staring at him.

"Come over here. Now!" It is a peremptory order in a deep gravelly voice and it never dawns on Harry to disappear while he has the chance.

"You're here to cause trouble, right?" the little man says, eyes locking into Harry's.

"No sir, I just wanted to watch," Harry answers nervously.

"Just wanted to watch, eh? You're as inconspicuous as a giraffe," the short man laughs, turning to his larger friends and the police captain who form a half circle around Harry.

"Has anyone told you that you have a German accent?" the little man says. "When did you come over?"

"Four years ago, sir."

"You don't look Jewish, too blond. Are you Jewish?"

"Yes sir. Half-Jewish, my mother was."

"Was; as in *dead*?"

"Yes, sir."

"And your father?"

"He brought me over. But I go college in Massachusetts. He doesn't know that—"

"That you're here. And you're still telling me that you're not here to cause trouble?"

Harry nods, apprehension growing when the little man unexpectedly glances at his fists.

"Hold out your hands, kid, and open them slowly," the raspy, Lower East Side accented voice says, giving Harry an order, the police captain now watching intently.

Harry nervously obeys; he has attempted to hide a taped roll of pennies in each hand.

"Well look at that," the little man laughs. "You're half Jewish and you're not here to cause trouble, eh? Dumb Jews like you are a dime a dozen. Taking them on by yourself, eh? How much do you think those pennies would help you? Let me tell you how much; it wouldn't have been enough to hurt those assholes; but you sure as hell would've pissed 'em off. More than enough for them to kick the living shit out of you. Bandages for weeks. Right, Captain?"

The captain, a slight Irish accent in his voice, nods sympathetically. "These boys play rough, son. You've got to think first before you get involved."

The little man grins again. "Well, kid, we're not here to watch their parade either. We're here to piss on those bastards."

Then he turns to a large beefy man, Harry's height but thirty pounds heavier. "Open up the medicine kit, Tommy," he says and turns back to Harry. "Kid, listen carefully. There *is* going to be trouble and if you want you can be in the middle of it, but you've got to stay near Tommy. Pay attention to him when things get rough. And drop those two rolls in the street, now."

"I can't, sir; they're all the money I have," Harry blurts out. "That and some nickels for the subway. To get me into the Bronx so I can hitch back—"

"Well I'll be damned, we have an idealist here, boys," the little man says, shaking his head and smiling. Then he reaches into his pocket and hands Harry a twenty. "Now drop the coins in the street, take the money, and hold out your hands." Harry does so, then feels Tommy slide brass knuckles onto them.

Knots of Brownshirts leave the Second and Third Avenue 86th Street elevated train stations and the Lexington Ave. subway stop and strut east, confidently smiling and enjoying the sounds of their boots striking the pavement in unison, each group commanding their little section of the sidewalk, locking arms with the joy of bullies, pushing aside anyone who wasn't nimble enough to get out of their way.

As they near Harry, he hears, "Hitler's a cock-sucking faggot!" The short man shouts. The fact that Hitler isn't married or publicly seen with a female partner has produced intense speculation, one of the few subjects causing unease even among his most ardent followers.

"Homos! Faggots! Cock-suckers! You Nazis are homos!" shout others, picking up the chant. The Brownshirts angrily push aside the crowd to get at the voices.

Harry moves forward, only to feel Tommy's hand on his shoulder. "Stay with me, kid, there's another group of 'em just behind these bastards. They're gonna' be ours."

Only now Harry realizes that the good-looking man has silently taken a position on his left; he has picked up bodyguards on both sides.

The first wave of Brownshirts rush in, fists flying, as often as not landing on the hands of brass-knuckled longshoremen. Out-of-uniform police wade in with nightsticks and blackjacks, knowing they'll be thanked the next time they go to confession. Brownshirts are quickly writhing on the ground, pummeled with kicks and punches. Welts form and bones break as their arms are pulled behind them, then locked with handcuffs. Bleeding, they are dragged off and left sitting, legs sprawled, under a Chinese restaurant's large "Chop Suey" sign. Later they will be literally heaved into a paddy-wagon, booked, and possibly jailed overnight. The Irish judge that they'll be taken to will be less than sympathetic.

As Tommy foresaw, another half-dozen Brownshirts are coming up fast, "Follow me, boys," their tall, heavy-set leader yells.

"He's mine," Tommy grunts, catching the Brownshirt leader's eye as the two close. On the left, an older, shorter Brownshirt hesitates seeing Harry bearing down on him. He stops, places both feet firmly on the ground, draws back his right arm and swings. Harry leans away, jumps forward, pushes the man's arm down with his left hand, scraping the man's cheek with his right hand. To Harry's surprise, this seemingly mild poke draws multiple lines across the man's face oozing blood. The Brownshirt, realizing he'll need stitches, appears paralyzed.

I've been waiting for this, Harry thinks as he puts his left foot forward and swings his right with everything he has into the Brownshirt's ribs. A crunching sound follows, then an "Oh" and a high pitched "Aaah!" as the air leaves the man's lungs quickly, followed by the horrible pain of a fractured rib or two. Instantly, he collapses into a blubbering mound.

Next to him, the good-looking man in the sports jacket has downed another Brownshirt with a vicious brass knuckled rabbit-chop to the back of the man's neck.

Harry turns toward Tommy, who is evenly matched, at best. No sooner does the Brownshirt leader block Tommy's swing, then he cocks his right to hit back. It is then that Harry jabs the man's face with his right; one, two, three, each shot drawing blood. The Brownshirt turns to face Harry, but before he can do anything Tommy bends low and delivers an uppercut to the balls. As the Brownshirt doubles over, his hands on his crotch, Tommy lifts his foot and gives him a vicious push-kick to the knee. As the leader rolls to the ground, balled up and helpless, an off-duty cop stands above him, rapidly striking the man with his club.

No Marquis of Queensberry rules here, Harry thinks, but the street fighting is far from over as, from the Second Avenue El, another half-dozen angry Brownshirts emerge.

"We've got company," Tommy shouts, charging forward, Harry alongside, other longshoremen only steps behind. Like their comrades, these Brownshirts are flabbergasted by organized resistance. Half will never see forty again, and years of beer drinking aren't conducive to fighting—beating priests, yes; street brawling, no. However, what ends any uncertainty is the sight of bone-breaking billy-clubs. Quickly, they fall back, but trip over fellow Brownshirts. Harry delivers a few punches, but discovers no elation beating the fallen. To his relief, police whistles sound. As Tommy's boys fall back, Brownshirts lying on the ground are kicked and clubbed, then cuffed. Two who made it into a German delicatessen are dragged out by the man in the sport coat and a cop. In turn, the two are pounded by other cops.

Tommy walks Harry over to the little man.

"He did great," Tommy says, breathing hard. "Got me out of a little scrape too."

"Good for you, kid. And I see that you got a nice red badge of courage for yourself."

"Not my blood," Harry says, grinning.

The short man pats Harry on the cheek. "Well, it's time for you to head back to school. Capiche? You're lucky as hell that you didn't get into real trouble," he says, winking at Tommy. "The captain just told me that we've had our fun for the day. Good luck to you, kid."

With the short man's twenty dollars in his pocket and a warm handshake and pat on the back from his good-looking friend, Harry turns towards Grand Central Station and Amherst with a satisfied smile; while he has mixed feelings about beating fallen Brownshirts, he has accomplished what he set out to do. A happy smile crosses his face. Instead of hitch-hiking, he can take the train back and even eat in the dining car. Talk about an unusual combination: he is both richer and wiser.

Chapter 18: Dinty Moore's, 2:45 PM

Now, seven years later, in uniform and with a major's gold oak leaves, Harry stands, trying to recall the two men he'd briefly met that Sunday in Yorkville. It was so long ago, but it was his first taste of blood. Something he had never forgotten, but after years of real killing he recalled it as almost innocent. Then he remembers where he is, standing in Dinty Moore's and the short man is talking to him.

"I remember you now too," says Meyer Lansky. "Before the war. Uptown in Krautland. You were looking for a fight and we helped you out. I even gave you twenty—"

"He asked to see you Meyer," Dinty whispers loudly.

"And here I am. You're among friends, Major. And look at that, the Eighty-Second Airborne no less! We watched your Fifth Avenue parade Saturday, it thrilled my kids. Now I'm remembering who you are. Let's see, you'd lost your mother. She was Jewish, right? Your accent's almost gone and you've grown too. Look at your shoulders and neck. Well, no more business for us my friends, we have an honored guest. Dinty, we'll need another plate of your Irish Utility stew. And a chaser, Major?"

"Jack Daniel's would be fine, thank you, sir. And my name is Strong, Harry Strong."

"Dinty, set up another place between me and Ben and Harry, there are no *sirs* at this table." Lansky points around the table introducing his younger brother Jake, brothers Albert and Tony Anastasia, Frank Costello, "Socks" Lanza, and Moses Polakoff. The one name he purposely slurs, Harry learns later, is the U.S. Inspector of Ports. These men, by law and muscle, control every commercial dock in New York harbor. Lansky makes no effort to introduce the others who sit in chairs against the wall and aren't eating; the bodyguards.

Harry's only mistake is to ask about Tommy. The table is quiet until Ben explains that Tommy was thirty-four and in terrific shape when Pearl Harbor was bombed. He enlisted in the Marines December 8, but didn't survive Tarawa.

Harry's plate arrives quickly; an Irish "utility" stew but filled with expensive, large chunks of undoubtedly black–market veal and kidneys, an occasional potato, carrot or celery slice added for decoration. It is perfectly cooked and with just the right touch of wine. Irish utility stew? This is about as Irish as matzoh-ball soup, Harry thinks.

What is apparent is that the table is fascinated by the minutia of his experiences; Sicily, Normandy, the Bulge, German concentration camps, and of course women. On the latter, he is asked to compare Sicilian women with other countries he'd been in, and does he have a girlfriend in the states. No, Harry says, thinking of Stephanie Pringle, she married someone else, but he doesn't think of Ilse when the question is asked. A few times Lansky interrupts to tell the others not to ask so many questions so that Harry can get a chance to eat.

About 3:30, as lunch ends, Lansky turns to Harry and suggests that he might like to use the men's room. Standing in front of a urinal, as Harry begins unbuttoning his trousers—the Army still not trusting zippers—he feels his hands shaking. Slipping into a stall he takes a huge breath, forcing himself to do so silently. He has seen how combat hardens a man's eyes, and most of the men inside, especially the bodyguards, look no different. Are they talking about me now? My God, what have I gotten myself into?

Ten minutes later, as Harry waits outside, smoking a cigarette and very much alone, the lunch breaks up and Lansky, after quickly speaking with Dinty, motions Harry inside.

▲

Decades earlier, the diminutive Meyer Lansky, his life dependent on it, learned to read a man's eyes. Now, in front of him sits a combat veteran, physically imposing and clearly intelligent, but who nevertheless is apprehensive. But why is he here? Izzy wouldn't have sent him over without a reason; something's up.

"So, what can I do for you, Major?" Lansky asks, suddenly all business, the smiles and artificial camaraderie of lunch replaced by a neutral expression. A waiter enters, silently clearing the table but leaving a fresh decanter of coffee and new cups.

"In May, just before the Nazis surrendered," Harry begins, "I came across something I shouldn't have." With that, after explaining how he knows Izzy, the paratrooper begins his story: how he'd killed the German—to which Lansky gives a satisfied grunt—and his belief that he, Major Strong, now holds valuable stamps, most likely taken from Jewish owners.

"Why do you think that?" asks Lansky. "Can you be one hundred percent certain?" Each question he asks is important, although sometimes he mixes subjects. From hundreds of meetings over the years, Lansky's very survival is based on often innocuous questions, careful listening, and above all reading the other person's eyes. Now he smiles with his mouth but focuses on Harry's eyes.

"Not one hundred percent, no," the young man carefully answers. "But look at it this way. I'm finding triplicates of valuable stamps and five copies of one stamp worth five hundred dollars. Also, many of them are in 'mint' condition, which means they were never mounted in a stamp album. No individual would buy so many, and the cost for a stamp dealer's inventory would have been astronomical because there's such a very slow turnover in their business. No, I'm certain these are from dozens of different collections."

So far so good, Major, Lansky thinks to himself, nodding. And he certainly knows that turnover is everything. Like in the jewelry business, where low turnover requires high margins.

"Also," Harry continues, "whoever collected these chose *nothing* inexpensive. I'm sure any individual collector or dealer will invariably have God-knows-how-many low value stamps."

"Keep on," Lansky says, "I'm understanding you."

"Most stamps are issued in a series; the series in total having far higher value than the individual stamps; just like a straight in poker. For example, in 1894, the U.S. printed a 'Famous American' series of sixteen stamps ranging from a blue one cent Ben Franklin to a five dollar green John Marshall. I'm making the numbers up, but perhaps a million Franklins printed, but only ten thousand Marshalls. Today a mint Marshall stamp is worth almost a hundred times more than a mint Franklin and a connected block of four Marshall stamps—"

"Might be worth five hundred times more—" Lansky cuts in, finding himself increasingly engaged in the conversation.

"And to date I've found two blocks of four Marshalls plus a half-dozen singles."

This is getting better by the minute, Lansky thinks, wishing that he knew more about stamps. Luckily, he knows people who do.

"What about those upside-down planes I've heard about?" Lansky asks.

"They're called the 'Inverted Blue Jenny,' named after a World War I training plane. In 1918, out of the tens of thousands of pages printed, one, 100-stamp page was printed upside down. Nothing similar was ever found. Most of the time when the Post Office screws up they make it a beaut, sometimes a million errors—which thus have no value because they're not unique. But not the Blue Jenny. A stamp collector saw it at a post office and the rest is history. Today each is worth tens of thousands of dollars, blocks far more."

"Too bad you didn't get one of those." Lansky says. He finds himself increasingly caught up in the story. And, of course, it is always fun to think about the *what ifs.*

"No, sir. I didn't get one; I've counted *seven*, and one is a block of four."

Lansky leans back and looks at Harry. Well I'll be fucked, he thinks. This is unbelievable... if I'm being told the truth. So far, the kid seems to be honest, or at least believes his own story. And hell, it's not like he's some stranger walking in off the street: I've seen him walk into trouble before. There's got to be a gimmick somewhere in here, but where is it?

Chapter 19: Dinty Moore's, 3:45 PM.

"OK, let's go over this again," Lansky says, asking Harry to tell the story backward, from the time he tossed Hermann Seis's body away. It's an old interrogation trick he learned from an ex- detective who ran murderers down. He'd asked the detective how he was so effective without beating the crap out of a suspect. For whatever reason, the detective said, people with false stories—when asked to go from the end to the beginning—became flustered, especially as you speed up the questions. How many times has he, Lansky, flushed out liars this way?

Three minutes into Harry's telling the story backwards—Lansky is unable not to laugh out loud about when Harry describes using Lowenbrau as a disinfectant—he puts his hand up. "Stop, let's talk about the stamps' value."

"According to the 1940 *Scott Directory*—that's the bible in the stamp business—based on the stamps I've recorded so far; the list value is well over three million dollars."

"So, for planning purposes you're talking in the six to ten million range?"

"I think that's safe. Moreover, the value can only go up. During the war, hundreds of stamp collections were destroyed by bombings, fighting, and by collectors—especially Jewish ones—hiding or burying their stamps before they were rounded up and murdered. Right now, those stamps are rotting in the ground, their location forgotten."

"Could a counterfeit trade in these stamps be developed?"

"Theoretically yes, realistically no. For an exceptionally valuable stamp, a buyer insists on verification. He'll check the engraving quality to compare it to authentic stamps, look at the paper stock, perform color and glue analysis, and other tests including fluorescent lighting. It's one thing to do all that work if you're going to manufacture thousands of ten dollar bills, another for a handful of stamps. Anybody walking into fifty stamp dealers' offices with an 1869 black and red, Lincoln ninety-cent stamp wouldn't make it past the third dealer and—"

"Even if he sold a few, it would drive the stamps' value down," Lansky cuts in, leaning back and closing his eyes. Where's the flaw? "Let's see if we agree. First, we *are* dealing with Nazis who needed ready money, but gold is too heavy. This means cash, diamonds, or stamps. Also, the Nazi you killed likely had associates. If they're still alive, at some point it'll dawn on them that their courier isn't about to materialize. They'll make inquiries, come up with a big fat zero, but then they'll start working backward: who last saw him and where. With luck, his body never showed up or was too waterlogged to identify. But with bad luck he could've surfaced," Lansky says, smiling at his own pun. "However, there's one good thing working for us—"

Harry looks surprised.

"That this happened in East Germany. Whoever's looking for the stamps isn't about to saunter back across the Elbe and ask too many questions. What we must assume," Lansky says, not realize the increasing number of *we's* he's using, "is that someone, somewhere has a list of the stamps. Not keeping records isn't very German-like, is it? I'm guessing the dead man's friends will wait for us to put the stamps on the market and cross-check their lists."

"Does that mean we wait, Mr. Lansky?"

"Yes and no. I'm not afraid of selling a small portion every six months or so, although for a few years even that might be risky. I assume you have a safe deposit box?"

Harry nodded, "The stamps I've identified went in yesterday— "

"Your first goal is to list and deposit them, but don't go to the bank often. And under *no* circumstances are you keep that list in your apartment. Every update you make goes into that safety deposit box. And I do *not* want to know the bank's name. Kapish? More questions?"

Harry shakes his head.

"OK, then; here's what I want you to do. Keep only keep a small percentage of stamps in your apartment. Then, remember that the most effective hiding places are those in plain sight. What's more natural than a soldier coming home who's acquired some stamps? Leave the stamps in cigar boxes on the table with whatever else a collector owns. Just be sure things aren't too neat or too messy and a cluttered waste-paper basket will add to the illusion."

"Now, here's what we're going to do," Lansky says. By now he has formulated a plan to further check Harry's veracity. Lansky knows he's gone as far as he can and realizes he needs support from men who know the stamp business.

"On Thursday, at 10:30 a.m., we'll meet at the Automat across from Bryant Park at 42nd. Bring two envelopes with, say, ten American and ten European stamps. Each packet should be worth about $ 1,500. I'll bring a friend who'll have a chemical kit—"

"To an Automat?"

"Why not? He'll go to the men's room and pour heavy duty Lysol on the floor. That'll stink up the men's room enough so he can use his own chemicals and magnifying glass to spot forgeries or incorrect watermarks. You don't want a French stamp on British watermarked paper, do you?" Lansky is pleased with himself. He's already sounding like an expert, isn't he?

"With everybody complaining about the smell, nobody will realize that my friend, who is sitting on a crapper, is actually testing your stamps." Lansky pauses, he's about to throw the kid a curve. "However, you have to brace yourself; the stamps might not be worth a penny."

Lansky watches the shock in Harry's face. All through his interview, the young major has been trying to keep a poker face but now all Lansky sees is anguish.

"Oh, shit," Harry mumbles.

Lansky laughs but Harry has just passed another test. Any other reaction would've been suspicious. "Remember," Lansky says, "it's always possible something's phony. We wouldn't be here if I didn't believe *you* think the stamps are genuine. And didn't your Nazi friend die because he thought so? But did somebody switch the stamps on him? Ever think of that? When it came to screwing people, those bastards thought of everything. They were far worse than my closest friends."

Abruptly Lansky switches subjects, "What will you do with the money, I'm curious?" It is another test; Lansky believes that a man not thinking about the money and what to do with it can't be trusted or his mind isn't working quite right.

"I've given it a lot of thought, sir. If I'm not putting the cart ahead of the horse, I'd like to keep some of it for myself, of course. However, since the stamps were taken from Jews—who I've got to assume are dead—I'd like to think about some way to give it back."

A huge, unaffected smile lights Lansky's face, "Does *Haganah* ring a bell with you?"

"Of course, they're the military wing of Palestine's Jewish settlers—"

"And they need money for arms, ammunition, explosives, and trucks. So, here's what I suggest." Lansky is talking so softly that Harry strains to hear him, but at the word *suggest* he involuntary shudders. He is about to be told what he can keep.

"Would you consider a split of sixty—thirty—ten?" Lansky begins, enunciating each word to prevent any misunderstanding. "Haganah gets the sixty, you thirty and me ten," which I will give to Haganah, Lansky adds silently. This type of opportunity rarely comes along. I can help my own people and, even better, use the Nazi's own money in doing so.

"With all due respect, why so much to Haganah?"

"Because we're Jews. Your mother's family has been wiped out, hasn't it?"

Sipping his coffee, Harry nods.

"I was born in Grodno, Russia, my father immigrated in 1909 and some of the family followed. At home, I have photos of my school friends, relatives, and my grandfather, a community leader. My mother's family was there for 400 years, even before the Great Synagogue was built. My father's family history was almost as long. Of the 25,000 Jews in Grodno before the war, do you know how many are left today?"

Harry doesn't have to be told.

"Effectively zero and the synagogue has been destroyed, too. Since you're part Jewish I'll tell you something my Sicilian friends can't fathom. Every day I feel the guilt of my survival and success. I made money during the war while they were being massacred; shot, hung, burnt alive in buildings, tortured, and raped to death. The few who managed to escape to the woods starved, froze to death, or were torn apart by the dogs used to hunt them down."

"For my mother's family," Harry says, "it was Dachau or some other camp, but their end was similar. And I sure as hell feel guilty too, never knowing until it was way too late."

"With my contacts," Lansky says, "I attempted to find survivors in Grodno. So far, a half-dozen. Not a single relative or family friend among them. Seven years ago, when we first met, I knew that bad things would happen, but this..."

"During the war, I did the best I could. I worked with Luciano protecting the docks. The Germans played hell with us in WWI, but nothing this time. The few who tried were turned into fish food. But damage; nothing. And strikes? Never a one. That fucking John L. Lewis led a coal strike while you were fighting, Harry, but every day we loaded the ships."

"You know what Major, I haven't stopped," Lansky continues, sipping his now cold coffee. "Do you know that arms being shipped to Trans-Jordan and Saudi-Arabia are getting lost or mishandled on the docks? One recent machine gun shipment fell into the Hudson while other crates are mislabeled and wind up in Haifa. How strange! Nevertheless, such little steps cannot be taken too often. Today our friends in Palestine desperately need American dollars. You can help them and I can help you. I look forward to our new association."

Lansky finds himself liking Harry. In fact, he's envious of Harry's father. Here he, Meyer Lansky, who lacks nothing, has his oldest son Buddy—the bright one—saddled with a painfully crippling muscular degenerative disease that bends his left leg a little more each year. And his second son, Paul? A boy without physical incapacity, but who is less active than a sloth.

The two stand, smile, and shake hands.

"By the way," Lansky asks, "under the new GI bill, how much money will you make?"

"They'll pay my Columbia tuition and give me sixty-five dollars a month for almost four years. Since I'll be in my Dad's apartment, that's enough to keep me going."

"No, you'll need more. It might be a while until our first sale; I'm going to advance you $1,500. That way you won't be under any financial pressure."

Chapter 20: Nan O'Malley

As Harry and Lansky walk from the back room towards Dinty Moore's entrance, Harry feels himself relaxing as Lansky speaks with more animation. Reaching the bar, Harry stops in mid-stride as if a referee's whistle has suddenly blown: sitting at the bar twenty feet away are, quite simply, two of the most stunning woman he has ever seen. The woman nearest him has long hair covering her shoulders, marvelous crossed legs, a tight skirt whose hem is above her knees, a white blouse, cashmere sweater, and an inexpensive fur coat.

"Wow," Harry mumbles to Lansky, repeating the hackneyed Bob Hope line he'd often heard, "If that's what I was fighting for it sure as hell was worth it."

"Then you shall meet them," Lansky says. "But the blonde is strictly off-limits; she's dating one of FDR's sons these days—among others."

"But the other; with the reddish-brown hair?"

"Nan O'Malley; nee Miriam Silberman: a good Jewish girl who graduated from some women's Ivy League school and is working her way into show business. She's already an understudy in *Oklahoma!* And on her way up. Let me introduce you."

"Wait a second till my heart stops racing—" Then he feels Lansky's hand on his arm walking him forward.

"Best not to worry," Lansky says. What he doesn't say to Harry is that earlier he had *suggested* to Dinty that Nan would be a nice home-coming present for the paratrooper.

"Nan," Lansky says, "this is an old friend, Harry Strong. He went to Amherst—"

"And I was Smith, class of '44," Nan says, turning to look at him over her shoulder, then swinging around on the bar stool, looking him in the eye, then throwing her long, glistening hair over her shoulder and giving the jut-jawed Eighty-Second Airborne paratrooper a dazzling smile. "That means we're practically kissing cousins. What year were you, Harry?"

"I would have been '42, but I left when the war started," he hears himself say, however his words seem to be coming from the end of a long tunnel.

"I want to hear more but I don't like bar stools, can we sit?" she says and leads Harry to a table. Is it his imagination or does she roll her hips slightly so he can see her spectacular ass? Here they order drinks—Coke for her, more coffee for him.

"So, tell me who you are, Major Harry Strong."

"Just another G.I. looking for a good time. What else could I be?" he laughs, his voice returning as he tries to focus on her face and not on her high, magnificent breasts.

"Well, for one you're a major in the Eighty-Second and I watched your parade Saturday. Maybe you're even polite sometimes," she laughs. "And you were born in Germany—right?"

"Yes. Do I still have an accent?"

"Not much, but it's there. It sounds quite sophisticated, actually." She pauses a second. "Therefore, given the accent, Amherst, and your rank, the odds are that you're Jewish."

"I'm half-Jewish actually, my mother was. My dad and I are Lutheran. Mr. Lansky said that your real last name is—or *was?*—is Silberman. That's Jewish too, isn't it? Whole? Half?"

"I'm like Ivory soap," Nan laughs, "99 and 44/100 percent Jewish. However, I don't think either of us has ever spent much time in a synagogue. But didn't I read that 'there are no atheists in foxholes?' You *were* in foxholes, weren't you?" she says, arching her eyebrows.

Harry finds himself increasingly unaware of what is going on around him. Nan's blonde friend is still at the bar talking with another woman, a few businessmen have been given tables,
and a second bartender has arrived and is fixing drinks.

"I'm the fastest foxhole digger in the Army. That's how I won my medals. While atheists dig foxholes, when an artillery round lands next to you and the dirt and body parts stop falling on you, lo and behold you emerge a practicing something or other."

Harry realizes that Nan has put a hand on his. Does that feel nice, he thinks, letting her warmth caress his hand.

"So how did you get here originally?" she asks.

"By ship," he answers, pausing with a goofy smile as she pretends to whack him. "Dad, my sister and I slipped out in '34." Later he will tell Nan how his dad hid valuable stamps in their shoes.

Harry looks around again and realizes that everyone has vanished except for Nan. He begins to feel that he's been whisked away to some enchanted land where only she exists.

"Dad's German name was Strölin," Harry says as he tells Nan that his father's second cousin, Elliott Speer became a minister and headmaster of the Mount Hermon School.

"I know it. It's also in the Connecticut River Valley; forty miles north of Smith."

"So, I went for an interview and was accepted. Dad liked the school because it was so isolated. He said it would be more difficult for the Nazis to track me down— "

"It was that bad?"

"No one was sure how pissed the Nazi's were. Dad's a *very* good engineer and designs production lines. Now he's in some godforsaken place in New Mexico—he won't say where—although I assume he isn't living with the Navajos."

Nan nods, from her smile and eyes Harry can tell that she's enjoying listening.

"A week before school opened in '34, Speer had me over for dinner and the first thing he said in German was we wouldn't speak German again."

"So, you were thrown into the water and expected to swim?" she said, touching her imitation pearl necklace and rubbing her neck exactly where Harry wants to kiss it.

"Hell no," Harry laughs, "they expected me to flounder. And flounder I did; I didn't start *thinking* in English for two years. Anyway, the next night he was in his study, when he was murdered by a shotgun blast—"

"I remember that! First page of the *New York Times* and the *Schenectady*

Gazette."

"Dad wanted to withdraw me because he believed it wasn't coincidental. I'd been there only four days and his cousin was murdered. How could it be a coincidence? Even the War Department was worried."

"And it wasn't ever solved, was it?"

"Never formally, no. A disgruntled faculty member was identified, but proving it? Maybe if the FBI had been called in sooner..."

"Did it affect you?"

"I was scared, of course, but the FBI said there was no connection, and after living in Germany I was really enjoying feeling free again."

"No other problems?"

"I didn't say that. Lots of problems. Like learning English. In fact, everyone was too friendly, almost condescending. Worse there was that little thing called *puberty*— "

"Tell me about it," again the dazzling smile as Nan looks at his eyes, slowing running her index finger in a circle over the rim of her glass.

"Except for summers, I barely saw my Dad although my sister lived close by. I spent most vacations with faculty members or at the homes of student friends."

"Well, I saw too much of my father. He worked for General Electric in Schenectady. During the Depression, GE cut his work week to three and sometimes two days; he was home often. While he didn't drink, he *munched* loudly and frequently; *munch, munch, munch—*"

"Like Bugs Bunny?"

"More like Oliver Hardy eating cream pies with his hands," she laughs and then begins to tell Harry about herself. "I was born December 30, 1923 which meant I was always the youngest in my class. Then I skipped a grade and was even more miserable; less coordinated, smaller and the last to understand jokes and styles. My small circle of friends; well, we called ourselves 'The ROs' for *rejected outsiders*. At night, I prayed I could be somebody special."

"You're joking?" Harry mumbles sympathetically, then catches the bartender's eye. "Would you like something to eat?" he asks Nan.

"Roast beef on rye and a coke, Frank" Nan says when the waiter comes over.

Roast beef? With rationing still in effect, Harry is surprised. Then he remembers the "Irish utility stew," that Nan hadn't looked at the menu, and that she knew the server's name when she ordered.

"The same," Harry nods, then turns his attention back to Nan. "So, you never thought you'd be somebody special?"

"No, junior high was terrible and my freshman year was even worse. I wasn't asked out once and when I tried to be a cheerleader—well, I was humiliated. But the last laugh was Mother Nature's because as a sophomore, everything changed in a few months."

Well, that's sure as hell true, thinks Harry, for in front of him sits this tall 5' 8" woman with greenish-blue eyes and a figure that would give Rita Hayworth a run for her money.

"Suddenly, smitten boys were following in my wake, hoping for a smile or that I'd at least wear tight sweaters more often—and everything was tight because I grew so quickly."

Harry finds himself fighting every instinct not to instinctively glance down.

"My voice also changed and I discovered I could belt out a song. Suddenly I was in every play and musical at Nott Terrace High School and that got me into Smith. After graduation, four of us found a one-bedroom apartment here. Then I volunteered at the Stage Door Canteen and won a talent contest jitterbugging and singing Joan Merrill's 'You Can't Say No to a Soldier.' That led to chorus work, *Oklahoma!* and modeling."

Harry listens as Nan, animated and energetic, describes the night Celeste Holm was ill and, as her understudy, she sang, "I'm just a girl who cain't say no."

The bartender arrives with the food and Harry leans forward to remove his wallet.

"Not tonight, soldier. Dinty says tonight's on him."

"Are you sure?" he begins. But both the bartender and Nan smile as Harry leans back. I'll be damned, he thinks as Nan resumes talking.

"But I've also learned I don't have what Hollywood wants. My arms are too thick and I'm too tall. The final nail in my coffin was a screen test with Xavier Cugat; the only thing going right was that his breath had dissipated by the time it reached my nose."

"But you've done well," Harry says, noting her expensive silk blouse, loose cashmere sweater and sophisticated earrings, necklace, bracelets and rings.

"That's from modeling. I was on the cover of *Startling Detective* a month ago—"

"No kidding. Can I get a copy?"

"Only if you'd like to see me strangled. But I need the work to dress the part. I can't go to the Stork Club and say hello to Sherman Billingsley wearing the same clothing twice, can I?"

"Of course not, but I've never heard of this Sherman whatever-his-last-name-is."

"Well, today he's the be-all and end-all of society. Walter Winchell and Harry Conover have their own tables, and Sinatra's a regular. The Stork is where Joe DiMaggio proposed to Dorothy Arnold. But the drinks are watered down, the food's worse, and the band's overrated."

"And nobody's ever proposed to you there?"

"Proposed to no, propositioned yes," she says as they both laugh.

An hour later—or whatever time it was in his now upside-down Salvador Dalí world—Harry realizes that he'd fallen head over heels in love.

▲

In reality, Cupid has also shot Nan O'Malley. This is the man she's been waiting for. She is overwhelmed by Harry's carriage, eyes, voice, smile, intelligence, and the shy way he looks into her eyes. Quickly, Nan returns to her college self, not the showgirl who leans forward when men light her cigarettes or gently touch the inside of a man's thigh when no one is looking. Instantly, Harry is Nan's best date ever, a real person who is everything she has dreamed of; not the son of someone rich but a person who, like her, has been through hell as an early adolescent. She quickly transforms him into a knight on a white horse who stops in front of the pavilion where she is sitting, dipping his lance to receive her scarf, and then unhorsing the evil King John's champion.

Nan hopes to God that Harry genuinely likes her. Even if it's for only one night, she tells herself that she'll remember him for years. Then, like the clock striking midnight for Cinderella, it is 7:30 p.m. and Dinty's bar is jammed, the noises of conversations, laughter and tinkling glasses rushing in. Where did the three hours go?

"Walk me to the St. James Theater," Nan says. Leaving Dinty's, they lock hands as Nan instinctively leans her head on the inside of Harry's shoulder. Her posture invites Harry to put his arm around her waist which he does, squeezing ever so slightly.

"Meet me here at eleven?" she asks when they arrive at the stage entrance. Nan turns to Harry. "Please kiss me." she whispers.

"Eleven," Harry says, as their lips meet. An instant after their tongues touch both draw their heads back. Nan is breathing hard, her heart pounding. She turns in front of the dressing room's staircase, runs up the stairs, and turns to see if Harry is still watching her. He is.

▲

This is going to be a long 3½ hours, Harry thinks as he walks up Broadway to the Pepsi Pavilion and listlessly sits in a corner. Everything is moving in slow motion; even his wristwatch seems to have gone on strike. But even as he replays their conversation in his mind, the one question he doesn't ask is why Nan happened to appear when she did.

Just after 11 p.m., Nan emerges from the St. James, sighing with relief when she spots Harry who has acquired a box of black market dark chocolates. The two hug, kiss, and hug again. Nervously, Harry asks if she might like to come back to his apartment. Nan's answer is another hug and kiss. A cab is hailed, the Morningside Heights address given, the cab driver barely turning on the meter before the two embrace.

Fifteen minutes later, they are in Harry's father's apartment, all but tearing each other's clothes off. The following morning the two slowly shower together, have delicious, soapy sex, and delight in their youth and staying power, each certain that they're meant for each other.

Chapter 21: Hanover, West Germany, January 16, 1946.

About the same time that Harry and Nan are showering in New York City, thousands of miles to the east it is late afternoon on a small farm south of Hanover. Not four weeks have passed since the winter solstice and, as the sun that was never high on the horizon begins to set, SS general Franz Seis finds himself staring into the barrel of a Colt .45.

Seis has been on the run for eight months, his capture a high priority for the American Counter Intelligence Corps (CIC). After leaving his brother Hermann and the others, he cautiously worked his way west. Nearing Hamburg, with heavy fighting underway between British and die-hard German units, he decides to cross the Elbe near Lauenburg. Here he joins thousands of refugees at a bridge manned by Allied officials looking for Nazis like him. Most men are ordered to remove their shirts; the CIC looking for the tattoos the SS routinely used for its own identification purposes. Those with tattoos are arrested while others are held because their documents are questionable or they look or act suspiciously.

Fortunately for Franz Seis, he is physically unimpressive. He wears thick glasses, rumpled clothing and sweater vest, and looks to be fifty. At first glance, he could be mistaken for the pre-war Konigsberg professor he'd been, not the *SS Brigadeführer* of one week earlier. On reaching the check point—apprehensive refugees pushing and shoving while keeping track of property and children—the first thing Seis does is to absent-mindedly ask in broken English where he can purchase real tobacco for his battered brown pipe. Thus, the harried inspectors wave him into Allied territory.

In early 1945, SS officers who committed war crimes—the handful that didn't fall under the definition of "oxymoron"—begin planning their escapes. A shadowy organization soon developed, popularly called ODESSA (*Organisation der ehemaligen SS-Angehörigen*). In all, ODESSA smuggled out thousands of SS officers from Germany into Spain, Portugal, South America, and the U.S.

Because of the stamps, Seis chooses to remain in Germany, his cover provided by an elderly couple. The two own a small dairy farm where, during the war, daily work was performed by Soviet POWs. With British occupation, all but one cow is confiscated and the Russians sent home to Stalin's paranoid embrace. For Seis and the couple, his arrival proves beneficial; they offer refuge while he performs their menial farm work.

In 1945's fall, Seis contacts his sister Marianne, a respected Heidelberg pediatrician, to let her and his parents know he is safe. Then, in October, Marianne has a visitor, ex-SS officer Frederick Hirschfeld, who asks for her help in removing not just his, but other SS tattoos. The two became lovers, then spend a weekend in Stuttgart where she removes SS tattoos from more than 150 men. Weeks later she learns that the CIC has captured most of them. Perhaps because she is in love, she never suspects Hirschfield. Then he brings her the best news possible; he has arranged work for Franz with a leather-goods dealer. Delighted, Marianne gives him Franz's address.

▲

That afternoon, Franz Seis is sweeping the barn when his broom frays. Sitting down, hunched over and shivering, he re-lashes it for further use: nothing goes to waste that winter in Germany. Distracted by a task he knows nothing about and a foot of snow that absorbs most sounds, Seis never hears Hirschfeld's car arrive. Thus, he is caught totally by surprise as he looks up to see Hirschfeld and two German-speaking American CIC's enter the barn.

"Don't move! We're the CIC! We don't want to shoot you!" Hirschfeld commands from inside the open barn door, twenty feet away as he points his Army Colt .45 at Seis.

Seis is so flabbergasted that his glasses fall off, causing the three to laugh.

"There will be no trouble, gentlemen, I am unarmed. Do you mind?" he asks, pointing to his glasses on the soft dirt floor. Slowly placing them back on, he absently asks, "How can our Germany ever recover if we aren't given time to repair it?" Sighing, he examines the broom, holding it at the neck, and shuffles forward, the picture of an old, defeated man. The two assistants holster their pistols while Hirschfeld lowers his .45, pointing it to the ground.

Without warning, Seis, now only feet away, takes a fast step forward, ramming the broom's handle into Hirschfeld's abdomen, just below the rib cage. Hirschfeld collapses while Seis, in a fluid motion, yanks the broom back, swivels, and hits one of Hirschfeld's assistants across the ear with such force that the broom handle cracks, the man spinning backward into the barn's interior. As the third man fumbles to retrieve his pistol, Seis charges into him, throwing him back to the wall, the broom neck high. When the man tries to push the broom away, Seis rams his knee into his testicles.

Hirschfeld, breathless and on his back, attempts to prop himself up until Seis grabs the .45, pressing it against his head. However, as Seis tries to pull the trigger, he realizes that the safety is still on: the three have never intended to kill him! Seis knows that, by killing three CIC, the hue and cry will be overwhelming. Better to take their car; the farmhouse has no phone and he'll have an hour's head start. Just in case, though, he decides to keep the .45.

Running forward, Seis bursts through the barn door. Even the weak sun is magnified by winter snow and his eyes are accustomed to the barn's gloom. He is in full stride as he reaches the barn door. What he hasn't noticed, however, is that waiting outside the barn is a fourth CIC officer named Baker. Too late, the sprinting Seis realizes that Baker's foot is sticking out and about to trip him. The next second he finds himself sprawled on his stomach, the air gone from his lungs, a beefy American kneeling on his back and Hirschfeld's .45 well beyond his reach.

"I told you that he wasn't Denny Dimwit," the 230-pound, former football player and Chicago detective hollers into the barn, expertly pulling out handcuffs and snapping them on Seis's wrists. Only then do Hirschfeld and the two CIC men stagger out of the barn. Looking up, the CIC officer, of Polish descent, delivers vicious kidney punches with his fist and elbow, catching Seis totally by surprise. Seis shrieks in pain and will piss blood for a week. However, as intended, there will be no marks on his angry countenance when he is photographed later.

"Well, fuck face," the American whispers in German into Seis's ear, "the next stop for you is Nuremberg and the hangman's noose." Then Baker throws a hood over Seis's head.

▲

In Heidelberg, a month later, Dr. Marianne Seis is found crawling on a sidewalk. Rushed to a hospital it is discovered that she has been poisoned. However, following an official autopsy, the verdict becomes pneumonia. In Heidelberg, locals are of three minds pointing to the ODESSA, actual suicide, or the CIC. Regardless, the results are the same: Franz Seis is imprisoned and his sister, who once too often told the wrong person too much, is dead.

Chapter 22: New York, Thursday, January 17.

Harry arrives at the Automat opposite the Public Library ten minutes early. He cannot suppress a smile after a second night of magnificent sex. Unlike Berlin, this is not the copulation of clinging, desperate people, but rather is exquisite, no-holds-barred, slow-motion sex.

Lansky is already seated at a table reading the late morning edition of the business-oriented, establishment Republican *Herald-Tribune.* On his instructions, Harry wears civvies; a college suit which no longer fits in the shoulders.

"May I assume your obvious contentment has something to do with a Miss O'Malley?" Lansky asks. "You two looked like old friends the second you met."

"Things are going much better than I could've expected," says Harry. An uncontrolled, lopsided grin crosses his face. "I can't help thinking how lucky I was that she was there just as we left. And how much I appreciate your introducing us."

Lansky smiles. Harry does not know that, in a few hours, Lansky will meet with Dinty Moore who is furious about Nan leaving him. On the phone with Lansky, Dinty lost his temper, cursed Nan and made threats. More than once a girl who left Dinty wound up badly beaten. It was all Lansky could do to calm him down.

"You have your stamps?" Lansky asks, all business. Harry nods and says he's also written an erasable colored cross on the back of each stamp, which brings a smile to Lansky's face. The crosses are very lightly marked with different colored pencils—easily erasable—so no one can switch stamps on short notice.

The man they are expecting arrives. He is six feet tall, rail thin, about sixty and wears a hat, earmuffs, scarf and heavy overcoat. His face is as dried out as if he'd spent his life living under a strong sun. He nods to Lansky, but then shuffles over to a change counter's enclosed booth. As Harry watches, for the man's dollar in an instant he receives twenty nickels, the hands of the woman making change moving faster than any card dealer.

"Montclair 'Smith,' " Lansky whispers, "was a wealthy stamp dealer but between the Depression and, shall we say, 'impatiently' playing poker, he lost everything. Then certain irregularities were uncovered and the professional stamp associations expelled him. Now he's a middleman in the stamp black market, but he still loves stamps—almost as much as poker."

Montclair sits down with a cup of coffee, never asking Harry's name. Lansky explains to him that Harry has acquired certain stamps that, *if* genuine, have value. As a personal favor, Lansky hopes Montclair will test their authenticity, then hands him the stamps.

Montclair takes the stamps, places them in his briefcase, bows briefly, and disappears behind some pillars.

"Do you trust him?" Harry asks apprehensively.

"Montclair has much to gain but far more to lose. At his age, he has nowhere to go. Your idea of colored pencil marks on each stamps' back also sends a message."

"While we wait, I want to ask you a personal question if you don't mind," Lansky says as Harry nods. "What do you want from life? I know it sounds intrusive, but I have my reasons."

"Well, I've certainly thought about it enough, but I keep on getting stymied. I was good at what I did in the Eighty-Second, but I became someone I didn't know or like. That's why I'm starting at Columbia Business School. I'm hoping to find some answers there."

Across the Automat the low hum of conversation ceases. Heads begin turning as a foul smell wafts from the men's room. Harry and Lansky just grin.

"But if you could do anything, what would it be?"

"I'd like to escape for a few years to Paris in the 1920s... No, I just don't know yet. Sometimes I still wake up and wonder what happened to the foxhole I'd dug."

"Don't worry about it," Lansky smiles. "Nobody ever went wrong with a business degree. Everything will fall into place after a while, you'll see."

▲

Ten minutes later, Montclair returns, smiles, sits, and nods with pleasure. "Other than your 'cross' young man, the stamps appear genuine. I'll unreservedly certify them, Meyer. And it's impossible to tell who previously owned them. Congratulations."

"But how does my young friend sell them?" Lansky asks.

"Meyer, this is the first time we've discussed this subject, so permit me to tell you about *my* business. Stamps are different, let's say, from diamonds or gold, which are *commodities* governed by international factors. Uncertainty drives up value, but with world-wide stability or when new gold deposits or diamonds are unearthed, then their prices drop."

"Stamps, on the other hand, are finite. Take the one-cent 1856 black on red British Guyana. Only one exists and commands $ 100,000. There are a thousand stamps that are worth more than almost any diamond. While stamps are easily hidden, they're also vulnerable to water, fire, disintegration in humidity and fading if exposed to light. Every precaution can fail; a famed British stamp dealer, Stanley Gibbons, covered his bets during the London Blitz by putting its stamps in different vaults, but one direct hit cost him millions."

Harry nods—Montclair is repeating what Harry's father had taught him.

"To add to the war's mysteries," Montclair continues, "How many Jewish collections were lost? We know the Nazis were very thorough in whatever they undertook. I assume," he says, looking at Harry, "you stumbled upon some of these. Were the stamps in albums?"

Harry shakes his head.

"In that case, there is no possibility of identification unless you could speak to the man you acquired them from."

"No, he's quite dead."

"Do you wish to discuss how to sell these?" Montclair asks Lansky.

"Not yet. If you are selected to sell all or part I will be in touch with you soon."

▲

"Now, at two," Lansky says after Montclair leaves, "we will meet Aaron Abramson—"

"Of Romanoff and Abramson?" Harry cuts in. "My God, he's as big as they come."

"Yes, he is, isn't he? However, my sixth sense anticipated Montclair's approval and I also have a sense of urgency about this. Montclair's good at the technical level, but Aaron has an unsurpassed overview so you'll meet him in a few hours. What will you do until then?"

"I need to buy two decent suits that fit. Do you have any suggestions?"

Lansky, always the conservative peacock, smiles with pleasure at being asked. "For you, Rogers Peet at 49th and Fifth is nearby and perfect. They cater to younger men and will fit you at a fair price. Ask for Abe Rosenbaum and say I sent you; it will speed up the tailoring," he laughs, smiling at a private joke. "And tell Abe about the Eighty-Second, his two sons were in the Marines."

Chapter 23: New York; 1944, 1946.

It is September 1944. Nan is being interviewed by Dinty Moore in his large office above the restaurant. He holds out a chair in front of his desk, offers Nan a cigarette, and begins. She is certain what he will ask, but he broaches the subject ever so delicately and patiently listens to her questions. Slowly, he describes the differences between a *prostitute* and a *courtesan*; which is what he has in mind. Listening to him, it sounds genteel, not coarse. As Nan feels herself relax, Dinty explains that she'll meet men weekday afternoons at a nearby apartment. The work will not interfere with *Oklahoma!* and Dinty will pay $1,200 a month besides tips.

Nan is surprised how quickly she agrees. After all, she thinks, this is short term; it's not like I'm taking marriage vows. And $1,200! This is too good to be true.

But it is too good to be true. The maids cleaning Nan's bedroom also collect film taken from behind multiple mirrors with Berning Optics cameras, a firm specializing in *Luftwaffe* night gun cameras modified for the Gestapo. Through Swiss contacts, Lansky has circuitously purchased the hardware that will ensnare military officers, government officials, politicians, businessmen and, with luck, an occasional District Attorney.

Chapter 24: New York, 1946.

After leaving Harry, Lansky walks over to Dinty's office above the restaurant. He then patiently sits across from Dinty and lets the Irishman vent his anger. But Lansky is unable to hide his amusement that this man, older than his father, is so upset. *Too* upset.

"Dinty, speaking as one old friend to another, haven't you left out something?" he asks.

Dinty looks perplexed and holds his hands out, palms up as confusion crosses his face.

"Isn't the real issue that you like Nan? At seventy-six you have a schoolboy's infatuation. How many times must I tell you to stay away from women you manage? Do I not remember a certain pregnant hatcheck girl? Did you fuck Nan on your huge couch? Or were you screwing her until Major Strong came along? Out with it, I want an answer."

Dinty's face turns bright red. "No," his voice almost a whisper. "She seduced me—"

"*She* seduced *you*, did she?" It is all Lansky can do to keep a stern look on his face as he fights not to laugh. "A porpoise wanting to be fucked by a whale?"

"I pay her extra to come in once a week to undress slowly and then... But it's more than that."

"Dinty, let me explain the facts of life," Lansky's sandpaper voice is unusually low for he is angry. "So, she blows you and says nice things to you? You are aware, aren't you, that you're part of things larger than you'll ever know? I like you, but first, last, and always we have a *business* relationship. How often in the *Daily News* or *Mirror* do we see a friend lying in a gutter or a restaurant, legs sprawled, half the head missing as police stand around laughing? Do we not receive calls from wives whose missing husbands are swimming in Jamaica Bay, their feet in concrete? All because they'd poked their noses into something that wasn't their business?"

Lansky, who knows Dinty is not stupid, sees that his friend's face has turned white.

"Let me be candid," Lansky says and pauses. "Because of Nan, you have become overexcited, and overexcited people frequently make mistakes. Do they not? People who make mistakes accidentally upset apple carts. And you are part of a very, very large applecart."

Lansky speaks slowly, carefully watching Dinty's eyes. "Let us review our relationship. To get your restaurant high quality steaks, officials are paid off with money or women. Even with the war's end, distribution remains expensive: refrigerated trucks have mechanical problems, old tires explode, and dependable drivers are few. Worse, Governor Dewey wants big name restaurants raided. Never forget that I have personally exerted every effort so that *your* restaurant has never undergone such a public humiliation. In exchange for our efforts, we ask you to assist us in certain ways, shall we say, in the selection and grooming of young mares."

"To date, I feel your work has been above reproach and my associates are of the same opinion. But now, and if I'm to be totally candid, I'm the one responsible for Nan's leaving. I personally like Major Strong and wanted to give him a 'thank you' gift. It never crossed my mind that the two would fall in love, but they have, haven't they? We both know hit-by-lightning love cannot last, but, while they are under its spell, they will be irrational. It would be easier to part the Red Sea than to separate them, right? Nevertheless, if Major Strong learns about you and Nan, he will kill you; just as he has killed others when he has lost his self-control. And I've watched him hurt others."

Dinty eyes squeeze shut as his fists open and close. I've never seen him so frightened, Lansky thinks. Good.

"Nan will be missed," Lansky continues, "but you will continue to harvest attractive, ambitious girls to replace her. Also, important business understandings have been made with Major Strong. Let me say this slowly: from now you will regard Nan as you do my daughter. If any problems arise, I *will* look to you first. On the other hand, if I'm angry enough, perhaps I won't bother to ask. Kapish?" Lansky says, smiling as he gently slaps Dinty's cheek.

Dinty tries to say something, however only "But, but..." emerges which stops when Lansky shakes his head.

"Thank you for your time, Dinty. Oh, if you would, please have the kitchen bring me a corned beef on rye, two sides of slaw, sour pickles and a pot of Columbian coffee, no cream, no sugar." Lansky walks behind Dinty's desk, sits down and picks up the phone. His business satisfactorily completed, he waves Dinty out with the back of his hand.

▲

Harry's 2 PM appointment is at the 604 Fifth Avenue Childs (between 48th and 49th), an upscale restaurant chain suited to the distinguished-looking man who joins them. Seventy-one, Aaron Abramson wears a homburg and a camel's hair coat. He is a former criminal defense attorney and American Philatelic Society president. With his thick white hair, Roman nose, strong chin and mustache, Abramson is still often mistaken for the late John Barrymore.

Later, Harry discovers that, in 1928, Abramson represented Lansky for a youthful "indiscretion"—hijacking at gunpoint a truck filled with kitchen and bathroom tile. In fact, Abramson had little to do when the terrified truck driver, placed on the witness stand, failed to identify Lansky. Despite their age difference, and whatever had been done earlier to extort the truck driver, Abramson took a shine to his client and the two became close over the years.

Lansky introduces Harry, emphasizing his service in the Eighty-Second. After chatting a few minutes and ordering coffee, Abramson comments on Harry's mild accent and from there quickly deduces his family story. Showing increased fascination, he listens as, prodded by Lansky, Harry tells how he had acquired the stamps, emphasizing their likely Jewish origins.

"Nothing is surprising when it comes to Nazis," Abramson says. "Although we've been far from perfect. German civilians report stamps stolen at gunpoint by our officers. You know, we captured a Nazi 'gold train' in Austria—gold, silver, paintings, icons, and stamps too—but everything disappeared, the American general in charge involved up to his rotten neck. I've also been asked by the Army to review a Leipzig incident where one of our medical teams, no less, stole stamps worth $150,000 from Germans."

"But for stamps like Major Strong possesses," asks Lansky, "what category are these?"

"This can be murky. If the stamps are in albums saying, 'Property of Moses Cohen, Rotterdam,' finding survivors becomes paramount."

"But every stamp I found was loose. Not a scrap of documentation."

"While selling is easier, you must remain cautious. Large numbers of stamps suddenly dropped into the market will invariably raise questions and lawsuits, spurious or not. However, a combat veteran like yourself, by telling a *reasonable* story, might safely sell a portion."

"For discussion's sake," says Harry, "Let's assume I have 500 times more stamps."

"I'd sell some this year and the remainder over the next two or three decades."

"What if we sold more now?" Lansky asks. "I'm quite curious about this."

Aaronson scratches his ear and sips more coffee before he continues. "What we must factor into any analysis is *privacy*, which you, Meyer, recognize more than anyone."

"But you'd represent us?" Lansky asked.

"Of course, I would consider it a privilege to auction them off for our firm."

"Then also consider this," Lansky says, looking Abramson in the eye, "most of the money will be going to our friends in Palestine."

"Then I will give this even more serious thought. Rest assured, I'll discuss this immediately with Baron Romanoff. He's my partner, Harry, and you'll soon learn that our friends in the Holy Land desperately need all the money and munitions possible."

Chapter 25: New York, Saturday, February 2, 1946.

Seventeen days after they meet, Nan and Harry are married in New York's Episcopalian Little Church Around the Corner, on 29th Street between Madison and Park. The small, romantic church had long since passed the 5,000-marriage mark since Pearl Harbor. When Nan asks the Reverend Randolph Ray how many he will perform he answers that six "is a quiet mid-week schedule, but before today ends I will officiate ten."

Nan looks and feels glorious in a white two-piece suit and light apricot blouse, wide brimmed white hat with white veil, and heels. Facing Ray, in his twenty-second year as rector, Harry stands ramrod-straight, immaculate in his khaki uniform, the Silver Star, Bronze Star and Distinguished Service Cross medals and various service ribbons and badges displayed on his chest and a major's gold oak leaf on his shoulders.

Afterwards, the bridal party is whisked uptown to the Plaza Hotel and a reception Lansky is hosting. Toasts are washed down with a rare 1918 brut champagne (a fine year but with limited production given the vineyards' proximity to WWI's trenches), followed by caviar, prime beef, Belgian chocolates, other wartime rarities, and finally a wedding cake with a bride and a paratrooper groom. There are no charges. The first round of post-war strikes has begun and hotel workers are unionized. As prices spiral, unions need little encouragement to strike. In fact, any reasonable suggestion Lansky makes brings a management sigh of relief; they know that a good word from him will make future labor negotiations that much smoother.

▲

In the Frank Lloyd Wright suite overlooking Central Park and Augustus Saint Gaudens' equestrian statue of General Sherman, the marriage is greedily consummated. Once Nan is sleeping, Harry tiptoes to the window, realizes it's snowing, and looks at the white-covered statue. Lighting a cigarette, he lets his mind wander; it is something he's been unable to do since meeting Nan. Everything has become so rushed and furious. Even his marriage proposal, which was made seconds before ejaculation. "I want to marry you," and Nan's response as they climaxed, "Oh God, yes!"

Idly he wonders about Ilse. Has she been as lucky? Is she in bed with someone? He hasn't thought of her in ages and he finds himself wanting to tell her about Nan. Except he doesn't really know Nan, does he? Yes, she's gorgeous and intelligent, but who is she really? Or for that matter, who is he? Back in bed he sees Nan's chest's rise and fall, takes in her animal scent and the heat from her body, then slides next to her and gently kisses her.

Like other young marrieds, there is no time for a formal honeymoon. Two days later, Nan is back to work at *Oklahoma!* Harry, his moment of introspection forgotten, returns to his father's apartment and the rest of his life.

Chapter 26: Baron Ivan Romanoff.

At precisely 9:00 AM, Wednesday February 6 the phone rings. Harry and Nan rapidly untangle. He reaches the phone by the fourth ring, answering with an incomprehensible grunt.

"Sorry to wake you," Meyer Lansky says, business-like.

Harry indicates he has heard, while Nan sluggishly rolls over, kissing his shoulder and running her hand over his side, grasping him. For a second he wriggles like a fish on a hook, smiles, then pushes her away with his free hand. "It's Mr. Lansky," he whispers.

"The Automat between Columbus and Amsterdam on 72nd Street."

"Yes," says Harry, now fully awake.

"Ten AM. Wear one of your new suits, not your uniform, and bring your safe deposit key with you." Harry repeats the instructions, then the phone line clicks dead.

Thirty minutes and a quick shower later Harry is out the door, Nan's smells hopefully off him. Only then does he wonder why Lansky called. Moreover, why had he been so brusque? It wasn't like him. Had he imagined it or had something unexpectedly gone wrong?

▲

Indeed, something has: the moneyman behind Lansky has become suspicious. Sipping coffee and eating a slice of just-made Dutch apple pie, Lansky gently explains the problem. A key individual simply cannot comprehend that Harry's story is real.

"Amateurs don't stumble across Captain Kidd's buried treasure or Mussolini's Swiss bank accounts," the man told Lansky the previous evening. "Something's going on that I instinctively distrust. It is entirely possible that our enemies, and there are many, have set a trap. Who and why I cannot say, but knowing my own weaknesses, baiting a trap with stamps has the highest chance of success. Your sixth sense is unfailingly good with Jews and Sicilians, Meyer, but there's a chance that this young man, whom I fear you like too much is, at best, a gullible pawn. Let's hope this is the case, but nevertheless I desire to meet him and need to take his measure without his having time to prepare."

"But..." Lansky's voice had trailed off.

The man who had advanced him millions in cash over the past decades raises his hand and shakes his head. His decision has been made. "Tomorrow morning, Meyer, while he is enjoying his honeymoon, will be best."

▲

Over coffee, Lansky hides his concern. More than once, he ate with a person who later vanished. "Yes," he'd told the police, "I saw him that morning, but..." Lansky has reserved a table at Peter Luger's always crowded Brooklyn steak house where he will be seen by dozens. At 3 PM, he will take a cab to Dinty's, tipping heavily so that the driver remembers him. Now, as Harry sits in front of him, content and at ease, Lansky tries to appear relaxed.

"Harry, you are to go to your safe deposit box and select forty valuable stamps from six countries. They are to include Imperial Russia, the U.S., Great Britain, and any three others." Lansky gives Harry an address and says that he is expected by noon. "If there is any problem in this request, you must say so now."

Harry smiles and nods, never realizing that his life is in danger.

▲

There are five known facts concerning "Baron" Ivan Romanoff: he was Russian, played brilliant chess, loved stamp collecting, performed magic tricks, and was a gregarious fraud. His birth name was Ivan Petrovich Balitnikoff, the illegitimate offspring of a Russian sea captain's daughter and a half-Jewish son of a Scottish tea merchant in Saint Petersburg. Born in 1874 and an artillery officer, Romanoff was badly wounded fighting the Turks at the protracted battle of Sarikamish in 1914-15.

No longer fit for combat, in 1916 he traveled to the U.S. to purchase weapons but never returned home following the Russian Revolution. In America, his name became Romanoff and he claimed to be an illegitimate grandson of Czar Alexander I. Broke, he hustled chess matches, performed magic tricks in bars, purchased stamps from Russians emigres, and became associated with arms dealers. He soon perfected selling to one country, then informing its neighbor. Unlike J. P. Morgan, who, when America's Civil War began, sold defective Belgian rifles to his own side (the Union), Romanoff never dealt in shoddy equipment. Yes, he did sell the same equipment twice, but the weapons always functioned. Romanoff armed both sides in the Spanish Civil War, small monarchies, and feuding South American countries. Making millions, he dined with Russian nobility (usually faux like himself) and moved into a magnificent Park Avenue penthouse.

In Manhattan, Romanoff taxied every morning to his office in the Graybar Building on Lexington and 43rd. Then, on a fine fall, 1938 day, as he strode from his apartment to a cab, a man rushed forward, firing a .32 revolver. One bullet plowed sideways through Romanoff's mouth while a second tore off his left ear. The building's doorman tackled the shooter, a Spanish Republican named Carlos Zabalza, only to be wounded himself. Traffic stopped and screaming began. Zabalza stumbled to his feet, looked at the crumpled Romanoff who appeared dead, then from one spectator to another and put his revolver in his mouth. This final shot caused the day's only fatality, but at sixty-four Romanoff had had enough. The following day he announced his "retirement" from a hospital bed and turned his energies exclusively to philately and women.

Years earlier, Romanoff had become friends with Abramson. The two formed Romanoff & Abramson, a stamp dealership which initially shared modest offices with Romanoff's arms operations. At first, the firm had only one important client: Edward H. R. Brown, America's wealthiest philatelist. When the upside-down (inverted) Blue-Jennys were first sold (1920), it was Brown who purchased the entire sheet of one-hundred stamps for $20,000.

Despite having lost a leg, Brown, all 6 feet 4 and 350 pounds of him, caroused with the best. Prone to falling, he entered speakeasys with two prostitutes, one holding a spare cork prosthesis which hid a bottle of bootleg, the second helping Brown. Most mornings, he took his chauffeured car and a pile of cash to Nassau Street's stamp dealers where he was known to spend $10,000 a day on stamps. In the afternoon, an assistant mounted the stamps in albums which

Brown seldom, if ever, examined. Finally, the Good Lord took him, his will specifying that, for his estate, Romanoff was to sell his stamps, the date set for 1946.

▲

As Abramson and Lansky explained to Romanoff the details of Harry's stamps, the baron became increasingly dubious. Thus, that Wednesday, Harry finds himself in Romanoff's southern facing penthouse. A butler in striped pants ushers him in. Harry notes a library with ceiling-high bookcases and potted palms before he enters a magnificent living room. Here sits a concert hall quality Steinway piano, Russian Orthodox icon altar paintings, miniature diamond encrusted gold coaches, and assorted Fabergé eggs. On the walls hang paintings from the brushes of Pieter Bruegel (the younger), Jacob van Roisdael, John Constable, and Thomas Cole.

A muscular servant, Sven, Romanoff's bodyguard, makes no effort to hide his shoulder holster. Standing alongside Romanoff are two large, peaceful-enough looking thoroughbred Russian wolfhounds, animals that in the flash of an eye can tear a man apart.

"Mr. Strong, please hold your hand out so that Nicholas and Alexander—they're named for my great-uncle and grandfather—can sniff you. They are amazing animals, you know, each weigh over a hundred pounds. Before the Great War, I watched them hunt wolves. While they appear docile... Good boys, now sit," he orders.

"I've heard much about you, young man," he says. Romanoff's voice rumbles, his English spoken in a disconcerting Russian-Scottish accent. He wears a white shirt, tie, sweater-vest, dark slacks, and fur slippers under a Japanese silk kimono. Shaking hands, his huge, thick fingers encircle Harry's. The baron moves slowly, his white-bearded chin seemingly meeting his upper chest, large brown liver spots on his face and hands. Carefully he lowers himself into a leather wingback chair, pointing to an Empire Period seat for Harry.

"I was told that Napoleon once sat on that, but antique dealers are like stamp sellers: born liars if you don't know their business—sometimes even if you do. Unlike poor Napoleon, who ran afoul of my grandfather, you've had the luck of the Gods by blundering into one of stamp history's most valuable collections. Then you turned to Meyer Lansky. He is a singular man, as honest as in his own way as Abe Lincoln, fully trusted by some of this country's most despicable personages—myself included," Romanoff laughs heartily, enjoying his own joke.

"By the way, did you know Meyer is in the jukebox business? He secured an exclusive Wurlitzer agreement for Manhattan and, for his Italian friends, cities along the coast. However, considerable capital is required; each Wurlitzer costs $1,100 so I help with that. Meyer is the best partner an investor could select and his 'sales associates' are equally knowledgeable."

Harry smiles. He doesn't have to guess how effective a broken-nosed, cauli-flower-eared six-foot, 300-pound "sales associate" with a monosyllabic vocab-ulary can be.

"Before we take you on as a client, young man, I want to review how you acquired these stamps. While I instinctively feel that you're telling us what *you* believe to be true, I must warn you that I've dealt with swindlers and charlatans for sixty years. If, during our conversation, I detect a lie, evasion, or failure to correct me when I make an obvious error, I will regretfully ask you to leave and instruct Messrs. Lansky and Abramson to terminate their relationship with you. Do we understand each other?"

Harry nods, hoping that he isn't sweating noticeably.

"Nevertheless, before you become too nervous I have asked—ah, here is Bernard now—to bring you a Jack Daniel's and a chaser; I believe you're par-tial to that. But let me examine the stamps you brought with you."

Romanoff begins looking through them, nodding his head in approval and sometimes nodding and smiling. Then he stops abruptly and holds up one stamp.

"Do you know what this is?" He asks, holding up a red Australian two-pence stamp.

"Of course, its's a 1936 engraving of the Duke of Windsor, while he was still Edward VIII, before he abdicated."

"What else do you know about it?"

"I remember reading that they were all destroyed. Clearly, however, they were not. I have six of them, but for all I know there are six thousand."

"Only a handful survived. Even I have never seen one. Nor has any other *bone fide* philatelist. You certainly have had amazing luck. Perhaps even been too lucky. And so, Herr Heinrich Strölin, it is time for us begin," Romanoff says, switching to fluent, rapid-fire German, "I believe that you were born in Hamburg?"

Harry answers the questions as best possible. Romanoff misstates facts he is expected to know and switches from German to English in mid-sentence. Questions often relate to the geography and history of where Harry lived or served. What is unique about the barns of the Connecticut Valley? They have open sides to let fresh air dry the tobacco leaves. Where was Harry on Kristallnacht (November 1938)? At Amherst. What did Berlin's Nettelbeckstrasse and Manhattan's Nassau Street have in common? Before the war, both were where their country's stamp dealers were concentrated.

Gradually Harry feels himself relaxing, whether it's his second Jack Daniel's, Romanoff's outgoing energy or the feeling that he's on a radio quiz show, he isn't sure. Nevertheless, at times Romanoff has Harry reeling: "Please describe a *satcheleer*."

"I have no idea; what is a *what?*"

"*Satch-e-leer.* They're salesmen who specialize in carrying stamps from dealer to dealer. Say Dealer X specializes in German colonials, but purchases a collection with British items. As so many stamp dealers are one-man operations, they can't afford to leave their offices too long. So, what do they do? Why, they turn to a *satcheleer*—actually, *briefcase-a-leer* would be more accurate—to sell the stamps to Dealer Y, a British Empire specialist— "

"Does the *satcheleer* get a commission?" Harry asks.

"Yes, and you correctly answered by *not* knowing the answer. But, please; indulge me as we continue our little game." Half an hour later Romanoff is smiling, then laughs, and finally—as his eyes water—he slaps his thigh with glee, all the while having Bernard refill Harry's glass while he quickly catches up with his guest.

"Enough!" Romanoff says unexpectedly. "Heinrich Strölin, you've convinced me. What I have decided to do is to sell some of your stamps and Edward Brown's *simultaneously*. Now pay attention, not all auctions are similar. Unlike the machine-gun speed of, say, a cattle auction, stamp auctions slow as the value increases. Even a too-quickly raised hand is considered gauche. Rather, a professional buyer will scratch his knee, stroke an ear lobe, or discreetly raise a finger to indicate interest. Best of all, watching Aaron Abramson is like Arturo Toscanini directing the NBC Philharmonic Orchestra. He coaxes every dollar out of buyers, plays one bidder against another and as often as not performs philately's greatest miracle: selling stamps at higher prices than Scott-listed catalog values."

Romanoff glances at his side table, finds the little platinum bell he is looking for, and rings it vigorously. "Bernard," he calls, "please phone Mr. Lansky. He's at Peter Luger's. Tell him that Mr. Strong has passed his test with flying colors." Harry, somewhat confused, keeps a poker face, never realizing that if Sven had been called in, the bell would have tinkled for him.

Chapter 27: New York, 1946.

Like so many wartime romances, neither Harry nor Nan has the slightest idea whom they married. What comes after a whirlwind romance and a fairy tale wedding? However, life soon falls into predictable patterns. Monday through Saturday, Harry waits for Nan to emerge from the St. James Theater after *Oklahoma!* ends. The two eat a late cafeteria supper at Hector's, Bickford's, or the Automat, then catch the IRT subway home. Weekdays, Harry is up at 7 AM for classes. Nan stays in bed or does light grocery shopping (although she can barely boil water), takes clothes to a Chinese laundry, or reads before going downtown.

Sundays are reserved for themselves; museums, visits to the Bronx or Central Park zoos, twenty-five cents to rent a Central Park rowboat, and, in bad weather, a quarter each to see a four hour double feature at an uptown Loews or RKO. Once home there is sex; wonderful and glorious for, as Nan confides to her *Oklahoma!* friends, Harry is *fantastic* in the sack. Of course, she's no slouch either.

Early on, Nan's chance for the number two female in *Annie Get Your Gun* ends when she indignantly refuses to "accommodate" a critical producer. Her agent, Hyman Garfinkle, is beside himself ("nobody cares if you just got married"), but somehow arranges a second meeting. Nan, her thespian future on the line, accedes but is "disciplined" by being relegated to the number four female role. Only then does she realize that she has learned two lessons; there will be similar requests and that she has placed her career over her marriage.

In late 1946, Lerner and Loewe's *Brigadoon* begins casting with Nan thoroughly motivated. Her *Wow!* performances on stage and couch win her the number three role and a bright future. But the day after her final "audition," Nan discovers she's pregnant, and tearfully withdraws. Above all, she wants Harry's baby; abortion is out of the question.

▲

Harry, his unused muscles beginning to twitch in 1946, begins realizing that sports and the outdoors had been his salvation for pent-up anger. At Mount Hermon and Amherst, he turned soccer fields and basketball courts into demolition derbies. Even in tennis he liked nothing more than to aim vicious serves and volleys directly at his opponent. Now, however, he has no outlets; he lives in a claustrophobic apartment and, at Columbia, he is glued to small goddamn desks in ancient classrooms.

"What's bothering you?" Nan asks, but Harry cannot find the words. For both it becomes sex yes, inner feelings no. Few recall that, twenty-five years earlier, veterans of literary bent migrated to Paris (Dos Passos, Fitzgerald, Hemingway and Steinbeck), calling themselves "the Lost Generation." Harry has no such friends and, in fact, no real friends. He doesn't mind the grade competition inherent in classrooms, but, unlike sports and the military, there's no associated camaraderie offering satisfaction for good teamwork. Leadership skills mean nothing when a spot quiz or essay examination is given.

Moreover, loathe as Harry is to admit it, marriage has further isolated him. As Columbia fills with ex-GI's, Harry unsuccessfully searches for a familiar face. While most veterans in business school are driven by Depression memories, Harry has nothing similar motivating him. For him, success is not about achieving secure middle-class status, but doing something *for others*. But what? And how?

Homework at Low Library at least permits him to fidget, drink water, or wander over to the Broadway Chock Full o'Nuts for coffee, but this is of little help. Then, mature co-eds in two-tone loafers, white socks, plaid skirts, not always loose sweaters, and mock pearl necklaces drop by his table. Finally comes the co-ed who forces him to point to his ring and say, I'm married. "But I can tell you're not happy," the redhead says. "And I have my own apartment." What most astonishes Harry is, as soon as he begins this affair, sex with Nan again becomes passionate. Hey, explain that one? He marvels. Nevertheless, these frolics bring on waves of self-loathing.

During his free time, Harry finds himself captivated watching construction. He yearns to hold the levers of a steam shovel or bulldozer, captain a tugboat, to do physically dangerous but mentally challenging work. Soon he is questioning his decision to major in marketing: is he essentially learning to sell soap? And his minor? Banking. Despite each course's fancy name, the classes all seem to be about accounting methods to shortchange clients and evade taxes. He cannot but help but wonder: is this what America's all about?

▲

By 1946's end neither dares acknowledge the need for more space—from each other. Harry's father's apartment is simply claustrophobic. Visitors, especially with Nan's pregnancy, seem to arrive more frequently and always stay with them. Harry's father from New Mexico, his sister and her husband from Michigan, and Nan's mother from Schenectady.

Then, on their first wedding anniversary, Harry hides a blue envelope under Nan's pillow.

"Go ahead, open it," he says, standing back, hands around her expanding waist when she discovers it.

"It feels like metal. But it's not a coin," she says, lifting the envelope to get a better feeling its weight. Then the object begins sliding. "More like a key."

"Could be. But you won't know until you open it."

"Should I close my eyes?" she says, her smile indicating that she knows something nice is about to happen. Eyes closed, Nan opens the outer envelope, finding a second layer of heavily folded, thick paper. "It is a key. But to what?"

"Is it?" he teases. "Who knows? But open your eyes and don't rip the paper."

"It looks like a house key ... And it's a diagram for a two bedroom ... Oh my God! Harry! It's for us, isn't it?"

"Dad's being reassigned here, so I thought we'd move out, have something bigger for the baby. Also Mr. Abramson sold some of my stamps. We'll discuss that later, but the building is on Riverside Drive and 79th. We're on the fourth floor with a living room facing the Hudson."

▲

Getting a decent apartment in 1947 New York City often involves years on waiting lists. But like everything else after the war there are lines and then there are *lines*, the kind Meyer Lansky knows about. Prior to the stamp sale, Harry says he wants to contribute an additional half of his share of the stamps to Haganah.

"So, you have a favor to ask me?" Lansky asks.

Harry blushes. Yes, he has a favor to ask, but he has also come to an important decision as the date of the first stamp sale draws closer. To Harry, he increasingly looks at them as the blood money of murdered Jews. He wants none of the money, he tells Lansky.

"Nonsense!" Lansky replies, all but losing his temper. "There's such a thing as too much idealism. You risked your life for your country and, without your intervention, those Nazis would be buying villas in Buenos Aires today. You *will* keep a certain percentage because it is the right thing to do and because I say so." Eventually Lansky and Harry settle on ten percent. Thus, in early 1947, Harry receives a $53,575 check and, simultaneously, Haganah becomes the recipient of over $482,000 in untraceable cash.

Only after the haggling is completed does Harry mention Nan's pregnancy and his difficulty finding a larger apartment. Lansky smiles again and, like some genie emerging from a bottle, he snaps his fingers. Lo and behold, two weeks later, Nan opens the envelope.

Harry is so relieved by Nan's happiness that he waits a day before saying that he has decided to drop out of Columbia and has lined up full-time employment.

Chapter 28: Munich, Germany, 1945–46.

Tall, lean, and with a pleasant if nondescript face, Rudy Spangler left the Seis brothers at Falkensee April 24. Knowing what he does about the Seis brothers' looting, their operations, and their brutality, he feels lucky to be alive and hopes to never see them again. Rudy successfully crosses the Elbe, and then, despite needing a cane, walks 350 miles through a destroyed Germany, eventually reaching his grandparents' undamaged home outside Munich. Because of his wounds, he is quickly "de-Nazified," and then, in August, hired by the Americans as a translator.

Rudy has common sense intelligence, threatens no one, and manages well. With women not being allowed supervisory positions, and thus far less job competition, he advances quickly. By 1946, he manages a staff of twenty-five female translators.

After the first war, Germany had its own "baby boom" of which Rudy was a product. Now, however, well over half the males are dead, physically or emotionally mangled, or—quite literally—in Siberia. For Rudy, who wishes only to settle down and marry, there is no shortage of eligible women, many of them widows. For women, finding a German mate is like buying an automobile during a prolonged car shortage; each part needs to be carefully inspected for proper working order and, if something is amiss, determine its importance.

Every morning, Rudy promptly arrives at work to watch over his harem, one of whom is a thin-lipped, handsome, high-breasted, twenty-two-year-old widow, Ingrid von Scharnhorst from the Teutonic Knights' city of Königsberg in East Prussia. Ingrid and her late husband Wilhelm represented mid-level Prussian aristocracy. An officer in the 21st Panzer, Wilhelm did not anticipate survival and had the connections to find safe work for Ingrid. Trained as a nurse, she was assigned to a soldiers' rest facility-hospital at Munich's Schloss Nymphenburg Palace. War or not, swans swam gracefully in its artificial lakes and waterways—at least until hunger overcame aesthetics.

With the American occupation comes new employment as a translator and she is assigned to Rudy's office where he quickly becomes her confidante. For the infatuated Rudy, Ingrid is a giant social step up, one otherwise unobtainable. For Ingrid, in a nation where women have no professional opportunities, a German male making respectable money is superior to Americans with Hershey bars and slam-bam-thank-you-ma'am sex. After she makes certain that Rudy's working parts function, she knows he means security in this upside-down world in which she also wants children and a reliable father.

Almost from the first day of their marriage, Rudy's surgically repaired hip proves unequal to Ingrid's bedroom requests. Doctors prescribe aspirin, rest, and the patience to settle for less; not quite the answers Ingrid seeks. Sadly, each is too embarrassed to discuss and try other ways to satisfy. Nevertheless, by mid-1946, Ingrid is pregnant.

In August 1947, Rudy slips into Vaduz, Liechtenstein, the sixty-two-square mile German-speaking principality of 13,000. His purpose is business—from under the noses of the Seis brothers, he too stole stamps, but those of lesser value. After successfully selling some of his stamps, he and Ingrid resign from their translation work and rent a rebuilt two-story shop and residence just off the *Marienplatz*, Munich's business center for 800 years. Not until its opens do they realize the curious interest Americans have in Nazi stamps, particularly those featuring Hitler, swastikas, or both. For twelve years, Third Reich stamps were printed by the billions, but half were never mailed. The two happily sell these to Americans at twenty-times their cost. As for Rudy's remaining stamps from the Seis days, worth tens of thousands, they gather dust while rising in value.

If Rudy is honest with himself, he is overjoyed by Franz Seis's capture and sincerely hopes that the bastard will hang. Fingers crossed, he follows the Nuremberg *Einsatzgruppen* Trial with unfeigned interest. Finally, twenty-two of the Nazi's worst murderers are sentenced; four are executed, ten given never-to-be-carried-out death sentences and two receive life. Seis and the remainder are given a lenient twenty years. However, the increasingly hot Cold War leads Rudy to correctly assume that Seis will be released sooner rather than later.

With seemingly no choice in the matter, Rudy tells Ingrid in detail about working for Seis, sparing nothing, including the massacre of the stamp compound's prisoners outside Berlin. When released, he says, he is certain that Seis will make a bee-line for Munich.

▲

But why, Ingrid wonders as she listens, does Rudy so fear Seis? Unless Ingrid is badly mistaken, will not Seis need Rudy's help after his release? Seis is intelligent enough, she says, to comprehend how little he knows about stamps. However, Ingrid finds herself disgusted by Rudy's attitude. "What has the war done to you?" She asks. "You were a *Fallschirmjäger*, the bravest of the brave. Is there something else you're withholding? I want you to know exactly what your share of the stamps was."

"My understanding was that Bormann was to get twenty percent, but if the Führer demanded more, Bormann's share would increase. Himmler, Darré, and Backe would each get ten percent regardless. Neither Goering or Goebbels were involved."

"So, half would go to men who did nothing?"

"That was the way business was done in the Third Reich. You know that. The Seis brothers would get the rest, my share coming from them. And now the Führer and Himmler are dead, Hermann Seis has disappeared, and Bormann is dead or hiding in South America. Backe killed himself, and Darré has cancer. Effectively, only two of us are left."

"So, what does that leave you?"

"I can't say, I never discussed the specifics with Franz."

"You never *what*? What kind of *dummkopf* are you? Tell me you're joking."

"No. He said he would 'take care of me' when the time came. I didn't dare push him. How could I? Franz Seis had three assistants, two too many. After Gottfried died, I expected Ulrich to be shot. But how could I be sure? I knew stamps best, but when you worry, everything's upside down. Also, I was a witness to when Seis and I removed stamps—"

"*Removed*? Listen to yourself; you're still in denial. Just say 'stole.' I'm your wife. You acquired everything through intimidation or theft. Right? When will you realize you were Seis's accomplice, not a bystander witnessing a crime?"

"But I *was* a bystander. I was forced to work for him. He often joked about killing me. I couldn't read his mind. Until he and Hermann shot Ulrich, I lived in constant fear."

Finally, Ingrid knows. Franz Seis treated her husband just as Ivan Pavlov manipulated his dogs: fear, reward, fear, reward, reward, fear, reward, fear, fear. Until this moment she hadn't understood the degree of Rudy's emasculation. Ingrid takes her husband's hand to comfort him, then leads him to bed. Riding him, she wonders if it will produce a second child and idly ponders the steps to find a new husband. She'll let Rudy down gently, of course, but she's had enough of being the man of the house. How she yearns for her dead Wilhelm!

With their second child's arrival in early 1949, Ingrid begins to experience frequent depressions. Given her classic Nordic looks and carriage, she soon finds solace when she ceases her practice of turning her back on flirtatious males.

But what about the stamps? Given that Seis isn't about to be executed, perhaps he can help Rudy track them down. No, before she does anything too rash she must be certain if the stamps can—or cannot—be recovered. Until then, with so many millions at stake, she'll tread cautiously; the stamps are simply too valuable to do otherwise. In the morning, she'll have Rudy contact Seis to arrange a meeting. After all, Landsberg Prison, where Seis and the other *Einsatzgruppen* have been sent, is no more than an hour away.

Chapter 29: 1947, New York Interns.

If there is one thing that New Yorkers have always been guaranteed it is physical change. Yet, since the Depression there had been virtually no significant development; the "Empty State Building," as the world's tallest building was called, typified New York. Yet, to the observant, a land rush has begun. With increasing momentum, stately Park and Fifth Avenue mansions, ethnic neighborhoods, and Gilded Age monuments are sold, demolished, and replaced.

While no developer has a monopoly, "Big Al" Beckendorf, is second to none. A roly-poly, ex-NYU lineman, he is a bald, cigar smoking, 5 feet 9, 250-pound bundle of energy with ideas flying off him faster than Gene Krupa can drum. If many economists expect post-war America to return to Depression days, Al is a classic American optimistic, his bull-headed, never-despair leadership even making money in the 1930's. In early 1942, with the war at its worst, he goes on a buying spree, three years later selling the properties for ten times what he had paid.

Al borrows to the hilt and sometimes beyond it. He takes advantage of every tax break, and doesn't mind bending the rules; "lawyers are a dime a dozen, a good corner property is a large diamond," he tells the *Times* after fending off one inquiry. Al works with Jews, Irish, Sicilians, and WASPs. Once, he boasts, he spoke with Frank Costello on one phone and Nelson Rockefeller on a second. He takes pride posing for *Life Magazine* talking into two telephones simultaneously and places the photo prominently in his office.

Like so many of his ilk, Big Al is first and always a businessman, not a reformer. He has no any interest in cleaning the city's Augean stables. He knows when to say no and doesn't wince when he must acquiesce. Above all, he believes in "insurance." There's a big difference between a truck filled with wet cement arriving on time versus one sitting a mile away with flat tires. Friends of his friends control unions. Better that some workers on a project—and how he guffaws at the word *workers*—sip coffee all day than face "wildcat" strikes. Invariably, Al finishes his projects on time and under budget, graft built into his calculations. No one blows the whistle. There *were* rumors concerning a story a *Brooklyn Eagle* reporter was researching; he would've won a Pulitzer Prize for investigative reporting, but instead he disappeared.

By late 1946, if construction and development is in an ambitious young man's blood he will likely attempt to begin his career with Big Al at Webber, Sandman & Beckendorf. Not only does Harry Strong catch the construction bug, but he is overjoyed to find something that grips his imagination, where leadership counts. Now the only thing he must do is get himself hired. Who better to ask then Lansky? Over coffee, Lansky grunts his approval and, when Harry asks him not to do anything for him, he nods in the affirmative and smiles.

Nevertheless, just as there are lines and there are *lines*, there are smiles and there are *smiles*. Sometimes the latter include little white lies. Harry has no way to know it, but Lansky and "Big Al" aren't unknown to each other. Lansky strongly recommends Harry to Big Al, pointedly repeating that the former paratrooper specifically requested no favors.

▲

Big Al's office is between 50th and 51st on Madison. Harry becomes one of six hires, all combat veterans, one a Tuskegee Airman. Al believes that, being based in New York, employing Negros is critical. If Branch Rickey can sign Jackie Robinson, he can also hire a Negro, Lister Todd. Big Al's move isn't just daring, the second part of his announcement is unprecedented: all six will receive the same high starting salary of $75 weekly.

Their first day, the six are taken to a windowless storage room with one long table, six wooden chairs that came from a jury box, an ancient couch with no springs, and half a dozen rusted metal filing cabinets. When the six are shown to the room, everyone hesitates to take a seat. I don't give a shit where I sit Harry thinks, then walks over to a middle seat, his back to a wall and facing the door. Thinking nothing of it, he asks Lister to sit next him making one friend and getting two annoyed looks.

The six quickly discover that Big Al has no specific plans for them. "I need more good people," he says at their first meeting that morning, "You boys will start at the bottom, just like I did. Let me tell you a story: long before ol' Jake Ruppert bought the Yankees, he began work in his Dad's brewery and he didn't start at the fucking top."

Al puffs on his cigar, sits on Harry's part of the table, his shoes on Harry's seat while the displaced Harry is forced to stand. "Jake's dad had him wash fucking beer kegs, twelve fucking hours a day, six fucking days a week, for six fucking months. Now, I don't have any beer kegs, but I just bought two fucking office buildings. One's thirty-percent occupied; the other's worse. And you know what? They were fucking steals," he says grinning, his cigar bouncing with emphasis.

"Now let's see if you boys can get both filled by March 15, that's the Ides of March if you boys haven't read your *Julius Caesar*. Why? Because I'm selling them in April and getting bonuses on the percent of leased offices. Any questions?"

"How do we fill them, sir?" one of them, Jason, a former B-24 bomber pilot, timidly asks.

Harry winces, this guy isn't going to make it.

"GREAT first question!" says Al.

Harry closes his eyes, Maybe he's the one who won't.

"Remember," Big Al says, "it's always better to ask than to pretend you know something and fall on your fucking face. How do you rent 'em? Well, you ask someone around here who knows the fucking answer. It's that easy. Always look before you leap into a pile of shit," he says grinning as he carefully eyes each of the six.

"And no, you don't ask me, you ask my secretary. As far as you're concerned, she runs this fucking company and knows everything. Me, well I'm just a fat fucking figurehead around here," he says, roaring with laughter. "Yeah, just a fat fucking alliterative figurehead. Second: My birth certificate says, 'Alfred Grant Beckendorf.' There is no fucking *sir* on it. You boys will always call me *Al* and not 'Big Al' behind my back. And never, ever fucking call me *sir*. Do we understand each other?"

"Yes, *sir*," the six veterans automatically say, all but snapping to attention.

But does Big Al really mean filling up two almost empty office buildings? Yes. Current renters receive a fresh, free coat of paint, washrooms are upgraded, favorable long-term leases offered, and the buildings' entrance and concourse receive aesthetically pleasing but very thin marble sheathings. And new tenants? In pairs, the six enter nearby office buildings and surreptitiously photograph each building's framed public directory. This clandestine action is critical; property management firms fight to the death—or, more literally, in court—to prevent others identifying their tenants.

Harry is paired off with Lister, never giving it a second thought. Not until months later does he discover that two of the other six asked not to be seen with a Negro. One will be fired before training ends, the second given his last choice for permanent placement.

Chapter 30: Robust Capitalism.

The six interns are not sent out willy-nilly. They practice sales pitches and make trial runs with Al's secretary who, as planned, "flunks" them all. Then she suggests ruses that work and tells funny stories about ones that don't. She's also relaxed about their illegal activities: in 1947, no ex-combat pilot or paratrooper is going to be arrested by New York's Finest.

Thus, one fine morning, in freshly pressed suits, these foot soldiers of capitalism march into battle. They go from building-to-building, then door-to-door, politely asking to speak with office managers. Once in, they state the benefits of Al's new buildings and invite the managers to see for themselves. One in ten visits. Of that ten percent, another one in ten signs a lease.

▲

"So, you boys got one out of a hundred?" Big Al asks six weeks later over a champagne, caviar, and steak and lobster dinner at the Club Monte Carlo—which he owns. "Not easy on the shoes, is it? But you did better than I did the first time. With me, it was more like one in two-hundred, but those were Depression days. No 'thank you' steak dinners for me those days, just a fifteen-cent Nedick's breakfast special: coffee, watered down orange juice, and a donut."

Big Al is particularly expansive; he's made a million dollars that he'll leverage by a factor of six. Al, Harry, and Lister come with their wives, three others have "dates" Al has arranged. The sixth, Jason, isn't there—not having made the grade in Big Al's mind, he has "resigned." Dinner itself is a fraternity initiation in spirit and intellect. Earlier, Al tells Harry that he will be assigned to construction, the firm's gold ring. The job's key element is to manage and certify all aspects of construction from basements deep in Manhattan's bedrock to scaffolding hundreds of feet in the air. Harry doesn't find heights frightening; to him it's something less daunting than, say, jumping from a wobbling C-47 at night with one engine on fire.

However, the evening is far less enjoyable for Nan, who is now eight months pregnant. If she fears one thing from working for Dinty it's running into a former "date." Al was almost a regular with her, but she never asked or learned his last name or profession. At home, Nan frequently hears Harry say Big-Al-this or Big-Al-that, but never associates Harry's boss with Dinty's Al. Thus, when the club's maître d' bring Nan and Harry to the party's private room, she and Big Al instantly recognize each other. Fortunately, Nan is standing parallel with Harry, giving her a fraction of a second to compose herself. And, since Harry is looking at Nina, Al's wife, to introduce himself, he never notices the surprise registering in Al's eyes.

"It's Nan, isn't it?" Al says, as Nan and Harry came up to shake hands with him. "You were at the Stork Club's New Year's Eve Party a few years ago. She was the most beautiful girl in the room, Harry, but she wouldn't give me the time of day."

"Me, beautiful?" Nan says, giving Harry a bewitching smile. "He was with Tallulah Bankhead. Believe me when Tallulah wanted to be noticed *nobody* competed with her. Actually, Al was pretty cute with his full head of hair—"

Big Al laughs with relief and introduces his wife whom, thank God, he met after Tallulah. No male ever rode in the volatile Ms. Bankhead's saddle for very long. "I get over one man by getting under another," she once 'confidentially' told gossip commentator Walter Winchell.

To Nina, the incident is amusing for it's clear that her husband and Nan *did* know each other. After dancing with his wife, Big Al invites Nan to dance with him at which time he reassures her that their little secret will stay just that.

At their seats, each new hire finds an envelope. "Open them," orders Big Al, basking in his benevolent employer role. Inside is a crisp five hundred dollar bill. They all profess not to have seen a five hundred dollar bills before, but for Harry memories of Hermann Seis's five-hundreds and Ludwigslust come roaring back. Harry closes his eyes, pleads a headache, and goes to the men's room where he sits on a toilet, deeply inhaling a cigarette until he feels calm.

▲

Working for Big Al sometimes feel like watching a Marx Brothers movie when thirty people fall out of a small room or break a few hundred dishes.

Nevertheless, his assignments provide the rugged work Harry craved; five days a week, six when the job is behind schedule.

The first day he goes up high, Harry wears his old paratrooper boots and military slacks, tucking them in for good luck. Just after he reaches the building's still open twentieth story, he finds someone blocking his way: a bronze-skinned man, his height, and in a short-sleeve shirt that emphasizes his huge arms. As Harry has learned, since New York high-rise construction began, Mohawk Indians are the lead workers on tall office and apartment buildings and bridges—men known for their high-level fearlessness.

"Hey buddy," the man growls, indicating with his hand for Harry to stop. Harry doesn't have to be told he is a Mohawk. Other men, equally big, stand behind him, arms folded and impassive. The Mohawk points to Harry's boots and slacks, "You ain't no fucking paratrooper."

"Eighty-Second Airborne," says Harry. "*Major* Harry Strong. I wear whatever I want, whenever I fucking want to, *Kemosabe.*"

"Charlie White Eagle, Hundred and First Airborne, white man," the Mohawk says, salutes, grins from ear to ear and then shakes hands. Soon, Harry is opening his lunch box with the Mohawks, sitting on steel beams, and enjoying the view, because, like them, he is an *outsider.* Unsurprisingly, his nickname became "the major," but if at lunchtime he's one of the boys, the rest of the day he's their boss.

In time, the Mohawks teach him archery or *fishing* as they call it. For high rise workers, little is more dangerous than pigeons leaving slippery grayish-white souvenirs. Unfortunately, there's no foolproof way to rid new construction sites of pigeons. However, shooting an arrow into the air—and falling to earth (often with a dead pigeon attached) no one knows where—is not looked on with favor by insurance companies. What to do? Tying light-weight fishing line to each arrow provides the answer. Lunch breaks often become fishing time, Harry's archery skills slowly becoming acceptable to his newfound friends.

The camaraderie is very real in the dangerous world of skyscraper construction. In the era before regulations or safety equipment, Harry hears stories that, for every million dollars spent, there was one death. Five men died building the

Empire State Building and the Golden Gate Bridge claimed five times as many. Try as Big Al does to prevent it, his projects collectively lose a man a year. Harry hopes to God that 1947's death won't be on his watch.

▲

Daily, Harry has a hundred things to check. But what he finds most difficult is striking the subjective balance between protecting workers and pushing them. It is for Harry to say if the wind is too high, or when rain or cold become too treacherous. Skyscraper construction requires scores of discrete but inter-dependent skills. Harry also approves flooring, walls, plumbing, electrical work, water circulation, heating, air conditioning, window and door installations; the list endless. More difficult: contractors aren't averse to cutting corners. Harry must decide whether to turn a blind eye, cajole, threaten, or, as a last resort, does he terminate? Each time someone or a company is caught comes an escalating reaction: lies, anger, tears, bribery, and even physical threats.

On his first project, an on-site Union official, Paddy Quill, demands cash under the table. Harry has been warned about Quill, an old-time Irish-born Marxist who threatens a wildcat strike "unless I find $100 in an envelope each week." Harry begins to protest, but Quill's answer is to spit on the ground and walk away.

Harry sighs, walks down the street until he finds a telephone booth, calls Lansky, explains his problem and asks for advice. The next morning a Bricklayers' official is waiting for Harry. Sadly, he relates, the night before Quill fell down some steps and broke both knee caps.

Later, Lansky explains what caused Quill's accident. Unions, he tells Harry, are like armies, a chain-of-command structure where the leader's orders are inviolate. Quill's shaking Harry down—Harry is green and therefore Quill thinks he can get away with it—is like a rebellion because Quill has broken the private understandings between Big Al and the union. He, Lansky, did nothing other than call the union's president and explain the situation.

▲

Frequently Big Al arrives unannounced, for there is no project he doesn't visit. Once Harry is promoted, he knows the day will come when he is the man who must say "no" and explain why to Big Al. Everyone knows about Al's tantrums, but after calming down he'll pull out a hip flask and everything is forgiven and forgotten. Almost invariably, Big Al agrees—he has superb confidence in the managers he picked. In the rare case when the flask stays in Big Al's pocket, that manager is demoted or fired. With Harry, the flask is always pulled out.

Part IV: Discovery

Chapter 31: Landsberg Prison, Germany, July 1948.

Franz Seis is now an occupant of War Criminals Prison No. 1 in Landsberg am Lech, Bavaria, forty-five miles west of Munich. Coincidentally, Landsberg is the same prison where Hitler was incarcerated following his failed 1923 Putsch.

It is a hot afternoon when he is taken to a small, windowless room, a large, portable fan oscillating in the corner. Three men are seated on one side of a table, a single chair opposite them. One man is clearly Russian based on his ill-fitting suit, butchered haircut and unsmiling eyes. The other two, equally identifiable by the dress and carriage, are British and American.

"There's something familiar about you," Seis says to the American as he sits down. "But from where?"

The American laughs. "My name's Baker. I'm the guy who tripped you up when we caught you. I put a hood over your head so quickly I'm surprised you remember anything."

Well, you bastard, Seis thinks, there's no way I'll forget you now.

Baker offers Seis coffee and a Lucky Strike, then begins speaking. "We've uncovered a male skeleton that might be your brother's." Seis's pupils open wide, unable to contain his surprise and horror. So, Hermann is dead, he thinks, inhales deeply on his Lucky, then, mouth set, looks back at Baker.

"Our Red friends," Baker says with a wry smile, "found the bones a few miles west of Ludwigslust. Some East German *volunteers* actually," he says, smiling at the Russian, for the workers were undoubtedly prisoners. "They were repairing the Rögnitz Canal at a stone bridge and discovered the silt-covered entwined bones of a man and a woman where the canal was breached in '45. As you know, bodies remain of high interest to us. We're all still hunting for ex-Nazis and informally cooperate."

Baker pauses to let his words sink in.

"Forensic reports indicated that both had been executed, although by different weapons. The woman one in the back of the head and the male through the mouth. Our Russian friends had their technicians make what they could of the corpses, and we cross-checked surviving dental records. While the woman's identity remains a mystery, we think that the man's bones could be that of your brother. Were there any particular singularities to Hermann's teeth and jawbone?"

"Yes," Seis replies. His head and body feel hot, and his arms seem to be tingling. "During the first war, before he lost his foot—"

Here Seis stops as the three meaningfully nod to each other.

"Hermann was shot in the mouth by a ricocheting bullet. He lost two right teeth in his mandible and there was a small half-moon where the bullet passed through. The bullet grazed his tongue, giving him a permanent lisp, besides making an indentation where it stopped on the left side of his mouth."

"Something like this?" Baker asks. He reaches into his briefcase and in his right hand produces a lower jawbone that perfectly matches Franz Seis's description.

Seis instantly vomits; a hard, wrenching sound.

"That wasn't very sporting of you, old chap," the Englishman tells Baker, unable not to smile while the Soviet colonel's grin stretches to his ears.

"Fuck him," Baker says. "We should have turned the bastard over to you, Colonel Rosokovski. Your people would have dealt properly with him."

After Seis finishes retching, fan working or not, the awful smell engulfs the small room. The three men quickly call the guard and leave, laughing at Seis's discomfort but leaving behind the pack of Luckies as a token of their good will.

▲

Prior to seeing the jawbone, Franz hadn't been certain of Hermann's death. Through the sieve of prison security, he'd sent out feelers, but the lack of information he received back proved nothing. As for his incarceration, he'd soon adjusted to the prison's rhythms; dull American meals, decent cots, an excellent library, and a courtyard providing sunshine. And escape? While everybody dreams of escape, it isn't impossible. At night, Seis often reflects on Hitler's many mistakes, how the war could've been won, and what his role might have been. Ah, the old saw, if wishes were horses then beggars would ride, he thinks, smiling to himself.

About the only positive event is that his wife, Hannah, is divorcing him. At one time, they were a perfect Nordic couple, once modeling for a Goebbels's propaganda publication, *Völkischer Bedbachter* ("The People's Observer"). In 1938, Hannah had braided blond hair, attractive if smallish breasts, straight teeth and slim hips. In the photo Seis wore hiking shorts that emphasized his muscled thighs, the pair walking arm-in-arm, mouths firm and looking into the future. However, after her second miscarriage, she turned to chocolates and God, weighing over two hundred pounds when he last saw her. Seis believed that the Reich's inability to find chocolate substitutes was likely the cause of her later weight loss. With the divorce papers, comes the welcome news that she'd soon marry a GI.

Ironically, Hermann's death rekindles Seis's interest in stamps as he re-members what he'd *possessed* and held in his hands. Objectively he realizes that he is like the Count of Monte Cristo, living for revenge. But against whom? Unfortunately, Seis knows full well that every morning his cell's tiny GI shav-ing mirror holds the answer.

Previously, Seis had no interest in Rudy Spangler, twice rejecting requests to visit. He assumed that the stamps were lost and had never really liked Rudy, a man neither of special intellect nor able to order vintage wines. But now...

▲

"As it is, we have nothing to show for our endeavors, do we? Only Hermann's bones, I fear," Seis is saying to Rudy. They two are in an unsupervised room where prisoners meet with visitors. It is September 10, 1948, a pleasant, un-usually warm day.

"First, it's possible that the stamps somehow survived," Rudy begins. "Did you know that after your brother spent the night of May 1 in or near Parchim?"

Seis is astonished. "Parchim? Parchim? Why was he still so far east of the Elbe?"

"I don't know, but numerous soldiers saw him May 2. A mutual friend rec-ognized him after someone tried to steal his bike. When Hermann screamed for help some men retrieved the bicycle and pummeled the thief. Seconds later an officer arrived. He asked questions of your brother, the thief, and men who'd witnessed the incident. Then the thief was shot by the officer. Scores of otherwise despondent soldiers cheered; it was an instant tonic for morale. My friend, who'd been called up to serve in the *Volkssturm*, briefly talked to your brother but they said little more than 'good luck' before Hermann bicycled off."

"So, Hermann wasn't seen later?" Seis asks as Rudy nods. "That means something delayed him before he reached the Elbe. But why do you believe the stamps survived?"

"This is conjecture, of course, but some of the stamps that are on the master list might—and I emphasize *might*—have been sold in America."

Seis expresses genuine shock. "But you never had the master—" stopping in mid-sentence and smiling. "Good for you Spangler! So, you slipped that by me? But how?"

"I had the original and *three* carbons typed, not *two*. The word *copy* has two meanings; the second being *duplicate*. I choose your instructions of three copies to mean one original and three duplicates. There was a total of four copies, not three as I'm sure you intended."

Seis remains too flabbergasted by Rudy's tricking him to say anything. How much else had his assistant, whom he clearly underestimated, slipped past him?

"Both you and Hermann thought I was, despite being an officer and awarded the Iron Cross, unsophisticated and perhaps simple. However, there is an old peasant expression, 'be dumb with dignity.' I planned to full take advantage of this if I were discovered."

"Which would have saved you," Seis replies, shaking his head but smiling.

"I made no effort to take the third carbon copy home—"

"Good: because your apartment was searched."

"Which I anticipated. I simply left the third copy in one of the file cabinets—"

"Where if it were seen you could explain it away, right? So very sensible. And one day you left the compound and mailed it to your parents, Ja?"

"In mid-February. But the other copies, what happened to them?"

"I mailed the original list in a package to my wife the day after the workers were shot."

As if he had nothing to do with it, Rudy thinks.

"She claims she never received it. Who knows? Thousands of tons of mail were on railroad sidings that were bombed. In retrospect, it was stupid to mail it. But what else could I do? Drive 175 miles? Every town had road blocks—"

"*Ja*, even *you* would have been stopped by the Gestapo—"

"And asked why I wasn't in a car with a driver," Seis says, as both nod.

"If you don't mind my asking, what happened to the other two copies?"

"Bormann had one and he was with the Führer until the end. Perhaps it became part of Hitler's funeral pyre. However, until he turns up, all remains speculation."

"Which leaves one copy."

"Darré's copy was in his suitcase when he was captured. He placed the suit-case down before the first American questioned him. That officer didn't notice it—"

"There were fields of suitcases lying everywhere those days," Rudy nods.

"Darré's cell is in the same wing as mine. He says, and I agree, that had he been holding his suitcase they would have searched it and discovered what we'd been doing."

"So, we're better off with his copy lost?"

"Precisely. The best that we can hope for is that the Russians —"

"Used it as toilet paper!" says Rudy, laughing at the punchline to a well-known joke.

"Spangler," Seis says out of the blue, "it is time you went to America. You've learned all you can here. Which stamp companies would you like to visit?"

The astonished Rudy pauses a few seconds to consider the question. "There are a dozen good New York companies in the auction field. Thistleman & Chandler is the largest, then there is H. R. Harmer—they sold Roosevelt's collection—and John Fox, Robert Siegel—"

"No, I'm not interested in going to Jewish firms."

"Please let me finish. Then there's Eugene Costales, Peter Keller, Herman

Herst, and Carl Pelander among others. They've all sold stamps that are the same as the ones we possessed. However, and perhaps it is only coincidental, one company has consistently sold numerous stamps that were in our collection. It's America's third largest, Romanoff & Abramson.

"You said Romanoff?" Seis laughs. "The Czar's family? Ah yes, clearly a charlatan. And the other is a Jew. Is there not a better pair to handle stolen stamps? As an authentic dealer, you can meet with them and find out what you can. I'll take care of your travel arrangements," he says laughing again. "There's no shortage of ready cash in this prison."

Chapter 32: New York, October 1948.

Three weeks later, Rudy becomes the recipient of a round-trip ticket from Frankfurt to New York. There is one refueling stop in Gander, Newfoundland and the plane is to land at Idlewild International (the future "JFK") Airport, then open just a year. Along with the tickets is an envelope filled with cash and American Express Traveler's checks.

Rudy doesn't know it but, for New Yorkers, October has been like a large family whose favorite children have disappeared; the city has fielded no World Series team. Now, Tuesday, October 12, the city seems pensive as Rudy wanders through Manhattan with a tourist's wide-eyed, strained-neck look and a war-starved European's desire for fresh orange juice and pineapple. Reaching the Hudson, for two dollars, he takes the *Manhattan* around the island of the same name. The tour is a shock; Nazi propaganda spoke of extensive damage by its long range but non-existent bombers. Try as he might, Rudy is unable to spot any signs of the bombing, but is otherwise awed by the city's magnificent skyline.

Besides Romanoff & Abramson, there are a score of stamp dealers on Nassau Street, just north of where it meets Wall Street, with a growing number clustered north of 42nd Street. The plurality of these are at 505 Fifth Avenue, a narrow, nondescript, pre-WWI, mid-rise office building. Reaching it late that afternoon, Rudy realizes that walking into various stamp dealers in the same building on the same day with similar questions can only lead to professional gossip. He therefore decides to begin the following day with his first choice.

Just after 10:30 AM Wednesday, Rudy plucks up his courage, inhales and, shoulders arched, opens Romanoff & Abramson's door. Inside, he hands his business card to a friendly, grandmotherly type who is the receptionist and secretary.

Romanoff is in, she says, and seeing him will not be a problem.

▲

"So, how can I help you?" Romanoff inquires fifteen minutes later, sitting in his regal, maroon wingback chair, layers of clothing below his thick neck, looking down at Rudy from over narrow glasses, the very picture of a Caesar Borgia or Henry VIII.

"I live in Munich— "

"In which case, we'll speak German. And has New York opened your eyes? A most impressive metropolis, is it not? Unlike our old capitals, St. Petersburg— or should I say Leningrad?—and Berlin, each destroyed. And here? Other than one of our own bombers crashing into the Empire State building—you've seen that, haven't you?—not a minutia of damage and now with construction cranes everywhere."

The one-sided conversation continues for half an hour, Rudy fully enjoying his role as the day's official listener and a second cup of delicious coffee. Then the receptionist-secretary discretely enters and whispers something in Romanoff's ear while handing him a slip of paper.

"Well, shall we get down to business, Herr Spangler? It has been a pleasure getting to know you." This comes as a surprise to Rudy, for he has barely spoken. "My congratulations on your venture; courage is required to open a stamp business in the Old World these days. Your foresight in joining our American Philatelic Society and American Stamp Dealers Association has made it easier for me to check your *bone fides*. Are you here to purchase or sell?"

"First," Rudy says, "might we begin with a stamp that a client is interested in? It is Dutch, an 1869 King William III, twenty-cent, dark-green." This stamp, valued in the Scott Catalogue at $175, has been chosen because Seis acquired six during the war.

Romanoff pulls out a file, affirmatively grunts when he finds what he is looking for, goes to the door, and calls in an associate. He quickly writes out the name of the stamp, tells the man to retrieve it, and concludes, "and take Sven with you."

"Take Sven?" Rudy asks.

"My bodyguard. I have survived one assassination attempt— "

Rudy tries not to gulp as Romanoff continues, "Rest assured, no stamp of value is kept here. New York is not like America's Wild West but, I must regretfully acknowledge, armed robbery is increasing. Across the street is the Chrysler Building the Bank of the Manhattan Company has offices and a particularly large safe. We keep our stamps there. An ounce of prevention is worth a pound of cure, Ja?"

As they sit waiting, Rudy begins to relax. For the first time, he notices how expensive Romanoff's furnishings are; the hand stitched leather chairs, his mahogany bookcases, the highly polished, petrified wood appearance of his burled desk, the hand blown and carved glass ashtrays, and the Wedgewood coffee service. Rudy also notices that no street sounds penetrates Romanoff's office and asks why.

"Just before the U.S. entered the war," Romanoff begins, "the British assassinated a German attaché who was working at his desk in a Radio City office. There were two men, both firing from 200 yards. The first shot broke the window, the second—an instant later—hit the target in the head. As I was the previous object of Joseph Stalin's affections, and hearing the story, which was told to me as more than a cautionary tale, I had bullet proof windows installed and added a layer of steel insulation around this room as a precaution."

Sven and the assistant are back twenty minutes later, the Netherland stamps carefully examined with a magnifying glass, and Rudy chooses the least faded dark green. After appropriate haggling, a price is agreed to and, on instinct, Rudy purchases a second. Having gotten the better of the deal—Rudy not fighting particularly hard—Romanoff mentions he is a member of the Chrysler Building's Cloud Club, located on the 68th floor. It features, besides magnificent views, excellent Dover Sole and homegrown (by a member) pink grapefruit. Romanoff calls his secretary in, scribbles a note, and Rudy discovers he has a 12:30 reservation, although Romanoff, regrettably, will be unable to join him.

"If I remember," Romanoff says, "you indicated that you had another matter to discuss."

"Something of a more discreet nature I am afraid."

"*Afraid?* A most interesting word choice. The feeling in these old bones is that you're not a happy emissary either. And, pardon my saying so, but you're picking your lip, swaying slightly, and squeezing your fingers. So, what do you wish to ask, or are you more like a medieval herald that gallops with messages between two armies?"

"I have been asked, by a group of gentlemen to ascertain—"

"And might I expect appropriate remuneration if I assist them?"

"Naturally, the philately business has traditionally included finder's fees," Rudy nods.

"So, you're the philatelist. And the others? May I also assume that they're German, men who don't wish to be publicly identified?" Romanoff says, pausing. "First, you've arrived at my doorstep to discuss philately, not running guns to banana republics. Second, I'd be working with Germans—of some wealth and much *previous* power? Is this deduction correct?"

Rudy nods, "During the late hostilities, these gentlemen at one time found themselves in the possession of exceptionally valuable collection of stamps—"

"As did many. Thus, my next assumption; this collection isn't clothed in the garments of legality. But did I understand your use of the past tense correctly; that these gentlemen either no longer have the stamps and thus are *not* selling them?"

"Yes, they are *not* selling," Rudy says, noting with satisfaction the clear surprise on Romanoff's face. "The fact of the matter is that these stamps were stolen from them, from their messenger actually; a man who was murdered for the stamps."

"Oh my, this is a most troubling turn of events. Yes, I can see how the utmost discretion will be a prime requisite."

"Furthermore, we know when and where the man holding the stamps was murdered."

"And by whom? That too?"

"To a surprising degree, yes," Rudy answers. Romanoff remains silent. "The site was just east of the Elbe, west of Berlin, in or just outside a little town called Ludwigslust—"

"Near Wobelein Palace?"

"Exactly. The incident that concerns us occurred on the afternoon of May

2, 1945. The murderer was not a German or even a Russian, but rather, we think," Rudy continues, saying each word carefully, "an American. And, based on available records, we are certain that the man was a paratrooper, a member of the American Eighty-Second Airborne division."

Deep within the pupils of Romanoff's eyes Rudy glimpses a millisecond of recognition, then a return to impassiveness. There's no need to visit other dealers on his list. His trip is a success; now Rudy knows who is selling 'their' stamps. Perhaps he doesn't know all the details, but, as he and Seis will excitedly discuss at their prison meeting weeks later, perhaps he knows enough.

In fact, it is more than enough to confirm Seis's wartime foresight. Shortly after Martin Bormann dealt himself in, Franz Seis requested help, in particular, a Zeiss Ikon microdot system capable of printing a tiny identification on the back of each stamp. The Greek letter *delta* ("Δ") was chosen, the printing invisible to the naked eye or any philatelist's 10x magnifying glass.

Once back in Munich, Rudy borrows a college chemistry microscope. Sure enough, on the back of both of the Dutch stamps is a *delta*.

Chapter 33: New York, 1947 – 1950.

James Gavin Strong, born in May 1947, physically changes Nan as she gains five points and loses her hourglass figure. Everything is still there but their positions have slightly shifted; the best she can hope for is in that new, ill-defined business called television. Her face has changed ever so slightly as her cheekbones fully emerge, giving her an air of cool disdain. Better yet, there is a subtle drop in her voice and, though a bra has now become necessary, her face photographs marvelously. Nan realizes that she has gone from being youthfully pretty to regally handsome.

Three months after their son is born, Nan receives a barely controlled call from her agent, Hyman Garfinkle: Harry Conover wants to meet with her. Advertising *wunderkind*, Harry Conover! His is the modeling agency to be associated with.

Conover occupies half the eighth floor at 52 Vanderbilt Ave., across from Grand Central.

▲

In the waiting room, Nan notices movie posters of the 1944 color film *Cover Girl* starring Gene Kelley and Rita Hayworth. With music and lyrics ("Long Ago and Far Away") by Jerome Kern and Ira Gershwin it has a simple plot based on beauty contest made up entirely of Conover models. The waiting room consists of brightly painted benches that once sat in Central Park, visitors looking at murals of the park. Nan's eyes immediately light on one wall that has a ten-foot-long cartoon of a man selling colored balloons, each balloon autographed by a famous model.

I want to be up there, Nan thinks. As they sit, models and want-to-be's drop off portfolios, fidget and check shooting schedules. Phones constantly ring as Conover's secretary somehow orchestrates the comings and goings of beautiful women and fragile egos.

"The reason we're here," Garfinkle whispers, "is because of television."

Nan knows nothing about TV other than that Harry has ordered a top-of-the-line twelve-inch set. New York had 7,000 sets prior to the war, but military requirements ended production. (The Germans proved more imaginative: in France, they broadcast newsreels to convalescent centers from the Eiffel Tower.) Peacetime retooling saw no TV sets manufactured until late 1946. Then, almost overnight, the number skyrocketed into the millions annually.

All shows are produced in New York, technical limitations dictating live commercials. Shows employ second bananas and young vets, but for advertising, with the blind leading the blind, Madison Avenue turns to Conover. Only thirty-five, he is ambitious ("Somebody must learn this TV business"), a chain smoker with a bad heart condition, and, like Walter Winchell, he has his own Stork Club table where he drinks, not sips, champagne cocktails.

"We've known each other for years," Conover says enthusiastically, if inaccurately to Nan when she and Hyman enter. Nan knows him only slightly from some years before when, buttressed by Dinty's employment, she politely turned down his modeling offer of five dollars an hour. Conover's giant office is mahogany furnished. He is proud of his friendship with Orson Welles whom he'd introduced to Rita Hayworth years earlier. Impressively placed on his desk is the glass ball with snowflakes from *Citizen Kane's* iconic death scene.

"Nan," Conover says, "everybody's going crazy because of TV. Nobody's ever sold a product to people they can't see. My girls are the absolute best, but only for photos. I've made it a point to hire bright girls, but they have Southern accents, sound like hillbillies or come from Brooklyn. And often, even those who have perfect diction get in front of a camera and freeze. My wife says they look like they're being asked to give a blow job to a bull elephant.

"Another nasty thing about television: it doesn't like some people. Good-looking women often can't handle the extra make-up and heat from the lighting. It's so goddamn weird that they're using brown makeup and blue shirts! Inside a studio, it's like a Mummers Day Parade. Would you believe it? The advertising boys are desperate—"

"But why do you think that I'll work out if so many others haven't?"

"I really don't know, but somebody mentioned you the other evening. It was like a light bulb turning on. Your diction is perfect and I know you went to Smith. If I've learned one thing, it is that bright women are critical for commercials. My advertising friends tell me they need women—not pretty girls, *women*. Women who look like they have something between their ears. They want to see intelligence, plus some tit of course. So, I'm in the process of starting up a TV division and would like to give you a test.

"Another thing: your hair is perfect. Hair is another unpleasant TV surprise; light blonde hair doesn't work. The lights make the hair meld into the face—on the tube, you can't tell where skin ends and hair begins. It'd be funny if it didn't screw us up so badly. Black hair's just the opposite, it overwhelms the face and the background. Since we don't have trouble making color movies, we'll eventually solve the problem, but we're nowhere close yet."

"But what if it Nan doesn't make it either?" Garfinkle asks.

"Actually, that's the second thing I wanted to talk with you both about. If the test doesn't work, there are some interesting things happening these days that would fit Nan to a T. With all the GI's coming home, getting married, and having kids, like you and Harry—"

Well, he's done some homework, Nan thinks.

"There's a growing demand for models who aren't seventeen or eighteen and clueless. We need women who are attractive but don't look confused holding a vacuum cleaner."

"Like Tillie the Toiler?" Nan laughs.

"Well, Blondie's better, but you get the picture. We've got all these labor-saving devices, TV sets and cars that need to be sold. During the war, women didn't mind their men salivating over Rita in her black negligee or Betty Grable's legs. But now husbands and wives want the person 'talking' to them wearing nice, clean-cut clothes, good-looking, but who still have—"

"Tits. Like mine for example," says Nan.

"Exactly," says Conover, unabashedly looking at them and smiling approvingly. "I'll make some calls and we'll schedule the tests."

Within a year, Nan reaches TV advertising's A-list. Once TV sets are manufactured so that programming can be watched during the day (General Electric's "Daylight Television"), programming hours double. Nan models, does live TV ads or both for Admiral TV sets, Bendix washers and dryers, Coolerator refrigerators, Packard automobiles, and TWA airlines. In the process, she becomes a minor celebrity in her own right. By 1949, Nan is making as much money as in her Dinty Moore days. She is financially independent and beholden to no one.

1949 finds Harry and Nan moving into Big Al's 530-unit condominium, Manhattan House. This twenty-story high behemoth encompasses an entire block between Second and Third Avenues running north and south, and 65th and 66th streets going east and west. The project is risky until the noisy Third Avenue "el" is shut down, but Al considers it a "can't miss." Harry and Nan get in on the opportunity, choosing a 2,800-square foot, three-bedroom apartment with a den. There is no balcony, the last thing a couple with young children want.

Somewhere along the line, Harry realizes that their marriage bed has become obligatory sex. Almost as annoying, Nan's growing status means that evenings are spent going to seemingly endless—meaningless from Harry's viewpoint—cocktail parties, compulsory dinners, and opening nights. The two are also seen at night clubs holding hands and saying hello to gossip columnists like Dorothy Kilgallen, Ed Sullivan, Earl Wilson (a creep noted for literally measuring starlets' busts), and Walter Winchell.

Harry cannot say exactly when he began thinking of Ilse, but his musing takes a more serious turn after moving to Manhattan House. Where does Ilse live? Has she married? It's almost four years since he last saw her. If she's left Munich how will he ever track her down? He realizes that asking for help, just months after the Berlin Blockade has ended, is a long shot. For this, there are no strings that even Lansky can pull.

Harry is soon second-guessing himself. Had he done it earlier, he might have turned to UNRRA (United Nations Refugee and Relief Organization), a lumbering, 12,000-person agency operating just that after the war, but UNRRA has ceased operations. Harry spends weeks trying to find out where their records are being kept, only to discover that UNRRA was responsible only for the ten million *non-Germans* that fled west.

After this setback, Harry runs into a second roadblock. With the May 23, 1949 legal formation of West Germany, refugee issues that were previously administered by American, British, French, and private relief agencies now become the responsibility of the Bonn government. In fact, Harry is down to one last hope: his old commander General James Gavin. Gavin is now the Army's Chief of Research and Development, active in developing a modern army for the nuclear age, and not exactly the easiest person to see.

After two unsuccessful tries, he finally reaches Gavin's administrative assistant, a Lieutenant Colonel. Harry is unsure what to say. His reception is so frosty that, even over the phone, he can see the officer shaking his head and wondering who this nut is. However, out of the blue, after Harry mentions Berlin and 1945, the officer says, "Does the name Ernie Manfredi ring a bell?"

"Of course, Manfredi was my driver for most of '45, do you know him?"

"He's the General's chauffeur these days. Talks about you a lot. Listening to him you'd think that you walked on water."

"That's because I never asked how old his German girlfriend was."

The two laugh, trade "war" stories and, to Harry's relief, the Lt. Col. says, "Yeah, we'll get you in, but it can't be for more than five minutes. Let's plan for May 16."

Five minutes turns into lunch at the Pentagon's general officers' mess (for senior officers) as Gavin, fascinated with high-rise construction issues, peppers Harry with questions. Before the meal is over, Harry brings up the favor he needs to ask: he has recently discovered that Ilse had a child by him (not true, but a believable white lie) and wants to assist in some way, to do something proper considering that these days he's happily married.

Gavin laughs, "Well, Manfredi wins the bet. He said that was why you wanted to see me. To tell you the truth, we're crapping all over the mothers of these illegitimate babies—and God knows how many thousands of them there are—and then we wonder why the Germans get so pissed at us. And when the fathers are Negroes? We're like the old-fashioned father who shoves his daughter and grandchild out into the snowstorm. It's absolutely disgraceful of us, but give me all the information you have on her and I'll do my best."

Only later does Harry remember that Gavin himself was born out of wedlock. Thankfully, he hadn't put his foot in his mouth.

▲

Three weeks later, and just weeks before North Korea invades the south, Harry has Ilse's address and hits himself for being so stupid: she's still working in the Army's Munich translation office. Now, all that he must do is write the letter. He begins leaving Manhattan House earlier than usual, goes to his mostly unused office on Madison Avenue one early morning after another, trying to find the right words as one draft after another is crumpled-up and lobbed into a waste paper basket. Finally, he dashes something off and mails it.

Harry writes that he genuinely cares how she is, a bit about what he's doing, where he lives, and that he's married, but doesn't say when. He tells Ilse that he has two children; a boy named after Gavin and a girl, Suzanne. What he expects, if she receives the letter, he really doesn't know. For Harry, any reply will be welcome as, for the Nth dozen time, he daydreams about their relationship.

A month later his heart jumps when she replies. But it's short, sweet and typewritten; she's just been jilted by a brigadier general who, having proposed, once back in the states "discovered" that his wife won't divorce him. "I've had enough of Americans and Americanized-Germans," Ilse writes. "Good luck to you and your family, and have a happy life." The only positive thing, Harry reflects, is that she didn't tell me to fuck myself. But Ilse's letter is like being without an umbrella during a thunderstorm and waiting for a cab.

Chapter 34: New York, October 1949.

When the pro forma police investigation ends, the report indicated that, as occasionally happens at the end of a late-morning IRT run to the 242nd Street Van Cortlandt Park station, the subway's engineer was going too fast, daydreaming of lunch. Hitting the brakes violently, the almost empty train screeched to a stop, feet from the track's end. Most passengers in the eight-car train are standing in the front car closest to the station's only exit. The sudden stop is a bothersome, but not unusual for veteran strap hangers.

The ride, as it came out of the 207th street tunnel, had been uneventful on this delightful October 10, 1949 Indian Summer day. However, one man sitting in the front car has lost his interest in the weather or anything else for that matter.

Tall, thin, wearing a cheap blue suit and looking to be in his sixties, like many older riders he appeared to be asleep on the car's rattan-weave bench seat; his chin on his chest, and hands between his spread legs. One rider vaguely remembered his transferring to this, a local, from the 96th street express, but states that there was nothing that drew her attention. But, all witnesses agree, as the train's brakes were applied, that the man lurched forward, his arms and legs flopping in different directions when he tumbled into people. As his hat flew off, he came to rest head up, eyes and mouth open causing instant screaming and temporary pandemonium as riders, already off balance, tried to scramble out of the corpse's way.

Because 242nd street is the end of the line, two police cruisers were parked at the station's stairways. Why? Predictably, some not-too-bright miscreant believed that by going to the IRT's last stop he had planned a perfect escape. Thus, in under a minute, police swarm into the train, calming and questioning unnerved occupants.

From the dead man's wallet, the police find the name Montclair Smith. His pockets contain an address book, which a Bronx patrolman wisely ceases thumbing through on reaching the "L's." Lansky's name is underlined with a number following the word "private." The patrolman calls his precinct Captain, Cornelius O'Shea who, minutes later arrives, sirens blaring. O'Shea is due to retire and has been given this low-crime sinecure as a reward for common sense and knowing when to keep his nose out of other people's business.

Quickly, O'Shea reaches Lansky and soon Montclair's effects, including a package of strange stamps, are turned over to a Lansky associate. As Lansky informally requests, an autopsy is ordered but, as suspected, it reveals only an enlarged heart and nothing suspicious. Days later, as Montclair is laid to rest, O'Shea discovers a cash-filled envelope on his desk.

▲

That evening, Harry joins Lansky and Abramson at Montclair's west side flat near Hell's Kitchen, no larger than a cheap hotel room. Other than a pile of dishes, everything is immaculate. An air-conditioning system, acquired to protect the stamps, keeps the room cool and reduces the smell of Montclair's two-packs a day habit. Except for basketball plaques from Lawrenceville and Princeton ('04), the walls are bare. What the three look for, though, isn't memorabilia, but any indication of dishonesty. After careful searching, they are relieved to find nothing. What they do turn up, however, in a tiny medicine cabinet, is an envelope for Abramson in which Montclair, sicker than anyone knew, had listed his final instructions.

Harry is genuinely saddened, for, over the years that he knew him, Montclair not only faithfully sold his stamps, but also explained the hows and whys of the business. When Harry once asked Romanoff about Montclair's honesty, the baron jovially replied that the most sublime of all honesty-inducing potions is fear. Montclair was aware, Romanoff said, that if he were ever caught cheating, he'd find himself dog-paddling with broken arms and legs in Hell's Gate, where the tidal forces of the East River and Long Island Sound collided.

Montclair's death puts a hole in the sale of Harry's stamps. Each year Montclair sold some $150,000 worth of stamps, Harry's percent twice Big Al's salary. While Romanoff, Abramson, and Lansky make attempts to find a second Montclair, no candidate measures up in intelligence, philatelic honesty or financial desperation.

▲

Following the 1946 auction of Edward Brown's and Harry's stamps, what neither Romanoff or Abramson, both aging, can admit is that a certain lassitude sets in. Collections scooped up a decade earlier are lost. Then, at seventy-six, Abramson begins appreciably slowing, then is diagnosed with lung cancer. Harry visits every few weeks but, as often as not, finds him mindlessly watching "Howdy Doody." When lucid, Abramson tells Harry about Lansky, the son he never had. Lansky's influence, Abramson says, is partially based on his role as tax expert and arbitrator between feuding Sicilian families.

"In 1932," Abramson continues, "Al Capone went to prison for Federal income tax evasion. Nobody cared about him, but it scared the hell out of other mobsters, especially those who could barely read or write English. And guess who started reading the tax laws and pretty damn quickly understood them as well as anybody?"

"Was it Meyer Lansky, by some small chance?" Harry asks laughing.

"To the mob, Meyer became a goose that laid big golden eggs as he went over their taxes. On top of that, with 'Italian problems,' if Luciano decreed, 'see Meyer,' it helped both, for Lucky understood petty squabbles sometimes had 500-year histories. It was Meyer who listened and asked questions, then made his 'suggestions.' Most Sicilians were secretly relieved to have issues resolved peacefully because, under their code, backing down isn't possible. Of course, one unhappy person threatened Meyer, but Lucky made him disappear."

Abramson pulls out a cigarette, "Last one today," he says for the umpteenth time. "However," he continues, "if Luciano's deportation isn't overturned, a new generation of mobsters will gradually take command and Meyer's influence will wane accordingly."

Sadly, as with all terminal cancer victims, eventually came the day when it became necessary for Abramson to take painkillers.

Chapter 35: New York, September 1950.

Despite seeing Romanoff regularly, Harry is surprised to receive a message for him to drop by the Saturday after Labor Day. To his astonishment, as he arrives, Lansky emerges from a cab. The two briefly speak, both perplexed by Romanoff's unusual summons. Upstairs, the old man is, as so often the case, absorbed looking at a small pocket mirror, twisting his head from side to side for a better angle of his chin and mouth to see if any red hairs remain.

"The last of my red hairs," Romanoff sighs dramatically, looking at the two. "Once they are gone there'll be no proof of my Romanoff blood."

Harry says nothing, tries not to roll his eyes and nods politely as Lansky winks at him. Harry believes that the baron is no more a Romanoff than he is a Plantagenet.

"You've never believed that I'm a Romanoff, have you, Harry?" the baron laughs. "Why? Please be candid, we've known each other long enough now."

"Because I learned that he died in 1825. Even if he had fathered a child, a daughter, and she—your mother—had been born the next year, she would've been at least fifty-four when you were born, and that's physically impossible. Mathematically, you can't be a grandson, although a great-grandson is biologically possible."

"Ah-ha, the logical statement I'd expect. But who ever said that Alexander died then?"

"The history books say it was near a small Black Sea town of Taganrog— "

"And give the date for his entombment as 1826. Unfortunately, the books don't say that when his well-preserved corpse reached St. Petersburg even his family couldn't recognize him."

"Given the skills of Russian morticians," Harry says, "if anyone even recognized the body's sex it would have been a miracle— "

"Ah, the correct word, *miracle*! Now, pay attention: just after Alexander I supposedly died, a hermit priest appeared in the Crimea named Feodor Kuzmich. He had red hair, was tall, educated, fluent in numerous languages, and never lacked money. It is well documented that he was visited in 1837 by the future Alexander II, and that a half century later Alexander III laid flowers on his grave. It's also known Kuzmich left many written documents—"

"And now you'll tell me that the handwriting has proven to be the same."

"Of course," Lansky laughs, "otherwise the baron wouldn't have mentioned it."

"Indisputably, Kuzmich's handwriting. It is precisely the same as Alexander I."

"But if he were a priest, wouldn't he have taken certain vows?" Harry asks.

"Russian Orthodox priests don't take vows of chastity. Almost all marry. Those who don't are mistrusted. My mother was born in 1849, and was twenty-six when I was born."

"Did she meet Kuzmich?"

"She had vague memories of him. She was told that he was her uncle. However, the last time she saw him he gave her a gift," the baron said, reaching into his pocket.

"He gave her this; a gentleman's snuff box of all things. He told her it had always been good luck to him and he wanted her to have it. She was polite enough to decline, but her mother insisted. Here, Harry, look at it. Meyer, you've seen it before, I believe."

Harry finds himself holding a diamond crusted, three by two inch oblong enameled, box, a brilliant half-eagle, half-lion red griffin holds a golden shield and sword, surrounded by four gold and a four silver-like lion heads. "I don't want to appear rude, but I thought the Romanoff coat of arms was a double-headed eagle? And that's a strange looking silver." On the back was a badly faded French inscription which Harry found illegible.

"You're right about the double-headed eagle," Romanoff said, "but Alexander identified with a red griffin. And regarding the 'silver.' It doesn't look like silver because it's platinum."

"I thought—"

"No. German artisans began molding platinum in the 1700s. This is from Prussia's Frederick William II, Alexander's staunchest ally against Napoleon.

I've had this my entire life. The inscription's rubbed off, but it has a message of friendship from one monarch to another."

"Nevertheless, my snuff box has resulted in disturbing news. It is the reason I asked you both to see me. As you know, to verify any stamp's authenticity I use a 10x magnifying glass. When I wear a deer-stalker's cap, I even look like the great detective."

"Or his older brother, Mycroft?" Lansky asks facetiously.

"Oh my, yes, definitely Mycroft Holmes!" Romanoff laughs, his stomach shaking. Like Lansky, he is a passionate fan of the Great Detective, immodestly thinking he possesses many Holmes characteristics. "But please don't distract me; even though you're correct. By the by, have I ever told you about the time Sir Arthur and I dined at London's Waterloo Club?"

"Now you are the one distracting yourself," Harry says, as all three laugh.

"Of course, the stamps. A month ago, I purchased a jewelers' 20x magnifying glass to further inspect my snuff box. Then, being inquisitive, I examined some of your stamps and ascertained they are as we thought: genuine in every respect. But, on the back of each I noticed a minuscule dot. Being curious, I acquired a compound microscope; the type one sees in a decent college's science laboratory and has 100x enhancement."

From the set of the baron's jaw, Harry and Lansky brace themselves.

"The long and the short of it is this: our Nazi friends apparently marked—let me repeat, *marked*—every one of your stamps."

"How could they?" Harry asks, flabbergasted.

"I thought…" Lansky begins, as perturbed as Harry has ever seen him.

"We have inspected every stamp we sold, but never microscopically. God damn them and how stupid of us! How very stupid of me! Every one of them is marked with the minuscule Greek letter 'delta.' At 100x the delta's triangle all but jumps out at you."

"Which means?" Lansky asks, having almost instantaneously regained his composure.

"Which means that the Germans who stole these stamps will assuredly track us down."

"But doesn't it depend on the associates of the man I killed surviving?" Harry asks, apprehensive for his children as his mind begins processing Romanoff's findings.

"It gets worse, I fear," Romanoff continues, "but we are not without resources. Like my younger brother, Mycroft—," and with this he lets out a bellow of nervous laughter. "To continue; let us examine the evidence from that the past few days. The man you shot was not a courier as you assumed, but a high-level scientist in the Food & Agriculture ministry. The fact that, Walter Darré, who you captured that same day, led the F&A ministry for ten years no longer appears coincidental. I must now assume that, during the war, leading F&A officials knew about this and certain additional facts are known or can be surmised."

Harry and Lansky say nothing.

"The man who succeeded Darré, Herbert Backe, killed himself in prison. His death eliminates a critical person. More senior officials died in 1945 when a bomb penetrated the ministry's air raid shelter. Today, most others wanted for war crimes reside in Argentina and Chile where they'll likely remain. And those alive in Western Europe? All are small fish; men who undoubtedly weren't aware of the stamp operation."

"So how many are left?" Lansky asks.

"Two, Harry, only two," Romanoff answers. "First is Darré, the man you captured in Ludwigslust. He's been released from prison and is dying of cancer—"

"Might I assume," Harry says sarcastically, "that he has a thirty-year life expectancy?"

"In his case no. My sources state that his cancer is inoperable and that he never leaves his house. But, even if he has lost his interest in the stamps—which by no means is certain—we're still not in the clear. Far from it, I am afraid. My source recently learned that last year a man's bones were discovered just west of Ludwigslust and have been positively identified."

"More concretely," he said looking at Harry, "the coroner's report of the wound's location match what you first told me when we first met. Equally intriguing, a woman's remains were found entwined with his. Was she also killed by your men?"

"No, he was alone. We dumped his body in the canal, which had been breached, and the current took it away. And we first stripped his clothing and destroyed his ID's."

"As for the woman," Romanoff continues, "whoever she was makes no difference. More importantly Harry, you once told me the man's name. Do you still remember it?"

"Of course, Hermann Seis."

The baron sighed, "Harry, Hermann Seis's brother, Franz Seis, a Nazi butcher if there ever was one, will be released from Nuremberg later this month. Even more distressing, there's some indication he knows my name, Aaron's, and perhaps yours Harry."

Lansky leans forward, "May I assume there's something I can do?"

"There should be, but he'll be working for Allied Intelligence. It has been made very clear that he should be left alone. Unfortunately, our so-called 'Cold War' requires using men like Seis. However, under no circumstances should we tell this to Aaron. I think we can agree that the more peacefully he passes away the better."

Part V: Fall, 1950–Spring, 1951.

Chapter 36: Munich, Early Fall, 1950.

Franz Seis is released from Landsberg on a brisk, Friday morning, September 29. With the Cold War raging, Seis's freedom is conditioned on his joining West German intelligence. While his American jailers had been mostly easy-going and disinterested—other than preventing escape—overall conditions (food quantity, bedding, space, and medical care) were excellent, and with the knowledge that he should've been hung, Seis had spent most of his free time happily reading. But incarceration is incarceration. While Seis knows that he'll be asked to play a small, undoubtedly dull role behind a desk, it is preferable to Landsberg. Of course, if the Russians successfully invade and he's about to be captured, he can choose between suicide and execution. Now thoroughly bald and needing thick glasses, Seis wears a sweater vest and an old suit. As the final door behind him closes, he is equally ecstatic and apprehensive. In minutes, he will enter a world he doesn't know. Holding his small valise, he smiles bravely and squints in the sunlight, preparing to wait for a cab. How does one hail a cab in a small town like this? There will be no one here to greet me, not even the press, he muses.

▲

In Munich, it is Oktoberfest week. At precisely at 11 AM Tuesday, October 3, as three Americans in uniform marvel at the 1943-44 engraved, exquisitely detailed series of twenty-five stamps depicting German forces in combat and the equally striking woman behind the counter, the little bell above Rudy Spangler's stamp shop door merrily jingles.

Seis, wearing a new, wide-lapeled, dark blue double-breasted striped suit, shirt, tie, and shined shoes, enters the brightly lit shop. Rudy's store is twenty feet wide and thirty deep. A chest-high glass case dominates the room, a Mosler safe in one corner. Seis's takes in the racks of catalogues, albums, book cases with carefully labeled shoeboxes filled with German and foreign stamps, and a children's stamp section. The GIs are browsing, a middle-aged German woman with her child, an exquisite woman, and, *ah*, Rudy Spangler.

Rudy steps forward instantly. "Professor Doctor Seis," he says formally, instinctively bowing slightly and with great difficulty not clicking his heels.

"Spangler," Seis says holding out his right hand for Spangler to shake, "It is so good to see you in these surroundings. Is it always this crowded?"

"During Oktoberfest, there are always people. Perhaps an early lunch? But let me introduce my wife and children. Pauline!" he calls out to the children's nurse and family cook, "please bring in the children."

Seconds later the stout Pauline enters the shop with two children who've been carefully dressed and scrubbed in anticipation of Seis's arrival.

"This is our four-year-old son Max—"

"Named after your boxer friend, of course."

"And our daughter Victoria, almost two."

A genuine smile crosses Seis's pale face as he leans over gently tickling Victoria's throat,

"*Aach du lieber!* What a pretty girl you are. And what a handsome boy you are, Max," he says rubbing the boy's blond head, "I see you will be a great soccer player." Max delightedly puffs out his chest and flexes his muscles while his father smiles proudly. "My only regret," Seis muses, "is not having children and, of course, never seeing any in Landsberg."

The testosterone driven Americans remain dumbstruck by Ingrid Spangler. At twenty-seven, despite her waist being wider after two children, Ingrid wears a three-piece Dirndl outfit—a wide blue skirt, a tight light-blue bodice ending below her breasts, and a thin white blouse that alluringly clings. The Americans swallow, for, as Ingrid leans over identifying stamps they've pointed to, the low-cut blouse permits further glorious views.

▲

Assisting the off-duty soldiers, all non-commissioned officers with a reasonable number of dollars to waste this early in the day, Ingrid also can see Doctor Professor Seis staring at her, his hazel pupils equally enlarged.

Rudy, annoyed by the American trio's lecherous staring, excuses himself and goes behind the counter, seeing to the philatelic needs of the now glum GIs while asking Ingrid to speak with Seis until he completes the transaction.

"You are indeed the most beautiful of women," Seis says to Ingrid after polite small talk, "had I known so beforehand I would have demanded an earlier release."

"There are ten-thousand more attractive than me in Munich," she laughs, immediately noticing the powerful eyes that remind her of the Führer. She is quickly struck by Seis's old-world courtliness and instinctively wonders if the ten pounds she's added to her waist and bosom since Victoria's birth make her less attractive. "But it is still nice to hear someone like you say it. My husband speaks of you often—"

"Complimentary I hope."

"Very much so. We were so pleased to hear of your early release. The trials were such a travesty; a foregone conclusion meant to satisfy the American and British public. But, thank God it was they, and not the Russians. I trust that the Americans treated you well?"

"Under the circumstances, yes. Acceptable food and never a threat of torture; but we treated their prisoners as well as we could until the end. While Americans have the manners of barbarians, I shudder thinking of my comrades in Russian hands. Although, like so many, I sometimes wish for the old days..."

"We're not supposed to say that, you know—"

"But I understand that most do anyway. However, you are most fortunate Frau—"

"Ingrid, please. Don't make me feel like some old hag in a Bruegel landscape."

"—Most fortunate in your husband and beautiful children."

"The children *are* my delight. Given the last five years, I am blessed having such a *practical* marriage. But like so many of us, what I most loved has been destroyed."

"And if I may be so impertinent, where are you from? Do I not detect a Prussian dialect?"

"From what has now become Poland," she says, angrily spitting out the word. "I was born near Königsberg—"

"Where I taught—"

Seis steps next to Ingrid. She makes no attempt to keep a distance between them. That quickly, she thinks, but finds herself pleased. The two look at the Americans and Rudy. "Sadly, my family's ancestral grounds are now a collective farm that produces far less food—"

"But more reports I suspect. Never underrate the Russian ability to churn out reports at an amazing rate. We said, 'guns not butter,' while they say, 'reports not butter.'"

"Those are Rudy's sentiments exactly. The Russians make a mess of everything, steal our best people, and then try to cover up their errors by intimidating us further."

Seis listens intently, and then moves his leg slightly so that it, seemingly by accident, brushes Ingrid's calf.

Have I been that obvious? she wonders, but she finds herself excited by the prospect. If only, she thinks. Nevertheless, poor Rudy is Rudy—a wonderful provider but the dullest of lovers. How she misses her late husband, now six-years dead.

"But, let us talk of less mournful things. Don't you have an attractive wife awaiting you?" she asks, brushing Seis's calf in turn and letting her leg linger for a second.

Rudy remains absorbed with selling common, but expensive stamps to the Americans.

"My wife, I am happy to say, divorced me and has married an American. My gain; his loss. Beauty, as is well known, and if he has not discovered already, is only skin deep."

"But if I am as lovely as you gallantly said earlier, don't you think my beauty is only skin deep?" she laughs, now looking at him to see how he will react. Then she notices his long hands. He has the beautiful hands of a surgeon, she thinks, wishing them on her.

"It would be my distinct pleasure to find out some day." Their calves touch again.

"Will you be in Munich long?" she asks, both are poker-faced, looking at Rudy.

"I will be living here and work in Pullach for some time."

"Ah, serious work for General Gehlen nearby. I assume you knew him during the war?"

Seis nods as Ingrid continues. "A man like you will need company and I will introduce you to women who put me to shame. There are many, you will be happy to learn, who have tired of American companionship. But do you go to church?"

"No. I am afraid that twelve years of the Third Reich cured me of hypocrisy."

The little bell above the door jingles again as four more GIs enter followed by a father with two bored teenage children.

"Nor do I," Ingrid says, her mind now made up. "Rudy attends early services Sunday and then assists in youth Bible studies that go on and on. My Sundays are *so* dull, the children visit their grandmother's and Pauline is gone. Knock at the back door at eight in the morning."

Seis's nod is almost imperceptible; his face shows nothing.

"Rudy," Ingrid says loudly, "you and Doctor Seis have business to discuss. I will manage everything while you are out." Then she turns and curtsies slightly to Seis, holding out her hand for him to kiss lightly. "It has been so enjoyable meeting you Doctor."

"The pleasure has been mine, Frau Spangler," he says, putting his lips to her hand.

Later, with Seis gone, Ingrid finds herself thinking that Sunday seems so far away.

Chapter 37: Munich, Noon, October 3.

Franz Seis's first choice for lunch had been the Osteria Bavaria, Hitler's favorite restaurant.

"I've always wanted to go there," he tells Rudy, "but before the war I couldn't afford it, even though they never took advantage of their popularity."

"I am happy to tell you that it's still there," Rudy says. "However, while it has reopened, it is now called Osteria Italiana and no longer serves the Führer's favorite trout."

Seis smiles, shaking his head. "Then it's not for me. Frankly, I had hoped, just this one time, to sit at Table No. 7 where the Führer always sat, but it was too much to expect, wasn't it? And Italian food? What would he say?"

Seis walks like a tourist, looking this way and that. "So much damage, still," he says, as they stroll together, each having trouble hearing the other over the construction noise.

"And so much more has been repaired," Rudy says. "Nevertheless, I love hearing the jackhammers, pile drivers and drills. Everywhere we're rebuilding."

"A tribute to our Germanic energy and purpose. You know, other than being visited by a tailor Saturday, I've spent the last four days sleeping and reading. I was too tired to walk around, so this is first I've seen what's happening."

A short distance from Rudy's shop, Weisses Bräuhaus is opening for lunch. Weisses is on historic *Tal Strasse,* the site of a brewery for 400 years. Since the 1870s, the chalk colored building has produced *Weisses* (white) beer and superior food. As Rudy and Seis place their orders, the staff finishes setting tables, straightening glasses, and checking inventories. During Oktoberfest, business is expected until the morning's wee hours.

The Oktoberfest Bock Beer arrives and the two click their beer steins. not as equals but as business associates, enjoying the perfectly brewed lager. "To our fatherland's resilience," Seis says and immediately turns to business. "I am gratified how your stamp store is prospering. You have been blessed by it, a beautiful wife, and lovely children."

Seis pauses, then continues. "And tell me, were you able to begin your business by selling the stamps that you thought I was unaware of your taking?"

Rudy turns white, remembering how Seis shot Ulrich Schmidt years earlier, but Seis only laughs and puts his hand up. "Naturally I knew, but you were careful to take nothing of high value. You weren't greedy and a captain's wages were so low. Who knew what could happen, Ja? An errant bomb and all our efforts up in smoke. But you don't think this Romanoff & Abramson company is aware of our marking the stamps?"

"No, I'm certain that Romanoff remains unaware of our delta. Like an old man, his eyes briefly gave him away, but otherwise he wasn't suspicious."

Seis smiles even more as lunch arrives. The sights and smells of exceptional Bavarian cooking all but overwhelm a man who has been incarcerated for years and become accustomed to drab meals. He does his best not to appear greedy, but his zest is apparent.

"And you're sure the stamps are in America?" Seis, between bites, asks a second time. The waiter, discrete but attentive, comes by as Rudy signals for two more glasses of Bock.

"Unless they've been sold," Rudy replies. "They must still be in America. Who else can afford them? We know Hermann was on his bike and safely ahead of the Russians. Yet he somehow met a woman that, you said, his body was found with. That's what so confuses everything. Why did he stop when he was so close?"

"You knew my brother, Spangler. Do you think if he suddenly met an attractive woman he'd stop to fornicate when the world was falling apart?"

"Odd as it sounds, I think that's what occurred. The two somehow met while the road was temporarily blocked. With death so close those days, people screwed like rabbits. We must assume that Americans came upon them while they were, shall we say, fully distracted. One American saw the stamps and took them. Whether it was before or after they shot Hermann makes no difference. But he, or they, shot your brother, then raped and killed the woman. And the Americans there were none other than the infamous 82nd Airborne."

"Which is when Romanoff gave himself away," Seis says shaking his head.

"Yes, it makes sense. Those paratroopers were thugs, more than capable of what you suggest. Hermann always thought with his prick. He must've assumed he still had time to cross the Elbe. Here's a one-footed tortoise who he acts like he's the fable's fast hare—but he screws, not sleeps. You know how he constantly bedded the compound's Jewesses. 'Give 'em more food,' he'd say, 'nobody likes fucking scarecrows.' And his last deed ruined us all."

Rudy says nothing as Seis continues. "If I ever find the man who shot my brother, I'll make him wish that he'd been drawn and quartered and watched his own entrails being burnt. But how do you suggest we identify and hunt this person down? Can we visit larger stamp shows where some might reappear, say Amsterdam or London?" Seis asks, chewing happily, his mouth full of Wienerschnitzel as his brain explodes with the meat's exquisite taste and smell.

"I'm afraid we'd be most unwelcome. There are too many people who'd be more than happy to turn us in for our wartime activities. The West European tribunals haven't been as lenient as the American, especially if we're recognized while on their soil. Even British stamp shows pose similar risks. Something we never thought about in '42, did we? But can you raise the money for another American trip?"

Rudy doesn't know it, but money—hopefully—won't be an object. With Hermann's death confirmed, Seis has two Swiss accounts adding up to almost $600,000.

"So, what do you suggest?" Seis asks, despite having fully formulated his plans.

"Once I heard that your release was imminent, I began to discuss the issue with Ingrid."

"Do you feel she would be helpful in our endeavors?"

"If Ingrid thought that there would be some profit for us. She will want to know what percentage of any sales you might be considering for us."

"Right now, we might as well discuss shares of the wind, but if Ingrid wishes 100% of nothing I will happily acquiesce. Except for Darré, who's dying, we have no remaining partners. And new partners are *verboten*. There'll be men we'll need to pay, but none will receive a share of whatever remains."

A smile crosses Rudy's face. "So, we wouldn't be reduced further?"

"Yes and no. I will advance the money but expect to be paid back. But please tell Ingrid," Seis says, at the same time realizing that it is she who is pushing Rudy into being so unnaturally bold, "that there is a high likelihood we'll need help, and expensive help at that. The days when our uniforms alone persuaded stamp owners are long gone, are they not? Frankly, we'll need to retain a forceful 'assistant' or two if we wish to see our stamps again."

Rudy has a confused look on his face.

Seis leans forward, lowering his voice. "ODESSA. Until last week, I remained skeptical about them. But, minutes after my release, a car pulled up and out came a wartime associate, Werner R— well, his last name is unimportant. Werner had arranged a room at the Torbraeu."

"But how? I mean—"

"Like many former SS," Seis leans forward, his voice low, "who've been released, I received immediate help from ODESSA."

"So, the 'Organization of Former SS Members' is real. I've heard rumors for years."

The two smile as, glancing around, they watch the other tables fill.

"ODESSA made my arrangements and Werner presented me with an envelope filled with cash. 'You'll need a car, an apartment, and new clothes,' he said. 'We know you'll be working for Gehlen's *Bundesnachrichtendienst*. When will that begin?'"

"'8 AM, Monday, October 30,' I said," Seis continues. "'I've negotiated a much-needed vacation. I'll have a passport, then visit Switzerland, and shall repay you on my return.' With that, we had my first meal at Torbraeu's Schapeau restaurant. What a pleasure not to be eating from a steel tray! Do you know what American prison meals are like? One shuffles down a line holding these trays stamped with different sized indentations into which 'food' is shoveled with a large spoon. Someone said it sounded like cows' shitting. 'Plop! Plop! Plop! Next person!' And even more disgusting, many American so-called cooks and servers are Negroes! I'd always thought that Russian Jews—"

"Please!" Rudy cuts in. "Times have changed, especially in public places like this."

"Of course, of course," Seis says and leans backward. "Everything is still so new to me. I feel like that American Rip Van Winkle. Well, as to our plans. It seems ODESSA has members in America; U.S. citizens who were born there and are interested in 'temporary,' albeit dangerous work. They're the type of associates we'll need. Over there, the two of us could be thoughtful while they—"

"Bash heads together? If you don't mind my saying so, we've discussed stamps enough for one day, why don't we look at the pretty women and discuss Ingrid's plans for you."

"Plans for me?" *I thought she was explicit enough,* Seis thinks.

At that moment, the waiter arrives. "Gentlemen, we received freshly brewed *Doppelbock* this morning. "Might I recommend it to you?"

"A small glass for me," said Rudy, "I have work to do this afternoon."
"I am not accustomed to alcohol, but I'll have a glass anyway," said Seis, now realizing how tight he has become. *I'd better be careful; I could easily make a fool of myself.*

"Ingrid thinks," Rudy continued, "that you've been without female companionship long enough. She would be delighted to introduce you to a certain young lady and we'll all have dinner Saturday. The woman is striking, but not bawdy, and embodies German intelligence. She was to be married to an American general, who then decamped for his family in Texas—"

"So, he just left her? How typically American. The guards used to taunt us with stories about our women. And may I assume the American military did nothing?"

"Yes. She was told not to take the matter further or she'd lose her job. She worked for me when I managed their translation staff in late '45."

"And you didn't wish to take her out?"

The waiter returned with two foaming glasses of *Doppelbock.* "Our compliments, Dr. Seis, but please remember that the brewmaster makes this with 13-percent alcohol." The waiter places the two glasses in front of them, quietly whispers in Seis's ear "*Heil Hitler!*" and shakes Seis's hand. Seis acknowledges his sentiments with a nod and gracious smile.

"No," Rudy continues. "I'd met Ingrid before the woman arrived from Berlin. She wasn't seventeen when the Russians came and well... I don't have to say what she went through. Her mother and a sister disappeared and a younger brother was shot defending her. Eventually an American took her in and cared for her. She fully recovered years ago, but—"

"She's has had a difficult life and one must treat her gently," Seis nods. "Well, after five years in jail, she might be good for me. And perhaps me for her, if her expectations aren't too high," he laughed bitterly. "But she's intelligent, you say?"

"She'll challenge even you and isn't husband hunting. You two might make a good fit."

Yes, a good fit, Seis thinks, also relieved he has steered Rudy away from the topic of his specific percentage of any future stamp sales. Rudy had proved to be reliable and discrete. If he and Ingrid are not too greedy Seis can see them receiving twenty-percent. However, should they prove avaricious...

Chapter 38: Munich, Saturday, Early Evening, October 7.

Supper is at the multi-story, red-roofed, white painted Hofbräuhaus. Inside is a picture of German joviality. Smiling waiters and patrons wear traditional Bavarian dress. Women wear brightly colored *Dirndl* outfits comprised of wide skirts, bodices (above or below the breast depending on age), blouses, white socks and flat heeled shoes suitable for dancing. Men parade in *Lederhosen*, calf-length white socks with garter belts, four (not three) thronged suspenders with a wide belt across the chest (connecting the front suspenders), open short jackets, and hats of different shades of brown with a single, large bright feather.

The Hofbräuhaus, Munich's most famous drinking spot, dates to the 1500s. It was at its current location since 1828 and, although it was flattened by bombs, it had been rapidly and lovingly rebuilt. Hofbräuhaus' twentieth century well-deserved fame (or infamy) was entirely due to its being the site of Hitler's spectacular entry into politics. Destitute, in 1920, he gladly accepted low-paying Army intelligence work to infiltrate tub-thumping radicals. That February 24, listening to a speaker at the Hofbräuhaus, Hitler lost his self-control, angrily jumped up and responded. The rest, some say, is the decline of the West.

▲

The Hofbräuhaus consists of an open first floor, large second floor (where Hitler spoke) and a smaller third floor with private rooms. But this evening's seating is segregated; Americans and other foreigners on the first (where the food is prepared), and Germans and Austrians on the second. On the German level, an accordion player wanders among the tables, playing and singing student drinking songs.

As planned, Rudy and Ingrid pick up Ilse at her apartment and introductions are made at the Hofbräuhaus where Seis arrived earlier. As his request, for he wants privacy and not people pestering him, they are seated at a small corner table. Patrons enjoy the smells of a different beers, roasted pork, duck and goose, dumplings, schnitzels, sausages, red cabbage, potato pancakes, sauerkraut, gravies, and dozens of other Bavarian specialties. Soon the tunes change to *Wehrmacht* marching songs, more chanted defiantly than sung, as sweating, overweight men—many in wheelchairs—pound the long communal tables for emphasis.

Seis surprises himself by joining the singers, downs a quart of beer before dinner ends, and orders a second desert. He is as happy as a bachelor just out of prison can be, for alongside him sit two stunning women, Ingrid Spangler and Ilse Wallbillig. Almost instantly, the two present a tightrope-walking problem. He is enchanted by Ilse but, tomorrow morning, he will visit Ingrid. Their two feet frequently touch until Ingrid slides her hand inside his thigh and gently begins stroking him. Rudy drinks beer, as oblivious as he is cheerful.

Seis didn't anticipate how attractive he finds Ilse, her black hair glistening, clothing sensual but subdued, and, as Rudy promised, clearly intelligent. Not even twenty-three, she's the opposite of naïve, her 1945 Berlin experiences giving her a wisdom and sardonic outlook coming from the exceptional pain she experienced. Nevertheless, she smiles easily, has a devastatingly youthful figure, and acts unimpressed by Seis.

Finishing her second stein, Ilse laughingly turns to Seis, fully aware that Ingrid's hand is on his penis, "So, tell me why did the Americans jail you? I must admit to being curious."

Seis has anticipated the question, but not the effect of Ingrid's hand as he tries to keep his voice modulated. "The incident occurred in August of '41. We'd been fighting non-stop for weeks and I, as a good officer, was always first up and the last to sleep. That afternoon, after the loss of two dear comrades only hours before, we captured a medium sized village. It was like so many other Russian towns; almost medieval, most houses having thatched roofs. There were only dirt roads, a handful of trees, no running water or electricity, and a primitive, single-line phone system on tottering poles. Entering the town, I wouldn't have been surprised had we encountered Ivan the Terrible or Genghis Khan's Tartars."

Somehow, Seis completes each sentence, all his will power required to prevent him closing his eyes and gasping with pleasure. Then, leaning forward and holding his stein, he feels Ingrid's hand retreat as she smiles demurely. "As usual, we rounded up Communist administrators, Jews, suspected insurgents, Red Army soldiers in civilian clothing, and anyone in the local jail. Our orders, concerning Red officials, to be candid, were always the same: execute them. That afternoon I was asleep on my feet when some vodka was discovered."

"And you drank it like water?" Ilse asks.

"Almost. Afterward a lieutenant shook me awake to ask what to do with the prisoners. 'Kill them, of course,' I said, thinking he meant the Reds. When I awoke next morning, I discovered over 150 villagers were dead. As the C.O., I was responsible. I signed a report stating what had occurred and, of course, the Allies found it in Berlin's rubble." Seis stops, for between the beer and the stroking he'd almost said, "Their *only* piece of evidence regarding my 'activities,' " but catches himself in time.

"And the other officer, the one who led the executions, what happened to him?"

"Later he was at Stalingrad. Who knows what happened."

▲

To Ilse, Seis's story doesn't come as a surprise. When the war with Russia started, her home in Königsberg was less than sixty-miles from the Soviet controlled Lithuanian border. From June 1940, following Russia's uncontested Lithuanian invasion, fact-based rumors of Russian secret police round-ups, deportations, and summary executions drifted across the border. That Ilse was twelve meant that the stories of Soviet secret police (NKVD) atrocities were even more frightening. Then, when Germany invaded Russia a year later, it was similarly impossible not to hear about Lithuania's "glorious" liberation, the fact that Hitler had occupied a small part of the country (Memel, 150,000 half of them German or German-speaking inhabitants) two years earlier forgotten.

With the successful 1941 German invasion, Nazi propaganda played up Soviet killings, including the Katyn Forest massacre of 22,000 Polish military and police officers. Goebbels' propaganda machine had little trouble painting Russians as a brutish, Neanderthal-like people—a portrait that Ilse subconsciously accepted.

Coming as she did from an educated family, Ilse was horrified following Stalingrad and the Russian march west. Of Lithuania's Jews, what little she hears she thinks is factually upside down; the Russians must have done it. Her terrible experiences at the hands of the Red Army in Berlin only adds to her hatred of Russians. Her attitude towards Seis's story is not one of revulsion, but rather like so many from Prussia is: "Good, the bastards got a taste of their own medicine." Ilse has endured too many rapes and seen too many bodies of women and children lying in Berlin's streets to feel sorry for any Russians.

That Seis will soon be working for Gehlen's spy organization is another plus for him. In Ilse's mind, he'll be one of those putting his life on the line to stop further Russian aggression. Ilse has no idea that, in fact, Seis is personally responsible for the deaths not of 150 Soviet officials, Jews, and others, but for more than a hundred times as many.

Chapter 39: Hofbräuhaus, 9:30 PM.

With most of the eating ended, a traditional German Oompah band begins performing. Couples leave their tables for the dance floor, all enveloped in the blue haze produced by hundreds of smokers. The musicians play traditional polkas as the audience claps, cheers and stomps its feet to the lively tunes.

Two women begin to dance, soon followed by other female couples.

"What is this?" the surprised and shocked Seis asks Ilse.

"It's a last 'gift' from our beloved Führer: too few men. And many are wounded veterans who, like Rudy, are unable to dance," she whispers. "But *you* can and you *will* dance with me." With that, she stands up and pulls Seis from his chair.

"I haven't danced since I taught," he protests unconvincingly, but grins broadly when he stands up and downs the last of the beer in his stein as Ilse takes his hand.

"You'll remember in a minute; it's just like sex," she laughs. Seis is shocked, and then realizes Ilse said this only to watch his reaction and laughs along with her. Ilse's attractiveness brings stares, but the beer numbs his inhibitions. For the first time in years he feels young. Holding her warm hand, he openly examines her figure, happy at how easily he keeps up with her. Soon the band excuses itself while most dancers remain on the floor.

"I can tell exactly what is going through your mind," Ilse laughs, "men are so easy to understand. You want to bed both of us, right?"

Seis, taken aback, can say nothing, then is amazed to find himself nodding.

"But you can't, certainly not now. What Ingrid didn't tell me I guessed. When we excused ourselves earlier I asked her directly and she said I was correct. Just remember to use their back door. Don't be embarrassed, you're not Ingrid's first by any means."

Seis blushes, something that he doesn't remember happening in a decade.

"Poor Rudy's so naïve... but perhaps I'll have my turn later?" she asks, leaning over to unnecessarily straighten her short white socks, letting Seis look at her breasts.

"Just as you've stared at me, I've been examining you," she says, smiling co-quettishly as they hold hands. "However, I've made a determination you won't like. Going to bed with you too soon would be a mistake. It so happens I like you, but I recognize that, like all men, you have certain physical needs. Needs that prison-life has only made worse."

"For a million years," Ilse continues, "man's survival has resulted in quick physical release. Only elephants and lions can afford to leisurely procreate and they likely had their own predators once. I'm sure Darwin believed that, for us, having slow sex would've resulted in mankind's being either trampled to death or eaten. Survival of the fittest meant those who could—if you'll excuse my candid language—ejaculate fastest."

"So, we're here tonight because our forefathers discharged rapidly?"

"Exactly. Which worked until we lived in caves and had more time for exploration."

"Which means?"

"Foreplay. For women, the more the better and for as long as possible. It's something most men aren't capable of. Their million-year-old instincts get the better of them; they subconsciously feel they have only a few seconds before—"

"A five ton elephant squashes them or they become a saber-toothed tiger's lunch."

Ilse nods and laughs, "Which, today, invariably leaves women in general and me, in particular, unhappy. By leaving prison so recently—if you'll permit my switching metaphors—you're no different from the proverbial sailor who arrives home after a year at sea."

"So, I fall into the 'any-port-in-a-storm' syndrome?"

"No, *I* would fall into it: I'm the port and you're the storm. Biologically, anything else would be impossible, your protestations to the contrary are meaningless. Nevertheless, you also fall into many other classifications, which is why you're such an interesting person."

"Which are the classifications?"

"They are to be withheld until we get to know each better. Much better in fact. Which brings me to something else I've been thinking about the last few hours."

"And that is?"

"If you would like to, I would be happy to see you again. Since I'd be obligated to see to your more primitive needs, I would select venues that hold the promise of other couples. Men who are interested in me will undoubtedly join us, good taste requiring they also bring wives or girlfriends. I will engage in conversation the weaker sex, be they of a certain attractiveness—"

"To us both?"

"Exactly, I can't exclude you in the evening's most important decision, can I?" Ilse laughs, eyes sparkling. "Then I shall determine if the lady in question is happy and, if not, would she would prefer me or you. Whatever her decision I shall inform you."

"But I will not have you."

"No, but at the end of the evening you will have met five times as many women."

"But with me; will you dawdle like Penelope weaving her rug?"

"Months yes, years no."

"You don't know how selfish that sounds," Seis says, but his attempt to sound stern is broken by a wide smile.

"Of course it's selfish. But look around you. Do you think for a second that I can't have my own way? For whatever reason, fate has made me attractive and given us both good brains. I've decided that with you, Doctor Professor Seis, if I cannot have a special relationship I'd prefer nothing at all. As I'm sure Ingrid explained, I've been hurt too often to have another intelligent man use my body as his receptacle."

Ilse smiles. Seis smiles back. The music begins to play again when a tipsy, overweight man in his fifties and his reticent, younger wife joins the dancers. Winking at each other, the band breaks into a fast polka, then switches the tempo from fast to slow and back again, suddenly stopping. The fat man crashes to the floor as gales of laughter follow.

Seis looks at Ilse. "I'll be next, I fear. If you please, no more dancing, my legs are beginning to stiffen and I haven't had proper exercise in years."

Reaching their table, Ilse remains standing and looks at Ingrid.

"You will dance with me?" she asks, as Ingrid stands and smiles.

The band goes up-tempo as Ilse and Ingrid whirl around, wide skirts billowing. Other couples leave the floor knowing they are no competition. Without warning the Bräuhaus' overweight, slick haired manager—who claims to have been a Hofbräuhaus waiter *that* night in 1920—signals the band to stop, then scurries forward with two glasses of beer.

"Catch your breath," he says loudly, "and then everyone wants more."

"More! More!" shouts one table after another, beer steins pounding as clapping follows. The two drain their glasses, then signal the band to begin. Cheers and stomping accelerate as they switch from male to female roles effortlessly until the noise reaches a crescendo. Only by raising their exhausted arms does the music stop. Sweat dripping and giggling with delight they fall into each other's arms and embrace. Ingrid and Ilse's eyes lock, they kiss naturally without embarrassment; then long and passionately, each tongue inside the other's mouth.

▲

Back at their table Ingrid kisses Rudy while Ilse finds Seis's mouth. But, what most amazes Seis is the sight of each women's clear sexual excitement. He'd heard about this type of relationship in Berlin, before Hitler clamped down, but it was something he'd never seen. In Nuremberg, older prisoners told him about Berlin—especially Berlin—after the first war. It's this way in any country that loses too many men, he was told. Seis had read about London and Paris in the 20's, and devoured Hemingway's *The Sun Also Rises*. How many men in Germany are no better off than Jake Barnes he wonders? Munich tonight must be no different than the world back then: women all but having sex on the floor with each other. So, is this behavior yet another bill that our beloved Führer left us to pay? And who is he to object after so happily going to war in 1939?

▲

Seis is at Rudy's back door the next morning one minute after eight. He hasn't slept well, his mind still racing from the women's kisses, his impatience for the sun to rise, and an overwhelming desire that leads first to one shower, then a second.

Apprehensive, he barely knocks when Ingrid opens the door and all but pulls him inside. She wears tight American dungarees and a white silk blouse. At the stairwell, she slides to her knees, pulls his pants down, first taking him there. Yet, hours later, despite mutual coital glows, as both dress they instinctively know the relationship will be short. For Seis, he has reached the age when he wants to spend his weekends leisurely traveling, enjoying good food, and slowly having sex. Unfortunately, poor Ingrid is chained to her role of housewife, mother, and shopkeeper; a waste, he thinks.

Walking back to the Torbräu, Seis finds himself thinking of Ilse and wondering how sincere her words were. She'd let him walk her back to boarding house where she had her own apartments, but at the front door she wouldn't let him kiss her. But she did say, "I hope you will ask me out again." How, he thinks, he'd enjoy a bicycle ride and a quiet dinner with her. She is, he instinctively believes, his future, and must be courted accordingly.

Chapter 40: Munich–Lucerne, October 1950.

In prison, Seis daydreamed a thousand times about Lucerne and the money deposited during the war. He and Hermann were advised not to bank in Zurich, too close to Germany and swarming with Allied agents. After the war, it was thought that the Allies would extort Swiss bankers—men whose amorality might have taught the Nazis many a lesson—to turn over German accounts. Accordingly, Lucerne and the small private bank of Joachim W. Hauser was selected, a secret identification number given.

For years, Franz Seis despaired of ever seeing this money again. But, miraculously, the Allies left the Swiss alone. Never in his wildest imagination did Seis anticipate his early release or working for West German spymaster Reinhard Gehlen.

In 1942, Gehlen took over Army intelligence for the Eastern Front, quickly replacing a bloated staff. January 1945 saw Gehlen fired by Hitler for his pessimistic, but accurate Red Army reports. Meanwhile, he hid vast amounts of intelligence data making him invaluable to the west once the Cold War began. When West Germany achieved independence (1949), Gehlen became president of its Federal Intelligence Service, the *Bundesnachrichtendienst.*

▲

Four thousand miles away, Harry Strong meets with Big Al and finds himself assigned to Beckendorf's prestigious new building, a 530-foot high skyscraper on Fifth Ave a few blocks north of St. Patrick's Cathedral. Because of the property's financial and public relations importance to Big Al's growing empire, he will personally direct construction, but Harry will be the Number Two on the job. It is a huge feather in Harry's cap; for the first time a small photo and short announcement appears in the Real Estate section of the Sunday *New York Times.*

▲

Seis meets with Gehlen Monday, October 9, 1950 to discuss his forthcoming work overseeing the infiltration of Iron Curtain trade unions and the liquidation or safe passage of key Communist administrators. On this day, Seis trudges between offices, fills out forms, is photographed, and receives a passport and identification papers indicating his employment in a fictitious West German government reparations office.

Returning to his hotel, Seis is depressed. He misses his black uniform with its silver insignias, polished black boots, and death's head skull on his SS cap. Civilians no longer notice him at 100 yards and scurry off. People in tram lines don't avoid eye contact or part to let him enter. His glance doesn't induce terror on those whom his eyes light on, nor do they freeze when he cocks an index finger. Seis now feels small in his gray overcoat and dark suit, looking like the prototypical bureaucrat. Is he destined to become one? Will he be relegated to posthumous fame through a son? Perhaps he'll marry someone twenty years younger—say a first cousin—and become the aloof father to an unwanted child. Like Alois Schicklgruber?

The next morning Seis is on the 160 mile, 4½ hour Heidelberg train, carrying a small, caramel colored suitcase and ordinary attaché case. He could have taken a faster train, but he's curious to see the countryside and remaining war-scars. Also, a third-class ticket on a slower train saves him a few marks and, more interestingly, someone following him will stick out like a sore thumb; precisely the trap two overdressed men have fallen into.

In Heidelberg, with 100,000 residents, Seis makes no attempt to shake his tail. The city is Germany's warmest, mild enough for fig trees. Walking on cobblestone streets toward the Neckar River, he takes in the sights, sounds and smells, thankful that the city wasn't bombed. Seis had once lived and studied in Heidelberg, a university town, but today's students appear younger, less purposeful. How he longs for the Nazi banners that hung from hundreds of public buildings and private homes in the city's center! Perhaps it was a reaction to liberal student tendencies, but Heidelberg was always a Nazi hotbed.

Instinctively, his footsteps carry him to his favorite restaurant, *Zum Roten Ochsen* (The Red Ox) on the *Hauptstrasse*. The brasserie, owned by the same family for a century, hosted Otto von Bismarck and Mark Twain. Half a century later, American tourists ask to sit where Twain had. Not knowing any better, they are invariably delighted to be told that Twain's table is available and tip generously for being given whatever empty seat is available.

Seis is content to sit outside under an umbrella, sip beer, crowd-watch, and slowly eat the Red Ox's signature, hand-made *Maultaschen*, a beef-filled ravioli-like dish. Closing his eyes, he pleasurably remembers the sound of a thousand singing and marching Nazis, their boots striking the *Hauptstrasse's* cobblestones in unison. Seis vacillates between his obligation as a son and his desire to avoid what can only be a painful reunion. He knows his mother will be emotional and he's never liked his father. In all, it takes Seis two hours to finish and, having procrastinated long enough, slowly rises to take a combination of trolleys and busses to his parents' house. A few tables away, two men, different from those on the train but clearly American, notice him getting up, put down their coffee and simultaneously stand.

Seis walks over, smiles, tips his hat and bows slightly. "Gentlemen, rather than inconvenience you, I'm about to visit my parents. If you have an automobile, might I induce you to drive me there? If you don't have their address, I'll be happy to direct you."

▲

"Is that you, Hermann?" his half-blind, frail, and increasingly confused eighty-eight-year-old father asks from his wheelchair. Hermann had always been his father's favorite and Seis knows the frail old man is hoping against hope that the familiar silhouette will be his oldest.

"No, papa," his mother replies as she hugs Franz and begins crying. "This is Franz." And so the conversation goes, his father never understanding to whom he is talking. This once stern man, an ardent Nazi proud of his four-digit party membership number, had been employed by the party illicitly purchasing arms. Then, more to do with competency versus dishonesty, Franz thinks, his father was sidetracked into an insignificant administrative post. Gustav, his middle brother, an *Afrika Korps* officer captured in North Africa, is also there, driving from Hamburg where he works in commercial insurance. For dinner, Seis's mother has lovingly prepared goose—Franz's favorite. After his parents go to bed, the brothers talk far into the night. At no time does Franz mention "his" stamps.

▲

Two days later, Gustav drives Franz north to Frankfort am Main's *Hauptbahnhof* (railroad station). Franz tells his brother that he's going to Paris, to see what has happened to a wartime girlfriend and an infant placed in an orphanage in '43. It's best, Franz thinks, that he lies because he's sure police will question Gustav later. The necessity of Franz's duplicity is immediately obvious: their Volkswagen is being tailed by a trio of leapfrogging cars.

Once Seis reaches the colossal station, fully repaired from its wartime damage, he buys coffee, gives his pursuers time to spot him, walks to a ticket booth, then loudly purchases a third-class ticket on a Paris train leaving in two hours. However, Seis has a huge advantage over those pursuing him: two days earlier, in Munich, he'd bought a first-class train ticket to Lucerne. When his Swiss bound train is five-minutes from departure and with twenty-six tracks on the upper level, Seis begins a zig-zag course through crowds and around kiosks, slipping onto the train seconds before the 200 mile trip begins. At the Swiss border, he sails through, the only question by an indifferent official being if he has ample warm clothing.

Basel to Lucerne is sixty miles. Here he checks into the 19th century Hotel des Balances, located in a former wine district within the city's ancient walls. Seis isn't a man to worry unnecessarily, but that evening he tosses and turns, wondering if he's made any mistakes. Regarding Hermann, his mother had provided him with his brother's birth and death certificates. But is there something else? Something obvious he has forgotten?

And will the bank be friendly? Most Swiss hate Germans, their freedom coming centuries earlier with a successful rebellion against Germanic rulers. By 1940, Nazi invasion plans (Operation Tannenbaum) were an open secret. And what of the unpublicized bloody border skirmishes and planes downed by Nazi probing of Swiss ground and air space? With bad luck, someone in the banking house might have been a casualty. Worse, Seis does not have a single piece of paper proving his and Hermann's accounts. Despite being in the SS, during the war's later stages, any proof of Swiss banking was a sign of defeatism resulting in swift execution.

Thus, Friday morning at 10:30 AM, a freshly shaved but slightly haggard Franz Seis stands in front of a thirty-five-feet wide, four story brick building with a thick oak door and discrete brass sign stating only, "Joachim L. Hauser & Sons." Seis pulls on the heavy door, surprised by how easily it swings open, and enters. A young male receptionist in a pressed suit and perfectly shined shoes rises to meet him, asking how he might assist.

"I have a numbered bank account that was opened during the war," Seis says.

The receptionist bows slightly, asks Seis for a business card, offers him a chair and coffee, then excuses himself. Seis has no idea how long his wait will be. He idly looks around the room, assumes that he's being photographed, but is grateful for the coffee and pleased to see his hands aren't shaking as he holds his cup and saucer. He is halfway through when the receptionist and a roly-poly fiftyish individual in a gray, striped, double-breasted suit and red carnation in his lapel emerges with a broad smile and a firm handshake.

"Ah, Doctor Professor Seis. What a pleasure," the man says, bowing slightly. "We've been expecting you. Please follow me."

Seis is astonished, "How did you know I was arriving?"

"We are not that small a company," the man laughs and points the way to his large office with huge bookcases and mementoes of fishing trips around the globe. Seis is brought even better coffee and offered cigarettes of Turkish blends. The banking officer, Jakob Knüsel, rummages through a pile of string-tied folders on his polished desk. Knüsel smiles after finding Seis's file. "I see that you are employed by General Gehlen," he says, "now, how can we be of assistance?"

Chapter 41: New York, October 12, 1950.

New York City's Lenox Hill Hospital fills almost the entire block between Park, Lexington, 76th and 77th Streets. Its location in Manhattan's "Silk Stocking" district has seen to its growth and prosperity. Senior staff fondly recall that during the "Roaring 20's" it had been Babe Ruth's drying out place of choice. For those of the Catholic faith who've run out of luck, Donahue's Funeral Home is the next block down on Lexington. Immediately across from Donahue's is St. Jean Baptiste's church, an easy three step process for bereaved families.

On 76th and Lexington's northwest corner stands a florist shop and a "stationary" store; a cluttered business selling soda pop from a steel ice chest (refilled daily by a man carrying a huge chunk of ice on his rubber-aproned shoulder), papers, cigarettes, magazines, and other low margin items. Many speculate how the 70-year old owner, a grouchy, cigar smoking Latvian immigrant, Leonard Rappaport, manages to pay the taxes for the coveted site. But Rappaport easily frustrates Lenox Hill's expansion plans by the contents of a little black book. Each January he places last year's book in a safe deposit box, each holding over a hundred women's names. In fact, Rappaport is the middleman for safe, discreet, but thoroughly illegal abortions which are a necessity in high society, show business (like Nan O'Malley), and criminal families.

Rappaport never sees a client; rather, he makes all arrangements from one of his pay phone booths—the one saying, "not in service." The abortions are performed two short blocks away, at the Gotham Hospital, a boutique-sized building opposite the Carlyle Hotel. As often as not, Meyer Lansky drops by representing a Sicilian-American father to whom the disgrace of a bastard grandchild is an unmitigated catastrophe. At the Gotham, the pregnant daughter will not just survive the operation and later conceive, but, equally important, stain her wedding bed. But how? On the staff is a Hungarian refugee specializing in hymen restoration, a centuries-old procedure learned during Budapest's Turkish occupation. In fact, sacrificial pigeons are kept on the hospital's roof to supply each wedding night's verisimilitude.

Decades before, Rappaport and Lansky's father attended the same Lower East Side synagogue and the two fully trust each other. Today, Thursday, October 12, Meyer drops by to briefly chat with Rappaport, not about a young woman, but to have Leonard purchase stock for him in a company about to receive a large military contract; information derived from Dinty Moore's filming operations. Meyer hands Rappaport cash, encouraging him to also buy some. Meyer will invariably sell his shares after they double, and quotes the ancient Wall Street saw: "pigs get fat; hogs get slaughtered." However, this afternoon, he sadly tells Leonard, he's also visiting Lenox Hill's cancer wing for terminally ill patients.

▲

That same afternoon, two days after arriving in New York and fully recovered from his sixteen-hour flight, Franz Seis enters Romanoff & Abramson's offices. He is staying at the Biltmore, adjacent to Grand Central, having taken a room until Friday and is registered under his own name. Seis knows that the singular best disguise is to never hide; rather, to establish and publicly keep to a routine. Seis receives a 7:15 wakeup call, eats downstairs at 8:00, and reads newspapers in the lounge until 9:45. On Monday he walks to the 42nd Street Public Library where he spends the day reading and taking notes. At 7 PM he eats dinner in the hotel's ornate Bowman dining room overlooking Madison Avenue. After a leisurely coffee, he orders an H. Upmann cigar, compliments the restaurant's maitre d' and makes arrangements to have a young lady sent to his room.

Seis arrives at Romanoff & Abramson's office at precisely 1:15 PM. He knows that unexpected questions are most effective after lunch when people are often drowsy. Entering, however, it is obvious that something is wrong. The receptionist, a woman of grand-motherly age, looks up from her chair, eyes red from crying, as a young man, sitting next to her, gently strokes her hand and whispers to her.

"Oh, I'm sorry for the intrusion," Seis says. "Would it be better if I came back later?"

"No," politely says the young man, but surprises Seis with his crumpled work clothing in this clearly white-collar office building. "Is there any way we can assist you?"

"I'm looking for Aaron Abramson; is he in by any chance? I'm an old friend and wanted to drop by. We knew each other before the war."

"Aaron's in the hospital," the man pauses, "Well, more than that. He's not expected to survive the week. Cancer, I'm afraid. I arrived here from the hospital only minutes ago—"

The woman begins crying again, stands up, and excuses herself.

"I'm afraid Aaron's taken a turn for the worse. The doctors warned us, but the end is always unpleasant. By the way, there's something familiar about you, have we met?"

"I doubt it. The last time I was in New York was fifteen years ago," Seis smiles. "I was with the German delegation to the FIPEX stamp show. This is my first time back. I met Aaron then; a most decent man, considerate and well-informed. We stayed in touch until—"

The young man nods. "I wish I had better news, but visitors are still welcome, especially friends from the old days. Anything that can take his mind off... You'll only be allowed a short stay, although I'm sure he'll be delighted to see you." Lenox Hill Hospital's address is given, the corner florist recommended, and for the foreign visitor a cab suggested.

"Excuse me," says Seis before leaving and glancing down, "but your work shoes, they look like paratrooper boots. Are they by any chance?" He also notices that the young man wears an expensive if conservative gold wedding band.

"Yes sir, you're quite observant. I was in the Eighty-Second Airborne during the war," he smiles and puts his hand out. "My name is Harry Strong."

"And mine is Max Gruber; it is a pleasure to meet you, despite the circumstances." Seis bows slightly and shakes the young man's hand. "And I see you were an officer by your posture. West Point perhaps?"

"No, not West Point," Harry smiles. "But yes, an officer, a Major."

"You are related to Mr. Abramson by chance? And from Germany? I seem to detect both a slight accent and resemblance," Seis says, although he's never met Abramson.

"I'm afraid not, but since the war he's been second father. And yes, from Germany."

"Because of Hitler, all Germans have become refugees in one form or another, have we not? Prisoners in our own country. And, if I might ask, when did you flee?"

"My father took us out in early '33, when I was a boy."

"Jewish?"

"My mother was. My father is Lutheren, a decorated Great War combatant. And you?"

Probing, as Seis suddenly remembers, is a two-way street in America. For a fraction of a second he feels tongue-tied, then quickly composes his story. "I was fortunate. A skiing accident left me a mid-level factotum in the Food and Agricultural Ministry, stationed in Oslo and Copenhagen. Thankfully, it was the dullest possible employment during those sad years."

Seis shakes hands and says goodbye. Harry Strong, Major, Eighty-Second Airborne, he thinks. Is he a friend of the man who stole my stamps? He certainly doesn't look like the type of person who'd kill. But something's going on, he thinks. Despite Strong not looking Jewish, there are too many coincidences piling up.

Harry returns the handshake. Hadn't Hermann Seis been in the Food and Agricultural Ministry? And the more Harry reflects on it, the more this Gruber reminds him of Hermann Seis. As soon as the door closes he phones Lansky but, unable to reach him, only leaves a message that he'd called. However, he's running late to be back at his new construction project and doesn't think to call the hospital.

Chapter 42: Lenox Hill Hospital

Hat in one hand and floral bouquet in another, Franz Seis arrives on Lenox Hill's seventh floor. The indifferent middle-aged nurse, dressed in her starched-white uniform and cap, says Abramson has another visitor but he can go in anyway, although only briefly.

Just outside Abramson's private room, Seis puts on his gloves to avoid leaving fingerprints. Quietly knocking on the door, Seis hears a firm but quiet "come in." Abramson is half-sleeping and propped up by pillows.

A well-dressed man is sitting by the bedside but stands when Seis enters.

"I've been here long enough, Aaron" Meyer Lansky says, gently patting Abramson's hand. "I'll see you tomorrow." Lansky points to his chair for Seis to sit in, then leaves the room. Seis takes the vacant seat next to Abramson's bed.

Abramson, eyes now open, looks at Seis, confusion on his face.

"We met long ago, before the war at FIPEX," Seis says smiling. "My name is Abraham Cohen and I'm from Heidelberg. Do you remember me by any chance?"

Abramson shakes his head, not remembering the man or the stamp show.

This man has nothing left. Seis has seen enough over the years to know that death is only days away. The cancer's eaten the fat from his arms, and his face looks like a skull.

"I'm an associate of Simon Wiesenthal," Seis is pleased with the story he's invented and by Abramson's feeble smile of recognition. He's about to continue when the nurse walks in with a vase filled with the flowers Seis purchased. She looks at Abramson who's still smiling, puts the flowers on the window mantle with a half-dozen others, and quietly leaves.

"Dr. Wiesenthal instructed me to express his sympathies and hopes you're not in pain." Abramson smiles again, nodding his head to indicate there is no pain.

"I apologize for intruding, but Dr. Wiesenthal asked that I speak to you about a horde of stamps stolen from our people during the war. We're trying to locate the stamps and return them to any survivors."

"I understand," Abramson whispers.

"The man carrying these was shot as the war ended. We also know that the man who shot him was in the 82nd Airborne, apparently in the same Division as your friend Harry Strong."

Abramson groggily nods, then says, "The *Queen Mary*." Despite his confusion, deep within him he realizes something isn't right.

"The *Queen Mary?* Is that what you said? I don't understand."

"Harry... won the stamps... coming home..." Miraculously, Abramson remembers the cover story he, Lansky, Romanoff, and Harry arranged years earlier. "Playing craps... On the *Queen Mary*."

"Did Harry Strong win the stamps or was he the one who stole them?" Seis asks, instantly kicking himself for wording his question too sharply.

As if a bucket of water has been thrown on his face, Abramson is suddenly alert, his eyes open and bright.

"Who are you?" he gasps. "Who let you in? What in hell is going on? Nu—"

Seis grabs a pillow, throws it over Abramson's face, swings onto the bed, and kneels on top of the struggling, pathetically weak man. Don't damage his throat, Seis instinctively reminds himself. There's no chance Abramson has been heard, but nurses and guests wander in and out of rooms freely. Seis listens but no one is coming. Slowly he counts to thirty. Abramson stops moving at fourteen, but Seis cannot chance his regaining consciousness.

Standing, Seis carefully lays Abramson in a comfortable resting position, his face toward the window. Seis knows that in minutes the facial muscles will begin to relax, in half an hour his death will look entirely natural. Then he closes the door and slowly walks to the nurses' desk.

"That was quick," she says.

"He fell asleep almost immediately. Hopefully he'll be more alert tomorrow."

The nurse locks eyes with him, then shakes her head.

▲

So, Seis thinks, this Harry Strong acquired my stamps in a game of craps! This nice-looking young man won my stamps gambling. If that's not typical American luck! Hermann screws some girl in the grass, gets himself murdered by a sadistic paratrooper, who in turn loses them on the *Queen Mary*! Could *anything* be more stupid? More logical? More American?

Rather than take a cab, Seis walks over to the Lexington Avenue subway station at 77th street, watches for thirty seconds, slips the booth attendant a dollar for change, and goes through the turnstile. Four stops later he is at 42nd street and Grand Central. Here he has a shoeshine, smiling at the ridiculous sign saying, "Your shoes will smile, after an Izzy-shine." Seis looks at the wizened, clearly Jewish manager with barely concealed contempt, shaking his head at the number of Jews he sees everywhere.

Crossing the street, he stops for a cup of coffee and apple pie at the Automat, plunking in the requisite nickels with the zest of a little boy. Do New Yorkers know that Germans invented the Automat's vending machines and built them in Berlin? From here it is back to the library. Like Monday, he returns to the hotel, has dinner at 7 PM, and makes the same arrangements as the previous evening.

Reading both the *Times* and *Herald Tribune* Wednesday, Seis finds the obituary sections. He's delighted to see that the well-known lawyer, philanthropist, and philatelist, Aaron Abramson, died peacefully after a long illness. Seis sees no need to change his daily schedule before taking his scheduled Thursday plane home.

▲

Friday noon, October 20. Temple Emanu-El, at 65th and Fifth Avenue is home to New York's leading German-Jewish reform movement. The building itself follows a late Roman design used in Syria seventeen hundred years earlier. As Aaron Abramson's memorial service begins, the synagogue's fills with Beckendorfs, Harmers, Hersts, Lehmans, Loebs, Neubergers, Ochs', Saranoffs, the mayor, Romanoff, some Rockefellers, and hundreds of others.

Slipping into a rear aisle is a man as powerful as any of New York's print, financial and political leaders, but who cannot be seen with them. A few minutes later, a straight-backed young man enters. He is wearing a three-piece, striped, deep blue suit, looks around and nods to the man in dark glasses.

"There you are, Harry," the man whispers, taking off his hat but not his dark glasses. The two quietly talk, Meyer Lansky identifying the rich and powerful as they pay their respects to Abramson's family. "Something's been bothering me about Aaron's death. You were at the hospital until I arrived. How did he look to you?"

"He was obviously dying, although I never expected he would go that quickly."

"How much time did you give him?"

"A day or two before he'd slip into a coma or contract pneumonia."

"Just as I was about to leave, a German entered, someone I didn't know but who was wearing expensive clothing. He was about 5 feet 9 and middle aged, I never asked—"

"After I left the hospital," Harry interjects, "I went to the baron's office. Minutes later a German walked in saying he was an old friend of Aaron's. He was shocked to discover Aaron's condition and left saying he'd visit him at the hospital. It has to be the same person."

"Brace yourself," Lansky says, "but I think Aaron's 'friend' murdered him. One of the doctors on the floor noticed a slight discoloration around the throat and left eye—"

"Strangulation?"

"Strangulation *and* smothering, exactly. The doctor tried to suggest an autopsy to Penny, but she was so distraught by not being with Aaron at the end she didn't want to hear of it. By the time I found out, Aaron had been cremated."

Organ music begins playing as the synagogue hushes.

"Meyer," Harry whispers, shaking his head, "the German we met looked like Hermann Seis. And I let him walk away! With so much going on I just didn't put two and two together."

▲

Like many others, Abramson never truly believed that he'd die. When it came to putting his house in order he failed to tell Lansky, the baron, and Harry that, over the years, he'd purchased hundreds of Harry's stamps from Montclair. Equally short-sighted, like those who hope to be remembered by generations yet unborn, it never occurred to him that Penny or his children wouldn't want the stamps. Thus, amid the inevitable conflicts that no will can ever anticipate, the only category of family unity was to sell his stamps immediately or, more realistically, after the lawyers, accountants, and Uncle Sam scooped up what they could.

To sell the stamps, the baron recommended the internationally known auctioneers, Thistleman & Chandler, its roots stretching back a century. Probating Abramson's will, Thistleman's technical review, and the possibility of some long-forgotten relative suing led to the conclusion that the auction would be best held in parallel with New York's November 1951 Third Annual National Postage Stamp Show. Simultaneously, Harry decided to sell many of his remaining stamps, many motives in play—his failing marriage not the least of them.

The Abramson and "other" auction (Harry's stamps) promised to be one of the 1951 show's highlights. However, when Thistleman published the 256-page color catalogue, neither the baron nor Harry give it more than a cursory look.

Chapter 43: Munich, Late October 1950.

Returning to Munich, Seis joins Rudy and Ingrid in the Spangler dining room as he narrates his New York trip, omitting, of course, how Abramson died. The three harbor no illusions; after five years, many of the stamps are gone but it's also highly unlikely that any one firm sold them all. While Seis believes Abramson's dying assertion that Harry acquired them playing craps, he doesn't believe Harry possesses the sophistication to understand their value.

"Strong," Seis says, "would've been a reliable army *Stabsfeldwebel* (sergeant major) with us, but he's devoid of an officer's understanding. Once the stamps were his, he turned them over to Abramson, likely letting the Jew make a one-sided arrangement with him."

"But," Ingrid asks Rudy, "if Abramson ran Romanoff's auctions, how will the remaining stamps be sold? Given their value; if many remain, must not their sales flow through a well-known reputable dealer?"

"Why?" Seis wants to know.

"It would be like a local tennis tournament," Ingrid smiles shrewdly, "and trying to slip in a Wimbledon champion. It couldn't be done because it couldn't be done."

"Very true," Rudy nods. "Auction houses can't change their stripes over-night. Trust is only achieved after decades of effort. And the firm must be American. While Europe is recovering, few companies, even British, have the cash to acquire our collection."

"So," says Seis, "what does this mean?"

"It means," Rudy responds, "that I should begin contacting major American auction houses and request future catalogues as well as those from the past few years.

"I assume, Spangler, that you know which companies to contact."

"I'd start with Thistleman & Chandler; they're at the top of a list I threw together."

"Don't believe him," Ingrid laughs, "he spent hours on it."

"After that," says Rudy blushing, "there's Costales, Fox, H. R. Harmer—who sold Roosevelt's stamps—Herst, Kelleher's, Regency-Superior, Serebrakian, and others. Adding us to their mailing lists is only a bit more work. This should be done as a professional courtesy, especially as we're a small European company and haven't ruffled any feathers. Also, for legal reasons, all keep careful records. Larger auctioneers mimeograph copies of their sales. For them, it's helpful when you're competing to buy someone's collection that you can show how well your sales previously did."

"And once the catalogs begin to arrive?" Seis asks, pondering the likely expenses he must advance. "I assume this will be slow and tedious, like during the war?"

"There is no other way to discover if our stamps are being sold," Rudy replies, "other than comparing our master list with stamps being auctioned."

"Therefore, we'll have to hire people, won't we? A little bit different from our past requisitioning, isn't it? Must we actually pay people to work? What is the world coming to, my friend?" Seis chuckles at his own joke, then realizes how he enjoys laughing again. "And how many might we need?" he asks, bracing for the worse.

"One person," says Rudy. "He or she would begin the comparison work when the catalogs begin to arrive. A second to retype the master list—"

"Naturally. If something ever happened to that... And the typist would have other work to do." Seis nods, thinking out loud. "More than enough to keep her busy for months. They would have to work in your shop Rudy; carefully supervised by you and Ingrid. Such work would arouse no suspicion in a stamp shop. But when might this begin?"

"I will compose a form letter, subject to your review of course, and begin sending them to America. But the process is slow. I would suggest that we enclose a check for postage—"

"And why would that be?" Seis asks, annoyed as he pictures cash flying from his new Munich bank account.

"It will show that we are serious and recognize the high cost of mailing. The better the company the more expensive the catalogue. Many of these run hundreds of pages on quality stock. And today, higher valued stamps are often reproduced in color. A person expecting to pay $1,000 for a single stamp wants to examine it carefully before considering a bid."

"And the auction house needs the highest resolution photograph to place in the catalog. Yes, that's sensible. And might I assume that I'd have other costs besides salaries?"

"We'll certainly need a professional grade typewriter and some sort of typing table. To say nothing of a work table, some chairs, at least one bookcase, stationary, and— "

"And the list will go on, won't it?" Seis sighs. "What is the old British expression; 'in for a penny, in for a pound?' Well, let's see if we get any responses before we spend too much."

While Seis is pleased by his progress, he sees no reason to tell the Spanglers about how Harry Strong acquired his stamps. There is still something in Abramson's last words that strike him as odd. But what exactly is it? Try as he might, he cannot put his finger on it.

▲

Seis begins work for Gehlen October 23. The building is prototypically Germanic, a rectangular bureaucratic pyramid—like a Mayan or Aztec temple—where each upper, smaller floor represents higher administrative authority. Despite the depressing architecture, there is a sense of urgency caused by June's North Korean invasion of the south. Now, with Douglas MacArthur's advance towards the Yalu River, rumors fly that China might enter the war or that Stalin has a winter surprise up his sleeve. Is an invasion of West Germany in the offing?

Seis works one floor below Gehlen and soon discovers that the laborious double- and triple-checking that characterized espionage efforts four months earlier have evaporated. Quick answers result in downtime he wouldn't have considered possible. And for him, less paperwork gives him time to develop plans to return to America, to claim control of his stamps, and to avenge his sister and brother. This later quest is something that he is certain Harry Strong can lead him to for there seems no possibility that Strong has forgotten the name of a man he bested in craps. How he hopes that bastard is still alive!

▲

By February, Seis and the Spanglers are delighted to find that American stamp auction companies are responding to their request for catalogues. Although they arrive slowly—all standard mail is sent by sea—none have more than a handful of "their" stamps. A large auction house having a few similar stamps is written off as coincidence; what Rudy wants are numerous, bunched together stamps.

To do the research and typing, Ingrid selects two university students who know nothing about stamps. She, Rudy, and Seis assume that the less philatelic knowledge the students have the better; that way there'll be less "what's-this-all-about?" questions.

May 14's weather is unseasonably chilly. Ingrid, as always, briskly sorts through the mail, barely glancing at two catalogs. She silently hands them to Rudy who, preoccupied, gives them and other mail to one of the students. Already backlogged, the catalogues are placed, unopened, at the bottom of a growing pile. The names Thistleman & Chandler and H. R. Harmer mean nothing to the students. However, they do represent more work; enough has accumulated so that both will remain employed through the summer.

The following evening, as Rudy absent-mindedly closes the shop, he notices the unopened catalogues. He is not busy and, to an idle Rudy, large unopened envelopes are like chocolate to a child. He wonders why he didn't notice them earlier. Fifteen minutes later comes the "Eureka" moment for which he, Seis, and Ingrid have been praying.

The Thistleman & Chandler catalog runs 256 pages; the firm announcing not only the auction of the late Aaron Abramson as well as a large selection of pre-war rarities from a "private" source. As Rudy opens the envelope, he finds himself facing a cover with a dozen stamps surrounding Abramson's photo. But the stamps! My God, the stamps! Rudy tries to call Ingrid, but discovers he has no voice. Staggering, he trips, loudly crashing to the floor, simultaneously laughing and cursing like a sailor in a bar at 3 AM.

"Are you all right?" Ingrid anxiously calls.

"No, I mean yes," Rudy is in shock and pain, and his voice croaks. "Please come, hurry!"

As Ingrid enters she sees Rudy sprawled, spread-eagle on the floor with a lopsided grin.

"Look," he whispers, pointing with his finger to the catalog that is just beyond his reach. "Look, they're here!"

▲

Ten minutes later, Seis arrives, tie askew, his usual controlled look gone. As Rudy flips the pages, excitedly pointing to one stamp after another, Seis's face becomes a rainbow of emotions. After a few seconds of skepticism, he too is elated.

"Finally, after all these years!" Seis says, at first not realizing that he is speaking aloud. "Excellent work Spangler. Excellent." He is so overcome with emotion that he clicks his heels, shakes Rudy's hand, and bows to Ingrid. He is about to reflexively say, "The Führer would be proud," but catches himself in the nick of time.

A minute later, Seis is lost in his thoughts as his brain charges forward.

Despite having bedded him on a half-dozen occasions, for the first time, Ingrid finds herself "reading" his unguarded eyes. What Ingrid sees are the inward deliberations of a mass-murderer, the man who had so badly frightened Rudy years earlier. Ingrid doesn't have to be told that her and Rudy's lives are in danger as never before.

Chapter 44: Bonn, March 31, 1951

Frederick Hirschfeld, the man responsible for Seis's capture and Marianne Seis's death, now thirty-seven, has taken a new name. Now under the alias Nicholas Altrock, he manages the government's tax department reviewing small business returns. Invariably, he follows staff recommendations, careful not to make waves as he gradually learns what his sinecure entails. The position is courtesy of the Counter Intelligence Corps which, indifferent to Hirschfield's tactics, was pleased with its former employee's results.

Hirschfeld's divorce has been finalized and he lives in Bonn on the third floor of a walk-up, in a one-bedroom flat with a partial view of the Rhine. His small CIC pension and salary mostly go to his ex-wife and three-year-old twins. The apartment is sparsely furnished but teaming with piles of Bonn's *General Anzeiger,* the *Frankfurter Allgemeine Zeitung,* the U.S. military's *Stars and Stripes* (a good way to practice English), and numerous "boulevard" newspapers—tabloids sold on streets with sensational, easy-to-read news. While he wants to own a TV, alimony payments preclude such extravagance.

This Saturday, Hirschfield, who owns no car, decides to bike from Bonn to Cologne, an easy twenty-two mile ride. With luck, he might encounter a female biker riding with the same purpose. Assuming he again might be unsuccessful and forced to spend a night alone in a hostel, he carefully lays out the necessities that fit into his small bike basket.

Hirschfield finishes his preparations by 9:30 AM. and is beginning a second cup of coffee when he hears a knock on his door.

"Herr Altrock?" a friendly voice inquires.

Hirschfield (Altrock), who is expecting no one, decides not to answer.

The man knocks again. "Herr Altrock, I know you're in because no papers are outside your door. My name is Albert Funk and I'm with *Der Spiegel* ("The Mirror").

Hirschfield sighs, "Please slide your card under the door." There is nothing else he can do. *Der Spiegel* is a powerful weekly, its format copied from *Time* magazine. It first published in January 1947 and quickly became known for aggressive reporting. *Der Spiegel's* first great scoop, and the reason Hirschfield is living in Bonn, is that, when Bonn was selected over Frankfurt as West Germany's capital, the close vote was determined by Bonn's representatives bribing members of the *Bundestag*. No, Hirschfield thinks, bending down and giving the card a cursory look, with *Der Spiegel's* circulation of 250,000, cooperation can only help his career.

"Come in," he says, opening the door and bowing slightly, "and please excuse the fact that my cleaning lady didn't come yesterday— "

"No, no," says Funk. "I'm a bachelor too. But have I come at a bad time? Were you about to leave?"

Hirschfeld physically relaxes. Funk is four-inches shorter, carries a dull-brown briefcase, wears a sport jacket, slacks, and a green Tyrolian hat with a red feather. The combination screams: I am dull and boring without wealth or status. In short, a typical reporter. He asks Funk to sit, pours coffee, offers the better of two frayed chairs, then sits and takes out his pipe.

"Now, how can I help you?" Hirschfield asks.

"I am afraid that this might be an unpleasant subject," Funk begins. "First, before we begin, you should know that in any future article you won't be identified by your original name, Bonn, or even working for the government. As for my presence, *Der Spiegel* is in the process of investigating certain abuses by the American CIC when you were in their employ, Herr Altrock. Or should I say Hirschfeld?" Funk says slowly, as Hirschfeld stiffens in his chair.

"Perhaps it is better if you leave."

"Please," Funk smiles. "I wouldn't be here unless *Der Spiegel* had been given your name by certain citizens at the highest levels. You, and indeed a half-dozen like you, have been or shortly will be interviewed. Let me personally assure you that both Bonn and *Der Spiegel* are interested in American abuses, not in those who were pressured into carrying out our conqueror's orders. For this reason, only Hirschfeld's name will appear."

"And if I refuse; politely of course."

"Look around you and think of your twins and former wife. You cannot afford to retire, can you? It's impossible to start a new career without letters of recommendation these days, *Ja*? Or, and let us think constructively and look at the positive side of the coin; if you're interested in advancement, your assistance for this article would be noted by those who suggested that I call on you."

▲

In fact, it is Franz Seis who is sitting in front of Hirschfeld. He is using Funk's business card as the writer had approached him months before and left his card. Seis hopes that Hirschfeld will not double check, for the man must be fully cognizant of his own release from prison months earlier.

Seis finds himself energized by this cat and mouse game. He removes an American yellow legal pad and furiously takes notes, at times asking Hirschfeld to speak "a bit slower." For thirty minutes Seis asks and Hirschfeld answers, mostly honestly in Seis's opinion, questions relating to the CIC's successful plans to ensnare former SS members and Marianne Seis.

"Didn't she suspect something when the two of you were in Stuttgart removing SS tattoos that winter?" Seis asks.

"Afterwards she thought how stupid we'd been allowing over 150 men into the rooms we rented that weekend. Some of these men were so asinine that they wore their ankle length black SS overcoats! 'We might as well have advertised in the *Stuttgarter Zeitung*' Marianne said, but she never considered that our being spotted was anything but accidental."

"And so, when you told her that you had arranged work for her brother— "

"She was delighted. She jumped over and gave me a huge kiss!"

"Didn't you feel any guilt?"

"Of course, I felt guilt. I am human, am I not? But it was my job. Work that no patriotic German with any sensibilities and feelings could find satisfying. That winter the Americans forced us to do distasteful, disgusting things. You may quote me on that—"

"Are you sure?" Seis sips more coffee, does Hirschfeld know how bad it is?

"Yes. But not for attribution. Would that corporal Hitler had died in the trenches during the Great War! All our lives have been ruined by that mad bastard. Undoubtedly, if I hadn't been selected that winter to capture Seis, it would have been somebody else."

Seis might as well be listening to a recording. Hirschfield's answers, if not in a sing-song voice, are by rote. "Even though, I assume, you were lovers by that time?" Seis asks.

"Oh yes, from the first day we met. It wasn't planned, but was one of those things—*of the moment*. She was a few years older, but it made our two painful lives better."

"I am told she was in love with you, is it true? That always makes a better story for our readers."

"Yes, I think she was. She even hinted at marriage once, but I was still legally married."

"But were you in love?"

Hirschfeld leans forward, confidentially whispering. "No, not in love. I liked her, but why marry an older woman—she was my wife's age, you know—without money when there were so many younger, more attractive ones to choose from elsewhere? This isn't for your readers, of course, but she was magnificent in bed. A real find for me. I couldn't stop—"

In a natural motion, as if he is just standing to refill his cup, Seis is on his feet, takes a step forward, grabs Hirschfeld's arm with his left hand and yanks him forward, twisting his wrist just enough and using his right hand to make sure that Hirschfeld lands on his back. The move takes only a second and Hirschfeld, fighting to keep his balance, lands softly.

As if from far away, Seis is already judging his performance. Perhaps he has lost a step over the years, but then so has Hirschfeld.

"This is the second time I have bested you," Seis laughs.

Seis straddles the horrified Hirschfeld, his left hand on the man's jaw, holding the back of his head to the floor. Reaching his right hand into a pocket, Seis produces a 4½-inch Italian switchblade. The "click" of the knife's button, releasing the spring, seems to resonate through the apartment, the stiletto-like blade pinching the skin below Hirschfeld's Adam's Apple.

"And did you poison her too?"

"For God's sake, it wasn't me!"

Seis says nothing, waiting.

"A CIC officer named 'Baker.' He did it. He was the man I reported to."

"That was his real name?"

"None of them used their real names with us. They treated us like shit. You know that."

"Tell me about him," now applying pressure with his knife. "What was his first name?"

"I never learned it. He insisted I call him 'Captain.' I only knew that he was a Polish policeman from Chicago. He was the officer who tripped you the day you were captured."

Seis nods. "My sister. She was poisoned in your apartment?"

"Yes."

"Why?"

"Baker only said that it must be done. That if he'd been given permission I would've been dead too. Like most Poles he hated us Germans. Me, you, all of us."

"And you were there when she was poisoned? You watched and said nothing?"

"What could I do? I noticed him slip something into her tea but... it never dawned on me that... how could I stop him? I was helpless." Hirschfeld's fear and the knife at his throat are reducing his voice to a whisper.

"Did you sleep with her the night before?"

"Yes."

"And did you know all along what this Baker was going to do?"

"No. How could I possibly—"

This time the knife punctures the skin like a pinprick, drawing a few drops of blood.

"Yes. He told me beforehand not to be surprised if something unexpected happened."

Seis does nothing, he is thinking about something. For a moment, he seems to relax. Hirschfeld's breathing slows as he anticipates Seis rising, the information he wanted now given.

Seis slowly rises but without warning plunges the knife into Hirschfeld's throat, jiggling it like a driver switching gears in a complex clutch then, jumps back. Hirschfeld's neck becomes a geyser of blood as he wriggles over the floor. Finally, he gets to one knee as his hands try to stop the pain, the loss of blood, and the shock of knowing he is dying. Then he topples over.

An unexpected thought flashes through Seis's mind; Hermann would have been so delighted to see this. Seis walks to the tiny kitchen, scrubs his hands, the chair, his coffee cup and saucer, and quietly ransacks the room. He empties the dead man's wallet and gives the apartment a final visual sweep. Not until reaching his car and driving a few miles does he stop to remove the contact lenses and toupee, only then realizing how satisfied he feels. Not only has he avenged his sister, but he's also learned about this American policeman named Baker.

Chapter 45: A Chat with General Gehlen.

Nine days later Seis is asked to report to General Gehlen's office.

"You are doing excellent work, Franz," he says, "not that I expected anything less."

"Thank you, sir, and a belated happy birthday."

The spymaster gestures for him to sit, has coffee poured, then waits until the two are alone. "You have a good memory, my friend. I was forty-nine, April 3. At my age, one begins to realize how lucky I've been, alive and enjoying the blessings of this year's gorgeous spring. Do you realize my birthday also happened to be the day that the body of Frederick Hirschfeld, an SS comrade of ours, was found? Do you recall his name by any chance?"

"Of course. He was the man who betrayed my sister, myself, and almost two hundred former comrades. If he's dead, I couldn't be happier. I can only hope it was painful."

"It must have been the way his throat was punctured; a horrible, gaping wound. You'd thoroughly enjoy the autopsy photos, *Ja*? Unfortunately, you've become a logical suspect given your sister's murder, your recent release from prison, and your current access to confidential information. If I might possibly inquire, where you were the last weekend of March?"

"I was in Frankfurt am Main. Since I am single, I have no hesitation stating that I was with an unmarried young lady. Might I assume that her name is unimportant?"

Gehlen nods for Seis to continue.

"We stayed at the Steigenberger Hotel and—"

"Were undoubtedly seen by many people. Naturally, I would have expected no less and will be pleased to tell certain authorities just that. Theater tickets, hotel, and restaurant receipts, the usual all saved? Of course, they were. Perhaps one or two memorable moments over the weekend that no staff would forget. Correct?"

"Quite so. As a matter of fact, the cleaning staff accidentally damaged the woman's strapless brassiere. It temporarily caused a bit of a commotion and forced me to be firm with some of the hotel's employees. A most unfortunate incident."

"As I am sure it was," Gehlen says. Both men smile.

"Franz, privately I understand what you did and why. Hirschfeld was a disgrace to us during the war as was his later groveling to the Americans; a Judas who should've been dealt with earlier. Fortunately, the first people who went through his rooms fell under my bailiwick. When the Bonn police arrived, there were no fingerprints other than Hirschfield's, and the money in his wallet gone. His death has been recorded as a robbery that spiraled out of control."

Seis nods, relieved that the conversation is about to end and slowly rises to his feet until Gehlen put his hand up for him to sit again.

"Two things, Franz. First, while I remain in full sympathy with your anger at Hirschfeld, his superior when he worked for the CIC was—"

"A Captain Baker, I believe."

"Yes, and a man who's risen rapidly in American intelligence. He has an instinctive nose for the Reds. His contributions to our side were and continue to be significant. I've therefore taken steps so his files won't be available to anyone in West Germany, you included, without my written permission. If anything happened to him, I would be deeply distressed—"

"And I would find myself in East Berlin, at best."

"Good. It is important that we understand each other on this. Second, I have a token of my affection for you." Gehlen stretches his hand out to Seis who leans forward and finds himself holding a blank, upside-down business card.

"No, don't turn it over just yet," says Gehlen. "Do you know who this belonged to?"

Seis shakes his head and gestures that he has no idea.

"It was Albert Funk's, Franz. The next time that you decide to do a person in, please do *not* leave someone's business card lying around with your fingerprints on it."

Seis, his face red with embarrassment, can only bow his head.

"It *does* takes a while to get back into this business, doesn't it?" Gehlen smiles, then pauses. "Also, if I might; an additional word. Poor Mr. Funk died forty-five days ago while skiing in Austria with his wife. Ran into a tree; in front of a dozen people. Quite thoughtless of him, wasn't it? And thank you again for your kind birthday thoughts."

Chapter 46: New York, Central Park, June 1951

Central Park's biggest lake is crowded with boaters on this lovely June Saturday. Now four, Jimmy Gavin Strong sits excitedly in the rowboat's narrow bow giving directions and shouting warnings, the important work Harry has given him, while Harry rows contentedly. On the boat's back seat is two-year-old Suzanne, the correct, pretentious pronunciation of her name *Su-zon* according to her mother. Sadly, Harry thinks, Nan already has thespian aspirations for their daughter whose name she spells in the French manner. Suzanne, meanwhile, happily sings to herself, as her eyes dart from one exciting sight to another.

Saturday is Harry's happiest day of the week, alone with his children. Most of all Harry enjoys the rowing. Although it is not obvious, he is carefully watching both children and, as he smokes, he can let his mind wander. He knows he is not introspective by nature, but he wishes that his father and mother were alive to see their grandchildren. Poor Dad. He now knows that his father was involved in building and dismantling sites for A-bomb tests. It was sometime then that he contracted the Leukemia that killed him. Yet, so typical of his father, there was not just a stoical acceptance, but also a continual refusal to speculate as to its causes. "Overall, I've been a very lucky man," is all his father would say as the end approached.

This afternoon, Jimmy was told that they'll land on the one-tree hundred-square foot island. It's in the middle of the seven-foot deep, eighteen-acre lake built over swampland ninety-years earlier. Jimmy holds a small American flag and will plant it on the artificial island. Next, they will inspect other sights; the stream that enters the lake on 77th street, adjacent to it the cave with iron bars in front—installed fifteen years earlier to discourage public fornication. Nearby is another inlet where pirates landed, and a rock formation where saber-tooth tigers still lurk. At this point, Harry will growl ferociously as the children giggle in delight. There are other sights and stories, some of which might even be true.

In all, Harry will time their slow circuit so that the children are not in the sun too long. Once landing—always a dramatic occurrence—they'll go to the boat house's restaurant. Here they'll have a lunch that includes a hot dog, soda, and Dixie Cup. The latter is the meal's highlight as they open the chocolate-vanilla ice cream cup and see the picture under the lid. Afterward they'll walk home, or as far as Suzanne can make it, Harry invariably carrying her the last few blocks.

And, Harry knows, he's also been lucky. The children are his second life. Unlike Nan, he doesn't care in which neighborhood they live or the size of their apartment. Gradually, he realizes that he is seeing less and less of his Mount Hermon and Amherst friends, few of whom have been as financially fortunate and don't seem comfortable visiting. Evenings with them means an inexpensive restaurant and going to movies, or having a home cooked dinner and playing bridge afterward, things that Nan increasingly avoids. Nan's friends, all acquired since her Schenectady and Smith days, are in advertising, journalism, the theater—while some of them are interesting, he has nothing in common with most of them.

Saturday afternoons are also Nan's time off from the kids. Harry has learned not to ask what she does, although he knows she's invariably shops along Fifth Avenue. And their marriage? Harry is now aware that their mutual success is pulling them apart. Nan's live television commercials are done in "prime-time," including weekends. Other than formal two-week vacations where they rent beachside cottages in East Hampton, they often go without seeing each other for days.

▲

For Harry, Alice Denham is a pleasant accident. He and two contractors are having dinner at the Grotta Azzurra restaurant in Little Italy. The eatery, named after the blue grotto on the island of Capri, in its forty-third year, is the go-to dining spot for Italians and their descendants from Enrico Caruso to Frank Sinatra. The dinner itself, a low-pressure meeting, more congratulatory than negotiating, is to confirm certain details concerning the Teamsters' Union and 696 Fifth Avenue, Harry's new project. Representing the Teamsters' are Anthony Provenzano ("Tony Pro") and Johnny Dio (Dioguardi), both high-level members in Carlo Gambino's family. The three have just ordered their third bottle of rosé champagne and are feeling no pain as they finish the house specialty, *Lobster Fra Diavolo* and pasta.

Since the restaurant is on Mulberry Street, Harry delights them by reciting some stanzas from Dr. Seuss' book that he'd read to his children a few nights earlier concluding with:

> *... And that is the story that no one can beat,*
> *And to think that I saw it on Mulberry Street.*

Harry knows that both are, mistresses aside, family men. His bringing family into the conversation emphasizes that this is more than a business dinner—it's a meal among friends. They laugh and clap as Harry had hoped but, if truth be known, he'd spent half an hour earlier memorizing the lines.

Nevertheless, at times as they down their wine and pasta, their attention is drawn to the next table where a young girl, gorgeous and voluptuous, is having an agitated conversation with a boyfriend. Harry's eyes all but popped when he first saw her enter; neck-length black hair, tight jeans, a partially unbuttoned, tight, short-sleeved white shirt, no brassiere, and designer Lille Dache's "Flying Saucer" floppy hat worn at a ridiculous angle. The men at the table nudge each other, sigh and laugh but she is with a good-looking, thirty-something man with thick, jet-black hair, so that is that.

Or at least until the boyfriend leans over and leeringly whispers something in her ear. She slaps him in the face, hard, and begins to stand. The boyfriend, instantly enraged, moves first, simultaneously pushing her back into her chair with his left hand.

"You bitch!" he says, then punches her in the nose with his right hand.

Harry springs from his chair, whirls the ex-boyfriend around, giving a vicious uppercut to the man's diaphragm. Down the boyfriend goes, vomiting. Johnny Dio, a man not shy to take advantage of his movie star looks, kneels by the fallen man's side, removes the wallet, and takes out his cash. He knows the restaurant ownership, the Davino family, and speaking to them in rapid Italian, gave the Davinos the money. Then, keeping the young man's driver's license, he walks him out of the restaurant—none too gently once out of the dining room—makes sure he would never bother the girl again, and deposits him in the gutter.

Harry meanwhile sits down next to the girl, gently feels her nose, wraps ice inside a napkin, and stops the flow of blood. There will be some swelling the next day he tells her, likely a black eye, but nothing is broken. To ensure that there'll be no problems, Harry gallantly suggests it would be best if he took her home. Which he does, thus initiating an affair.

Part VI: Final Preparations.

Chapter 47: Munich, Summer 1951

In his office, Seis reviews Otto Klaber's files. He knows Klaber and remembers he is over six feet tall, has a lanky build, and hails from Cleveland, Ohio. Like a few thousand German-Americans, Klaber left the U.S. to fight for Germany when World War II began. In Klaber's case, he walked away from Purdue a year short of an engineering degree and was instantly welcomed by the Fatherland. Given the deeply held, often fanatical beliefs of those Americans who slipped into Germany, the physically fit often joined Himmler's *Waffen* SS.

Seis sees that Klaber's education and attitude immediately identified him as officer corps material. Klaber's requisite year of military experience began in the *SS Totenkopf* (Death's head) Division, including participating in the 1940 massacre of 100 Royal Norfolk Regiment prisoners who, trapped at Dunkirk, the Germans lined up against a farm wall near La Paradis, France and machine-gunned. Soon after, Klaber became a second-lieutenant and survived the disastrous winter of 1941 in which four-fifths of the division become casualties. Advancing rapidly, he was a major when he was badly wounded in 1943's epic battle of Kursk.

Seis discovers this because of German record keeping proclivity, the information remarkably thorough until the war's last weeks. In the murky days of April and early May 1945, ODESSA took control of most SS's files. One of their remarkably successful goals was to create new homes and hide these and other SS in the U.S. by using the identity of the dead German-Americans. These ex-SS then applied in the dead man's name for a "misplaced" birth certificate and social security number. Later these men found employment through the help of hundreds of U.S. businessmen who remained Nazi sympathizers. (Not until 1957 will the FBI accidentally uncovered the program, far too late to identify all but a handful.)

In the late 1940s, as Seis learns, a score of ODESSA chose to live in the hamlet of Yaphank, New York. Located in south-central Long Island, its sandy soil was unsuitable for sustained agriculture or indeed very much of anything. During

World War I, it became an Army training camp known for patriotic songs and a musical revue (*Yip Yip Yaphank*), written by draftee Irving Berlin. There, Berlin also wrote such numbers as *Oh how I hate to get up in the morning* and *America the Beautiful*. In the 1930s, pro-Nazi businessmen purchased much of the land naming it Camp Siegfried. Here, young American-Aryans happily saluted the swastika every morning and goose-stepped to their heart's content as they marched down streets named for Hitler, Hess, Goebbels, and Goering.

Following the war, most of the land became the Brookhaven Atomic National Laboratory. Nevertheless, a hundred or so homes in Yaphank remained part of a smaller sub-community. This enclave, supported by restrictive land covenants, effectively barred anyone—especially Jews and African-Americans—from owning property. The ODESSA members in Yaphank find themselves doubly blessed; not just alive but also living in an oasis of Nazi beliefs where, by avoiding politics and keeping to their own business, they are not bothered.

While most *Waffen SS* veterans want only to live out their days peacefully, others miss the excitement, bullying, and, yes, killing. Then, as Seis excitedly discovers, General Gehlen and his CIA counterpart, German-speaking Admiral Roscoe Hillenkoetter, agree to use Yaphank volunteers for classified "wet work" inside the Iron Curtain. While Germans remain hated in Eastern Europe, Americans are always, if unofficially, popular, and Yaphank's ODESSA, so clearly American, prove exceptionally effective. If many selected by the Gehlen-Hillenkoetter team are certifiable psychopaths, they are highly functional and not the monosyllabic, slobbering-at-the- mouth creatures Hollywood so often portrays.

One of these is Klaber, who, in 1943-44, while recuperating, briefly worked for Seis. Coincidentally, by mid-1950, after South Korea's invasion, Klaber begins receiving assignments in Poland, Lithuania and Latvia, the geographic area which is Seis's official bailiwick.

▲

In July 1951, after a successful Polish assignment, Klaber returns to Munich. Seis invites him to dinner at the Halali restaurant, Munich's most expensive. As Klaber knows Seis will foot the bill, he orders roast pheasant, other Halali signature dishes and "Jack in black," as American officers call Jack Daniel's Black Label. Seis, who can't expense the meal, ruefully watches while Klaber, smartly dressed, belts down a third shot before turning to business. Only then does Seis broach work in America, something prohibited by West German–U.S. protocols. Klaber is interested; he enjoys his profession and, being human, can always use additional money.

Quickly Seis reviews the history and goals involved.

"Stamp dealers?" Klaber says. "My God, we might as well deploy ourselves against children. This will be like the eastern front in '41! Wonderful days, weren't they, Franz? The happiest in my life, that's for damn sure. Stamp dealers, eh? I think I should pay you," the two then have long laughs comparing philatelists with the Jews and Communist party officials that they "ran across" that summer.

"But," Seis says. "The people you'll be calling on are wealthy and undoubtedly some will be well guarded. And the man who inherited the stamps is a former paratrooper."

"A dangerous character?" Klaber asks, his interested piqued after his fifth Black Label.

"Intellectually, no. He appears to be common enough, and coincidentally he's the man who won our stamps by playing craps with the man who assassinated my brother. But he is a strong physical specimen—"

"At least there will be one challenge for me—"

"No, I need him to talk. Afterwards... who cares."

Klaber sighs, for he enjoys besting physical equals. "Once you are in America, will we have time to adjust your plans if necessary?"

"At least a week. I'll also need considerable intelligence work on your part. There's another individual too; a Pole who poisoned my sister. He's working for the CIA and lives near Washington. For him, a suspicious death will result in an investigation by the FBI, CIA, and General Gehlen. Before committing yourself, think it through. I'll leave the U.S. afterward, but you'll have no such choice. Either way, I'll need your advice. I'm intelligent enough to know what I don't know about America and I want to avoid overreaching."

"Yes, neither of us wants to go beyond our limits," Klaber says as the waiter comes by to ask if there is interest in a dessert, coffee or an aperitif.

"All three," says Klaber as Seis inwardly winces. "Your crème brûlé with potted nectarine and mocha bean ice cream is always superb, your best Columbian coffee, and a good Austrian *Marillenschnaps* would be perfect."

"To continue," Klaber says after Seis orders coffee. "From what you've said; for me, murdering Baker, which entails only modest dollar benefits, is another story. This is especially true given your limited time in America. Therefore, I'd respectfully advise you against it."

"Is that a firm no?"

"On the contrary," Klaber grins. "It could be far more interesting."

Seis gives Klaber Baker's name and Harry's. However, the previous year he found to his dismay that in the Manhattan phone book were a dozen Henry, Heinrich and H. Strongs.

Chapter 48: Veronica.

Back in the U.S., Klaber spends over a week in Washington and then New York. Finding "Baker" is easy. After a few days stake-out of the modest, single detached home in an Arlington neighborhood of identical post war homes near North Quincy and Washington Boulevard, he discovers Baker works in the Pentagon. On his way there, he drops off his wife who's a coffee house waitress. They have no children, are homebodies, and aren't affectionate in public. In fact, from what he observes, not in private either. At night, the upper and lower floor lights go off hours apart. The only problem is that Baker frequently travels and is always armed. As for kidnapping the wife, she's Baker's age but quite stout. Klaber writes Seis that he feels Baker wouldn't care if Baker's wife went missing. Actually, he might even pay them.

Finding Harry proves more difficult. In fact, there are more Strongs in the phone book than Seis realized. Not until Klaber's eighth try does he hit pay dirt. This call is answered by a maid who says that Mr. Strong is at a construction site but that a message can be left at his office. Klaber calls Big Al's office, says he must send a business letter, and in return receives Harry's title (vice president and project manager) and corporate address.

Seis goes to the Madison Avenue address of what turns out to be an impressively designed block-long, twenty-one-story affair with set-back tiers of floors, ribbon-like windows girding the entire structure and looking, Klaber thinks, a bit like the multiple layers of a Swiss torte cake. As Klaber examines the building, given the number of people entering and leaving, he realizes that there'll be no easy way to spot Harry Strong. But didn't Seis mention that Strong was working on a construction site?

Klaber assumes Harry will take the Lexington Ave. and 68th Street subway stop, and for two days stakes out a rotating position in the shadows of the Third Avenue elevated train. Here he can watch everyone leaving 260 East 66th Street, which faces north. But no one matches Harry's description. Not until the second afternoon, by accident, does he spot at 65th street a tall man in a bombardier jacket and boots who's carrying a briefcase. The combination sticks out like a sore thumb. Klaber is too much of a professional to run or even walk rapidly, but he reaches 65th street just as the man turns into a south entrance of Manhattan house.

Thursday morning sees Klaber again in wait. He easily tails the unsuspecting Harry to 696 Fifth Avenue; an invigorating mile walk, for Harry sets a fast pace. The following morning, just after Harry has left and turns the corner, Klaber casually approaches the south-side Manhattan House doorman. This man is a beefy, officious Irishman—clearly an ex-cop who spent twenty-five years on the beat.

"Wasn't that Major Strong who just left?" Klaber asks, affecting a bit of hesitation.

"Yes, sir. Do you know him?"

"I thought I recognized him," Klaber says with a smile. "We were both in the Eighty-Second. Small world. So, he lives here, nice digs," he says, nodding with approval.

"May I tell him your name, sir?"

"Yes, please do. It's Harry Johnson, but I wasn't an officer so he might not remember me. But we both remember D-Day and the Bulge." Klaber smiles knowingly, recalling non-existent memories. "He's married now, I assume. And children?"

"Yes sir, a lovely son and daughter. The boy's in pre-school."

"Already? My god, how time flies." Klaber knows that he's asked all the questions he can from this professionally suspicious doorman. "Please tell him I'm still in the service but on leave," Klaber says, tips his hat and walks in the opposite direction that Harry went.

Children, Klaber thinks, this is getting easier by the minute. By noon, the doorman has already forgotten the brief, unimportant conversation.

Later, Klaber walks to the east side's 67th street public library. In nice weather nannies and mothers take the very young to playgrounds. He once abducted a three-year-old in Latvia and, after negotiations and returning the unharmed child, the distraught father, a high-level official, proved easy to extort. Now, far less is needed; this will be a one-time action: exchange the kid for the stamps, then kill the parents. He hopes that Seis doesn't want to kill the child—not that he personally minds, but because Seis doesn't understand how American newspapers feast on this type of story.

At the library, Klaber discovers he's only blocks away from the Rockefeller Institute and the city's St. Catherine's playground, named after a church that sold the property decades earlier. Later, sitting in the playground, he sees mothers and nannies (many wearing nurses' uniforms) wheeling baby carriages and coming from 66th street. The children are either infants or toddlers and many of the women seem to know each other. But none carry a sign saying, "I am Harry Strong's wife (or nanny) and have his child." It's another false path.

Nevertheless, the morning is pleasant. At about 11:30, his attention is drawn to two young mothers walking together, pushing carriages, wearing furs and engrossed in gossip. Having nowhere to sit, they choose an empty bench across from Klaber. One has red hair, is dressed to the nines, and looks like Miss Adelaide in *Guys and Dolls*. The second is a Veronica Lake, her long, lustrous light-brown hair falling over her right eye a siren's call. She is, Klaber thinks, not just a gorgeous woman but clearly a class act with a cute blonde daughter, perhaps two years old. Klaber's sure he's seen the woman, but where?

To hell with Harry Strong, Klaber thinks, his breath taken away. He wants to meet 'Veronica,' whoever she is. Hell! He'll find out her name even if it kills him. However, being the only male sitting in the park he knows he sticks out like a mustached Turkish weight-lifter in a ballet class. If he stays much longer, someone will ask a cop to speak to him because, until the child is a teenager, in the back of every mother and nurse's mind is that greatest of all horrors: kidnapping. Around the country, the number of incidents is rising.

In fact, within the precinct police station on 67th just east of Lexington, kidnapping is the greatest fear to New York's finest. A corpse is a corpse, but a missing child *might* still be alive. The public will feast on a kidnapping story for weeks if the family is wealthy or well known. It's therefore no surprise that, on pleasant days, St. Catherine's is invariably under loose but real surveillance, an extra cop on the beat and patrol cars driving by to and from the station house.

Thus, it is just a matter of minutes until a patrolman walks over, standing in front of Klaber and scores of watchful eyes. However, Klaber's immediate priority is to do nothing that will prevent his seeing Veronica again and, in fact, this will give him an opportunity to for her to focus on him. A few seconds into his brief, smiling conversation with the blue-clad officer, he slowly reaches into his back pocket and produces a business card that states his correct name, Yaphank address, and in larger type, "Translation Services." Speaking loudly enough so that Veronica should hear him, Klaber states that he's working at the Rockefeller Institute. His translation work is deadly dull, he tells the policeman; getting a smoke and watching little children play the perfect antidote. The patrolman smiles, relieved that there is no problem, and saunters away as mothers and nannies return to their gossip.

I'm going to meet her, Klaber thinks. He waits a few minutes, finishes his cigarette, folds up his early edition of the *World Telegram & Sun* and walks over to the two.

"You both have beautiful children," he begins, tipping his hat. The redhead, from Celtic blood and not a bottle, has no wedding ring and shows her interest with a meaningful smile. Veronica, who's wearing a ring, smiles politely but is otherwise aloof. But she's the one Klaber is after. After a minute or so the redhead asks if he works at the Rockefeller Institute and when he affirms this she volunteers that she and Veronica come to the park every Tuesday and Thursday. After a few more words, Klaber tips his hat and leaves, doing his best not to shake with excitement for, he realizes, there is no reason on God's green earth why he can't pursue Harry Strong and Veronica in parallel.

Chapter 49: June 1951, Baker.

The message, which wastes no words, catches up with Harry Strong at the construction site. "I'm in the government and need to talk with you about Ludwigslust." With it is a phone number and an extension. Harry calls, is put through, and speaks with a young woman who said she's been expecting his call.

"My boss said for you to choose a spot for early lunch tomorrow. He says it can't wait."

"What else did he say?"

"You pick the place and he'll see you, he knows what you look like Mr. Strong. Come as you are from the construction site. He won't wear anything fancy."

"Tell him 11:15 at Gittlitz's Delicatessen. It's on Madison between 53rd and 54th, the west side of the street."

▲

New York must have a hundred Gittlitz-like delicatessens doing business Monday to Friday from 6:30 AM until after lunch. It's a short walk for Harry, who's had enough lunches there to be considered a "regular." Overhead, fans from an earlier age whirl silently, Gittlitz unable to afford air-conditioning. Next to the cash register is Isaac Gittlitz, Jr., already sweating in the 90° heat. Standing behind the counter, men in white aprons prepare for the lunch rush hour. Directly across is a line of two and four-seat tables that run to the back. A half dozen-waitresses stand in a corner and in another a man sits smoking.

"Somebody's waiting for you, Major," Gittlitz says, pointing. Sitting at the rear table a large man slowly rises. Harry is fifteen minutes early, but Baker is waiting.

"My real name is Janusz Kaczanowski, but everyone calls me Baker," he says, enveloping Harry's hand in an iron grip. Harry notices the broken nose, thick hair, rumpled suit and, surprisingly, an Indian sachem's straight back posture. Baker is fractionally shorter, Harry thinks, but weighs forty pounds more and not much of it fat.

"Why 'Baker'?" Harry asks.

"I played semi-pro football while I was at the University of Chicago," Baker smiles slyly. "My sophomore year there, Jay Berwanger won the first Heisman Trophy for us. We'd a damn good team, but if I'd been caught we would've forfeited all our games. My pro coach's name was Howie Baker and by my using it everyone assumed I was his son. As often as not I played two games a weekend. It wasn't as if I could afford a gentleman's college like—say Amherst—or play tennis and soccer."

"Ever jump from a parachute?" Harry asks.

"Touché," Baker laughs. "While you were in the Eighty-Second I was with the Counter Intelligence because I spoke good German. Hell, you could have had my job—"

"And miss the good views I had floating down? With all those tracers coming up?" Harry sits down where Baker indicates, Baker's back against the wall.

"After the war, I got myself transferred to the National Intelligence Agency, and last year became part of something that you probably haven't heard of—"

"Like the CIA?" Harry laughs, then carefully inspects the ID Baker hands him. It is Baker's turn to be surprised when Harry removes a small 4x magnifying glass from his pocket.

"Well I'll be damned, I've never seen anybody this distrustful."

"It has nothing to do with trust, although in your case I'll make an exception," Harry smiles and hands Baker's ID back as both laugh. "Actually, it's because I collect stamps; you never know when you might see something interesting."

"Sounds like my hobby, baseball cards, but nothing after the '20s. I even have a 1909 Honus Wagner for my retirement." For the next few minutes the two, already getting along well, animatedly talk about collecting until the waitress came over.

"What's good? You're here enough, I see," Baker asks.

"Great roast beef on rye, right Mary?" he says looking up at the waitress. "Beats the Stage and the Carnegie delis hands down. Also, get the cucumber salad, it's a real picker-upper. And, go for the iced tea, it's homemade with a touch of orange juice. But, you're not here for lunch or to talk about stamps or baseball cards. Your message said Ludwigslust,"

"Well, maybe stamps a bit. Although I really want to speak to you about two murders."

"Hold on; wasn't this was supposed to be a friendly conversation."

"It is, but I wanted to grab your attention first—"

"Which you have."

"Then let me get to the point. First, I know all about you, Heinrich Strölin. Second, we have something in common that's real big and might get both of us killed. We're members of a very small fraternity. You murdered Franz Seis's older brother Hermann—"

Despite liking the big man, Harry feels like he's been run over by a cement truck. A Tom and Jerry cartoon flashes across his mind with Tom as flat as a pancake. Holy shit, Harry thinks, what doesn't this guy know? And what in God's name does he want from me?

"And I'm responsible," Baker is saying, "for the murder of his sister, Marianne. I'll get to that in a minute, but it was a German named Hirschfeld. The bastard actually poisoned her—"

Baker pauses as Mary comes over with the two iced-teas and a plate full of half-sour pickles. Baker takes one and crunches into it, "My God, I'd kill for something like this in D.C."

He waits until Mary leaves and then continues. "Unless I'm mistaken, Franz Seis knows who we are. First; he's sure I killed or gave the orders for his sister's death. Second; he doesn't realize that *you* murdered his brother but suspects you can lead him to the killer. He'd work you over and, even if he never found out you shot Hermann, he'd kill you afterwards. Not just to shut you up, but because he likes doing it. Of course, by then you'd be begging him to. He's not very nice when he holds the whip hand. He's already murdered one man this year—"

Harry looked at him, astonished. "And you let him go?"

"Seis had an airtight alibi. We have zero proof, and we're getting even less cooperation from our German friends. The man Seis killed, Hirschfeld, worked for me after the war. He kissed our asses and didn't mind being a turncoat. And apparently, he was a real sweetie in the SS. Nobody cared about him, but it shows that five years in jail hasn't kept Seis off the warpath. I wish you had killed both those Seis pricks. Instead of my treating you to lunch I would've given you a medal—"

"Lunch too, I would've hoped; medals aren't very tasty." It isn't a good joke Harry thought, but better than nothing. "But why do you think I killed his brother?"

"Because I happen to know that Hermann tried to pull a Derringer on you just before you went crazy and shot him in Ludwigslust. Not that anybody cares. But we've picked up some interesting things on telephone taps and conversations with Manfredi and Tonstad. Zilina died in an accident two years ago; he and his car got in a fight with a telephone pole—"

Harry shakes his head, he'd always liked Zilina... But why the interviews with Manfredi and Tonstad? How did this guy track them down? What the hell is going on?

"What I want to talk with you today is about the danger we're both in, and your stamps. We know about the stamps, where the money is going, and why. Everybody from HST on down couldn't be happier. Nevertheless, we've run across some things that don't make sense except that you've made an enemy who wants to put the *kibosh* on you."

"Well, I happen to know a bit about Franz Seis. I've heard about him, too. One of my stamp partners, Baron Romanoff, learned about him a few months ago."

"The baron found out because we fed him the information. But now we've picked up a lot more. Seis is coming here in November. While he still has no idea that you shot his brother, he knows that you acquired 'his' stamps. Believes it was in a crap game actually—"

"Who told him that?" Harry says, clearly shaken. "Only a few people know that story. Even Nan thinks it was a crap game. You don't tell your wife that your valuable stamps come from someone you shot. There was also a German woman in '45, but I said I'd purchased them from refugees. But somebody told Seis the craps story. Who the hell was it?"

"No idea, but..." Baker stops and smiles as Mary delivers the sandwiches.

"The big picture is this," Baker begins again, taking a moment to bite into the sandwich and smile with approval. "Over the years your stamps have resulted in tens of millions going to Haganah, the Mossad, and others."

" 'Tens,' there's no way that that's possible. The stamps can't be worth..."

"Stop a second. Your friends Lansky and Romanoff are far more imaginative than you gave them credit for. They haven't wasted the stamp money merely to buy equipment, they leverage the cash—all in beautiful green American dollars—to *bribe* government officials. Between Romanoff, who still knows people from his gun-running days, and Lansky there's hardly a country in the Americas or the Mediterranean where they don't have contacts.

"And why do they bribe?" Baker continues his rhetorical question. "Why, to more easily *steal* weapons and ammunition. We love it! Let me ask you a question: what South American dictator was coziest with the Nazis? The answer is Juan Peron, of course. So right now, while our favorite *caudillo* doesn't know it, if the Argentinians rebel, whoever breaks open the gun cases and ammunition boxes in his armories is in for a big fucking surprise: half of 'em are filled with bags of sand."

"But neither Meyer nor Romanoff have the time," Harry interjects.

"Lansky and Romanoff don't do the legwork, it's the people working for the Mossad who are filling up the freighters. And the Greek ship owners are in on it too."

Harry shakes his head, smiling in admiration.

"But where does Franz Seis fit into all this, you might ask? Right now, we're concerned he'll upset everything. We're sure he's coming to the U.S. this fall to go after me, you, his stamps, and maybe Romanoff. Who the hell knows for sure?"

"Can't you guys keep him out of the country?"

"Don't I wish. The reason he's out of prison is because he's got friends in very high places. Right now, he works for West German intelligence and he and Gehlen—"

"Reinhard Gehlen, the ex-Nazi who's their spymaster?"

"Exactly. They knew each other before the war. For planning, espionage, 'etc.,' Gehlen implicitly trusts him. Don't forget, Seis has a first-class brain. If you're willing to be objective, he's a very impressive guy. Actually, we need more men like him on our side these days."

"Do you also think that?" Harry asks. He's finished his sandwich and cucumber salad, is into his third glass of iced tea while poor Baker has barely taken a bite.

"What I think, unofficially of course, doesn't matter. But Seis's work has priority over my worries. While I assume he's a nutcase, he's *our* talented nutcase and we—me in particular—have to treat him with kid gloves."

"Does that apply to me?"

"Of course not, why do you think we're having lunch?"

Chapter 50: Munich, Late Summer, 1951.

Gradually, as Seis develops his plans for New York, he realizes that besides Rudy and Otto, he'll need at least two more ODESSA members. He'll also need a woman he can trust. When he first began to consider his options, he had Ingrid in mind. However, in the last few months she has been increasingly distant, but realizes that it's his own fault. Partially, the reason is his unexpected, blooming relationship with Ilse. Despite her flirting and friendliness when they first met, she has physically kept him at arms-length.

▲

"Why?" Ilse had answered Seis's question, drink in hand at, of all things, a Valentine's Day party that winter. "What's in it for me? I'm courted by younger men and women and don't need you for gratification. Until I feel you genuinely like me, our bedding is out of the question. You've stopped seeing Ingrid, not that I mind, and now that you've acquired a veritable stable of widows. I couldn't be more pleased." It's something she clearly finds amusing although he doesn't know why. "I understand that they're only too happy to join you on weekends when you motor to some romantic location. No, you don't need me. End of discussion."

Accepting Ilse's rules, Seis nevertheless takes her weekly to an opera, film, or a fine restaurant. Physically these dates are frustrating, although he thoroughly enjoys the conversational give and take. And, as she predicted, with her he meets other women—handsome, well-bred, and educated—who enjoy his company and bed. Adding to his mystique, it's an open secret he is employed by Gehlen.

Seis also acquires a new automobile. Because a Mercedes or BMW is too ostentatious in Germany, he selects a two-tone, red and black, Volkswagen Hebmüller Cabriolet. The car is both a two-seat convertible and an aphrodisiac. However, never for a minute does he consider dropping Ilse.

▲

As for Ilse, she genuinely likes the Seis that he presents. If his features are nondescript, and at times he looks ridiculous driving his adult toy with the top down, cigar-in-mouth, and gray Alpine hat with its red cockade, nevertheless his brain is absolutely first class. She soon understands why he became a *professor doctor* when so young, and that, in prison, he weekly read four or five books.

At times Ilse thinks of Harry Strong, but had she really loved him? It seems so long ago. And that God damned letter of his! The nerve of him. Talk about making her angry. She has no regrets for the letter she dashed off and tells herself she hopes he'll never write again; it hurt so much. Sometimes, however, she wishes that she'd had the patience to wait a few days before replying. To say how much she missed... But she banishes those thoughts, or at least until they unexpectedly pop up.

Reflecting on Seis, Ilse smiles more frequently. She is beginning to think about babies and instinctively believes he'll be a good father. In contrast to Ingrid, who feels chained down, Ilse wants children. It is clear proof, they laugh, that the grass is always greener somewhere else. But how to reconcile the cultured man she knows with his conviction for mass murder? Can she risk letting Seis slip away? Looking at him objectively—cold-bloodedly to be sure—she's been in Munich over five years and nothing better or, more accurately, no better German bachelor has come along.

Finally comes that magical evening in early June when Ilse decides to unlock the door. Over a candlelight dinner, Seis says he considers her his best friend. "I've grown comfortable with you. I feel free to ask you for advice and know that you'll keep my secrets."

"Franz," Ilse says after a long puff on a cigarette, "in two weeks it will be our summer solstice weekend, the longest days of the year. Since the war, it has become an informal holiday for younger people. We still have time to get a good room; why don't we visit the Austrian Alps and spend a weekend there?"

Seis is speechless.

"From all your conquests, surely you know a good location," she laughs. "Once there you could tell me who you took in the past and how good she was. Perhaps we'd have the same room, or walk by the same waterfall and make love on the grass. You do make love outdoors, don't you? I mean in the sunlight. It can be so exhilarating with the right—"

"Are you are toying with me?"

"Of course not, Franz," she says, taking his hands in hers. "I couldn't be more serious. It is time we became lovers. But there will be one strict condition."

"Which is? Devious women like you," he laughs, "always have a catch, don't they?"

"Naturally. Mine is that you'll relinquish all your other girlfriends. Quite frankly, I'm curious to see how you'll react to being with one woman for more than a few weekends."

"And I'll expect the same. Does this mean you'll live with me?"

"Don't be silly, not for some time. I wouldn't suggest this if I didn't think that we were compatible, but I really don't know. Can you truthfully say you do? Haven't we often discussed the Führer's despicable attitude that most women were breeding animals. I'd be less than candid if I didn't tell you that I'm concerned that you subconsciously retain this Nazi temperament. However, the only way to find out is for us to begin an affair."

"So, your purpose is to see if I measure up to your standards?" he laughs. "Don't forget, I also have mine."

"My instinct tells me that you will be well satisfied," she says, taking his hand. "I've learned, personally and anecdotally, that your generation of our 'master race' is similar in bed to the British, not the French or Italians. Yes, the German male can impregnate, but too often his imagination is limited and his temperament prohibits giving pleasure. Or, equally important, acknowledging pleasure. No," Ilse says smiling demurely, "our males are as inferior to their Mediterranean counterparts, just as they are substandard to U. S. Army Negroes."

"But despite these complaints you're still willing to risk it with me?"

"Risk it, of course not. But teach you, absolutely. And, unless you want more coffee, I'd suggest that we begin this evening."

▲

In weeks, Seis finds himself laughing and smiling broadly, at times surprised by his own contentment: Seis's first wife, Hannah, while attractive, was orderly, contained, and without warmth. Only after he proposed did she say yes, but she always insisted that sex be quick. She'd been taught marriage meant never saying no at night, but foreplay embarrassed her. Hannah seemed no more excited by sex than by the completion of her weekly laundry—something she approached with equal seriousness. And Ilse? She jokes, laughs, and always encourages second couplings. Seis well remembers Hannah's disgust when he once suggested it. Not only does he discover he's far happier, but it also begins to register that, at times with Ilse, his resolve to recover his stamps is diminishing.

▲

Gradually Seis's plans for New York, like a multiple-phased attack, begin to merge into a unified whole. To seize Strong's stamps and discover Hermann's killer, he needs to hold Strong, his wife, and their children hostage for at least eighteen hours. To carry this out, Ilse will stay with the children and their mother. However, considering what will likely transpire, he doesn't wish to tell her any details until they reach America.

After determining his strategy, Seis begins thinking through his expenses. The highest cost will be three round-trip tickets (himself, Ilse, and Rudy) from Munich to Amsterdam to New York on a non-stop KLM Lockheed Super Constellation. He's amazed these planes can hold sixty passengers and cruise at 330 mph, not much slower than the war's first Messerschmitts. Seis will stay at the 2,000 room Commodore, upscale but not luxurious. It's on Lexington and 42nd, with an indoor Grand Central Station entrance and a half-mile walk along Park Avenue to the stamp show. Slipping into Switzerland for a day, Seis closes his Lucerne account and purchases two one-way tickets from New York to Buenos Aires.

▲

When Ilse is alone, she increasingly mulls over the obvious: Seis is inching towards marriage. But does she really want to marry him? Even more troubling, going to America reawakens her day-dreams about Harry. She once placed him on a pedestal, but who is he after almost six full years? Has his hair receded or his waist expanded from all the steak Americans eat? If she did see Harry again would his conversation be dominated by descriptions of mowing the family lawn or pulling out his wallet, as Americans strangely do, and showing pictures of his family? Could it be that he's already failed and become morose or an alcoholic? And why did he write? He must have been unhappy, but why?

Ilse knows that she has changed. She continues working for the Americans, but, still only twenty-three, she has Rudy's old job and manages a stable of translators. Her office reads every message from East German strongman Walter Ulbricht (his secretary's typewriter is secretly wired to an Allied teletype machine that repeats every key stroke), and she's begun mastering Russian. For the first time in her life, the shortage of intelligent, young German males is beginning to work in her favor. If she doesn't marry and have children, she has been told that she has a bright professional future.

However, Ilse's most nagging problem is knowing that Seis is on his best behavior. The chase does that to men. He brings flowers, recites opera librettos and takes her to lectures. But is this the real Franz Seis? What of the stories Rudy told Ingrid? Ilse knows Rudy fears and secretly hates Seis, but how has this colored his stories? If the wartime atrocities Seis was accused of initiating did occur, the man is—or was—reprehensible. How, in God's name, might their children turn out?

Yet, each weekend is like a honeymoon. To use coarse American idiom, she finds fucking him delightful. Marvelous as their relationship is, it leaves Ilse more quizzical about Harry. She'd love to see and speak to him again; to see if today's Harry measures up to the Seis she knows. New York will be the perfect opportunity, but like an idiot she tore up Harry's letter after answering him. Regardless, can she let a four-month affair six-years earlier ruin her life? Then, wasn't she just another desperate person hoping to survive?

Chapter 51: New York, August 31, 1951.

Harry is now effectively managing the largest of Big Al's projects, a fifty-story behemoth spanning the entire front of Fifth Avenue between 53rd and 54th. Big Al, superstitious, prefers addresses ending with three or seven, but as the building is on the west side of Fifth, it must be an even number between 680 and 698. Al chooses "696" which, he says, has seven-threes and therefore will be exceptionally lucky. But at 696, if anything can go wrong it does. Accidents seemingly come out of nowhere. One amputation (a man's foot squashed) and numerous injuries and accidents make everyone feel that the project is jinxed.

Of course, there's also theft. No matter how many sweetheart deals Big Al negotiates, "petty" theft is never fully controlled. Harry's fully aware that construction sites present tempting inventory, especially after the Korean fighting begins. The military scours scores of Pacific islands for usable left-behind equipment, while arms production sends metal prices soaring. By late 1950, sleepy watchmen have been replaced by outdoor lighting, trained dogs and armed security guards, patrol cars passing by intermittently.

Yet, even with fencing topped with concertina wire, double locks, and paying off the mob (insurance companies informally consenting), inventory disappears. Occasionally, a theft is sufficiently large to make the newspapers. A truckload of GE lighting equipment vanishes into thin air one weekend, the thieves adding insult to injury by painting "Killroy was Here!" the explanation point, being the middle finger.

And then there are payrolls. Workers are paid, in cash, on the last Friday of each month. On these days, Harry begins the morning opening his office safe and strapping on his webbed military belt, Army regulation holster, and a loaded .45 Colt. Two men from Lansky's private security firm stand guard when a Brink's armored truck delivers the cash in canvas bags.

Despite these precautions, on August 31, after the Brinks truck leaves and workers line up, a stolen, large-bodied Yellow Checker Cab halts on east-facing 54th street. Four men, all from an Irish Hell's Kitchen gang, stride into the construction office brandishing a sawed-off shotgun, automatic pistols and a canvas duffel bag. Caught by surprise, there is nothing that Harry, his staff, or the security men can do except "freeze" as they are told. As one thief stands guard with a shotgun, two take the Brinks sacks and scoop-up the table's cash and everyone's wallet. The fourth man, pistol in hand, slides from desk to desk, yanking out phones.

In little more than a minute the four are out the door, padlocking it from the outside, another indication of careful planning. The robbers are back in the cab seconds later having committed the perfect robbery. So far.

Harry, with five others, adrenalin rushing through them, pick up the 200-pound oak work table in the middle of the office as if it were a feather mattress. In unison, they rush the door, smashing the hinges so forcefully that the flimsy building, held in place only by gravity, threatens to collapse. Three of the men, like in a silent film comedy, topple through the door when it bursts open.

Harry, pistol now in hand, emerges first in time to see the get-away cab. Because of a red light, it is unable to cross Fifth Avenue's heavy, two-way, north-south traffic. Instead the cab makes a screeching right turn into Fifth Avenue and heads south.

Once on Fifth Avenue, the driver hits the pedal while merging into the moving traffic. A split second later he realizes that the "open" right-hand lane is, in fact, blocked by a flat-bed truck unloading prefabricated latticed steel flooring. Frantically the cab's driver swerves left, only to be rammed by a car in the lane he's trying to enter. The crash sends the cab careening back into the right lane where it hurtles into the truck's rear.

As men unloading the truck dive out of the way, the left side of the cab hits one worker, throwing him into the traffic. In all, almost a dozen cars and delivery vans on Fifth, coming in opposite directions, hit their brakes and crunch into one another; each steel-bending collision sending up plumes of dust. The worker knocked off his feet is hurled into the fender of a squealing car, pushed forward, fortunate not to be run over.

At the same instant, the right side of the cab rams into and under the truck's rear left platform. Most of the impact takes place above the cab's engine in the front right seat. As the metal frames pierce the cab's front right window, the man sitting next to the driver is thrown forward. In the instantaneous thud that follows, he is decapitated in a Vesuvius-like explosion of blood as his head lands in the middle-back seat. Simultaneously, the driver is first catapulted forward, his head lacerated by the steering column and steel horn (a separate disk inside the steering wheel), a fraction of a second later whiplashed backward, his spinal cord crushed.

As horrified pedestrians watch, Harry, Lansky's security guards, and angered workers come churning around the block. Harry's .45 is drawn, its safety off, as he concentrates on the now motionless Yellow Cab. From the back seat, two men tumble out. The man in the middle seat, covered with blood and all but holding the decapitated head, is too stunned to move.

The first man, somehow still holding his shotgun and wobbling like a drunk, nevertheless gets to his knees, his trembling hands trying to steady the weapon to shoot the man charging down on him. It is Harry. As he shakily raises his shotgun, Harry's instincts take control, while everything unfolds in slow motion. Twenty-feet away, Harry looks into both barrels and leans back, like a ball player slowing down the instant before reaching a base.

Harry's body comes to a sudden halt as he spreads his legs for better balance, and fires. His first shot plows into the sidewalk, inches in front of and alongside the man's thigh, but bullet fragments, tiny chunks of pavement, or both hurtle into him. The man shudders and rocks backwards while Harry's arm is jerked up from the pistol's backlash.

All sound around Harry has vanished; he is oblivious to honking horns, people screaming, and distant police whistles. In front of Harry, the shotgun holder wills himself back up, locking eyes with him. Harry sees a determination that on rare occasion he'd encountered during the war; I am going to die, the man's eyes say, but I will kill you first.

Steadying his right hand with his left, before the man can shoot, Harry aims by instinct and squeezes off two more rounds. Each of the heavy caliber .45 slugs plow into the man's upper chest. He is hurled backward, doing a somersault and landing head up as his body comes to rest. Harry steps forward, .45

defensively pointed, kicking the shotgun aside. For a few seconds, he stands over the gasping man whose fountain of blood splatters him. Is he trying to talk? Harry wonders in the few seconds before the man die.

One thoroughly dazed stick-up man quickly surrenders, or at least tries to. However, before the first patrolmen arrives, he is mercilessly kicked and punched by the construction workers. In the cab's backseat, the final robber sits motionless with a severed head and two money-filled, blood-covered canvas bags.

Harry hasn't been so maddened since Ludwigslust. As the police arrive, his anger subsides in a huge *whoosh!* and he realizes that he is standing in the middle of Fifth Avenue, a literally bloody .45 in his hands. Blank-eyed and dazed as if in a collision, Harry is unable to think in English; only German words enter his mind. He attempts to walk back to the construction building, only to be gently stopped by some of his Mohawk friends.

The story is the life blood of that day's afternoon newspapers. "Beckendorf's Posse," the *World Telegram and Sun* calls them. The *Journal-American* has a photo of the crushed cab; a robber sitting in the back seat with the decapitated man's unattached head partially visible. The photo alone is good for an extra production run of 25,000 copies.

Soon Big Al is on the scene along with lawyers, Brinks representatives, union leaders and police brass. Harry, as can be expected, is the center of attention from both the Fifth Estate and the Police. The latter closely question, then congratulate him.

▲

The following Friday Harry finds himself in Big Al's office, door closed. All week, he has been apprehensive, and while the legalities and insurance aspects of the robbery are being settled, he knows Big Al does *not* like the attendant publicity and especially the paperwork. More ominously, after Harry enters, Big Al doesn't smile or say anything; rather, he simply motions for Harry to sit. On top of his desk is a large white envelope tied with a rubber band.

Big Al lackadaisically flips the envelope to Harry. "Open it," he grunts.

Inside are ten one hundred-dollar bills.

"Is this my severance?" Harry asks, expecting the worst.

"No, asshole, it's a bonus and you're being promoted."

"For killing that guy?"

"No. For saving the company a lot of money and letting a shit-load of punks know not to fuck with us. That's what the money's for. Second, I'm promoting you. This has been going through my head a couple of months. I want you finishing Six-Ninety-Six, but after that..."

Harry's emotions have screeched to a halt in one direction and accelerating in another.

"Here's what's happening," Big Al continues. "We've reached the point where the bankers are telling me that we're too small to be big and too big to be small. No more money, they say, until there's better fucking management. As if I couldn't handle it, the pricks. From here on in it's strictly a suit and tie for me. They want full-time managers for the Boston, D.C., Denver, and Manhattan construction projects. That means Manhattan's going to be yours; your Six-Nine-Six, the lower Broadway building, and the two that'll break ground next year."

Harry sits there, a crooked smile on his face.

"Think you can handle it? Well I do and your Uncle Meyer does also. He's an even better judge of character than I am."

Harry is unable to do anything other than nod yes.

"Good, but don't think for a second that I'm not going to be all over your fuckin' ass."

Chapter 52: Munich, September.

Not until late summer did Seis dare approach Gehlen. "So, you need two full weeks, Franz?"

"I would prefer a third but will make do with less."

"May I assume that this time you'll be traveling further than Bonn?"

Seis nods.

"Might by any chance your destination be the U.S.?"

"Yes, actually New York."

"But not Washington?"

"I have no plans to be in Washington," says Seis, who has already given considerable thought to how he might kill Baker.

"Nevertheless, Franz, I will contact Allen Dulles before you leave and inform him that we have reliable information that an attempt will be made on Baker's life. If that isn't acceptable, then there can be no American 'vacation.'"

"You have my word that I have no interest in Baker."

"Good. And you will be traveling by yourself?"

"No," Seis said, surprised by the smile that he can't control.

"So, might I therefore assume that you will be with the same Ilse who's broken so many Munich hearts? A lovely lady. I'm tempted to reread her dossier just to look at the photos."

Seis smiles again. It is a happy one, far different than Gehlen has ever seen.

"Permission granted. That's all then," Gehlen nodded, indicating the interview is over.

Seis rose and was about to get up and say thank you when Gehlen scratches his head a second and put up his hand.

"Oh, the vacation time you requested. I am told that it overlaps with a New York stamp show. Are you planning to attend?"

"Yes, in fact with my friend Rudy Spangler."

"Of course, your aide-de-camp in the war's last years. He manages a popular stamp store here in Munich with his wife, Ingrid. My poor secretary has so many dossiers to keep track of these days. And so, Franz, among your other—shall we say hobbies—you've become a philatelist?"

"Very much so. As harmless an avocation as one can imagine."

"So it is, so it is. Although, years ago, I never would've guessed you would find it so stimulating. Nicely illustrates how wrong I can be, doesn't it?"

After Seis leaves Gehlen sighs. Seis is so caught up in his stamp chase that his work is suffering. Gehlen will meet with the CIA chief in a few weeks. Perhaps, after dinner, they'll make a little side bet concerning Seis's ever returning to work, although he, for one, doubts it.

▲

Seis, Ilse, and Rudy arrive in New York Friday, November 9. Seis is almost bubbly; he has money, a plan, and ODESSA support. While he isn't optimistic that most of his stamps can be found, his stratagem includes receiving hundreds of thousands of dollars from Thistleman & Chandler, Baron Romanoff's remaining stamps if any, and the name of his brother's killer from Harry Strong. After that, combined with the money from his Swiss account he'd have almost a million dollars and be on his way to Argentina. Hopefully with Ilse. As for Rudy, he has no specific plans but prefers giving him some hush money versus killing him.

Saturday morning, after a night at the Commodore, Seis sends Rudy and Ilse on a day-long bus tour of the city while he goes to the 42nd Street library's reading room. After dinner, Rudy and Ilse go to the Broadway musical *The King and I*, while Seis meets with Otto Klaber and his Yaphank associate, Dieter Schmidt.

Seis finds Dieter physically impressive. An inch over six feet, thick-necked, and with an athlete's sloping shoulders, Seis immediately begins looking at the best way to utilize his size; he is certainly a match for Strong which neither he nor Otto are. Like Otto, Dieter slipped out of the U.S. in 1939, serving as an NCO and an officer in the SS Panzer Lehr Division until being wounded in the Bulge. Now, he tells Seis, he's a carpenter and handyman in Yaphank.

Otto won't admit it but, having worked with Dieter, he's slightly afraid of the man. The second time they met, Dieter became annoyed by a fly. "Did you know that flies take off by jumping backward? Once you know this, capturing them isn't difficult." He then proceeded to trap the fly with his left hand and removed a pair of tweezers from a pocket. "I love this, that's why I always carry tweezers" he laughed and slowly began to detach the insect's wings.

Otto removes some newspaper stories from a large envelope. "Our friend, Harry Strong," he tells Seis, "has been in the headlines lately. As you can see, he's no pushover and might even legally carry arms. It might add a twist to your plans."

"Well, well, well; he's no pushover or coward," Seis nods after reading them. "He'll be like a cornered wolf, a bear, or a bull... Yes, like a bull. And we shall weaken this bull too. Just as *picadores* runs their lances into a bull's shoulders, so we shall weaken Harry Strong before the *banderilleros* and the matador take their turns. Can you find two additional men quickly?"

Otto and Dieter nod as Seis outlines his plan. First, he, Otto and Rudy will visit Thistleman & Chandler on Monday. A week later, there will be a second Thistleman visit followed by a visit to Romanoff's office that same afternoon. Simultaneously, Seis explains, the two *picadores* will call on Harry Strong at his work site.

"As Strong is beaten," Seis continues, "he's to be told that we want our stamps back. When Strong limps home, he will be shocked to discover that we have invaded his home and are holding his wife and children hostage. When he sees us, it will be the second of a one-two punch, and psychologically devastating."

"You two, will choose the *picadores*. They are to weaken Strong, but are not to break any bones. Hospitalizing him would badly upset my timing. Nevertheless, because this type of thrashing often results in blood accidentally being splashed about, Dieter, you will wait at the site in a car and drive the two to where they can catch a train to Yaphank. Also, you must be sure that they have available different colored overcoats, hats, and shoes."

"Why so much?" Dieter asks laughing. "And shouldn't I be a *picadore*?"

"Anyone can inflict a beating. I want you to manage it correctly. Which is why they'll need extra shoes and overcoats. If you don't have them, assuredly, someone will notice blood and ask questions. Fate invariably decrees that without taking proper precautions there will be problems. And Dieter, after dropping them off, I want you to come to Strong's apartment. Before everything is over, we will need another firm hand."

As Seis finishes his planning, he indicates that six pistols will be needed, "silencers" a necessity for all. "If possible, a Walther P38 should be obtained for me. The hostages, including the children, will be kept overnight in Strong's apartment. Tuesday morning, you two will accompany Strong to his bank and all remaining stamps will be retrieved. When you return, Strong and his wife will be shot. Any household staff and the two children will be shot—"

"But they're infants," Otto blurts out.

"Of course. There's no need to shoot infants who are too young to identify us. But the others, yes. There are to be no witnesses."

Otto and Dieter nod, considering the money Seis is paying, they have anticipated bloodshed.

Chapter 53: October 10, 1951.

It is only a few hours after the Yankees have won their third World Series in a row, this time defeating Leo Durocher's Giants, and, with the children tucked into bed, Nan tells Harry they need to talk.

Nan is wearing a tight maroon polo shirt and rolled up shorts. The two sit at opposite ends of the living room's wide sofa with drinks in hand. "You know how much I love you."

Harry reaches for a cigarette but forgets to offer Nan one, "Is this what I think it is?"

"Yes. I'm not happy and haven't been for some time."

Oh shit, Harry thinks, this is going to be worse than I suspected.

"You've given me everything I've asked for or needed," Nan is saying. "Even more money than I thought possible. I love my children, my work, and going to bed with you. But I feel empty. I want more, and I want to do more of what I want to do."

Harry starts to speak but Nan raises her hand. "Listen to me. I know you don't like benefits or opening nights and absolutely hate nightclubs, but I love them. I love putting on a low-cut dress and jewelry and making the small talk you hate so much."

"But we go anyway, don't we? Saturday night—"

"You didn't want to go to the Asch's. You don't like Anne and think that Jonas—"

"Is a horse's ass."

"That's my point. Can you truthfully tell me—"

"But I went, didn't I?"

"Please, look at this from my viewpoint. How much fun do you think I'm having, knowing that you're miserable. You mope around with a long face and don't even realize it. Right?" She says, looking into Harry's eyes, throwing him on the defensive.

"And there's something else these days," she continues. Harry realizes his tasteless Scotch is gone and pours himself another, his mind registering that his ice cubes have melted.

"Oh?"

"Actually, a somebody else."

The word *somebody* is what Harry fears. When it is a some*thing,* Harry has always made things right by giving her a gift or carrying her off to the bedroom. But *somebody*? How is he supposed to respond?

"He's an editor, Harry, the number two man at *Cue* magazine."

"*Cue*? You're kidding me. The only thing *Cue* does is list things. Nobody *reads* it."

"You're wrong, Harry. Its circulation ran past *Saturday Review* earlier and now it has more New York area readers than any other weekly."

"So, do you want me to advertise in it?"

"No. Listen to me, you big lummox," she says, unable not to smile. "God, can you ever evade subjects. They're tripling their editorial content. Not just movie and theater reviews, but concerts, art exhibits, fashion; you name it. Mort told me the other evening—"

"You're seeing Mort Glankoff? He's the goddamn editor and just got married. We went to his wedding for Christ's sake! Is he already trying to bang you?"

"Harry, it's not Mort. I'm *seeing* Frank Sussman."

"Jesus fucking Christ, Sussman's over fifty. We've met..." but now the effect of Nan's spider bite is spreading through his body. He feels himself weakening and his tongue seems like a dentist just injected his mouth with Novocain. He knows Sussman; in fact, he likes the man. Dropped out of high school to enlist in World War I, saw combat with the Rainbow Division, and then went to Princeton. Worked for the *New Yorker* and joined *Cue* a few years back. Married, a family, but long since divorced.

Aaah, the magic word *divorce*. But Sussman? He's Harry's opposite. Not tall, *maybe* Nan's height, dresses like a college professor with a pipe, brown tweed jacket with leather elbow pads, slacks, loafers, and half-a-head of unruly gray hair. The last time he'd seen Sussman he'd paid no attention while he and

Nan talked and laughed uproariously. He hadn't thought twice when Nan returned, eyes sparkling.

"How long has this been going on?"

"Almost a year."

"Have you slept with Frank?"

"Yes. We began just before you started with Alice what's-her-name."

"Alice Denham? You know about her?"

"Why are you so naïve? Of course I do. Since there was Frank for me I didn't mind Alice for you. With a face and figure like hers, she's got to be good for any man's ego. By the way, are they real?" Nan asks, laughing at Harry.

"Yes, and fuck her, she doesn't mean anything to me. Have you told your mother?"

"Yes."

"So, I'm the last on the block to know. What about the children?"

"We've run into Frank a few times in Central Park."

"Run into? Sure you have." Time for another Scotch, he thinks, reaching for the bottle for the third time.

"Harry, put the fucking drink down and pay attention to what I'm saying."

"Don't worry, I'm listening to every word. With bated breath."

"Damn it! Stop being sarcastic. For what it's worth, I still love you."

"But why? Why is Frank better than me?"

"He's not better than you, Harry. I don't want another you. Frank's better for *me*. It's all about me and my children."

"They're *our* children, God damn it! Or do you have another surprise?"

"No. Of course, you're their father. What I meant to say is that you and Frank live in different worlds. I don't like yours Harry—look at all the people you associate with. The fact of the matter is that I love Frank's world and *that* world is better for *our* children. Can you tell me it isn't? Frank's world doesn't have anything to do with money. In the end, I suspect—no, I'm sure—you'll be more successful and make so much more—"

"I don't give a rat's ass about success or money."

"I know that, which is one reason you'll wind up on top. You'll be Big Al's number two and all the others who're backstabbing each other will wonder why. You're happy because—"

"I have you, the children, and a job I like. Why shouldn't I be happy?"

"Maybe you're happy, but I'm not. You've seen to my *basic* needs; children, food and shelter, and Lord knows great sex. But my *mind* wants more."

"You didn't mention money."

"Don't be sarcastic. Money has nothing to do with this. After you run out of stamps to sell, I'll make more money than you. Then, my divorce lawyer says, we'll split our assets plus I'll get alimony and child support. So, you see, it's not at all about money. But I've had enough of zoos, natural history museums, and European history books for a lifetime."

"But I'm a good father, aren't I?"

Nan nods and Harry sees that she's trying not to cry. He's also trying not to cry. Not to scream. To have the suddenly warm room cool off.

Harry sits, head down, confused and defeated. What had he read about Abraham Lincoln when he lost to Stephen Douglas? "I'm too old to cry but it hurts too much to laugh."

Nan stands, kisses him on the forehead and takes his hand. "Get up, we'll talk more in bed." However, tonight, when it ends, Nan can't stop crying and Harry finds himself shaking. Even Nan wrapping herself around his back and squeezing him tightly as he lies in a fetal position doesn't make things better. Other than combat, this night is the absolute worst since his mother died.

▲

The next morning Nan finds herself relieved and as happy as she's been in years. Her lines from the previous evening, many of which she'd rehearsed with Frank, had gone almost flawlessly. A bravura performance. She's well on her way to having her own New York literary salon. Now the only thing Nan must do is follow her attorney's advice and screw Harry into compliance. It will be the best of both worlds for her for he *is* far better than Frank.

Chapter 54: Monday, November 12; Thistleman & Chandler.

The week following the 1929 stock market crash, Artemis Ward Chandler departed this earth leaving behind a half-million dollars in debt from stocks purchased on margin and an open twenty-third story window overlooking Wall Street. Since that day, all Thistleman & Chandler correspondence and telegrams were signed or sent by a Thistleman, father or son. Thus, Franz Seis smiles with delight on Wednesday, November 7 upon receipt of Robert Seabury Thistleman, IV's reply to his telegram: his plan is moving forward.

The previous day, Seis contacted Thistleman, under the guise of a Federal Republic of Germany's War Reparations Board's Inspector, Gehlen's non-existent organization. In it, Seis telegraphed that November's stamp auction had just been brought to their attention. Sadly, the agency believes that many of these stamps were stolen during the war. Proving this allegation will take a short time. Seis states that he expects his message to be regarded as confidential. So that the auction can be held, he hopes that a meeting will be possible. Closing, he notes that he'll be staying at the Commodore beginning November 11.

▲

Thistleman & Chandler's offices are on the fourth floor of Chase National Bank's headquarters, a thirty-eight story structure completed in 1928. While the bank chose a Pine Street address, it also fronts Nassau Street. For practical purposes, this means that not only did Thistleman & Chandler's 1942 move from 116 Nassau Street have the protection of Chase's bomb proof vaults, it remained in the very heart of the city's philatelic district.

Monday, promptly at 10 AM, Seis, Rudy and Otto are whisked into a small, mahogany paneled conference room. Six deep maroon leather chairs have been arranged around a rectangular table, the polished bookcases filled with stamp catalogs and reference volumes.

The three are barely seated when a cadaverous, seventy-one-year-old man enters in a three-piece Brooks Brothers suit with a gold watch chain, *Phi Beta*

Kappa key, and fob. Thistleman has on pince-nez glasses—famously worn by Teddy Roosevelt—and a high collar, all of which emphasize the cavities under his prominent cheekbones and the shiny dark bags under his eyes reflecting nights of worry.

The Thistlemans didn't arrive on the *Mayflower*. However, they were among the first contingent of the Massachusetts Bay Colony in 1629, aboard *The Lion's Whelp* when it sailed up to the Indian settlement of Naumkaeg. The *Whelp*, one of five heavily armed ships carrying 300 devout Puritans (fanatics, if one is less forgiving), who, after quickly ridding themselves of the Algonquians, renamed the site Salem. Indeed, the family's genealogical history, *Thistlemans in America* (1888), states that Uriah Thistleman accused one woman of witchcraft, testified against her and two others and, without doubt, watched as the three were hanged.

Two hundred and fifty years later, Thistleman IV usually beats out his competition for valuable collections for, when it comes to stamps, no one in philately has a better mind, sense of timing or deeper pockets. Publicly, he is modest and self-effacing, although behind closed doors he is like his ancestors: a prototype Puritan, devoid of humor and compassion.

Better yet, as Seis discovered examining General Gehlen's archives, wartime German Intelligence compiled lists of Americans to be eliminated or rewarded. Among the latter, Seis found a thick Thistleman dossier stating the annual dollar amount of his 1930s support for the German-American Bund, Yaphank's Camp Siegfried, and the Lindbergh-America First movement. There are also photos and correspondence relating to Thistleman's April 1939 visit to Berlin shortly after Czechoslovakia's annexation. This part of the file included a cocktail party photo by Leni Riefenstahl showing Thistleman IV, eyes all but adoring, looking at the Führer as they are introduced. Before returning the dossier, Seis pockets the photo and other documents.

▲

"Good morning, gentlemen, I'm R. S. Thistleman," the American blue-blood, hoping to exude an air of confidence, begins. "Permit me to introduce my chief administrative officer, Lars Enkell, and the man who'll be our auctioneer later this week, Patrick Cassidy. Please have some coffee, and, since you have come all the way from Germany I've had fresh squeezed orange juice prepared."

Seis introduces Rudy Spangler and Otto Klaber whom, he says, can assist in translation. He pointedly notes that Klaber lives in Yaphank, a comment causing Thistleman to immediately stiffen. It is the first of several nasty surprises that Seis has in store. With the introductions, there are the slight bowing of heads, handshakes, and artificial smiles. A secretary serves pastries, coffee, and the orange juice. Rudy drinks his first glass so quickly that she pours a second serving before leaving the room.

Seis is quickly impressed by the straight-backed Enkell, obviously Finnish, who has almost white hair and eyebrows, pale eyes and skin but, strangely, no Uralic accent.

"You're Finnish by birth?" Seis asks.

"Racially Finnish, but born in Red Wing, Minnesota."

"By your posture," Seis smiles, "might I assume you participated in the late hostilities?"

"Very much so, I fear. I was a student in Helsinki when the Russians invaded in '39. I had two options, return to Minnesota or use my skills as a marksman and skier."

"And chose the latter." Like all Germans, Seis always has been impressed by the fighting qualities of the Finnish who held off an overwhelming number of Russians. "Your defense of your country was remarkable, your small forces cut the Russians to pieces that winter."

"When panicked men without camouflage and wearing boots in knee deep snow are faced with white-clad skiers holding hunting rifles, the answer is always the same," Lars replies evenly. "By the same token, as I personally discovered, skiers cast shadows in sunlight and stand little chance against spotter planes armed with machine guns. My right eye is glass."

"Quite so, quite so," Seis nods with sincere sympathy, "I myself felt lucky to have lost only two toes facing them." The two talk another minute, both former comrades in arms against the Russian bear. No matter how much the Germans despise Russians, it is nothing compared to Finnish hatred of their neighbor and former overlord.

Well I seem to have made a friend, thinks Seis. Discussions are inevitably easier when you have an objective opponent.

▲

Thistleman nods for Seis to start. During the early part of the war, Seis begins, and in the Nazi looting that followed, stamp collections of Jews and Gentiles in conquered countries were seized. However, given the magnitude of the theft, the Germans needed technical assistance. Because German males were needed in the war effort, what to do? The most accessible resource, Seis explains as heads nod, were Jews held in concentration camps.

"But how do you know this?" asks Thistleman, almost sarcastically.

"Because I am here by knowing things that I shouldn't," Seis answers, smiling like the proverbial Cheshire cat. "Also, one of the camp's officers survived. You may be sure that his story has been verified and cross-checked before we contacted you."

"But to continue. These Jews, to a man and a woman, were fully aware that they'd be eventually executed, not just for being Jews, but for knowing about this secret operation. The stamps' value, we estimate, is now well over ten million U.S. dollars using conservative 1950 Scott Catalog estimates. We believe that you are in the process of auctioning off some of those stamps that were stolen."

Seis pauses to let his story sink in. Rudy, nervous, gets up and pours himself a third or—Seis wonders—is it a fourth glass of orange juice?

"What were these poor Jews to do?" Seis asks. "Somehow, under the very noses of their captors, they marked a microscopically small symbol on the back of each stamp. Lettering so small that no human eye could see it nor could a philatelist with a 10x magnifying glass."

"Can I prove this? In our exchange of telegrams my final message listed twenty-five stamps that you are about to auction and we believe were stolen by the Nazis. We, for our part, purchased a Bosch & Lamb optical microscope. Spangler, would you please..."

▲

Rudy is increasingly disturbed by his role in Seis's theatrics and disgusted by his story of how the Jews—all murdered in cold blood by Seis—are being given credit for marking the stamps. If they knew the truth, he thinks. But what can I do? Not that this Thistleman deserves anything. He reminds me of a thin Heinrich Himmler, especially with those glasses of his.

Rudy, nervous as seldom before, is thinking about getting another glass of juice. He hasn't not had fresh orange juice since before the war. After the war, Americans imported orange juice in cans. And who could forget the name of the brand, named after their famous Mickey Mouse. But, thinking about oranges, his mind has drifted.

"Spangler..." he hears.

▲

Spangler opens his wide briefcase, then carefully removes a carefully-wrapped optical microscope that includes a rotary head with three lenses of 25x, 50x and 100x magnification.

"I know this sounds like a magician's trick," says Seis, "but you've possessed the stamps for months or years while, at no time, we have never had physical access to them. Now, if you'd randomly select five of the twenty-five that you have. And, as there is always the possibility that these will reveal nothing, we'll go home and apologize for wasting your time."

Seis does not have to be told that any chance of his leaving the United States with a significant amount of Thistleman's money depends on the next few minutes. If for any reason the stamps are not marked, he has wasted thousands of dollars and will return to Munich, a lesser man with no future. Yes, he will live comfortably, marry Ilse and have children, but the rest of his life will be on a prescribed, ordinary path.

Thistleman nods to Lars who randomly opens one of the five envelopes that has been removed that morning from Chase National's vaults, takes five stamps, and places them face down on a white sheet of paper. Lars smiles, removes his own 10x magnifying glass, looks carefully at all five, sees nothing and shakes his head.

"Spangler," says Seis, "would you please take one of the five stamps that Lars just examined and place it on a specimen glass and then in the microscope? Thank you; now please set the microscope at the 25x magnification and let Mr. Enkell examine it a second time."

Lars looks, "Well, I can see some sort of a dot."

"As we expected," Seis says, as smoothly as possible, his gamble now reaching its zenith. "Mr. Thistleman?" Thistleman shakes his head and Seis continues.

"Spangler, please turn it to 50x magnification, and let Lars look again."

Lars takes the microscope. "My God. It *is* there. There is a *delta*. I can see it clearly. Those poor Jewish bastards, but at least someone has discovered what happened."

Angrily, Thistleman all but grabs the microscope. He turns to 100x magnification and, looking carefully, can only shake his head as his lips involuntarily press together.

Chapter 55: Thistleman & Chandler, 11 AM.

"It is an open secret that this Thursday will be the best attended and most publicized auction since the President Roosevelt's collection was sold by H. R. Harmer," Seis says twenty minutes later, after the nineteenth of the first twenty-five stamps are found to have *deltas*. "And why did H. R. Harmer beat you out five years ago?" he says, looking at Thistleman and pauses. "Especially when your firm was almost twice Harmer's size."

Seis's question is rhetorical: he is goading Thistleman and the man's face becomes incrementally redder as he attempts to control his growing anger and humiliation.

"Did it not have something to do with Harmer's efforts throughout the war on behalf of the Allies? Or perhaps was it the fact that you and your father were closely associated with certain political elements that were not looked on with favor by the late President?"

Seis slides a folder over to Thistleman, who can read German well enough. Thistleman hurriedly looks through, then all but slams it shut and pushes it back across the table, daggers in his eyes. In it are Nazi records indicating that through Chase Bank, in a complex transaction, Thistlemans (father and son) acquired $750,000 of *Rückwanderer* (returnee) *Marks*. In short, the German war effort was strengthened by acquiring American dollars paid for with stolen Jewish money, the facts known to the Thistlemans and others.

"My reading of the *Reichsbank* documents shows that you, Chase, and hundreds more American Nazi sympathizers placed your wartime bets on both sides. As a German, I must admit to being slightly jealous." Seis looks around the room, thoroughly pleased with himself and the additional materials he's uncovered in the New York Public Library's reading room.

"Now, given these financial materials and the stamps that you have examined to your satisfaction," Seis says, "I fear that your Thursday auction must be cancelled—"

"Like hell it will!" Thistleman interjects, almost sputtering. "You have really gone too far, Dr. Seis. There is no legal way that the auction can be cancelled and I assure you that I will not. I really think that you gentlemen—"

Thistleman rises to end the meeting.

"Please sit down R.S.," Lars says gently. "I think that there is more bad news to come. We need be fully apprised of it before we act too hastily. With your permission, may I also look at the folder Dr. Seis handed you?"

Thistleman nods. Seis passes the file to Lars who looks at it for a minute before returning it. "If past is prologue, R.S., I think we need to listen to the rest of what our visitors are about to tell us."

"Thank you," Seis says. "Permit me to apologize for I'm sometimes unable to be as tactful or concise in English as I wish. Naturally, if you would like to return these stamps to your safe deposit facilities and bring up another twenty-five or even a hundred that are slated for auction, you'll likely find a similar high percentage of marked stamps. Therefore, despite my not knowing how the *New York Times* or the *Herald-Tribune* select their stories, the *delta* and the files you've just examined more than likely will compel their immediate attention. There's no question that while these Jews knew they were going to die, they desperately wanted their fate known. Furthermore, this is exactly what our attorneys will explain to a judge—"

"What judge? What attorneys?" Thistleman barks with a high-pitched screech.

"Ah, that. As you might recall, in 1920 President Wilson appointed John Foster Dulles to the Allied War Reparations Commission. Dulles argued against, but was unsuccessful in reducing Germany's post war payments. However, under the 1924 Dawes Plan—for which Dawes received the Nobel Peace Prize—Dulles used American money to finance new business development in Germany, the profits of which went to Great Britain and France. And they, in turn partially paid off their loans to the United States. Robust capitalism at its best, eh?"

"Why I happen to know this story is because my father became a friend of Mr. Dulles. The two worked together for over a decade before Hitler unilaterally stopped payments."

"Permit me to continue slowly, for the relationships are rather complex. As you also must know, Mr. Dulles' firm, Sullivan & Cromwell established a Berlin office and reluctantly withdrew from its German clients before the recent war. In fact, many still retain their suspicions concerning S & C's objectivity even after war was declared. Does it not stand to reason that little could be better for S & C's image than working *pro bono* to see that these stamps, stolen from Jews, at long last result in some good?"

Out of the corner of his eye Seis spots Rudy about to get another glass of orange juice and shakes his head. Has the man no self-control?

"Dulles is still with Sullivan & Cromwell, who are located only blocks from here. I've no hesitation leaving this office and walking over there this minute. On arriving, I'll present myself at Dulles's door and explain to his secretary who my father was. If Dulles is out, I'll knock on the door of their senior corporate law partner. He is a German Jew and lost many of his family. Given the terrible things done to the Jews, I've no doubt that I'll be shortly in somebody's office and will have S & C representing not me or our Reparations Board, but rather millions of dead Jews. Taking one consideration with another, to paraphrase a Gilbert and Sullivan song, a stamp auctioneer's lot is not a happy one, is it? By this time tomorrow, I am certain S & C will have had an injunction issued to stop the sale."

"Lars," Seis asks, "you know the American legal system far better than I do. How many *years* are we talking about before a final decision might be reached?"

Lars gives a harsh laugh, "A minimum of three; but, with bad luck, if our Supreme Court became involved, four or five. Also, R.S., we must consider, the impact that such publicity would have on our corporate future."

For the first time Thistleman & Chandler's auctioneer, Cassidy, speaks. "There would be no more auctions I'm afraid, R.S. This story would effectively put us out of business. We could expect Jewish boycotts plus investigations by the ethics committees of some of our professional associations. Speaking personally, to salvage my career, I'd be forced to resign later today. Lars too." Head down, Cassidy holds his hands prayerfully as he shakes his head.

"Do I have any options?" Thistleman asks, shoulders slumping as he looks at Lars.

"Yes, I believe we do," Lars answers looking at Seis. "First, and foremost, have you forgotten Dr. Seis that any publicity means that the stamps will be in litigation for years? That means all of us at this table will be hurt equally. Have you considered that?"

"Of course," Seis replies evenly. "But as a government agency, we will continue drawing our salaries. We are fully prepared to wait for as long as the international legal process takes."

Seis is about to continue when he notices Rudy pouring yet another glass of juice. "Get me one too," he smiles, for he has the rest of the day to carry out his bluff. "Perhaps though," he says to Lars as he looks around, "you would point us to the wash room while you gentlemen can talk privately. The facts are on the table. It is up to you to decide how to treat them."

▲

The negotiations are brief. Thistleman capitulates minutes after the break concludes. Almost crying, he agrees to pay Seis 57½ cents per dollar for each *delta* stamp sold at the auction. Since he is also obligated to pay Abramson's widow and Romanoff—which include Harry's stamps—any significant delinquency on his part will lead to the collapse of his business. Not including upfront costs and unmarked stamps, Thistleman can now look forward to an expenditure of some $1.60 for each dollar in revenue; in short, a bath of monumental proportions even if the minimum bid price were accepted for every sale.

And stiffing Seis? Thistleman is not a violent man and has no desire to lock horns with ODESSA, whom he realizes that Otto represents. He agrees that Spangler will attend the auction, noting each sale and perhaps bidding at times to artificially raise prices—a violation of every philatelic ethical code. All payments will be due in cash, in one week, at 10 A.M. at Thistleman's office. The final amount determined by Rudy, Seis, and Lars over the weekend. Seis emphasizes that, given the amount of cash, besides he and Klaber, other gentlemen from Yaphank will join them.

"Oh, and one more thing," Seis asks, "please have more fresh orange juice brought in."

Meanwhile, for as long as it takes, Spangler and Lars will microscopically examine each stamp to be auctioned so that there is no question as to which stamps were marked.

▲

Seis also announces that Otto will stay in the event he's needed and is pleased to see Otto nodding. Seis doesn't realize it, but by asking Otto to stay another day, Otto can drop by St. Catherine's Park Tuesday and visit with Lori, the redhead whose first name he's learned, and "Veronica," who was friendlier the third time he saw her.

▲

As for Thistleman, he knows he's being extorted, but doesn't know how to respond. What he does know is that he soon will be selling at least a half-million dollars in stocks and bonds from his father's fast-shrinking patrimony.

Chapter 56: New York, Thursday, November 15.

The massive Seventy-First Regimental Armory on Park Avenue and 34th Street is capped by a 150-foot tower modeled after an Italian medieval design, the turreted main building four stories high. The main drill hall alone is 39,000 square feet, its curved roof sixty feet high. For the show, 30,000 philatelists will visit 225 booths, or *bourse* as philatelists call them (from the medieval Latin word 'purse'), displays, and auctions. Most exhibitors buy and sell stamps, and so if there is one shoebox (the standard way stamps are filed) there are ten-thousand, each holding some 250 packets of stamps. In short, millions of stamps are for sale.

Attendees at this third National Postage Stamp Show, mostly men, knowing that there is no interior heating, wear heavy overcoats and hats. As the armory's massive doors swing open, the crowd, paying 30¢ each, surges in.

From the floor, hundreds of men stand in front of their displays, the atmosphere immediately changing as attendees enter and get their bearings. Some collectors make a bee-line for a favored vendor, wanting to be the first to purchase or resolutely check out a dealer's inventory. In minutes, friends meet, questions are asked, and sales begin. As most attendees' smoke, the air is transformed into an immense blue cloud slowly drifting to the ceiling.

Also in attendance are uniformed police, private guards, detectives, and IRS and Bureau of Printing and Engraving agents. Their role is simple: protect the estimated $25 million in stamps on display, or to be sold or auctioned off. Indeed, theft is the industry's bugaboo. Since the war, with sad frequency, newspapers report well-planned break-ins; among others the American Stamp Company ($75,000, 1948), General Stamp ($100,000, '49), and a burglary ring caught after $700,000 in thefts ('50).

▲

Weeks earlier, Romanoff had told Harry that he wanted to attend the stamp show, but not Thistleman's auction. Like Roosevelt in '45, the baron now wears the mark of death. Dark blotches cover his face and hands, he has lost weight, his jowls sag, half-moon black rings droop beneath his eyes and, barely able to stand, he is effectively confined to a wheelchair. With Sven pushing and Harry alongside, the trio slowly roam the armory's huge floor.

Veteran stamp dealers realize that this is likely the baron's last public appearance. Frequently fortified by cognac, his mind works perfectly and he is at his best remembering names, recalling incidents, and telling stories—some true—as he visits each booth.

Just after leaving H. R. Harmer's booth and after a long, hilarious chat with the firm's patriarch, the increasingly deaf, irascible, eighty-three-year-old Henry Ravell Harmer, Sven wheels Romanoff sharply into an aisle, accidentally bumping a distracted attendee. The man, although not to blame, in keeping with the conference's civility, immediately apologizes.

"Don't I know you?" Romanoff asks as he, Sven and Harry look at the person.

"Yes, we met four years ago, sir" says the clearly surprised Rudy Spangler, bowing.

"Permit an old man's confusion, but I'm trying to recall our conversation."

"I was interested in a particular Dutch stamp, which you had. Then you, having negotiated so well and suspecting I had little money left, were kind enough to send me to the Cloud Club for lunch," Rudy replies, making the story as humorous as possible.

"But there was something else. You were a *Fallschirmjäger*—"

"A *Fallschirmjäger*? So was I," Harry cuts in as he professionally looks Rudy up and down. "And you have a paratrooper's build."

"Until Crete."

"You were wounded there? Your cane?"

Rudy nods twice.

"But you said *until*. You were a *Fallschirmjäger* before Crete. In Belgium?"

"At Eban Emael."

A smile of recognition and professional admiration comes over Harry's face. He instinctively likes this man and Eban Emael was the combat parachute equivalent of Mount Everest. "Fort Eban Emael? An amazing story, landing in gliders on the roof of a covered fort and then blocking their air vents."

Rudy modestly nods, "I would've preferred that to Arnhem. The fort's roof was actually quite empty."

"I always admired Max Schmeling for his saving Jewish children. He was also a *Fallschirmjäger*. Did you ever meet him?"

"We were wounded together. He is my son's godfather. And you, no bad wounds?"

"Little ones, starting with a bad landing in Sicily— "

"Then you were in Gavin's Eighty-Second? Remarkably able. Did you meet him?"

"I knew him well enough so that he is godfather to our son, James Gavin Strong."

"And my son is Max Schmeling Spangler," Rudy says.

The two shake hands, acting like old comrades. Harry wishes they had time to sit down and reminisce for he instinctively likes this man, his former foe.

"A pleasure to meet you, and to see you again, sir," Rudy says, bowing slightly to Romanoff and excusing himself, "but the auction I'm attending begins shortly."

As Spangler goes, Romanoff turns to Harry, signals 'come here' with his hand, and whispers in his ear. "Now I remember why he visited me; he'd no real interest in Dutch stamps, he wanted to know about *yours*."

▲

Mid-afternoon, Friday, November 16. At CIA headquarters, Baker is ordered to immediately see the European section head. After reporting, he is bundled into a waiting car and driven to Bolling Air Force Base, a site on the east side of the District of Columbia's Anacostia River. No phone calls are allowed. He is told that someone will take his car and pick up his wife, informing her that he's been sent overseas. The reason for the urgency is not explained. Not until he's well on his way to Europe does he learn that General Gehlen has received information that Seis, now in the U.S., plans to kill him. Not until late Monday will Baker have access to an overseas phone.

Chapter 57: New York, Saturday, November 18.

For scientifically inexplicable reasons, people often sense when they are being stared at. Later Harry feels *something*, turns rapidly and sees two men looking at him. Both men pretended they hadn't been noticed, but he's met one before. Where had they met and why did he look so familiar? Not until Saturday, two days later, eating lunch in Romanoff's apartment, does it come to Harry.

"He looked like Hermann Seis, I'm sure of it," Harry tells Romanoff and Lansky. "He was the person I met the day Aaron Abramson died."

"So," says Lansky to Romanoff, "the man who questioned you about our stamps is in New York again. Then, someone who looks like this dead Seis fellow also shows up." Lansky leads the long discussion, asking both Harry and Romanoff a host of questions about Spangler and the man they assume is Franz Seis.

"Well, I can't say that it isn't entirely unexpected..." Romanoff says, his sentence trailing off.

"Do you think they know what I did to Hermann?" Harry asks.

"Let's assume so. By the way," Lansky says, "where are your children?"

"At home," he begins, but the weight of the impending separation, divorce, and Nan's romance comes gushing out.

"And there's nothing that I can do," Harry concludes. "Nan's got me by the balls, I've had a part-time girlfriend for almost a year that she knows all about. She hired a private detective a few months ago and has photographs of me entering Alice's apartment and silhouette of us undressing. I'm screwed blue and tattooed. I saw an attorney yesterday and discovered that, under New York law, unless I can *prove* adultery on her part, she'll raise the two children."

"Theoretically only, Harry," Lansky asks, "Do you want to prove she's also been adulterous? After all, she says she has." Lansky sees no point telling Harry at this moment about Nan's working for Dinty Moore years earlier. Harry learning now that Lansky set him up with a prostitute, now the mother of his two children, is *not* going to help their relationship. To Lansky, continuing to sell the stamps and raise cash for Israel remains his first objective.

"No," Harry answers, "I'm too tired to fight. She's going to marry this man and I'm just as guilty. Anything that came out in court will only screw up the children down the road. I prefer losing some money to having shit flung all over a courtroom."

"You're doing the right thing," Lansky says, relieved. "And you can count on me to make sure her lawyer doesn't screw you over."

▲

"Harry," Romanoff begins after calling Bernard to bring in more coffee, "I want to tell you a story about my good friend, Rudyard Kipling."

Harry and Lansky smile to themselves; both have discovered that, as often than not, the more famous Romanoff's purported friends are, the less likely it is that the baron knew them. But both agree, as Romanoff often comments, that "good stories shouldn't be ruined by facts."

"Rudyard told me," the baron begins, "that he'd been to Hartford on business—he was living near Brattleboro, Vermont then—when coincidentally a Shriner Circus came to town. For whatever reason, one of the elephants went wild and badly injured a trainer. When the elephant couldn't be calmed down, the circus manager realized that they'd have to shoot the poor beast. As elephants represent considerable expensive to train and feed, the manager, faced with this financial loss, announced he'd publicly execute the poor beast, and began selling tickets for the event.

"Kipling, already well-known, got wind of the plan and became incensed. He called the editor of the *Hartford Courant* and next the mayor. Soon the three were at the circus, meeting with its manager, and standing in front of the huge bellowing beast. Kipling told me it was one of the largest elephants he had ever seen in captivity."

Harry isn't surprised at the creature's exaggerated size; a pygmy elephant, for example, would never have done for one of the baron's stories.

" 'Where is this elephant from?' Kipling asked the manager," the baron continued.

" 'I believe near Bombay,' was the answer.

" 'Excellent,' Kipling replied, 'I was born in Bombay and am fluent in Bombaiya.'

"With that," Romanoff continued, "Kipling took off his shoes, socks, tie, and jacket and walked up to the elephant, his posture and walk every bit as slowly as on a hot Indian day. As he approached the beast he began talking softly to it in Bombaiya. The agitated animal immediately ceased to roar and paw the ground and, in minutes, it had wrapped its trunk around Kipling as it would a baby pachyderm.

"Kipling returned to the three men he had just left and explained that there was no need to shoot the animal. After hearing Bombaiya language and seeing clothing like an Indian's, the pachyderm became calm. However, in the future, Kipling said, even if no one spoke Bombaiya, the elephant's handlers should not wear jackets, shoes, or ties in its presence."

"But what happened to the beast afterward?" Harry asks.

"I never asked," Romanoff answers, shrugging his shoulders. "For all I know, with a little bit of bad luck it was hit by a locomotive when the circus moved to New Haven. But it's far more likely they publicly shot the poor animal in Buffalo or Toledo; someplace where Kipling wouldn't have heard about it. However, Harry, you're probably wondering about the point of my story."

"Perhaps I was wrong," Harry smiles, "to assume that there would be no lesson."

"My brief to you is this: You, Harry, are the elephant while Nan has become the avaricious circus manager. My friend Rudyard is long gone, Harry; what we need to find for you not someone who speaks Bombaiya but—"

"Rather," Harry says laughing, "someone who speaks German?"

"Exactly. But enough of Kipling," says Romanoff. "Yesterday afternoon I received a message stating that Franz Seis and his assistant, Spangler, would like to see me Monday afternoon."

"Well," Lansky says, "let's discuss what we need to do."

Chapter 58: Sunday Evening, the Commodore Hotel.

Ilse and Seis are entwined on their bed at the Commodore Hotel. Neither is dressed as they lie under crumpled sheets, the smell of cigarettes slowly dissipating the odors of love making.

For Ilse, the past week has been a marvelous experience. With Seis busy during the day—at meetings, the stamp show, or the Public Library—she visited the Statue of Liberty, took the ferry to Staten Island, rode to the top of the Empire State Building, and marveled at the collections in the Metropolitan and Natural History museums. Without objection from Seis, who spent Saturday with Rudy at Thistleman's office, she went by herself round-trip via train to Albany. This way she could compare the Hudson (America's Rhine) with the real thing as well, as visiting the famed Keeler's German restaurant for lunch. Back that evening, she and Seis ate at Gallagher's Steakhouse on 52nd Street (where "New York" strip was first cut) and, holding hands, they strolled back to the Commodore via Broadway's Great White Way.

Ilse rolls over next to him. "You've more good news, don't you?" she asks. "Since Monday I've never seen you happier. Now you're acting as if you just jumped over the moon."

"Rudy and I finally completed our work at Thistleman's. They'll be paying us tomorrow morning. We'll be getting more than I expected."

"Do you want to tell me how much?"

"Of course not," he says laughing and kissing her. "But it will be over $125,000 in American cash." Ilse has no way of knowing that the actual figure is almost four times higher, but to her the number still seems incredible.

"So, your trip is now a total success?"

"I have almost reached my goal, but I am not quite there yet."

"But why is Otto Klaber joining you? It means something risky, doesn't it?"

"Tomorrow morning, I will be carrying more cash than I'd like. Otto can best see to the money's safety. Also, remember that this past Monday's success wasn't guaranteed either," he says, kissing the nape of her neck. "But it turned out well."

"However, tomorrow involves greater risks, doesn't it?"

"Really?" Franz answers as Ilse realizes he has other thoughts on his mind.

He is about to say something when Ilse laughingly slaps him. "One subject at a time," but she lets him take her hand and place it between his legs. "And how much more money can you gain by this?"

"It is not just the money; a significant number of my stamps remain unaccounted for. And, after so many years, I might finally learn how Hermann died."

Ilse knows the conversation is almost over, for Franz places his mouth on her breast.

"Why, Franz? Why pursue it further? What happens if something goes wrong? If the people involved aren't as malleable as Thistleman?"

"Don't worry," he says, momentarily pulling his head up. "I won't be involved in anything dangerous. In fact, tomorrow evening, we'll be having dinner with one of the gentleman and his wife at their house."

Ilse wants to ask more, but then becomes distracted by a more intimate kiss and caress.

▲

With Ilse asleep afterward, Seis is annoyed at himself for not discussing marriage and Argentina. If he's honest with himself, there could be some danger tomorrow. How many people has he known who carried their luck a tad too far and, like Icarus, flew too close to the sun? What would he stand to lose by returning to Germany with Thistleman's money? If he does nothing else, their lives will be beyond comfortable. As for losing face with Otto and Dieter, he has half a dozen good reasons to call things off, and, after all, they'll be paid handsomely. It will be something to think about when he awakes.

Part VII: Monday, November 19.

Chapter 59: New York, Morning.

Romanoff's office in the Graybar Building has shrunk to 600 square feet, papers packed in stacked boxes, the last staff discharged. Now there is only a small anteroom, washroom, closet, and Romanoff's 15' x 20' office. After a light lunch at his desk, Romanoff prepares himself for the interview he'd anticipated since he first met Harry Strong. Sven is armed and expecting trouble, and Romanoff has willed himself together.

At 1:15 PM, Seis and Rudy knock. Seis, trusting no one, carries the black leather valise holding American dollar bills containing the faces of Presidents McKinley ($500) and Cleveland ($1,000), the total coming to slightly over $457,000.

Seis introduces himself to Romanoff, specifically stating that he is a *doctor professor*. It is a title he seldom uses, but he knows that the European educated Romanoff will understand its importance.

"Ah, and Mr. Spangler too," Romanoff says, going along with Seis's War Reparations charade. A smile crosses his face. "Years ago, I spent some time with a Conrad Seis. By chance are you related?

"My father."

"Excellent. I knew him in the Third Reich's earliest days, when the French attitude toward German rearmament was decidedly negative."

Seis's eyes widen with interest. It was when he was beginning "in university," all but oblivious to his father's work for Hitler's government.

"Your father wasn't well-known, I mean no disrespect, of course," he says to Seis who acknowledges the comment with a nod, "so he traveled without concern. We arranged for new Mausers and other weapons to be shipped from the Oberndorf factory to Buenos Aires or Valparaiso. While German arms limitations were strict, the Mauser company was permitted to sell overseas to third parties. So, across the Atlantic rifles went, then sat in warehouses. After more paperwork and 'thank you's' to local officials, the arms returned to Germany after traveling 15,000-miles. But, you ask, how did we bring rifles *to* Hamburg? Because they were now in cases labeled 'sardines' or 'corned beef.' "

"And when they were opened?" laughs Seis, clearly charmed.

"Out came Mauser rifles and ammunition; a cornucopia of weaponry needed for the rifle clubs that were 'spontaneously' springing up everywhere. Your father was an excellent negotiator, fluent in Spanish, and a man of discretion. I was sorry to read about his death this year. If your mother is still living, please offer my condolences. Perhaps she'll remember my name."

It was, Romanoff thought, a fine performance if he said so himself. While he had shipped Mausers and what not via South America, he'd never worked with Conrad Seis. Nevertheless, he knew the man by reputation—an arrogant Nazi prick.

After listening to Seis explain his fictitious goals, Romanoff can only laugh to himself, but Lansky had counseled candor. "The person you want to speak to is a Harry Strong. In fact, I took the liberty of calling him after receiving your message last week. He'll be happy to meet you after work."

Seis is stunned. All his machinations have been unnecessary. It is too late to prevent Harry's being beaten by Dieter's bully boys, but he's made worse mistakes.

"Let me tell you what I know," Romanoff continues. "As a stamp buyer—and let me be candid, albeit immodest—with my international reputation, it was imperative never to acquire stamps I knew to be stolen, and Strong's stamps presented numerous ethical questions."

Seis and Rudy sit motionless, at rapt attention.

"Major Harry Strong was in the 82nd Airborne," Romanoff begins. "After the war ended, the 82nd was sent to Berlin for garrison duty. Because he spoke perfect German—"

"Perfect German?" Seis asks.

"Yes. Harry is the former Heinrich Strölin, born in Stuttgart and half-Jewish; not that he looks it. His father left after Hitler took power."

Seis nods, trying not to show his anger that a Jew has acquired his stamps.

"When the 82nd returned on the *Queen Mary* one evening he joined a craps game—"

The two nod in agreement. So far, so good, Romanoff thinks, carefully watching Seis's eyes. "Harry was doing well, so sometime that evening he became what is called 'The Bank.'"

"The bank?" Rudy asks.

"Yes. That is what Americans call the player who holds the money and directs the game. Meanwhile, the officer who had acquired the stamps kept losing."

"And wouldn't quit," Seis says, and shakes his head. "There are so many people like that. They're always certain that their swayback horse can defeat the thoroughbred. I assume that, when the gambler became desperate—"

"Just so. The officer returned to his quarters and came back with the stamps. Harry was an amateur collector and didn't need to be told their value. One look sufficed. Because he was the bank, he loaned the officer $1,000; the stamps his collateral."

"And the officer lost that too," Seis says, shaking his head. "Do you know anything more about this person? Who he was or how he had acquired the stamps?"

"I inquired no further. Like Admiral Nelson at Copenhagen, there are times in philately when turning a blind eye towards a commander's signal is the only practical approach. My assumption has always been that the stamps were originally acquired from Jews, but from whom and how often they exchanged hands before reaching Harry is a mystery."

"I'd have expected no less," Seis laughs. "And this Harry—"

"Has other interests these days."

"If I might inquire, what does he do professionally do?" asks Seis, whose question is rhetorical.

"Nothing concerning stamps. For a year he went to graduate school, but like so many men who have seen combat, sitting in a classroom all day proved irksome. In the years since, he's done quite well for himself in the construction industry. As we speak, he is atop a new building on Fifth Avenue, hundreds of feet above the ground. I get dizzy just looking up."

"As do I," Seis smiles. "But how were his stamps sold?"

"Through our now closed business. With my partner's death, all that remained were sold last week. However, Harry isn't naïve. You will be pleased to know that he had no trouble guessing the source and remains troubled by it."

"But that didn't stop him from keeping the money, did it?"

"On the contrary, he kept just enough to pay for his graduate studies and rent. Like us, he considered these stamps 'blood money.' We, Romanoff & Abramson kept *nothing*. Every penny of expense was born by us."

Seis has had enough. Ilse is right. This man is dying, he thinks, I have $450,000 from Thistleman, and am seeing Strong tonight. Rudy can sit with Sven so that nothing happens when Otto arrives.

"I have only one more question," asks Seis. Where did the stamp money go?"

"Of course," smiles Romanoff. "First, we made sure that we conformed to American law. But you asked where the money went. By chance, does the name *Haganah* ring a bell? And now the Mossad."

"The Palestine Jewish terrorist organization?" Seis answers, his face getting red. "Do you mean to tell me that you gave the money to those bastards? And the Mossad?"

"I mean to tell you just that," says Romanoff, inwardly happy. He wishes he had one of those new Polaroid cameras to capture Seis's look of disbelief. "Fortunately, its successor, the Mossad, also delights in untraceable American cash. Our goal was never complex; we wanted to help surviving Jews. Was there a better way so that those murdered didn't die in vain?"

"So, that is what you expect me to tell Bonn when I write my report?"

"Precisely that. Harry Strong won the stamps playing craps aboard the *Queen Mary*. I'm certain he can even give you an exact date."

▲

In shock, Seis glances around. He needs to compose himself before he explodes. So, this Romanoff is a Jew too! He's given the money from 'my' stamps to Haganah and the Mossad. Calm yourself. Breathe slowly and concentrate on something else. Glancing around, he realizes that he didn't notice one object when he entered: on a book shelf is a reproduction of a Greek vase showing Ajax and Achilles playing dice during the Trojan war.

"I believe that amphora is from the school of Exekias," Seis says pointing. "As you know, Hitler believed the Greeks to be the fountainhead of Aryan civilization. In school, we studied them carefully. Even when he invaded Greece he refused to let our *Luftwaffe* bomb Athens. That original amphora is now in the Vatican, although counterfeits are also frequent."

"This is, of course, a reproduction," Romanoff laughs. "However, there is an excellent counterfeit sitting in my library. There was a time when I thought that I had hoodwinked the Vatican, but now I keep the bogus example as a reminder that I'm not infallible. Nevertheless, watching Achilles and Ajax playing their version of craps is always enlightening."

"Yes, it is, Baron Romanoff; yes, it is." Seis says and begins laughing so hard that Rudy becomes concerned.

"It's there, Spangler," Seis says. "There. You don't see it, do you?" he laughs again, then turns back to Romanoff. "No, my dear sir," Seis says, "I am afraid that behind your desk is the fatal flaw to your imaginative story concerning how Major Strong won *my* stamps. And you've just told me what it is."

Seis is about to say something else when, despite their door being closed, the three hear knocking at the office's front entrance. Romanoff puts up his hand as Seis and Rudy turn to look. "Sven, see who is there," he calls. "And please continue, Dr. Seis."

"Unfortunately, I have always felt that there was something wrong with the 'craps' explanation. At first, I couldn't put my finger on it—"

"At first? I don't understand," Romanoff says. "When did you originally hear the story?

"*When* makes no matter now, but might you be interested to know what the flaw?"

"I'd be delighted," says Romanoff, feeling his heart beating faster than he wants. "However, it appears I have forgotten to take my medicine. If you don't mind handing me both those bottles," he says to Seis, pointing to two a few feet away.

"And some water too," Romanoff says. Rudy stands to fetch a glass. "No there's no need for you to go. Sven might as well do something to earn his money."

"Sven," he calls out," would you bring in a glass of water, please."

There is no response until Otto Klaber appears and looks at Seis.

Romanoff can only mutter "Oh."

"Otto," Seis says, "please bring the baron some water. And, if I might be so bold as to say it, baron, I'm afraid that Sven is no longer in your employ."

Only then does Romanoff realize how incredibly stupid he's been.

Chapter 60: Craps.

Sven's death had been instantaneous. Hearing the knock on the door, he opened it, and saw Otto holding a pistol with a silencer. Otto pulled the trigger, then leaped forward, grabbing Sven collapsing body before closing the door. There is blood and urine to wipe up, but enough closet space in which to place Sven's standing corpse for a few hours.

"Thank you, Otto," Seis says as Otto enters Romanoff's office with water. "And if I might ask? What do the pills contain?"

"The tiny one is nitroglycerine; the larger ones contain codeine."

"A good choice," said Seis, as he nods to Otto. Romanoff puts the nitroglycerine tablet under his tongue until it dissolves. Then he swallows three codeine pills, the effect of which he knows will make this last conversation of his life bearable.

"Might I ask for a cigarette?" Romanoff asks, "my doctors have made every effort to block my access to smoking. Even poor Sven wouldn't purchase them for me."

As Seis watches, Romanoff says "ashtray" and slowly reaches into a desk drawer soon fingering not just an ashtray, but also his cyanide capsule. Palming the capsule, an easy trick for an amateur magician, he places the ashtray on the desk's top, leans back in his chair, and takes a deep puff of the cigarette Seis lights for him.

"If you might," he says to Seis, "let us be as civil as possible. I can assure you I have no weapons in my desk; that was Sven's role. You are welcome to look, but I will find this conversation more tolerable with Otto outside."

Seis has no reason to look. To him it's apparent that Romanoff is almost in shock and poses no threat. He nods for Otto to leave.

"So, shall we discuss the flaw of Major Strong's account?" Seis asks.

Romanoff says nothing, the codeine is beginning to have its effect. Meyer offered me help Saturday, he thinks, and what did I do? I turned him down. As Harry also did. Did I secretively want to die this way versus having my heart stop without warning?

"Like yourself," Seis is saying, "I am somewhat of a linguist."

"Yes, but how does that impact Harry's winning the stamps?"

"Few upper-class Germans play craps and educated German Jews, never. Perhaps peasant Jews, but can you imagine Sigmund Freud or Albert Einstein on their knees rolling dice? Major Strong holds a position of business responsibility. And what was his father?"

"A senior engineer working for Ferdinand Porsche—"

"Dr. Porsche? That's exactly my point. Would a father, especially an engineer employed by Dr. Porsche, permit his son to sink to his knees and roll dice? Or a Jewish mother with high aspirations for her son? Think about it. Major Strong wouldn't have learned, least of all acquired an expertise in such nonsense. Craps on a felt covered table in Monte Carlo is one thing, but a dank, crowded troop ship on the high seas, even the *Queen Mary*, is another."

"Craps is a game of luck that every soldier plays," Romanoff says resignedly.

As the two continue speaking in German, Rudy sits all but stupefied. So, he too will finally learn how Hermann lost the stamps.

"No. No Jew such as Strong would risk his wartime savings gambling on a troopship. I am afraid your friend lied to you. I have learned many times over that no Jew tells the truth, especially concerning something of value. You must search to find the lie, but it is always there. Of course, *you* could've made up the story to sell the stamps. Did you?"

Romanoff shakes his head. The story had been Lansky's idea, a poor Jew growing up in a slum who told stories about playing sidewalk craps with Lucky Luciano.

"And there's something else you should know. The man who acquired these stamps, someone in the 82nd, did so only after brutally murdering my brother Hermann. His front teeth were smashed, the pistol placed *in his mouth* when he was shot. He was carrying the stamps for me, Rudy, Herbert Backe, Walther Darré, and Martin Bormann. Did you realize that?"

"How could I?" Romanoff answers weakly. His heart is speeding up again and he places a second nitroglycerine under his tongue while he and Seis say nothing.

"My actions always have been about the stamps *and* my brother," Seis continues. "I am independently wealthy and the stamps are—what do Americans say—'frosting on the cake'?"

Romanoff nods, all but kicking himself. By not understanding Seis's motivation to avenge his brother, he and Lansky have also placed Harry and his family in mortal danger.

"Now," Seis says, "to show you that I appreciate your contributions to the Third Reich decades ago, do you have any last words before I call Otto back? I'm in no hurry."

"Yes, a few. Did you know that my good friend Orson Welles is also a magician?"

Although they both know who Welles is, Seis and Rudy are confused.

"Rudolf, if time permitted I would pull a silver dollar from behind your ear, but let me show you both something else I taught Orson."

"*Oh my,*" Romanoff thinks, putting his hand to his mouth without hesitation and crunching the cyanide pill forcefully before swallowing the almond smelling liquid.

"Dr. Seis, you are a dead man too—" He had thought there would be more time to say something else, but he feels his body beginning to shudder. And, as if from very far away, he is conscious of the strange fact that he is having trouble thinking of words.

▲

Seis dives across the table, but is far too late. The old man's body arches back, throwing him over the top of his wheelchair. Then Romanoff's eyes roll back as his final convulsions end.

Seis shakes his head. I shouldn't have said I knew he was lying, he thinks. I lost my temper before finding out everything I needed. What if Major Strong is just a straw man? Am I meeting someone who really knows what happened to Hermann?

Otto bursts through the door, carefully placing his head next to the dead man's mouth.

"Cyanide?" Seis asks as Otto nods.

"Yes, and we must be careful now," Otto says. "American offices have women clean-up every evening. We can't hide Romanoff's body, but we can make it appear natural. The police will be here, but if we're lucky the closet might not be opened immediately. Downstairs are American 'drug stores.' I'll purchase something they call *witch hazel*; it's an all-purpose liquid medicine with a pleasant, not a chemical smell."

"I suppose that you have done this before?"

"Oh yes, more than once."

Seis smiles. "Well, it would be best if we begin cleaning this office immediately."

Chapter 61: Triborough Bridge, 1:30 PM.

Less than five air-miles from Romanoff's office, Dieter Schmidt is sitting in a DeSoto, "lifted" only hours before. Now it sits on the Triborough Bridge where traffic has all but halted. Dieter has not yet reached the highest part of the bridge's arc, but, to his right, a mile away, he can see the toll booths and the rotating lights of police cars, tow trucks, and ambulances. To his left, is the uncompleted East River Drive that also has a jam at the 96th Street exit. He doesn't know what has happened there either, but he now estimates that, despite leaving Yaphank early, he might be two hours late in reaching 696 Fifth Avenue.

Alongside Dieter in the middle seat is Hasso Bittrich, a longtime, thoroughly reliable friend. Bittrich is large, has a mean streak and was *Panzer Lehr*'s champion light heavyweight boxer which left him with cauliflower ears and a certain slowness of speech. However, he is slow to anger and surprisingly careful, almost cagey. The third passenger is Milwaukee-born Klaus Stutsman. A 1941 leg wound saw Stutsman, built like a fireplug, successfully apply to the Gestapo where, until the war's end, he was assigned to SS prisoner interrogation—work not for the squeamish. Dieter has decided that, on reaching 696 Fifth Ave. and confronting Strong, Stutsman will administer the beating.

All three smoke and fidget, but there is nothing they can do to speed up traffic.

Chapter 62: 696 Fifth Avenue, Mid-Afternoon.

696 Fifth Avenue is Harry's most prestigious project. The building's design, he proudly tells visitors, isn't one smaller rectangular cube placed on top another to conform to city zoning requirements. Rather "Six-Nine-Six," like so many near Rockefeller Center, is perpendicular from top to bottom. The structure is "recessed" from Fifth Avenue and both side streets, giving pedestrians the feeling of a plaza, the planned visual enhancements including raised flower beds, long marble seating, and a small fountain, all facing Fifth Avenue.

The steel framework, rising 535 feet, was completed as scheduled the previous week. A brief "topping out" ceremony has been held. A small fir tree—in keeping with an ancient Scandinavian/pagan tradition—is placed above the highest beam. Not surprisingly, Big Al has planned a large party at his Club Monte Carlo for the Tuesday after Thanksgiving.

For Harry, the gathering presents a quandary. How will he explain Nan's absence? It's one of the first ramifications of their separation that is beginning to hit home. Indeed, it seems scarcely a minute goes by without his wondering what will happen to the children, and how much, other than loss of face, does he still really care about Nan? Sometimes, on a clear day, standing alone on the top of the unfinished building, the magnificent view unparalleled and soundless, he knows that the answer is no. Harry is not angry at her nor angry at himself, there was love at first, but as Nan more clearly recognized, he tells himself, they have grown in different ways, taken divergent paths. It was as if they'd been together, walking along the Continental Divide in Yellowstone Park, and each had taken one of the tiny streams from Isa Lake that lead to different oceans.

▲

By early afternoon, Harry feels the tension from Seis's presence in New York. Earlier, a telegram from "Baker" reaches him saying that he's in Europe and Seis is in New York. Harry is angered by its contents: big fucken help the CIA is, he thinks, now telling me to be careful. Thanks for nothing. There's also a message from Lansky brought by a runner: "I'll in the lobby of Manhattan House by 4:30 acting as your attorney. Wait for me there."

Harry feels the muscles in his neck tighten and his mouth goes dry. Switching from coffee to soda pop doesn't help. Sometimes pictures of Alice Denham pop into his mind. She's ambitious, gorgeous, and self-absorbed, but he and Alice have no future. It's almost the same as when he met Nan, pure ego and passion. He'd thought that with her living in Greenwich Village, where he's unknown, he could carry off the affair. But now his lawyer is telling him that this little tryst means Nan will take him to the cleaners in court, especially if Alice's "artistic" nude pictures are shown.

▲

3:30 PM. Across the street from the construction office, Dieter Schmidt pulls the DeSoto over and lets out Klaus Stutsman and Hasso Bittrich. The two enter, and find five architects working. Two others drink coffee while reading the *Journal-American* and *Daily Racing Form*. Finally, the younger one looks up. Union foremen, Stutsman thinks with disgust, but politely asks where Harry Strong is. The man, annoyed that he's been bothered, without asking who they are, indifferently points to a construction elevator grunting, "He's up top,'" and returns to his paper.

The two then wait until a man saunters out of a john and confirms Harry's location. "But I gotta take you up myself. Union rules, you know. I hope you boys ain't planning on staying long; it's colder 'an shit today." Klaus and Hasso have worn inexpensive raincoats and hats, cheap scarves and thin socks that offer no protection against a wind chill that exponentially grows as the heavy-duty, open-sided construction elevator slowly rises. When the elevator finally stops they're hugging themselves.

On what is to be forty-ninth floor, the wind fiercely whips a small American flag, but nothing offers protection. A score of workers, wearing seamen's Peabody jackets and hoods under safety helmets, are busy welding or laying down the steel lattice over which concrete will be poured. Fifty-feet away a tall man is clearly in charge, gesturing to three dark-skinned workers with the high cheek bones of Indians. As they talk, little white vapor puffs come from everyone's mouth. In a month, it will be the year's shortest day and the sun, already low on the horizon, offers no warmth.

Klaus and Hasso carefully watch their feet as they walk across thick wood planking, quickly reaching the man who seems surprised seeing two "civilians" so high up.

"Whoever you guys are," says Harry Strong, who steps in front of the Mohawks, "this is no place to be. You're gonna' freeze your balls off. And who let you up here anyhow?"

"You Harry Strong?" ask Klaus, not bothering to answer.

"Yeah, that's me. But who are you? Nobody's supposed—"

"We came to talk to you about your stamps," Klaus cut in. Then his right hand, brass knuckles on it, comes out of his pocket.

"What stamps? What the hell—" Harry is saying when Klaus sucker punches him in the lower groin, bringing him to his knees. Harry's jacket, thick as it is, doesn't prevent Klaus's punch from taking most of the air out of his lungs. As he doubles over, Klaus elbows him with an uppercut to the jaw, further numbing him.

"Hey?" one of the Mohawks says. All three step forward, only to see Hasso holding a pistol with a silencer pointed at them.

"Just back up and no one will be hurt," Hasso says. "This is a private discussion. It's got nothing to do with you boys."

Klaus slowly pulls Harry up, smiling when he sees how wobbly the man's legs are.

"This is all about the stamps you stole, my friends want them back," Klaus says, this time smashing Harry in the side, but not hard enough to break any ribs. Harry, gasping for breath, is about to roll onto the lattice-work while Klaus steadies him on his feet.

"Do you get the picture now? You pissed off the wrong people. Next time leave well enough alone. And for that I'm going to kick the shit out of you." There'll be no broken bones per Seis's orders, but Klaus's kicks and punches will leave some nasty black and blue marks across Harry's body.

After another uppercut elbow to Harry's jaw, Klaus takes a half step back, anchors his left leg and begins a swinging motion with his right foot. Yet, at the same instant, he realizes that something is hurtling towards his face. Klaus instinctively leans back, but the tip of his nose is torn off by an arrow. As his hands reach for his face, which seems to have erupted in blood, a searing pain explodes in his left thigh. Slowly, he stands, doubled over in pain, then he becomes aware of a new form of agony that is even worse: the notched arrow is suddenly yanked out of his thigh. Slowly, he begins to topple over.

Hasso, hearing Klaus's scream, whirls his head around and sees two, three, four, then a half-dozen men with drawn bows and arrows. His pistol is pointed at the Mohawks, but then he notices an arrow on the ground, slithering towards him like a snake. Almost hypnotically his eyes follow the arrow with a thin black line attached to it. Its point is red and there are little white specs that appear to be Klaus's flesh, his companion now bellowing in pain.

For a second, Hasso does nothing as Klaus continues writhing on the ground. A few yards away Harry is slowly rising to his knees. Hasso slowly raises his pistol and begins pointing it at Harry. Fuck Seis, Hasso thinks, I'm going to shoot this bastard.

Three arrows hit Hasso almost simultaneously. One goes completely through his upper left wrist. A second arrow passes through his raincoat, partially entering his left thigh from the side. The third plows into the tiny gap between his right shoulder blade and upper arm bone—where it looks like the hemispherical head of a ballpeen hammer.

Hasso, momentarily held upright as the Mohawks yank their arrows out, is barely aware that he had dropped his automatic as two more arrows punch into him. The first plows into his stomach. The second slams into his throat, splitting open his carotid artery.

"Whoever you are, you're dead if you don't put your hands up," Harry gasps to Klaus. Indeed, Klaus can see that he is not only surrounded, but that Hasso is rapidly dying.

Stupidly, Klaus reaches for his automatic.

▲

"Charlie, come over here," Harry calls as best he can from an awkward kneeling position, bent forward, his hands on his knees as he tries to pull air back into his lungs. Charlie White Eagle, the group's foreman, is already running over to help.

"You O.K. boss?"

"Get me some water, then give me a minute, but I'll be OK. Maybe."

Water downed, Harry smiles, then points to the bodies as other Mohawks crowd around. "We've got a big god damned problem. Anybody got any ideas?"

"Do we call the cops?" Charlie asks.

Harry shakes his head, every motion causing him to wince. The Mohawks look from one to another, shrug, and say nothing. They have instinctively defended Harry, but going to the police and subsequent newspapers stories—the August robbery is still fresh in their minds—is something else. Also, never spoken, is the fact that many Mohawks feel that they're second class citizens. If Harry tells them 'no police' that's fine with them.

"I can get rid of their bodies in a few days," Harry says, hoping that Lansky will think of something. "But what about tonight? Don't you bury your dead in trees?"

Charlie laughs. "No, white man. The Sioux do, but us sophisticated Mohawks prefer burial mounds, like the Scythians. That won't work up here, but..."

Part of the clean-up includes placing Klaus and Hasso's loosely tied bodies on a light-colored tarpaulin above the elevator shaft. Charlie explains to Harry that birds of prey—young falcons (older ones fly south in winter), ospreys, hawks, kites and kestrels—will discover the bodies before they totally freeze.

"We'll cover 'em up during the day," Charlie says, "but the birds will pick at 'em during the night. Wednesday afternoon, with Thanksgiving coming up, we'll leave 'em uncovered. By Monday the only thing we'll have to do is throw some bones in the fire."

Harry nods. "You boys split their money, let anybody who wants them take their pistols, just burn their wallets, clothes, and everything else now."

▲

Sitting across the street and smoking, Dieter waits, increasingly apprehensive as fifteen, then thirty minutes go by. Not until after 4:30 does he notice a group of men, grim-faced, emerge from the freight elevator. Two of them support an injured man who they gingerly walk to Fifth Avenue, then help him into a cab. Something's wrong, but Dieter cannot leave his two friends stranded. He waits another half-hour, shakes his head a final time, and then drives in heavy traffic to Harry Strong's address.

Chapter 63: Late Afternoon, Manhattan House.

Manhattan House's lobby, larger than many hotels, has square columns finished with Vermont granite and walls covered with large mirrors. Ilse, sitting quietly on one of the French Empire reproduction couches in the majestic lobby, is amused by this ostentatious architectural mish-mash. Taking into consideration everything she's seen this past week, it's just another example of American wealth and power. As people come through the building's entrances, she carefully watches their dress and carriage, attempting to guess their wealth and occupation. Clearly, no one who lives here is poor.

And what is she doing in this pseudo-palace? She still doesn't know other than she, Seis, Rudy, and Otto Klaber are waiting for someone before holding a business meeting. However, the glow from the previous night is gone; for the first time, she's seen the usually docile but happy Rudy shaking his head, whispering to Seis, and refusing to look her in the eye. Just a few minutes earlier Rudy stood and seemed about to walk out until Seis jumped up and forcibly took his arm. Something is clearly wrong and even Seis's "I've got everything under control" smile to her cannot allay her worries.

Seis has just given her a 14-karat white gold with diamonds Longines watch and, looking down, she sees it's minutes before 5 p.m. Glancing about, for the first time she notices a small man in a double-breasted alpaca overcoat sitting by himself. He catches her eye for a second, smiles and nods as she politely reciprocates.

Only then does Ilse see the uniformed doorman and an elevator operator hurriedly walk to the 66th street entrance. A tall man is having trouble walking as he enters the building. Both Manhattan House employees are clearly concerned. The doorman, the taller of the two, takes the man's left arm, supporting him as he tries to walk. He doesn't appear to be drunk, Ilse thinks, but maybe he is injured; because of his fedora hat and the way his head hangs down, his face is obscured. Has he been hit by a car, she wonders?

"Are you all right, Mr. Strong?" the elevator operator asks.

"Nothing's broken, Roberto. Just a little accident at work," The man says, trying to smile, but wincing nevertheless.

Ilse feels a chill going through her. *Mr. Strong?* From the corner of her eye she notices that Rudy, Otto, and Seis are standing and watching, Seis nodding and exhibiting the slightest smile.

Ilse also stands. Staring at the man's face, she is still as a statue other than her eyes which are blinking rapidly. Is it? Can it really be?

Twenty-five feet away, the man stops walking and focuses on her.

Seis's head is swiveling back and forth. Does Harry Strong know Ilse? Why are they looking at each other that way?

"Harry! Oh, Harry, is it really you?"

"Ilse? Ilse," he says with a goofy smile despite his split lip. "What are you doing here?"

The elevator operator and doorman look equally confused.

Ilse jumps up and runs to him, stops for a few seconds, makes a half-laugh and half-cry sound, then throws herself into his arms. "I never thought I'd see you again," she repeats over and over. Then she hugs him as tightly as possible, kisses him on his bruised cheek, and puts her head on his shoulder. "My God, how I love you," she whispers, as surprised as Harry as her words tumble out.

▲

Seis feels like King Kong has swatted him. For a few seconds, everything is pitch black, he feels dizzy, his stomach is squeezing, and bright speckles of light pierce his closed eyes as the weight of Ilse's betrayal overwhelms him. Then his eyes reopen. I've been cuckold by the American who saved her in Berlin, his brain illogically thinks.

Had not Ingrid, and Ilse too, for that matter, told him the story? Surprise gives way to anger. The two won't live to enjoy this reunion, he thinks with instant determination. I'll make that whore pay for this humiliation. Damn her. And with all those people watching us.

Seis pulls himself together, stands, walks over to Harry and put his hand out. "I am Professor Doctor Franz Seis," he begins, trying his best to appear composed. Everyone tries to smile as introductions are made, Harry visibly shaken when Seis "introduces" Ilse as his fiancé, but smiles on seeing his fellow paratrooper, Rudy, again.

Meanwhile, the short well-dressed man, having watched everything, stands then walks over to join the five.

"Permit me to introduce my attorney," Harry says, seeing Lansky.

"Augustus Meyer," says Lansky, handing Seis and Rudy business cards. The cards read "Buckingham, Windsor & Meyer, Attorneys" have a phony address and phone number, and were printed up years earlier as a birthday joke from Lansky's late friend Bugsy Siegel.

There are mutual insincere bows, handshakes, and smiles that courtesy requires.

My God, Seis thinks, this Meyer looks like the worst sort of Russian Jew. They've taken over New York like cockroaches. But his anger and hurt is directed at Ilse. So, this is her Berlin savior. It was always, "there was someone in Berlin," and now "someone" is Major Strong. I will kill his children, Seis tells himself, and let them watch, knowing that they were the cause.

"I think we should go upstairs rather than talk here," Lansky says, not realizing how much Seis wants the same thing.

"Perhaps I should wait a few minutes for Dieter?" Otto asks Seis, who nods.

"Are you going to be alright, Mr. Strong?" the white-haired, thin-mustached elevator operator Roberto solicitously asks, ushering Harry, Lansky, Ilse, Rudy, and Seis into the roomy cab. Like all unionized personnel in upscale apartment houses, Roberto wears a white shirt, tie, and a dark blue uniform that gives him the look of a hatless railroad conductor but without the watch and fob.

Looking around him, Seis angrily turns his thoughts on Roberto. Typically Italian, Seis thinks, trying not to shake his head in disgust. A useless race for the last 1,500 years. Hadn't Mussolini's antics contributed to Operation Barbarossa's delay and the North African sideshow? But Americans do one thing right: they give them work suiting their abilities.

"Is Mrs. Strong home?" Harry asks as they walk toward the large elevator. For Harry, every step, indeed every word is painful. He knows he'll be better, but at this moment he finds that concentrating is difficult despite his joy—yes, joy is the right word he tells himself—of having Ilse standing next to him.

"With the children," Roberto answers. Reaching the sixth floor he opens the elevator's doors as the smell of paint becomes stronger. Harry looks confused and is about to say something when Lansky makes it a point to melodramatically sniff the air.

"No complaints I hope, Roberto," Lansky says.

"A few from the seventh floor, sir," Roberto answers. "But there's no good time to paint an apartment, is there? Everybody wants the painting done overnight, not in the winter and not in the summer, and never *now*. All without any smell. Can't be done, can it, sir?"

"Maybe someday. And there are always miracles, are there not? Otherwise what would be the point of praying," Lansky says, a bemused smile on his face.

Seis does not approve of an attorney talking with building help as if they were equals. Perhaps it's because the man is a Jew. Yes, that is it. Strong certainly doesn't converse informally with this man, but of course Strong is half-German.

Entering the apartment, the smell becomes overwhelming. Splattered tarpaulins cover the living and dining room floors, each one a Jackson Pollack-like splash of colors. Protected furniture is huddled together, lighter items stacked on couches. Heavy, five-gallon cans of paint, some opened, are near step ladders so that the painters can reach the ceiling. Nan comes out of one of the children's bedrooms, nods to Harry, and politely shakes hands with Seis, Rudy, and Ilse, their names meaning nothing to her. For Lansky, who she has always liked, she has a genuine hug. What leaves Harry perplexed, however, is that Nan hadn't said a word to him about the painters.

"Miss Wallbillig," Lansky suggests as he looks at Seis for approval, "why don't you stay with Nan and the children while the rest of us talk in Harry's den." Seis nods and the four file into the room. Harry is about to take his chair from behind his desk where a side drawer contains a 1918 Savage .32, ten-shot automatic, a rare pistol and marvelous device for close fighting. So near yet so far, he thinks.

"Please, Major, move your chair around front where we can be more informal," Seis says with a polite smile and bow of his head. "Your sitting behind that desk will make us feel like we're having an audience with you, not a friendly exchange of ideas."

Chapter 64: Harry's Apartment, 5:30 PM.

A few minutes later Otto enters the apartment and joins the others in Harry's office.

"No sign of Dieter," he says to Seis, puzzled.

Harry—every muscle hurting—delicately moves his chair so he faces Seis. The five are sitting in an elongated U; Harry closest to the door, Otto opposite Harry, Rudy and Lansky on a couch (Harry's fold up bed), and to the right is Seis in a separate chair. At Seis's feet is his valise with Thistleman's cash and from which he removes a Walther P-38.

"Doctor Seis," says Lansky, lighting a cigarette, "I believe that you requested this meeting, how can Harry and I be of assistance to you?"

"Let me be candid and start from the beginning," Seis says, determined to make every word sting Harry and his Jewish attorney. Seis describes acquiring stamps in Poland, his responsibilities had Great Britain been invaded, and his "cleansing" role during 1941's drive to Moscow. Without reservation, he speaks of the stamps taken from Jews and Gentiles alike, unabashedly telling of removing Jews from death camps to assist his operations. When describing the March slaughter of the compound's Jewish prisoners, Rudy interrupts, "Please, doctor, the particulars of that horrible day do not have to be repeated."

"Yes, I have spoken long enough, Rudy. It was a shame that you had to bear witness to the executions, but did I not tell you at the time that your presence wasn't necessary? However, perhaps now Major Strong could give us the details of—"

With a knock on the door, Dieter enters the room looking flustered.

"Ah Dieter," Seis says. "Congratulations. From the looks of Major Strong's face, your two companions clearly spoke with him. But why are you so late?"

"Because his friends have disappeared," Harry cuts in, but his attempt to smile aggravates his split lip. "With luck, they are in Valhalla."

"Kaput, eh?" Seis sighs. "Otto, if you would give Dieter your seat. Please fetch him some water and see how the painters are doing. Kindly nudge them along if you would. Then look in to Mrs. Strong and Ilse and see to their and the children's comfort."

Otto closes the door and Seis continues. "Major Strong, later we will discuss how you disposed of Dieter's two associates. But for now, if you would, I would appreciate your telling me if you were in Ludwigslust and did you meet my brother the day he was murdered? I have no intellectual problem with one person, by chance, killing another in battle and then searching the body, in Hermann's case removing our stamps. However, the torture of a man, even in the heat of war, I find repulsive. We were given grim orders and carried them out, but never with the intent of protracting a man's death. Nevertheless, since Hermann was my brother, I'm not disinterested in how he died and who killed him."

Neither Harry nor Lansky say anything, both sitting motionless. Rudy is equally silent, desperately thinking for a way to talk Seis out of his obvious intent, but knowing that there is nothing he can say or do that might save their lives.

"As I now know," Seis is saying, "Hermann died near Ludwigslust, where you were, Major. I also know that in arresting Walther Darré you acted in a thoroughly correct, proper military manner."

Harry looks surprised and Seis continues. "You see, Darré also participated in our stamp venture. He told me this, having no idea who you were, while we were both imprisoned in Landsberg. So, you see, when I hold the scales of justice, I do so impartially. Regarding my brother, the forensic records indicate he was shot from inside his mouth, not through it, and after his teeth had been smashed. By any chance were you there at the time of his death?"

Harry had been prepared for this question since that 1945 afternoon, but now, as his eyes lock with Seis's, he finds himself too exhausted to keep the lie hidden any longer.

▲

"Yes, I was there."

"And you did nothing to stop it?"

My God, Harry thinks, the prick is assuming one of my men did it. It won't take much to blame it on Russ, or Manfredi, or even Pete, who's dead. They were all hotheads too, weren't they?

However, what Harry finds himself saying is not what he'd expected. "We had all returned from the Wobelein death camp; in fact, we'd left only hours earlier. May I assume that during the war you visited a death camp or something similar?"

"Yes, not infrequently, and supervised the construction of smaller ones in Russia and the Ukraine." Seis looks around as if he has completed a large meal and is waiting for coffee and cigars. "However, I will not excuse my answer with the modifier, 'I am afraid.' Regarding those facilities to rid the world of the Jewish presence, most of us felt back then that the Final Solution was the correct approach."

"But did you ever see a camp where the prisoners were dead or literally starving to death and without water for days?" Harry asks. "Where the dead were neatly stacked like so many cords of wood? And, with flies covering their bodies, the stench unimaginable."

"Yes, I can see where that might prey on your American sensibilities."

"No, Herr Doctor Professor, on my *German* sensibilities. I am a one hundred percent product of Germany, coincidentally half-Jewish as your brother Hermann surmised. In fact, my Jewish mother died because of your crackpot Nazi ideas."

"Harry, speak slowly," Lansky interjects. "You're getting red in the face, count to ten."

"So, may I surmise that one of your men, or even you, shot my brother?" Seis asks.

"Something had happened to Hermann when we first saw him," Harry continues. "We were in Ludwigslust's town center, a small butcher shop that also doubled as the post office. We'd found a few cases of Lowenbrau and we were drinking when Hermann staggered in—"

"Exhausted and his foot bothering him?"

"Exactly. He said he wanted our help in crossing the Elbe and was willing to pay us."

"And pay you too much?" Lansky asks.

"Way, way, way too much—over $5,000 in American dollars and British pounds. He said he was a Food & Agriculture ministry courier carrying important papers for Admiral Dönitz's government. I assumed that these were important papers, and I began going through them."

Seis nodded, "To see if your General Gavin might be interested? And, if I may ask, what was in the papers that made them so valuable?"

"That's the point; on the top was a study about potatoes. Potatoes? So, I began looking carefully at the others. The reports were pseudo-scientific studies about the medical treatment of near-death, badly wounded men. The research was performed in concentration camps with prisoners who'd been purposely shot, or burnt, or half-drowned. Hundreds were involved."

"The actual number was 714," Seis interjects in a monotone. "But what was Hermann doing with the reports? They were supposed to be destroyed before we left Berlin."

"Perhaps he double-crossed you," Lansky interjects, "It has been known to happen, you know."

▲

Seis, shocked, shakes his head in disbelief. The little Jew is right. Hermann betrayed me. Betrayed us all. Until this moment his older brother's actions made no sense, but without warning everything falls into its logical place. All along, Seis thinks, my God damn fucking brother planned to sell out to the Americans and keep the stamps for himself. That bastard!

"So, you found the papers and began to leaf through them. Then what, Major?" Seis asks, his voice shaky and high pitched. How he wants to scream at Hermann!

"Even though there were three of us and all armed," Harry continues, "he went crazy. In the scuffle that followed, I broke your brother's front teeth with the Walther I'd taken from him earlier."

"And?" said Seis. "Please, continue if you would."

"Your brother wouldn't stop cursing us, kicking, trying to punch, and calling me a Jew again and again. It was insane, a one-footed man picking a fight with three paratroopers."

"My stupid brother. His whole life was one of near misses. Invariably, he managed to antagonize someone like you, Major. He constantly wrecked his chances finding the pot of gold at the end of the rainbow. I won't ask; but as you apparently dispatched two of my men an hour ago, and since I have just seen your temper, and wherefore you admit holding his Walther... *Ipso facto,* by the facts themselves, I therefore will assume it was you who pulled the trigger."

Seis looks around the room as if speaking to a jury. "And do you know what? I do *not* blame you. You were carefully selected for personal characteristics that are so admirable in wartime. And, after your own difficult day, you were angered beyond control. Might I ask what my brother specifically did to so anger you?"

"It was his smugness about his 'scientific' research and—"

"No more is necessary. Believe it or not, I am glad that he died at the hands of an intelligent man for a sensible reason, not because of screwing some simple-minded fräulein in the grass as we had suspected. No, my brother stabbed me and the rest of my associates in the back, getting himself killed for his efforts. Because Hermann didn't live up to our trust or his responsibilities, all of us are in your apartment today. All so unnecessary; so very, very unnecessary."

"Nevertheless," Seis says with a sigh, "As I'm sure you understand, and as distasteful as the subject is, I still have my family obligations, don't I?"

Chapter 65: 5:45 PM.

For Nan, sitting in the same room with Ilse and the children is awkward. When she arrived at Manhattan House, she had been amazed to see Meyer Lansky sitting in the lobby waiting for her. He explained to her that, on his instructions, their apartment is being painted. Nan was flabbergasted, but as Lansky did not offer an explanation, she knew better than to ask. Her children are fine and having a wonderful time watching the painters when he last peeked in. However, now that Nan is home, he suggests she send their nurse off. Also, he, Harry and some others will arrive upstairs about 5 PM. for an important meeting. What Meyer couldn't warn Nan about, for the simple reason he didn't know, is that one of those joining them will be Ilse.

▲

Ilse, virtually in shock after seeing Harry, finds herself having difficulty remembering English. Nan, having no idea who she is, prattles around making small talk, and with no way to cook, fixes a supper of peanut butter and jelly sandwiches for the children. Only after they are nestled in front of the television does Ilse sympathetically remark on Harry's injury.

"Construction work is always difficult," Nan says. "Something goes wrong two or three times a year."

"But Harry's a pretty 'tough cookie' isn't he?" Ilse asks.

"That a funny word choice," Nan smiles. "It's one of Harry's favorite expressions."

"Harry's the one who taught it to me."

▲

As instructed, Otto walks into the living room where the four are painting. They seem to have run out of steam, having made no discernible progress since everyone's arrival. If truth be told, this should not be a cause for surprise. The four are no more painters than they are police. In fact, the quartet work for Carlo Gambino, a protégé of Lucky Luciano. Together, their "rap sheets" include charges relating to, and occasional convictions for, armed robbery, assault with a deadly weapon, breaking and entering, extortion, kidnapping, manslaughter, larceny, possession of stolen property, racketeering, grand theft, and, of course, homicide.

The dining and living rooms (all told 40' x 23') are split by two, wood-framed glass doors. In turn, the dining room connects to a kitchen which opens to the apartment's rear "service" entrance. Along the hallway, opposite the dining-living area, are three bedrooms. One striking difference between Manhattan House and gracious pre-war apartments is that no "maid's room" exists; the practice and pregnancies slowly diminishing.

In the living room, Otto realizes that a cheap AM radio is playing Frankie Laine "hit" songs. Since he is primarily supposed to keep an eye on the painters, Otto says nothing, but when *Mule Train* comes on, he mouths the words, his hand cracking an imaginary whip and singing "Haa! Haa!" along with Frankie.

"It's one of my favorites, too," says Salvatore, one of the painters, grinning.

"Any coffee around?" Otto asks, still cracking his imaginary whip.

"Yeah, but we made it hours ago, and it tastes like shit," Salvatore laughs. "It's in the kitchen. You'll find a cup just above the coffee pot."

Otto walks into the kitchen, pours himself coffee, comes back out, sips some and begin to laugh. "Hey, it tastes like you guys made it with turpentine. This stuff *is* bad. You don't mind if I take some home to my wife?"

Salvatore and the other painters laugh. Be one of the boys, Otto thinks to himself. He didn't want to scare them away, but the sooner they leave the apartment the better.

Five minutes later, the coffee gone, he decides it's time to also get them moving.

"You boys are working late," Otto says, hands on hips, attempting to act nonchalant. If it hadn't been for the pistols that he and Dieter are carrying, he would have opened his double-breasted jacket. However, the vapors of the heavy lead-based paint make breathing difficult. He knows he looks ridiculous standing there and sweating with his jacket buttoned. The fact that three five-gallon paint drums of an off-white color paint are open isn't helping matters.

Perhaps they hadn't heard, so he repeats himself. "I said, are you boys working late?"

"Being paid overtime. We hope. But I'm not the boss. Hey, Dominic!" he calls.

Dominic, a squat, wide-bodied, thick-necked, man with huge hands, a prototype "villain" in professional wrestling, hears Salvatore and he and the other two painters amble over.

"He wants to know how late we're going to be working," Salvatore asks.

Dominic scratches his head. "Real late, this is a rush job. That's all they told me. The boss is coming over maybe about eight, then we'll know how much longer, but a couple of weeks ago he had us going until midnight. You get some fancy-shmantzy woman with a bug up her ass that a color's not right and then she's got a big party coming up. That's what's going on here, I think. But who the fuck knows? We're getting paid extra, that's what counts."

Inwardly, Otto groans. He wants the painters gone so all the happy horseshit between Seis and this guy Strong can be ended. Then he remembers the original plan which is to hold the wife and two kids hostage, then force the big guy to go to his safe deposit box the next morning.

So far so good, the only surprise being his yid lawyer who looks like Meyer Lansky, the guy who's the Mob's brains. That's odd too, isn't his name Mr. Meyer? Otto scratches his head. And, oh shit, he almost forgot, but Seis wants him checking in to see the guy's wife.

"Where are the women and kids?" Otto asks.

Dominic points to a bedroom. "But try and be quiet, I think the kids just went to sleep."

Otto walks to the door, hears two women talking and knocks quietly.

"Come in," he hears a voice whisper.

As he enters, Otto's eyes sweep around the room. He sees Ilse, a collection of toys and mobiles, dolls and teddy bears, and two sleeping children on a small bed.

Only then do his eyes alight on... "*Veronica!*"

"You!" she says, instantly recognizing Otto from seeing him so recently in the park, but further confused by his calling her "Veronica." However, she recovers before Otto. "Why are you in my house? Have you been following me?"

"No. Really, you don't understand—" Otto wants to crawl under a bed and hide.

Nan, half hysterical, turns to Ilse. "I've seen him three or four times. Last week in the park when I was with… Oh my God, he wants my children!"

"You bastard," Ilse instinctively snarls in German, standing protectively in front of the children. "Get out of here. Now!"

Otto is thunderstruck. He shouldn't be in the apartment, but how could he have known?

Behind him the two women, knowing that something is terribly wrong, push some furniture in front of the door but, because it is the children's room, there is no telephone.

Chapter 66: 6:00 PM.

Otto backs out of the bedroom, hands over his face, his eyes seeing nothing, and staggers into the living room, dazed. His world has been turned impossibly upside-down. "Veronica" is Harry Strong's wife. He knows he has no future, but like the chivalric medieval knight-errant who has been mortally wounded, he is determined not to let Seis harm Veronica or her children. He *will* save them if it's the last thing he does.

"Hey buddy, you O.K.?" Salvatore asks. "You look like you've seen a ghost."

"I have," Otto says. My own, he thinks.

From somewhere Otto remembers Harry's friend. "That short guy inside. The lawyer," he asks Salvatore. "He looks a lot like Meyer Lansky, doesn't he?"

Salvatore cocks his wrist and whispers, "come on," also motioning for Dominick and the other two painters to follow him. Like conspirators they walk into the dining room where they can't be seen or heard. Salvatore scratches his head, and turns to Dominick, "The short guy, does he look like Meyer Lansky?"

"Naah. More like Lansky's twin brother," Dominick says. Salvatore and the other two laugh like it's Bob Hope's best joke ever.

"No, I'm serious," Otto says. "He *does* look like Lansky. I've seen Lansky's pictures enough."

"You know, now that you mention it, it does look like him," Salvatore replies.

"Yes, it's Lansky," Dominic says. "But why do you ask? Do you want his autograph?"

However, Otto doesn't laugh; he is speechless with fear. If it is really Lansky... If Lansky and this guy Strong are killed, then he and Dieter will have to kill the painters, none of whom look like pushovers, Veronica, and her children too. The cops and the mob will swarm the place and his fingerprints could be anywhere. And what about the elevator operator? And if the mob catches him? They'd pull out every finger and toe nail, rip out his balls, pluck out one eye, and leave the second in so he can watch the real fun begin when they get serious.

Otto's arms and legs feel like they're made of lead. "I gotta get out of here," he mumbles. He is in such a daze he doesn't know which door to take. Instinctively he opens the jacket of his double-breasted suit to make sure he still has his automatic and extra clips.

Only then does Otto realize that Dominic is giving him a funny look. "Say, fella', I don't want to be rude or nothin', but isn't that a rod you're carrying?"

"No, of course not." The word *no* is Otto's reflex answer, but what he really needs to do is pull the damn thing out and let 'em know who's calling the shots. However, his hesitation gives Salvatore and Dominick the few seconds they need. Without a word, Salvatore's arms grab both of Otto's as Dominic, seemingly from nowhere, places a knife against his throat.

Otto still has one slim chance. He stands still, waiting for an opportunity, trying to think exactly what type of attack will catch them off-guard. Then, to Otto's surprise, Salvatore drops his arms and jumps a step back, producing a police baton from a back pocket.

Otto whirls quickly, but has not completed his turn when the baton smashes into his face. It is a testament to Otto's strength that he doesn't topple over, but Salvatore's next shot is to his right kneecap. As Otto falls, Salvatore jerks the baton up and into his stomach, below the rib cage and just under the heart. A second later Dominick, now holding Otto, pulls his head back. Salvatore swings the baton into Otto's Adam's Apple striking his throat so hard that no miracle will ever let words emerge again.

"So, are you the fella' that killed Mr. Lansky's two friends today?" Dominic asks. "You looked real tough a few minutes ago," he says, pushing the knife into Otto's discolored skin with his right hand and reaching under Otto's jacket, his hand emerging with the pistol.

Otto knows he should try and wriggle free, but the pain, coming in terrible waves, has left him helpless. The grip on his arms tightens pushing him backward so that he is off-balance when Dominic moves the knife under his right eye and pushes through the skin.

"Now let's see what's in— Well looka' here Salvatore, a fucking ice pick also," Dominic says, tossing it away. "I don't think you'll be needing this, pal. You thought of everything, didn't you? Except for one thing: you're a dumb, stupid fuck."

It is then that Otto dimly feels the presence of a man behind him, but now he is having trouble breathing, throwing up as he simultaneously gasps for air.

"Put him on the floor," Dominic orders, turning to pick something out of a metal utility box. Otto is on his knees, silently screaming as Salvatore forces his knee into Otto's back, his hands gripping Otto's jaw. Dominic returns to Otto's line of sight, kneeling, so that Otto can see him. In his right hand is what looks like a child's skip-rope with two handles on the end. But this is not a children's toy, it's made of wire: a garrote.

"End of the line, fuck face," Dominic says. Then he hands the garrote to Salvatore. Salvatore throws it over Otto's head, crosses the ends, and twists.

Chapter 67: 6:10 PM.

Minutes later, Seis, growing impatient that the painters have not left, sends Dieter to find out what the delay is all about. "Now let us all sit quietly for a few moments."

No one can possibly know it, but Dieter has only minutes to live.

The room is silent until Rudy clears his throat. Seis, still holding his Walther, looks at him, "Were you about to say something—" he begins to ask. Despite being smaller than Seis, Lansky lunges at Seis's right arm, hitting it with a downward chopping motion and sending the pistol spinning to the thick carpeting where it lands at Rudy's feet. Rudy simply leans forward, then picks it up, seemingly in slow motion.

"Well, gentlemen, we appear to be back where we started," Seis says, giving Lansky a murderous glance.

▲

"No," say Rudy. "I've had enough," leaning forward and handing the Walther to Harry. It's one thing to extort the sanctimonious Thistleman, but it has taken all of Rudy's self-control to stay with Seis after Sven's murder and Romanoff's all-but-forced suicide. When Romanoff said that the stamp money had gone to Israel, Rudy had secretly applauded. Now, in Harry's apartment, knowing Seis, he's sure that the Jewish lawyer will be tortured to get Harry to turn over any remaining stamps. Rudy knows that Seis, Otto, and Dieter will kill the lawyer, Harry, and Harry's wife sometime later. And Ilse? He has known her six years and considers her a family friend. Rudy has witnessed Seis killing Ulrich Schmidt in cold blood and that same murderous look came into Seis's eyes when Ilse embraced Harry. And he certainly doesn't have to be told that his own life is danger. After all, why does Seis need him now?

Harry takes the pistol, involuntarily wincing from the continuing pain.

"Well, well, well," smiles Lansky, putting two fingers in his mouth and giving a whistle that he'd learned as a boy on the Lower East Side. "Dominic, Salvatore, come in here."

"Those painters," Seis begins, "are no match for..." However, his hopes collapse as Dominic and Salvatore enter Harry's office with drawn guns, each with silencers.

"Is it done?" Lansky asks.

Dominic draws his forefinger across his throat and nods.

Lansky exhales slowly, looks at Harry and smiles. "A bit dicey, wasn't it?"

Seis can only bite his lip. But he still has one last card to play.

Chapter 68: 6:20 PM.

"Dominic, please join us and sit behind the desk, I wish to ask Dr. Seis some questions," Lansky says, looking at Seis. "So, you don't like Jews in general and, I assume, me particularly. Since it makes no difference now, tell me what your plans were after you acquired the stamps. I assume you couldn't have gone back to Germany?"

"There were never plans for returning to Germany. I was going to keep the stamps and go to Washington—"

"Why? Surely not to see the sights."

"To avenge my sister's death. The man who ordered her to be murdered lives there."

"Baker?" Harry asks.

"Exactly."

"And after that?" Lansky inquires.

"To Argentina. Even without the stamps I had enough money to live a civilized life. In the back of my mind I always assumed that my stamps were mostly sold."

"Then why did you come to New York?" Lansky asks. "Why have you been tracking us down since Rudy came here years ago?"

"Pride. I had become forgotten in the Third Reich," he says, speaking slowly because he needs every minute possible so that the others will think that he's given up. "Advancement was impossible after Heydrich died. I am told that my current work with German intelligence is important, but it's little better than a sinecure. I'm under no illusions. I'm still good but there are a dozen others who can carry it out. Do you think I don't hear the whispers 'Why is he here?' And the answer, 'Because he's a friend of the boss from the old days.' When I reached Argentina, I wanted other Germans to tip their hat to me."

Seis still has a two-shot Derringer and he watches as Harry thrust the Walther pistol underneath his belt. Therefore, his first shot will be for Dominic. This so-called guard has stupidly placed his pistol on the desk; well out of Seis's reach but where Dominic can't reach it quickly either. With his second shot, Seis will hold the others at bay while he recovers Dominic's automatic. The odds are not as he would like, but he has the element of surprise.

As Seis speaks, with his right hand he slowly scratches his right ear lobe, then the left side of his chin. The Derringer is now just inches away, in his left inner pocket.

"I know what you have in store for me," Seis is saying, "but perhaps we can come to an understanding. I have a half-million dollars in a Swiss bank account and an equal amount in my briefcase here."

Seis all but gives a sigh of relief as Lansky, falling for the bait, sits upright, then leans slowly over to retrieve Seis's briefcase. Rudy and Harry also follow Lansky's movements as he begins to open it. Dominic is no different. He leans as far forward as possible to get a better view, placing both his hands firmly on Harry's desk to hold his weight.

Seis has just finished saying "in my briefcase" when his hand grasps the Derringer. Pulling it out slowly at first, as if he has finished scratching himself, he pivots and sends his first bullet through the right eye of the astonished Dominic, whose head is no more than six feet away. Seis's mind is working so quickly that he has time to congratulate himself on his splendid shot before Dominic's upper body collapses on Harry's desk and lands on its chin. Seis's last impression of Dominic is that the man's left eye still retains its astonished look.

Seis swings his body and arm back to cow the others.

▲

Despite his pain and the ten feet between them, Harry is already on his feet even as Seis shoots Dominic. Hermann Seis had two Derringers, Harry thinks during the slow-motion fraction of a second that follows, why didn't I frisk his brother? Harry has forgotten the Walther in his belt, but after one full step he is in full stride and launches himself at Seis.

Fully off the ground, Harry plows into Seis with wrists crossed and elbows in front of him like a football lineman. He drives the surprised, six-inch shorter and fifty-pound lighter Seis between the chair and the corner of his desk. As his elbows crash into Seis's chest, both men fall awkwardly. In the second before he hits the ground, badly jolted and falling backward, Seis's involuntarily pulls the trigger, the Derringer's last shot harmlessly discharges into a bookcase.

Despite this, the tiny pistol does not fall from Seis's hand. Seis recovers first and begins to wriggle free from under Harry's weight, punching and chopping at Harry's neck and shoulders. At the same time, Seis swivels the nine-ounce Derringer in his fingers so that he can use it as a hand club. For Harry, although he is on top of Seis, the pain from his afternoon beating almost immobilizes him so that, at first, he can do little more than hang on.

Closing his eyes to the pain, Harry's left hand grabs Seis's right wrist, which is holding the Derringer. He doesn't have the strength to stop Seis entirely, but what would have been stunning blows are reduced to inconsequential jabs. However, Seis left hand is free and, amazingly, Harry can hear the thud of Seis's left fist connecting to his neck and elbow. Yet, because of the adrenalin flowing through him, each punch is painless. Despite still fighting for his life, the ridiculous thought—that he is going to be very sore in the morning—flashes through his mind, followed by what a stupid thing it is to think about that at a time like this.

While Harry knows that other people should be helping him, every second he wrestles with Seis seem like minutes. Only then does he remember he still has Seis's Walther tucked into his belt. With what he knows is his final effort, Harry sets his legs, arches his back and pushes his head under Seis's chin. Only then does he reach for the Walther inside his belt.

Somehow Seis understands what Harry is trying to do, but, in his desperation to land a knockout blow, the Derringer slips from his fingers. The only think he can do is desperately rain short punches on Harry's upper arms and shoulders.

Finally! Harry reaches the Walther, thrusts it into Seis's cheek and gasps in German, "Do you want me to kill you like I killed Hermann?"

Chapter 69: 6:30 PM.

Seis stops struggling as Harry finally hears the welcome sound of the other painters sprinting into the room. One helps the half-conscious Harry untangle his body from Seis's. Salvatore takes one look at his friend, the dead Dominic, and cursing, sends a salvo of punches into Seis's stomach, taking all the air out of him.

"Stop it!" Lansky orders, breathing hard. "Tape his mouth and wrists behind him, and then go through his jacket and pants."

As if from far away, Harry examines the Walther, only then realizing that the safety catch is still on.

Two painters hold down the still struggling Seis while Salvatore expertly ties his wrists behind him with tape, then angrily slaps more tape over Seis's mouth.

A wallet and billfold quickly emerge containing thousands in cash, which Lansky pockets. "This is for Dominic's family," he says. After that come smaller items from Seis's pockets: hotel room keys, a lighter, cigarettes, and then a strange oblong object.

"Let me see that," Harry demands. The item Harry has noticed is a rounded pill box with an enamel red griffin mounted on platinum.

"So, Doctor Seis, you're not just a killer, but you're also a petty thief. Is that why you left the classroom for the SS; you were thrown out?"

One eye already swelling, Seis does not answer.

"Salvatore," Lansky says quietly, "See that Mrs. Strong and that Ilse woman are all-right. Tell them everyone's fine and I'll explain everything to them in a few minutes."

As Seis sits on the floor, Lansky peers into Seis's briefcase, his eyes momentarily widen, and then he quickly snaps it shut.

"What about his man Rudy?" Lansky asks Harry.

For a few long seconds, Harry looks Rudy in the eye. Then the two, brother Fallschirmjägers, nod to each other.

"He's OK," Harry says and smiles. "He's been around. He'll keep his mouth shut."

"In that case," Lansky says to Rudy, "you're to go back to Germany immediately. Last plane tonight or the first one tomorrow."

A tight, but grateful smile crosses Rudy's face as he wipes away his sweat.

"Harry will help you and advance you any money you need," Lansky says. "Harry, on second thought, give him five thousand more from Seis's briefcase. The prick certainly has it."

Then Lansky turns back to Rudy. "There will be people asking questions so pay attention to what I am going to tell you. You are to say that you met with me this morning at the—"

"Commodore Hotel."

"Yes. You met me—and you *are* to use my name for your own protection— this morning at the Commodore. Just after I left, so did Seis and Ilse. You did *not* see them again—"

"I think I understand—"

"No, let me finish. There was no Otto and no Dieter. You will say this and no more to any German or American authorities who question you. Do we fully understand each other?"

Rudy nods.

"Harry," Lansky says, "You, Ilse, and Rudy are to leave immediately. And you are not to come back here until Thursday. Check into the Commodore under your own name; if anyone asks, it's because of the paint smell. Ilse will take everything of hers and move into your room. This is for everybody's protection, of course," he says, winking at Harry. "I'll also have Seis's belongings removed and his bills paid."

"What about Nan and the children?" Harry asks.

"I'll make arrangements for them at the Plaza and have them taken there. You can call them tonight. But I want you, Rudy, and Ilse to leave immediately."

▲

After Lansky has ushered the three out of the apartment, he goes to the children's room to speak with Nan. Soon, one of the painters, changing back into civvies, escorts Nan and the children to the Plaza.

Twenty minutes later Lansky returns to the living room where he sees Seis and grins. But it is not in a nice manner, more like an orca swimming in the open sea just behind an unsuspecting pup seal. Like the fastidious man he is, Lansky carefully removes his jacket, vest and tie, taking care to fold each item before placing them on a chair on the other side of the living room.

Seis, his hands tied behind him and sitting on the floor, carefully watches. More than once, Lansky guesses, Seis has been in his position.

"Help him stand up," Lansky tells Salvatore. The big man gets behind Seis and easily hoists him to his feet.

"Now cut his tape." Salvatore knows what is coming, Lansky thinks, but does Seis?

Seis bends slightly forward so that the tape binding his wrists can be cut. He is now standing fully erect, his hands in front of him as he flexes his wrists and back, then begins instinctively puts his hands to his mouth to remove the tape.

As Seis's body relaxes, Salvatore, takes a full swing with the rubber hose, connecting with the back side of Seis's knees, the thud of the hose and cracking cartilage muffled by the room's thick rugs and paint tarpaulins. As Seis crumples, the duct tape still over his mouth, Salvatore swings again and again, perhaps a dozen in as many seconds, connect with Seis's arms, legs and ribs.

"That's for Dominic, you fuck," he mutters.

"No head shots," says Lansky, then motions with his hands for Salvatore to stop.

Salvatore kneels next to Seis and looks at Lansky, who nods again. Salvatore removes a blackjack from his back pocket and, one at a time, seizes Seis's hands. In a rat-ta-tat style he smashes Seis's fingers. Following another nod from Lansky, he jerks Seis's head back, and delivers half a dozen carefully aimed hits to Seis's jaw, nose, throat, and ears. However, none of the blows will leave Seis unconscious.

Seis, lies motionless, dazed and in shock as Salvatore rips the tape from Seis's mouth so that he can throw up through his shattered mouth. Like any animal near death, he instinctively tries to escape. For a few seconds, he crawls in the direction of an open, half-empty, five-gallon can of paint, almost knocking it over.

Lansky kneels alongside the man's shuddering body, pulls Seis's head up and twists it until the two men's eyes lock.

"You are very, very lucky that we do not have more time," Lansky says slowly in English. "But now you are about to die at the hands of a Jew." He is rewarded as Seis twitches, then almost imperceptibly nods that he understands.

Lansky, Salvatore, and a second painter pull Seis further up, his shoulders now atop the paint bucket's side, then Lansky pushes Seis's head into the thick white muck. For a few seconds Seis kicks franticly, but Salvatore and another painter firmly hold his upper body in place while simultaneously keeping the paint bucket steady.

In a few seconds Seis's arms and legs collapse. Lansky stands, nods to the other two to take a step back, only then noticing that because the paint is so thick there are no ripples when the few remaining air bubbles rise to the surface.

Epilogue: Mount Hermon,
Massachusetts, 2003.

Saturday, May 25. Despite her increasing frailty, Ilse Strong and her four children smile for the school photographer as she holds a silver-plated shovel on this warm spring day. Ground is being broken for the two-story, state-of-the-art 9,500 square foot Harry Strong Memorial Language Arts Center on the Mount Hermon campus. Besides the cash bequest in Harry's will, the only surprising stipulation is that Harry's excellent copy of Sixth Century B.C. Greek amphora showing Ajax and Achilles playing dice be displayed in the new building's main lobby.

Across the Connecticut River Valley, trees are finally reaching full bloom with numerous shades of soft green as spring advances into the low mountains. School officials make short speeches, Ilse nervously says a few words, and a few survivors from the class of '38 briefly reminisce about Harry. The small crowd politely claps, and the ceremonies end.

Ilse's mind drifts back to that November 19, 1951 evening when she saw Harry for the first time in almost six years. As far as Ilse could tell, his divorce later with Nan was amicable. The only thing that Harry told her was that Lansky stepped in and, after a short, very candid chat with Nan, personally adjudicated the details for both parties.

Ilse stayed in New York and was soon employed as a United Nations translator. Shortly after his divorce from Nan, she and Harry married. By this time, Harry had had enough of New York and, through General Gavin, joined a large construction firm doing business with the Pentagon, retiring as its CEO in 1982. Until lung cancer from his smoking took hold, he and Ilse split time between homes in New York, Florida, and a cottage overlooking the Rhine.

Poor Big Al, Ilse thought. She always liked the man, but the 1953-54 recession, short-lived as it was, wiped him out. He made numerous comebacks, but all failed. Big Al retired for good in 1971 and died in his Yankee Stadium box seat during a 1976 Red Sox game.

As for Meyer Lansky, Ilse never met him again. His name often appeared in headlines, but under government pressure he gave up his U.S. gambling interests and moved to Florida. Ilse knew that for the last twenty years of his life, Lansky lived modestly after his Cuban holdings were confiscated by Castro. It was not impossible, she thought, that on more than one occasion Harry had "loaned" him money.

The first half of Nan's life ended abruptly when her second husband, Frank Sussman, suffered a stroke on the night of his sixtieth birthday. After he passed away, and though Nan was financially independent, her third marriage was one of financial convenience. As far as Ilse knew, Harry's two children with Nan had had good lives. James Gavin Strong was the academic dean at a small private college in Ohio, and Suzanne, after a brief flirtation with show business, became a housewife and mother.

Ilse lost contact with the Spanglers as Ingrid blamed her for Seis's mysterious disappearance and her lost chance at wealth. Decades later, on business in Munich, Harry visited Rudy's successful stamp shop and the two had more than one friendly drink at the Hofbräuhaus. Harry learned that Ingrid had three more children but became increasingly bitter and died suddenly at fifty-two. Rudy also volunteered that after his return to Germany in 1951, General Gehlen personally interviewed him. However, hearing Lansky's name, he gave a sad, knowing smile and terminated the meeting.

And the cash that Seis had extorted from Thistleman? With first Abramson and then Romanoff dead, Lansky realized that he no longer had a role to play. Almost all Thistleman's cash went to Israel, Lansky only too happy to inform him of the details after the Abramson and Romanoff estates were fully paid. Harry turned the last of his stamps over to the Israeli government in 1952 and never opened a stamp album again. And the money from his percentage of the earlier stamp sales? Harry had invested it wisely.

Appendices

A. What's Fact, What Fiction.

- 18 Pine Street, Chase National Bank's headquarters in 1951 (and Thistleman & Chandler's location) still exists but is now a condominium apartment building.

- 696 Fifth Avenue is imaginary. My first choice was 666 Fifth Ave., but as this (real) building is owned by Donald Trump's son-in-law, "696" it became.

- The 1951 American Stamp Dealer Association's conference was held at Manhattan's Park Avenue and 34th Street Armory, November 16-18. For fictional reasons, I added Thursday, November 15.

- Amherst College, founded in 1821, is part of the "Little Ivy League," and one of America's top small colleges. The *1940 WPA Guide to Massachusetts* offers a nice description and history.

- Herbert Backe (1896-1947), who replaced Darré, in the Food & Agriculture Administration was as cold-hearted as any Nazi. Backe was responsible for *all* Third Reich food production. See Collingham, *The Taste of War* below.

- Edward H. R. Green's surname was Brown (1868-1936). A legendary drinker, bon vivant, and philatelist, he wed a prostitute and was the son of Hattie Green, the larger than life tightwad who made millions on Wall Street. (See Flynn below.) Jackie Gleeson's playboy character, Reggie van Gleason, was likely based on him.

- Harry Conover (1911-1965). His star shown briefly over the modeling and advertising world. Before WW II, one of his best friends and fellow models was future U.S. President Jerry Ford. The 1944 movie "Cover Girl," almost entirely filled with Conover models, gets *** stars from Leonard Maltin, is occasionally shown on Turner Classic Movies, and wasn't half as bad as I expected.

- Craps or similar betting games with dice have existed thousands of years. An illustration of a *seated* Achilles and Ajax playing dice on a table is painted on a 2,550-year-old amphora attributed to the Athenian school of Exekias. His vases/amphora are characterized by black painting on a light tan or orange background.

- Walther Darré (1895-1953) was captured in Ludwigslust. Many crackpot Nazi schemes concerning Lebensraum and mass starvation trace back to him. At least ten million Russian POWs and east European civilians died when his theories were put into practice. As an administrator, he proved indecisive, ineffective, and dull.

- Alice <u>Denham</u> (1927-2016), Harry Strong's fictional girlfriend and July 1956 Playmate of the Month was well known to the first generation of *Playboy* readers. See her autobiography below.

- <u>Distances</u>. I have used miles, yards, and feet rather than the metric system.

- All <u>European Locations</u>; Heidelberg, Lucerne (Switzerland), Ludwigslust, Munich, and Nuremberg locations and institutions are real. I have attempted to include still-open restaurants and hotels and use current guide books for recommended menu items. The architecture of Gehlen's spy headquarters outside Munich is imagined.

- General James <u>Gavin</u> (1907-1990) was charismatic, an able battlefield tactician, and highly respected by Eisenhower. I have been as accurate as possible in describing him, affairs included. After the war, he was an influential, progressive player in the military-industrial complex. See bibliography.

- Reinhard <u>Gehlen</u> (1902-1979), his background and the Gehlen Organization are well-documented. He did hire Seis (Six) in 1950. See E. H. Cookridge in Bibliography.

- <u>Gold.</u> During the 1930s, the price of gold was set by the Roosevelt Administration at $35 an ounce. This figure lasted throughout WW II and until the Nixon Administration permitted the price to "float." As this is written (August, 2017), the price is over $1,300 per ounce.

- Reinhardt <u>Heydrich</u> (1904-1942) was the fastest rising and most cold-blooded of the younger Nazis and possibly posed a threat to Himmler. His death remains suspicious and might have been due more to Himmler's doctors than his wounds. Franz Seis (Six) was an up-and-coming protégée until Heydrich's death.

- The <u>genesis</u> of this fictional story reflects the actual looting of a Nazi post office by a late cousin, a WW II artillery officer. Returning from Europe, he gave me (then not quite eight) a few dozen uncancelled Nazi stamps which I still have and reference here; the twenty-seven 1943-44 engraved stamps of German armed forces in combat.

- President Franklin D. Roosevelt's stamp collection was auctioned off in multiple phases by the then and now highly respected <u>H. R. Harmer</u> company. In 1946-47 the sale grossed some $ 225,000.

- <u>Historical figures</u> (Martin Bormann, Allan and John Foster Dulles, Eisenhower, Reinhardt Heydrich, Hitler, Lucky Luciano, Frederick Porsche, Roosevelt, Ben Seigel, Stalin, Simon Wiesenthal and so forth), Hollywood and Broadway stars, New York gangsters, writers and sports celebrities are all used fictionally. A marvelous description of the pre-war Bormann vs. Heydrich infighting is in Philip Kerr's 2017 novel, *Prussian Blue.*

- Meyer <u>Lansky</u> (1909-1982) was a very real gangster although his relationship with Harry is, of course, fictional. Robert Lacy's excellent, biography (see below) describes his attempt to break up a Nazi rally. Lansky's mobster friends included Albert and Tony Anastasia (brothers who spelled their last names differently), Carlo Gambino, Frank Costello, "Socks" Lanza, Meyer's brother Jake, Lucky Luciano and Benjamin ("Bugsy") Siegel. Unlike Siegel, Lansky saw no future in Las Vegas, the worst mistake of his life.

  In the early '50s, Lansky focused his efforts in Cuba paying off President Batista. Lansky built a large casino/hotel which, following Castro's takeover, was confiscated. Over the years his influence gradually waned as a new generation of gangsters gained control. As this is written, and with the (temporary?) thawing of U.S.-Cuban relations his grandchildren were attempting to receive payment for the facility.

- <u>Looted Art Work and Stamps</u>. The Nazi's looted anything of value. To this day legal battles continue over stolen works of art. Numerous WW II histories mention stolen stamps, but no cache (such as described in this story) has ever been recovered or known to have existed.

- Shortly after the 82nd Airborne arrived in <u>Ludwigslust</u> and then discovered Wobelein concentration camp, the mayor of Ludwigslust, his wife and teenage daughter committed suicide. The small community (some 4,500 during the war, 12,000 today) can be found on detailed German maps. See Megellas (below) for a non-fictional account of the 3rd Battalion, 504th Parachute, 82nd Airborne Division where I have placed Harry's unidentified company.

- <u>Microdot</u> technology and its precursor, the shrinking photographic process, dates to 1870 when a Frenchman developed the technique to send messages via carrier pigeon from besieged Paris. After World War I, Emanuel Goldberg, a Russian Jew working for Zeiss Ikon in Dresden appears to have invented the technology. By WW II, Germany commonly used microdot technology for espionage purposes.

- For whatever reason, <u>Mohawk</u> Indians, an Iroquois tribe, have no fear of heights. They have taken the lead working on high level, difficult work on bridges, and office and apartment buildings for almost 150 years. Numerous books and articles about their skills are available.

- James "Dinty" <u>Moore,</u> Jr. (ca. 1869—December 1952) opened his restaurant (and later Prohibition speakeasy) in 1914. One regular was a popular cartoonist who created "Dinty" in a comic strip, which Moore thought was named for him. That the restaurant was one of Lansky's favorites is clear (see biography below), but I have fictionalized their relationship.

- The <u>Mount Hermon School</u>, located along the Connecticut River, is today part of the Northfield Mount Hermon School. Founded in 1879-81 by the evangelist Dwight L. Moody, the progressive vs. conservative educational infighting did result in the 1934 murder of its headmaster. Today it remains one of the nation's better preparatory schools. See 1940 *WPA Guide to Massachusetts*.

- The following <u>New York locations and institutions</u> are/were real: Manhattan House (designed by Skidmore, Owens & Merrill,1949-50), Club Monte Carlo, Dinty Moore's, Gotham and Lenox Hill hospitals, the Seventy First Regimental Armory and the Stage Door Canteen. Between 50th and 51st on Madison was the Look Magazine Building, constructed by the Uris family in 1950.

- Wartime <u>Nazi</u> stamps. By the war's end, English and American forces had captured over a billion Nazi Postage stamps. Rather than destroy them and increase the value of those that remained, millions were auctioned off (ca. 1948) and are today relatively commonplace.

- The escape of Nazis from Germany via <u>Rat Lines</u> to South America is well documented. The role by Catholic clergy in Germany, France, and the Vatican supporting these activities is controversial but sadly real.

- Although the <u>Romanoff</u> story of Alexander I and the priest Feodor Kuzmich being the same person is generally discredited by reputable historians, a novelist is under no such restraint.

- The <u>"scientific experiments"</u> supervised by the fictional Hermann Seis were undertaken by various Nazi doctors (think Joseph Mengele) on concentration camp inmates. See Jacobson's *Operation Paperclip* (below). As the Cold War intensified, the Americans and British begin to place beyond Russian reach scientists and engineers such as Werner von Braun. "Paperclip" saw over a thousand of these men—the majority with blood on their hands—brought to the U.S., and vitally assist western Cold War efforts, most becoming model citizens.

- The 1940 and 1950 <u>Scott [stamp] Catalogues</u>, available at the American Philatelic Society library, are the basis for the value of specific stamps mentioned. Today, the multi-volume, color catalogues are published annually.

- Franz Seis is the fictional name for Franz <u>Six</u> (1909-1975). Seis's titles, education, wartime experiences, account of his capture, trial, imprisonment, and work for Gehlen are dramatized but real. At Nuremberg (Trials #9) he was convicted and given twenty years. Six volunteered to testify at Eichmann's 1961 trial but was told that if he did, he would be arrested and tried himself. In his 2006 novel, *The One from the Other*, Philip Kerr states that in Smolensk, USSR, Six, "commanded a Special Action Group that had massacred seventeen thousand people (p. 334)." To the best of my knowledge, he had no interest in philately and died of natural causes. Seis's sister Marianne and brother Gustav were real. Her death is as described although who poisoned her is unknown.

- Elliot <u>Speer</u> (1899-1934), the headmaster of Mount Hermon died as described, this writer seeing still existent bullet holes twenty-one years later. His murder was never formally solved in large part because the investigation was badly botched by local police. Full length books are available discussing the crime and the likely murderer.

- <u>Stamps</u>. The red Australian two-pence of Edward VIII (Duke of Windsor) was yanked just before circulation began. For decades, the whereabouts of six known surviving stamps remained a mystery. In 2017, they were to be auctioned off by MossGreen of Melbourne. All other stamps cited are real, their prices as reflected in the 1940 and 1950 Scott catalogues.

  As of this writing, the <u>future</u> of stamp collecting looked ominous. A September 30, 2017 op-ed page article in the *New York Times* was headlined, "Stamped Out" with its sub-headline, "In the internet age, philately has lost its once worldly charms." The story went on to say that membership in the American Philatelic Society had been halved (to 28,953) in the past twenty years, and that the average collector today was 65 to 70 years old, an unpleasant demographic.

- <u>Stamp Dealers</u>. While Romanoff & Abramson and Thistleman & Chandler are fictional, all other companies, dealers, and Nassau Street's importance are historical.

- Dr. Karl <u>Strölin</u> (1890-1963), fictionally the cousin of Harry Strong's father, in real life was a good friend of Erwin Rommel. He was not the wise man portrayed by Sir Cedric Hardwicke in the film, *The Desert Fox*. A nasty racist, he joined the Nazi party in 1923 and, ten years later, proclaimed himself mayor, staying in power until the Allies were at the gates of Stuttgart. Harry Strong's family's name of *Strölin* was chosen because of its phonetic resemblance to *Strong*.

- <u>Sullivan and Cromwell</u>, founded in 1879, remains a powerhouse New York headquartered, blue chip law firm. William Nelson Cromwell (1854-1948) was as responsible as any non-engineer for the Panama Canal. He built up the international side of the law firm that was to include Alan (CIA) and John Foster Dulles. Domestically, it was every bit as powerful, perhaps the country leading establishment-GOP firm during the years when this story takes place.

- The 1952 <u>Volkswagen Hebmüller Cabriolet</u> that Seis owned had a production run of less than a thousand cars. You'd need one of Harry's better stamps to purchase one today.

- <u>Wobelein</u> (the German spelling is Wöbbelin), was the location for a temporary Nazi POW and then concentration camp from the fall of 1945 until it liberation on May 2, 1945. Photos of its prisoners appear in Gavin's autobiography (below). In doing research for this book, I had the distinct honor to meet a Wobelein survivor who lives in Northern Virginia.

- <u>Yaphank</u> was the site of a pre-war Nazi Boy Scout-like camp. A 2015 *New York Times* article reported on its restrictive covenants and American Nazi-sympathizers continued living there. In 2016, the FBI arrested a pro-Nazi father and son team for bomb making and plotting mass murder.

- The Nazi parades in <u>Yorkville</u> were real and represented only a small fraction of the German-American Bund's activities after Hitler came to power. While some sources indicate that this parade took place in 1939, once the war began New York prohibited such pro-Nazi activities. While Lansky's role is fictionalized, he is known to have participated in the fist-fighting at a Bund Madison Square Garden rally in early 1939 and later kept the docks safe from sabotage.

- New York developer "Big Al" Beckendorf's name makes more sense if you change the "B" to "Z" as in William <u>Zeckendorf,</u> (1905-1976). (See Bibliography.) Beckendorf is <u>not</u> modeled after Donald Trump. In fact, the 45th President wrote a blurb for Beckendorf's book and was born after this story begins.

What's Fiction.

Most major characters in the story are fictional including but not limited to Harry, Nan, Ilse, Rudy, Ingrid, "Baron" Romanoff, Big Al, "Baker," ODESSA members (Otto and Dieter), those in Harry's jeep (Manfredi, Tonstad and Zilina), and most other characters making brief appearances.

B. Suggested Further Reading

Albrecht, Donald. *Only in New York: Photographs from Look Magazine,* (2009).

Alford, Kenneth D. *Allied Looting in WW II: Thefts of Art, Manuscripts, Stamps and Jewelry in Europe,* (2011).
_____. *Nazi Millionaires: The Allied Search for Hidden SS Gold,* (2002).

American Philatelic Society, Library, Bellefonte, Pa.

American Philatelic Society, *The American Philatelist,* Monthly.

American Stamp Dealers Association, *The American Stamp Dealer & Collector*, Monthly.

American Stamp Dealers Association, [Third Annual] *National Postage Stamp Show Program,* November 16-18, 1951, New York.

Amick, George. *The Inverted Jenny: Money, Mystery, Mania; A True Story of Crime, Romance, Corruption and Greed* (1986).

Ascher, Kate. *The Heights: Anatomy of a Skyscraper* (2011).

Barron, James. *The One-Cent Magenta: Inside the Quest to Own the Most Valuable Stamp in the World,* (2017).

Beevor, Antony. *Ardennes 1944: The Battle of the Bulge,* (2015).
_____. *The Fall of Berlin,* (2002).

Cohen, Beverly and others. *What a Year It Was* [for:] 1945, 1947, 1951, 1952, 1953 (ca. 2001).

Cohen-Solal, Annie. *New York Mid-Century, 1945-1965: Art, Architecture, Design, Dance, Theater, Nightlife,* (2014).

Collingham, Lizzie. *The Taste of War: World War II and the Battle for Food,* (2012).

Conover, Carole. *Cover Girls: The Story of Harry Conover,* (1978).

Cookridge, E. H. *Gehlen, Spy of the Century* (1971).

Denham, Alice. *Sleeping with Bad Boys: A Juicy Tell-All of Literary New York in the 1950s-1960s* (2006).

Diehl, Lorraine B. *Over Here: New York City During World War II,* (2010).

Festerman, Dan. *The Letter Writer* (2016, fiction). (about 1942 New York City, Lansky and the mob).

Flynn, John T. *Men of Wealth* (1941).

Gavin, Gen. James M. *On to Berlin: Battles of an Airborne Commander, 1943-1946* (1978).

Gunther, John. *Inside U.S.A.* (1947, reprint 1997.)

Herst, Hermann, Jr. *More Stories to Collect Stamps By,* (1982).
_____. *Nassau Street: A Quarter Century of Stamp Dealing,* (1960).
_____. *Stories to Collect Stamps By,* (1968).

Jacobsen, Annie. *Operation Paperclip: The Secret Program that Brought Nazi Scientists to America* (2014).

Jones, Richard D. *Jane's: Guns Recognition Guide* (Smithsonian, Fifth Edition, 2008).

Kempowski, Walter. *Swan Song 1945: A Collective Diary of the Last Days of the Third Reich* (2015).

Kerr, Philip. *The One from the Other* (2006). This Bernie Gunther novel partially takes place in Munich in 1949 and includes a cameo by Franz Six/Seis.

Kopleck, Maik. *Munich, 1933-1945: A Guidebook,* (not dated, ca. 2000).

Lampe, David. *The Last Ditch: Britain's Secret Resistance and the Nazi Invasion Plans* (2008 reprint).

Lacy, Robert. *Little Man: Meyer Lansky and the Gangster Life* (1991).

Lichtblau, Eric. *The Nazis Next Door: How America Became a Safe Haven for Hitler's Men* (2014).

Life Magazine. 1938-1951, various issues.

Linn's Stamp News. Monthly and Weekly publications, various issues.

Megellas, James. *All the Way to Berlin: The 82nd Airborne's Most Decorated Officer* (2003).

Morris, Jan. *Manhattan '45,* (1987).

The New York Times, various issues 1938-1951.

Saikia, Robin, ed. *Munich: Capital of the [Nazi] Movement,* (Germany 1937, reprint 2008).

_____. *Weegee's New York, 1935-1960,* (1982).

The Forties: The Story of a Decade [from] the New Yorker [Magazine], (2014).

Tishman, John L. *Building Tall: My Life and the Invention of Construction Management* (2011).

Vassiltchikov, Marie. *Berlin Diaries, 1940-1945,* (1985). (Franz Seis/Six was her real-life boss.)

Wikipedia.

Works Project Administration. *The WPA Guide to Massachusetts* (1983 paperback reprint), and *The WPA Guide to New York City* (1992 paperback reprint).

Zeckendorf, William. The Autobiography of William Zeckendorf, (1987) New York construction after WWII. Nice blurb on the dust jacket by Donald Trump.

C. Acknowledgments

This book would not have been possible without the continued help and en-couragement of Amin X. Ahmad, whom I have had the pleasure of working with for several years. His energetic prodding, suggestions, and invariably com-mon-sense approach to fiction writing is greatly missed by all with his move to the Windy City.

Additional thanks go to participants in the 2015-2016 Bethesda Writer's Center's experimental "novel year" program. Fellow writers in the class were Cathy Baker, Michael Barron, Ginny Fite, Moxie Gardiner, Frank Joseph, Lauren Kosa, Kenny Robinson, Janis Villadiego and Stan Whatley were invariably candid (often painfully so) but that, of course, is the whole point of the program. The 2016-2017 class was equally tough and constructive. Many thanks to Sapna Batish, Julie Gabrielli, Jamie Holland, Rita Kempley, Hillary Meek, Donna Oetzel, Emily Rich, Ellen Sassman and Harry Specht. This class was marvelously led by Susan Coll, a novelist, and an active figure in Washington literary circles.

Many thanks go to the amazingly comprehensive research library of the American Philatelic Association in Bellefonte, PA (near Penn State) and to Scott Tiffney who went out of his way to be helpful before, during, and after my visits. Needless to say, the many mistakes that professional philatelists will find in the text are my responsibility but (I can assure you) would have been far worse were it not for the uniformly friendly APA staff.

My struggle with grammar will shortly enter its eighth decade, and I am thus deeply grateful to Katie Goldberg for her invaluable assistance in proof reading this manuscript, as well as designing the book interior and cover.

Among those who read through earlier drafts of this were my brother, James G. Lubetkin, and Daniel Bleiber, Donald H. Cady, Edward B. Dingledy, and Joseph Whitehorne. John McClintock (Mount Hermon '56) "introduced" me to the late Hans Deutsch who fled Austria in 1938 and arrived at Mount Hermon not knowing a word of English (very much like Harry Strong) and graduated in 1943.

Special thanks to my son Will for his technical help when I called in great panic about something or other. And, last but certainly not least, to my wife Linda for her patience, understanding and common-sense observations over the years.

About the Author

M. John Lubetkin, a native New Yorker, is a retired cable television executive, and has had a longtime interest in American history. He has published four books with the University of Oklahoma Press including the award-winning *Jay Cooke's Gamble: The Northern Pacific Railroad, the Sioux and the Panic of 1873*. John is a graduate of the Northfield Mount Hermon School, Union College (a history major), and NYU with an MA in government. John resides in Northern Virginia and still possesses the Nazi stamps that his cousin, first lieutenant William H. Green, "liberated" for him in 1945.

2007 awards for *Jay Cooke's Gamble*:
Western Writers of America, Little Big Horn Associates, Northern Pacific Railway Historic Association, and a High Plains Book Award

Made in the USA
Columbia, SC
01 February 2018